Richa

There can

May those be...

dreams come

true and

me

FOR THE
GLORY
OF LOVE

WORK on

some projects

together

[signature]

SWORDSLINGER

BOOK ONE:
FOR THE
GLORY OF LOVE

STEFAN DUNCAN

Swordslinger
Book One: FOR THE GLORY OF LOVE
Stefan Duncan
Copyright © 2013 Stefan Duncan
All Rights Reserved
Print version ISBN-13: 978-0615772561
Publisher: Raven's Light Publishing
Charlotte, NC
Published February 2013
Cover illustration: Artist Unknown
Editing: Howard Ward
Final editing and digital formatting: Karen Troutman
Available as digital e-book
Find out more about the author and upcoming books online
http://www.swordslinger.net/
http://www.stefanduncan.com

Dedicated

to

My Family

Table of Contents

"The true measure of a man is
if he will die for love."
Stefan Duncan

CHAPTER 1

SHOCK

Oh, yeah, the bad man cometh, Swordslinger thought. His palms twitched with anticipation to feel the weight of his sword and its lust for blood. He squinted his eyes beneath his worn fedora. His Nehru waist long frock coat was as still as a single fall leaf over a graveyard. He focused on the dark alleyway before him. A tin can rattled; and, a fat rat fled to the safety of streetlights yards away. The burn of ozone was in the air. The sultry heat hung over the city in a smothering hot blanket of moist air. Angry lightning lashed out into the night turning the inky darkness to white, then black again as the lighting zigzagged across the sky. Thunder rumbled. Gusts of wind rattled the marquees and overhanging canopies of the buildings that lined the streets.

The Swordslinger leaned against the wall of the dark alleyway, breathing heavily. His face was obscured in the shadow of a wide-brim fedora. Underneath the long black coat that seemed obscenely out of place on such a muggy evening, his skin was sleek with sweat. The muscles of his body were taut, bunched tight in anticipation of the battle he was about to face. A closer look revealed eyes bright with unshed tears. The dark figure appeared stunned, perhaps unbelieving of some unlikely event that had just occurred.

The man continued to rest against the wall, gathering himself, and lifted his face. The pale, yellow light from a distant street light illuminated the handsome, whisker-stubbled chin. He was trembling, and sharp teeth bit into the bottom lip in an attempt to use pain to force himself out of the mind-numbing shock.

An empty tin can rattled and skirted through the shadows as another gust of wind swept the alley. Lightning flashed, shifting shadows snatching and withdrawing. The man tensed; his dark eyes squinting as they anxiously scanned the surroundings.

The ozone was thick tonight, almost dense enough to feel, and fertile for a lightning strike. "Or a Rippling," the Swordslinger whispered through clenched teeth. He was no longer truly aware of his actions; he had placed himself on autopilot. Rational thoughts had overloaded, fuses blown, melted and locked in a myriad of tangled snakes in his tortured mind. He squeezed his eyes hard shut and his body quivered with emotion. His mind wanted to blank out the events of the past few moments. Where his heart had been was now a void, ripped out and thrown to the wind. No feelings in the tips of his fingers or from the teeth pressed into his bottom lip. The metallic humming brought the hair on the nape of his neck on end. The old but familiar electrical energy of flesh creating and fusing together had its own smell. This odor and hum penetrated the numbness, the shock, and the Swordslinger knew it was about to happen.

Swordslinger sprang from the wall, clenched fists held before him. From the depths of his devastated soul, the cry he wanted to scream became a raspy wisp of a single word, "Draconis."

Electricity crackled and sparked as it flowed through the fingertips of his hand, creating a ghostly silver-white shape of a sword. He felt the pull of his life force — the merging of flesh and bone and steel. A heavy scent of flesh, hot steel, and burning ozone consumed the air. Flowing electrical silver-white light began to solidify into the shape of a 42-inch blade. The hasp of the brilliant blade had been fashioned from the tusk of a Highland ox and was a thing of beauty in its own right. The blade grew heavy and began to descend, but the Swordslinger, as he had done hundreds of times before, snatched it by the hasp before it could hit the ground.

The white-hot blade shimmered as the cooling process began. The Swordslinger moved in a semi-circle, holding the blade waist high, anticipating a threat. He held the tip poised chin-high, muscles tensed. Waiting. Watching. Listening.

A sudden gust of wind spiraled down the alley. Paper and trash skirted across the narrow gash between the huge buildings. The bulb in the lamp that had partially lighted the alleyway popped and the light went out. There was only darkness now; feeding the fear of the knowledge that something deadly dangerous lurked in the heart of it.

"I know you're there," Swordslinger hissed. He brandished his weapon, moving it up and to his side. "You followed me, now finish the job. Come get some."

There was no sound emanating from the alley other than the Swordslinger's voice, only the distant wailing of a siren, the impatient honking of automobile horns along the city's busy streets.

The Swordslinger squinted, trying to force his gaze to penetrate the darkness of the alley. Nothing. There was no sound. No movement. Just an eerie quiet that was unsettling. He lolled his head back and sighed.

The screaming man burst out of the darkness with a sword held high in both hands. The mad charge caught the Swordslinger by surprise, but he quickly recovered and held his ground. He stood with knees slightly bent, his weight balanced for action, sword tipped forward. He would not give ground, any more than the screaming swordsman rushing toward him would yield. The intruder lifted his arms higher as he approached, ready to bring the sword downward with enough momentum to divide a solid oak.

"AHHHHHHHH!" The screaming attacker made his final move, leaping forward and driving the sword down hard and fast in a blow that would split the Swordslinger's skull.

The Swordslinger made a quick movement forward, then lithely sidestepped the charge, making a half circle with his sword, catching the descending blade from the top and forcing it downward with its own momentum. As the blade struck pavement, the Swordslinger smoothly slid his sword up the blade of the other and followed through with a killing slash. The decapitation was clean. And fatal.

The headless torso staggered several feet forward, its momentum not allowing it to fall to the pavement just yet. Agonizingly, almost as in slow motion, the body fell upon its knees and clasping hands released the sword. The body with no head fell forward, the severed neck pressing against the alley pavement. At first glance, it appeared to be a man kneeling on the ground with his head buried in a hole. Only the head was some 10 feet to the side, eyes wide open and staring vacantly into a private hell. The sword made a haunted, clanging sound that rang through the alley as it bounced on the pavement.

A sudden blinding electrical beam connected the falling sword with the one in the Swordslinger's hands. The shock startled him, his wrists jarred by the sheer electrical power. His own blade resonated in the gloomy surroundings, glowing, throbbing with white light … crackling and humming.

A shrill metallic scream pierced the night and the dead man's sword suddenly rose in the air and began traveling the beam of light toward the Swordslinger's sword. As he watched, transfixed in the gloom, the shining piece of metal attached itself to his own sword. There was the sizzling sound of hot metals fusing and the two swords became as one.

Prismatic light flowed and swirled around the sword. The myriad of colors reflected in Swordslinger's eyes as he observed this event with the utter fascination that he always felt as he watched the miracle occur. As the colors began fading, he lowered the sword, and then sank wearily to his knees on the pavement.

A sound from the end of the alley made him look up. At the entrance from the street, an elderly street person gawked. The old bum's bottle of cheap wine was held forgotten to his side.

"Go!" The Swordslinger cried his voice hoarse and scary.

The bottle of wine clanked and bounced once, ending on its side. The old man apparently realized the bottle didn't shatter. He stopped, turned and around to consider if his life was worth the risk of that one last swallow.

"Don't even think about it," the man with the sword growled.

"You want it, you can have it!" The drunk made a shriek and waddled hurriedly away like a duck with its feathers on fire, mumbling, "Crazy, crazy muther, bad man, cutting off people's head for a drink."

The Swordslinger turned back to the scene in the alley. He lifted the newly forged sword and embraced it in his arms. The heat and electricity from the weapon course through his ribs, causing him to gasp. The glow from the sword was blinding and he could feel the steel's separated molecules penetrate and mingle with the cells of his body. The merging was complete.

Swordslinger rose to his feet, removed the wide-brim hat and shook his long black hair loose about his shoulders. He took a deep breath, surveyed both ends of the now empty alley, and decided it was time to move. There was no time to grieve now. No time to harvest the pain of loss, the butchering of his brother.

CHAPTER 2

BROTHER NO MORE

The stench of blood assaulted his nostrils as the Swordslinger stepped from the shadowy alley into the dim lighting of the street. He took a moment to check his clothing for telltale spatters of blood, but the long black coat, the black pants, white long-sleeved, collarless shirt, and the calf-length black boots carried no reminders of the horror that had just taken place.

Even a casual observer would have noted the absurdity of his attire, although the long black coat was still stylish enough for this time. The rest of the clothing was dated; a retro outfit that would quickly draw undesired attention

The Swordslinger sniffed at the air, noting that the smell of blood must be from his mental state. There was a coppery taste in his mouth and he spat in an effort to rid himself of this.

"Time to move," he muttered to himself. "Gotta keep moving." He took one last glance at the body he had left behind and noted that the electrical surge that had fused the swords had turned the headless corpse into a human ash. *Ah, well,* he thought, *the wind will take care of that. No one would even be suspicious of a heap of scattered ashes. Just some street person playing with matches.*

The Swordslinger lifted his arm and stared at the fluorescent dial of his wristwatch. The green glow showed 5:45 a.m. So early, and already so much had happened on this day. The green sign at the corner he approached told him he was on Tryon Street. Somewhere near, he knew there would be a bank. He was going to need one. However, that couldn't happen before 9 o'clock. He had to be careful.

Reaching into a coat pocket, the Swordslinger dug out a thin black leather wallet. Inside were a photo identification card, a North Carolina driver's license, a Sam's Club membership card, two 10-dollar bills and two keys. He replaced the wallet and paused.

Standing near the curb of the street, the Swordslinger studied the surroundings. The sun still hadn't made its appearance and the area was shrouded in darkness, punctuated by the overhanging street lamps. A few early-morning risers were strolling on the opposite side of the street. A couple of street people were bundled in doorways, their meager belongings in bags that they used for pillows.

The Swordslinger sighed deeply, standing alone at the street corner, unmindful of the scattered raindrops that continued to fall. The sidewalk shimmered in the half-light, its wetness reflecting some of the all-night neon lighting from storefronts.

Finally, the tall figure began moving again. Crossing the street, the Swordslinger approached a bus stop shelter and, finding a vacant bench, wearily took a seat. He glanced casually at a street person stretched out on the bench across from him but sensed no danger.

He slumped on the bench tiredly, his head lowered into the folds of the black coat. His breathing was ragged and he forced himself to take slower, smoother gulps of the morning air. The near zombie state that he had found himself in after the incident in the alley was beginning to wear off. He closed his eyes, letting his mind drift. Mentally, he replayed the earlier scene, the scene from another world called SkyeEden.

"Ha! Ha ha ha! Brother, that looks like a hairless ox!" Samuel taunted. "Och, teaching ye to draw might as well be trying to teach our horse to sprout wings, fly, and play the pipes at the same time."

They were sitting under a blazing red maple tree. It was the first time since the night the meteor came that they had relaxed or even smiled. Though a quarter of a mile from the village and forge at their shop, they smelled of fire and iron.

"It's not that bad!" Robert said. "I think it is a fine drawing of our horse." He held the parchment arm's length and made a big grin. His eyes shined as brightly as spring green grass with cheeks peppered in freckles, always giving him a boyish demeanor, and charm to woo the girls. Samuel was a head taller.

"If you think that, brother, then chicken scratches in the dirt must be masterpieces to ye," Samuel said."

Robert playfully hit Samuel on the head with the scroll of paper. "I'll draw you to look like a frog and then maybe you'll hop away from here," he said laughing.

"Will you now?" Samuel continued taunting. "And how 'bout me hopping all over you!" He grabbed his younger brother and the two young men grappled, rolling in the grass. They struggled in a make-believe wrestling match that neither cared about winning. Samuel got Robert into a headlock and used his knuckles briskly across his head. "Why you-" Robert said.

"Ah, look … one last buggering before they die." The voice brought an instant response from the brothers and they broke apart, leaped to their feet and grabbed for their swords.

The figure poised before them was imposing. The man was more than six feet tall and muscular. The muscles in his bare arms were bulging, appearing to be chiseled from granite. He held a long blade that reached from the ground to his chest, and he was wearing a white jerkin and kilt of the Frasier tartan colors.

"You!" Samuel hissed, lips drawn taut over his teeth. Dexter Frasier! You die now!"

The big man's lip curled in a cruel smile. "Ah, such love we have for one another. Out of caring I feel compelled to ask, did your woman live?"

Samuel started to step forward but Robert held his arm.

"I killed. You killed. Yes, three of my cousins that day you put down. A part of them is in you now. When I take your essence and reclaim my cousins, it will be like a family reunion."

Samuel tensed, the muscles in his arm growing tight from the grip on the hasp of his sword. "Since her death, seeing you dead is my sole motive to live. No more words. Draw your sword. The world has had enough of you." He moved a step closer to his adversary, casting a quick look toward his younger brother to make sure Robert was not doing anything foolish.

kDexter's smile turned into a ghoulish smirk. "I think not, Samuel Donachee," he said, making a gesture with his free hand. As one, twelve more of the Frasier clan rose from the tall grass and gathered behind their leader. "I don't want to appear selfish," Dexter said, chuckling as he saw the surprise cross Samuel's face. "My friends want to play, too."

The group of ruffians formed a semi-circle behind Dexter, facing Samuel and Robert with weapons drawn and flashing in the sunlight. They might have been starving wolves surrounding two sheep.

"Ohh, this is beautiful, Dexter," Samuel hissed between clenched teeth, "The honor of the Frasier Clan at its finest, twelve against two. Fight me, you coward. . You and me one-on-one."

"Och, honor is just a word the overmatched use to build useless hope," Dexter said, laughing coldly. "I want your metal." Dexter motioned with one hand for Samuel to approach. Samuel kept his eyes glued to the semi-circle of men as they cautiously advanced toward him inch by inch. The odds were overpowering. Moreover, if he died, Robert died. He decided to play for time for an opportunity of any kind to present itself.

"Ok, Dexter," he said, "You want my metal? I'll give it to you and you let my brother go unharmed. He held out his sword with both hands as an offering. If you insist on fighting, I will take as many of you down as I can. But if you insist on harming my brother, I vow to you that I will not die alone." He stared icily at the men, who had now formed a circle around him and Robert.

"You're right, you won't die alone," Dexter said through an evil cackle. "Your brother dies with you." He turned his back to Samuel and stepped outside the circle of men.

"Killed a man bound in shackles, now have others do your killings, so brave are you," Samuel said, his knuckles growing white as he gripped his sword even tighter.

"You dare mention him in my presence? Oh, you think you hate me? Let me share a little of the HATE I once held for that man. Dexter's mad eyes blazed with fury. He whirled around, raising the 50-inch blade of his sword above

9

his head, and reentered the circle. "Don't let these peasants out of the circle!" he commanded. "They're mine!" Still yelling, Dexter made a mighty swing with his blade, swishing through the air with such force that it sounded like a scream.

Samuel moved quickly, seizing Robert by the arm and yanking him alongside. He leapt into the wall of men, swinging his blade with deadly precision. The men were caught by surprise and the first man the sword sliced into fell with a gaping wound to his shoulder. Samuel dropped to his knees, eluding the wild swings from his assailants, who were now finding their own movements hampered by their close proximity to each other. A scythe-like move with his blade cut through a pair of unprotected legs and there was a sudden opening in the broken circle.

Samuel shoved his younger brother through the break in the circle of men and shouted, "Go! Run!" Robert sprinted through the men with Samuel on his heels.

Dexter Frasier screamed in frustration. "After them!" he shouted. "Don't let the dogs get away!" He gathered himself and led the men in pursuit.

Samuel and Robert were running free, a few yards ahead of the yelling Frasier Clan. Samuel drew his sword up above his head and without slowing his sprint, hurled it ahead. The sword was spinning end over end when it was suddenly ensconced in a blinding light that seemed to emerge from the very earth. There was a shrill ripping sound and a portal to another world opened before the fleeing men.

The open portal loomed ahead like a tear in a curtain, tantalizingly near but still a few deadly yards ahead. "Faster!" Samuel shouted to his brother, now trailing him by a few feet. "Come on, Robert, we're almost there!"

Dexter Frasier was lumbering along in the wake of his quarry, but not gaining. He paused, gathered himself and heaved his blade after the two. "Rip him!" he shouted angrily. The blade sailed through the air growing white-hot as it left Dexter's hand. The sword suddenly began disintegrating in mid-air, re-forming into forty pieces of metal that had been melded into the steel. The hurtling stones were like drops of liquid metal which hardened into deadly spiked balls.

Samuel made a desperate leap for the portal, reaching back to grasp his brother's hand and pull him along. They almost made it. Then one of the spiked stones crashed into the back of Robert, making a sickening bone rending sound as it entered the young body. Spots of blood peppered Robert's shirt as two of the deadly spikes protruded through Robert's chest.

The last Samuel saw of his brother before the portal closed was the horror in his eyes. Robert's facial expression was one of bewilderment, shock and sudden, awful death.

"Hey, buddy, want to wake up and let these good people have a seat on the bench?"

The Swordslinger jerked his head up and opened his eyes to see a police officer standing over him. "No problem, officer," he said, rubbing the sleep from his eyes. He rose from the bus stop bench, sucked in a deep breath, and began walking. The police officer watched the tall man in the black coat moving away, shook his head and smiled at the soon-to-be bus passengers and resumed his foot patrol.

The sun was somewhere low behind the skyline. The Swordslinger checked his wristwatch and sighed. It was 9:10 a.m. and the Wachovia bank would be open for business.

A few minutes later, the Swordslinger had displayed his identification and been shown to the bank vault while an attendant waited near the door. Relief washed over the man in black as he counted out a thousand dollars in cash from a pile of wrapped hundred dollar bills. He eyed remaining bills and sighed. On his next visit to this land, he would have to bring more artifacts from the 14th century. Items that were of little value in SkyeEden sold quickly in the antique shops. He placed the money in his coat pocket and then reached back into the safety deposit box and took the key that lay there. *Good*, he thought, and stowed the key in his pocket as well.

Returning to South Tryon Street, the Swordslinger hailed a taxi and gave the driver the destination. The cabbie, an Italian who had made little effort to overcome the language barrier, nodded. He knew the place, about five miles outside the city limit. Nice fare.

"Hey, I don' wanna seema nosy," the cab driver said, craning his neck around to look at the oddly dressed man in the back seat. "But ain't cha a little hot in that coat? Heat index is 105 today. You gonna burn like a wrapped shish kabob."

"I like it hot," the Swordslinger said, his lip curling in a semi-smile. The brim of the big hat concealed the face and the cabbie studied him for a moment in the rear view mirror. Satisfied, he decided to mind his own business. Something about this passenger bothered him. Creepy bastard. You get all kinds in this business.

"Any power shortages recently?" the Swordslinger suddenly asked.

"Wha-?"

"Blackouts in the city? Power outages?"

"Nah. Not that I'm aware of," the driver said. Suddenly he was tired of this conversation. He would be glad when this ride was completed. Pickup and delivery was one thing. A fare to hell was altogether something else. Not today, my weird friend. The sooner we say ciao, the better.

The Swordslinger leaned back against the upholstery and watched the crowd of people moving along the sidewalks. Several times, he turned his head to check for a tail through the rear window. Nothing seemed suspicious.

You couldn't prove that by the cab driver. This ghoul in black was making him feel more uncomfortable by the moment. There was something very dangerous about the man in the back seat. It was like driving the streets with Death sitting behind you. He felt a spot between his shoulder blades begin to ache. He half expected a skeletal hand to tap him on the shoulder.

When the Swordslinger broke the silence, the sound of his voice spooked the cabbie to the point that he almost lost it. "You can let me out here," the voice said. And the cabbie could feel his own breath choking him. He braked the taxi to a stop before a desolate-looking building surrounded by a tall wood and wire fence that read, "Boston's Car Refuge."

The relieved driver took the twenty-dollar bill from the Swordslinger, mumbled "Thanks," and departed the scene with a flurry of gravel spewing from the spinning wheels. "Damn!" he mumbled, shuddering as he cast a final glance back in the rear view mirror. "That man's the walking heebee geebees."

As the Swordslinger entered the fenced area, a man sitting inside a small building with a large window jumped to his feet and came running out. The man was wearing a pair of dark blue mechanic's coveralls, and a soiled handkerchief was flapping from a rear pocket.

"Hey, man," the mechanic greeted the Swordslinger, "where you been, Sam? It's been weeks since you were here. Don't worry, though, everything is OK. I make sure of that. You gonna take her out for a while?"

"Aye," the Swordslinger replied. "I'll be gone for a few days." He picked his way through the graveyard of crumpled and rusting automobiles.

"Well, let me hose her off for you real quick then. It's been kinda dusty around here. However, the bike's in great shape. I've been taking it for a spin every couple of days just to keep it on point." The mechanic was almost jogging in an effort to keep pace with the Swordslinger's long strides.

"Aye, I'll wager you have," the Swordslinger said, chuckling.

They rounded a heap of junked cars, piled high in one corner of the lot. The sight of the shiny black Winnebago with the Harley-Davidson hitched to the rear end brought a smile to the Swordslinger's face. "You did well," he said, handing the mechanic two hundred dollars. "Here you go, my man. Now flitter away."

"You got it, boss." The mechanic said, and hurried back to his hut, casting a furtive glance over his shoulder to see the man in black climbing into the driver's seat of the Winnebago.

"Home away from home," the Swordslinger said, pressing his back against the form-fitted seat. He removed the hat and casually tossed it over to the passenger seat, then inserted the key into the ignition and smiled as the powerful engine caught and then began to purr like a huge cat. The cool air flowing from the air conditioning vents chilled the sheen of perspiration on his face. He left the engine running, set the parking brake and walked into the back of the vehicle, where he took a seat at a table. Several changes of clothing were hanging in the mini-closet. Numerous newspaper clippings and maps of cities were thumbtacked to a board on the wall.

Moving slowly, almost as in a trance, the Swordslinger pulled open a cabinet door and gingerly withdrew a 20-inch lightning ball that he placed on the table. He stared at the ball for a few seconds, letting the thoughts 'form themselves into coherence, then stood, picked up the ball and walked back to the front of the Winnebago. Working quickly now, he took a cord from the console and plugged one end into the cigarette lighter on the dash. The other end he plugged into a socket in the ball. A moment after the wire was connected to the ball; jagged lightning lines appeared inside the surface, striking the glass with unbroken streams. The lightning flashes grew more frequent as he watched, the lines dispersing in all directions.

The Swordslinger reached out a hand and touched the ball with the tip of his right forefinger. A new stream of jagged light converged on the other side of the glass ball and he sighed with a mixture of relief and dread.

Satisfied, the Swordslinger placed the ball in its custom-made niche on the console and turned his attention to a plaid cloth-covered box approximately the size of his palm. He took the box from the console and slowly opened it.

Inside the box were several items, but the Swordslinger ignored everything except the lock of red hair. He picked up the hair and stroked the smooth texture with his fingers. He brought the strands to his nose and inhaled, savoring the familiar scent. Immediately, he felt his heart begin to race. The image of Heather's face filled his mind. Sometimes he could see her so clearly, he almost believed he could touch her face, and he knew if he did, he would feel her breath. Heather had been the love of his life; as dear to him as his village that he lived to serve, honor, and protect. The vision of her made his chest ache. If only he could be with her now to share the grief that wracked his soul. He could bury his head on her shoulder, losing himself in the auburn hair.

Reality fought its way back. Robert was dead now, too. His brother's body was probably lying in the little vale where they had shared those last precious moments before the attack of the Frasier Clan. They had mistakenly thought they were safe, protected from stone robbers. Now young Robert was dead, the scroll with his painting of the horse still clutched in his hand.

The Swordslinger felt the tears running down his cheeks and swiped at them with the back of a hand. "Robert," he said softly in what was more of a moan than words. He shut off the engine of the Winnebago and, turning, opened another cabinet and withdrew a bottle of Jack Daniels. He removed the top, then turned the bottle up and took a long drink.

The Swordslinger was in anguish. "I'm so sorry, Robert," he said, his blue eyes filling with tears again. "I failed you!" He slammed a fist on the table and cursed.

For an hour, he sat unmoving, except for occasionally raising the bottle of Jack Daniels to his lips. He simply sat and stared. And mourned.

Finally, he shook his head and mumbled, "Shower, then bed. Tonight, Robert, I will begin."

But the crying wasn't yet done. The tears came again in the shower, washing down the drain with the soapy water. More than a year of bottled up grief was being released. Grief for his cousins, fellow clansmen, and his wife who had all been butchered by Dexter Frasier. Now Robert's body lay among those corpses. The sweet green beautiful land of SkyeEden was now soiled with their blood. He wept. He grieved. He hated.

Later, as the Swordslinger lay in bed, he closed his eyes and visualized the mountains … the Highlands. The sky was so blue, the grass so green, just a shade darker than Heather's eyes. But he couldn't concentrate on Heather's beauty. Instead, his mind turned to his brother, recalling memories from the short life. He began from the moment

15

Robert was born, when as a frightened four-year-old, he had stood in the next room, horrified and almost in shock as the cries of his mother tore at his young heart.

Robert was born, a healthy red lump of humanity that would become the closest thing to Samuel's heart. A few hours later, their mother was dead. The struggle of delivering Robert had been too much. Robert became Samuel's shadow. There was no mother, but the boys led a disciplined life, enforced by a father who worked hard as an ironsmith, but drank far too much. The elders of the clan were always available for advice, and Samuel never left Robert alone. They were as one.

Everything was peaceful in the village. The strife that had existed between clans had calmed and the men were not killing one another. A good growing season had yielded plenty of food and the raucous children were healthy. Samuel was a sturdy young man of 17 and when he wasn't spending time entertaining and caring for Robert, he was enjoying the sweet times he shared with Heather. Samuel and Heather had been best friends since they were tots, but this was their first romantic summer.

They walked in the gardens and talked until the shadows grew long. She laughed at him when he was dueling with stick swords and the other boy cracked him across the head. He laughed at her when she almost stepped on a frog and screamed. They were young and in love.

SkyeEden was paradise. It was a Highland heaven, until the night the stone came.

CHAPTER 3

NIGHT OF THE STONE

Nothing on earth compares to a summer's evening in SkyeEden. The stars are brilliant, twinkling in an array of colors and flickering rays of diamond dust. A field of tall grasses stirred in waves generated by the warm breeze. All of this created a memorable vista, but the moment was made special by Heather standing in the field with her arms outstretched toward her young lover, Samuel.

The young girl's cheeks were flushed, eyes sparkling even at ebb of night. She held out her arms, opened, and closed her hands like the gesture of a child wanting candy. Moonlight illuminated the face and the beginning white slopes of her breasts.

"Hold me, Samuel," Heather beseeched.

"Aye, lass, I will hug you until eternity," he said, laughing, "or at least until we faint from starvation."

Rushing to Heather, Samuel placed his hands around the tiny waist and lifted her from the ground, then slowly lowered her, feeling her tight young breasts press against his chest as she slid downward against his body. They kissed passionately and he ran his hands through her long locks of auburn hair. Being so close to her made him dizzy, as the passion became an insatiable hunger.

Suddenly, Heather spun from his arms. The thin cotton dress and strands of her hair swept across him. "Come," she said. "Come, I want you to see this."

"Heather, the only thing in this world I want to see right now is you."

"Follow me, it's down this path."

They moved along a path that entered into a wooded area predominately populated with oak trees. "Sit right here," Heather said, patting a moss-covered boulder. "I, my Lord, will perform for you."

"I think I am going to like this," Samuel said, as he watched her move into an open area. For the first time,

17

Samuel noticed the swarming fireflies. They blinked on and off as they darted among the branches of the trees.

Heather was into her role playing, making a deep bow and lifting her arms. Spinning slowly she left the ground in a graceful leap. Her body swayed as though moving to a sweet soft melody. The fireflies seemed to be drawn to her. When she moved her arms through the air, flashes of fireflies followed. Some of them began finding a perch on her hair.

Samuel laughed, a little nervously. Heather continued to dance and after a few steps, she had him mesmerized. She appeared to him as he thought a fairy might, weightless and graceful; the long ends of her sleeves waving like ribbons. Her movements slowed, becoming even more sensuous, her head lolling back and the dress swirling above her knees.

The scene was so breathtakingly beautiful, that Samuel lost sense of himself. He watched her spinning slowly, her hair flowing in long waves around her. The fireflies, seeming to number in the hundreds, moved with her, becoming an eerie part of the dance.

There are special moments in one's life; things that will be stored as cherished memories. This was one of those moments for Samuel. What he saw in Heather was not just a woman of flesh that he loved, but also a creation from the Highlands themselves. Woven in her bones was the dust of SkyeEden. Her hair represented Highland's passion to him. Her eyes, so light and pure, sparkled in the moonlight.

Heather continued the dance, widening the circle, gracefully skipping and pirouetting as she released flower petals from her hands to drift in the gentle breeze and mingle with the colorful fireflies. Samuel watched her movements, his mind wandering as he allowed it to absorb the dream-like scene. Heather was somehow deeply connected to the land he cherished. Her body was its soil .... Her breath its breeze .... Her eyes its green .... *This is why Highlanders fought so hard to preserve their land,* he mused .... *For moments such as this.*

His people were one with the land. After several generations of inner tribal warring, it was amazing that peace had settled upon them like a blanket of summer grass. An alliance was forming between the McGuire clan, the Donachees, the Frasiers, McGregors, and MacDougals. They lived in the northern end of the country, along the foothills and mountains of the Highlands. Warring foreigners rarely advanced this far inland. It was nice and lifesaving to finally have a time in which crops were not being stolen or burned to the ground. He breathed in deeply… *Oh, this is so right*, he thought. *This is how it should be.*

He watched Heather with fascination as her body swayed and moved rhythmically to the music. *Thank God no other clansmen could see her*, he mused, smiling at the thought. . The young men would be fighting among themselves to attract her attention.

Samuel reveled in the moment, enjoying the delicious knowledge that this girl was his sweetheart. Yes, she was his. All the natural beauty about her, the voice that was soft and tender, the infectious laugh and sense of humor that kept her eyes sparkling and your mind alert. But most of all, it was looking into those translucent green eyes. Holding that lovely angel's face inches from his own and drinking from the languid reflection pools was invigorating. The auburn hair contrasted perfectly with the pale complexion. He loved the way only a few minutes in the sun seemed to spawn a collection of tiny freckles across her nose.

Heather moved closer to him, her body still moving to the music, and extended an arm to within inches of his lips. Turning to him, she placed a palm flat on her midriff and began slowly undulating her hips.

"Heather," Samuel whispered, "is this dance legal?"

Heather laughed, continuing the sensuous movement, their bodies almost touching.

"Gypsies," she said, giggling softly. "Some of them came through earlier today. One of the girls showed me how to belly dance. Like it?"

Now it was Samuel's turn to laugh ."A Highland lass belly dancing in a field of grass and fireflies?"

"You don't like it? I'll stop if you object."

19

Samuel sat upright. "Nae, no, no. I like it. Oh, I do… It's just that it causes a stirring in my kilt and I don't know exactly what to do about it."

"Oh, really! Well, I have an idea," Heather said. She lifted one side of the dress up to her thigh and arched her eyebrows. "Come, my manly Scot." She laughed, then turned and fled into the tall grass. Samuel could barely see her head bobbing above the blades of the grass. In the moonlight, the blades glistened like glass.

"Heather," he called out, rising to his feet. He could no longer see the blades of tall grass moving in her wake. Then his heart raced as he heard the splash of water and a feminine yelp.

"Och, the water's not cold?" Samuel asked, breaking through into a small clearing and seeing Heather was now lying atop a grass-blanketed boulder in the stream.

"Are you cold?" she countered flirtatiously. "I'll warm you, big man. Are you not brave enough?"

Samuel stopped a few feet from the boulder, his eyes caressing the beautiful young body. "Would you be calling me a coward?"

"Yes, maybe. But I'll call you some sweet things if you'll only come out here."

"Okay, woman, clothed and armed, I'm coming."

Diving straight into the cold water rather than wading in and freezing by degrees seemed the better idea to Samuel. Still, when his body hit the water, it proved a rude awakening. The moment his head broke the surface, he could feel his body quivering with the cold. Ahh, but the prize waiting on the boulder in mid-stream was worth the momentary discomfort. He took a couple of powerful strokes, moving through the water clumsily with the claymore still attached to his back. The sword, still in the scabbard attached to his side, pointed toward the sky as he neared the boulder.

He heard the beauty on the rock laughing. "You swim like a bull with a stiff tail," she taunted.

"I think you mistaken another part of me" Samuel said as he shifted his kilt.

"Oh my, Mr Samuel! If someone was to see that, they might one day call it the Loch Ness monster."

Samuel reached the boulder and pulled himself up beside Heather. He didn't want her to know that he was freezing, but the tremors of his body betrayed him.

Heather laughed again. "You are my protector? Are you shaking with fear of climbing this tiny rock?"

"I am shaking in anticipation of putting you over my lap!" Samuel said with a mocking laugh. He grabbed the girl, who was pretending to struggle, and began kissing her passionately. "Wait... wait...." he said, pausing for a breath. He tenderly cupped Heather's face in his hands and lifted it skyward. "I just want to see you in the moonlight."

The green eyes seemed to become even brighter in the moonlight. A smile spread across the angelic face. Samuel's heart raced, his pulse pounding like a jackhammer in his head. In the pale light, Heather appeared dreamy and surreal. The look of passion and love in her eyes melted his heart. It was a feeling he could never put into words. But he tried anyway. "I love you, Heather."

"And I love you, me darling Samuel."

Samuel's eyes moved from the luscious lips to Heather's open blouse. He smiled when he saw the three freckles around her left breast. He kissed them, letting his lips linger softly. "Ah, my lucky charms," he murmured.

"Samuel, look at the sky. It's filled with stars. Do you know their names?"

Samuel paused, his heart still pounding. What was this? Another flirtation? At that moment, he was not thinking of astronomy, more like anatomy. Reluctantly, he rolled onto his back and looked upward. She was right, in the Highlands, especially on a mountain; a clear sky was rare. Yet tonight, there was no sign of rain or even mist, just a dark sky full of pinpoint lights.

"Look!" Heather said, pointing. "A shooting star!" The streak of blue-white light sped northeast and faded as quickly as it had appeared. Almost immediately, another meteor streaked across the sky. "What a beautiful night," she said, her voice a near whisper.

"Those are shooting stars from my heart," Samuel said. "Come here, woman..." He was almost pleading as he pulled Heather close and kissed her soft, full lips. Looking into her eyes, he began to lower himself for another kiss.

Heather's face was suddenly bathed in an almost blinding light. Her scream ripped through the quiet of the night and her eyes went wide in terror.

Samuel reacted by shoving Heather aside and drawing his sword. Instantly, he was in a fighting crouch. However, this was no enemy he could repel. The source of Heather's blood-curdling scream, a huge hurtling ball of fire, was tearing through the sky toward them. Its path appeared directly toward the young lovers.

There was no time to think. Nothing he could do. Helplessly, Samuel pulled Heather to him and shielded her body with his. He raised his sword in a futile defensive position and held his breath. The object was almost upon them. He closed his eyes, still holding the sword pointing in the direction of the oncoming destruction. The object grew even larger as it neared the couple and the area was a bright white in the eerie glow. There was a horrible screaming sound as the object neared, and Samuel suddenly realized that the screaming was coming from him and the terrified Heather. They prepared to die as the ball of fire descended like the wrath of an angry god.

Samuel knew he was shouting "Noooo!", but he couldn't hear his own voice anymore. The screeching and whooshing of the meteor drowned out his voice, even his thoughts. A sudden hot wind enveloped the two cowering on the boulder. The brightness of the light and the heat seared Samuel's eyes even through the closed lids.

Then, as suddenly as it had appeared, the fiery ball was gone, speeding past the petrified lovers. The sudden darkness and quiet left Samuel momentarily stunned, but he turned just in time to see the ball of flames pass over the peak of nearby Furley Mountain. It seemed to miss the peak by only inches.

A second later, the entire area was lighted up by a huge orange fire-flash as the meteor crashed into the mountainside. The explosion that followed was like a blast of thunder and echoed through the hills with deafening shock waves. The Earth trembled.

"Heather, run back home and tell the men to come to the other side of Furley Mountain. Tell them what we saw. I'm going to see what that was."

Heather gave him a quick kiss and slid off the boulder into the stream. "Be careful, Samuel," she cried and began trying to run through the water. Samuel dove into the stream and swam to the opposite bank. He figured the meteor had to have landed at least two miles away and it would take some time traversing the rough terrain. Crossing the mountain would be rugged going, but it was passable. He jogged, saving his energy, the wet kilt trying to cling to his upper legs. His jerkin felt like a second skin.

It was easy finding his way to the object. An eerie glow was being emitted from the area and Samuel simply headed in that direction. Twenty minutes later, he was rounding the slope of Furley Mountain. It was not a huge mountain, serving as a foothill for the larger ones on the horizon. Samuel came over a small rise and froze at the spectacle before him.

Several men had already arrived at the scene and Samuel was unable to discern the color of their tartans. There was a crowd gathering and more arriving as he watched. Samuel decided to remain on the outskirts and get a feel for the situation before approaching the glowing object. There were too many unknown men in this group. He found a small boulder and sat down, one hand poised on his dirk. Too many of his fellow clansmen had died for a lack of caution. True, the land was at peace now, but small bands of robbers and tinkers roamed about the hills and would kill for a man's scabbard.

As Samuel waited and watched, the crowd of onlookers continued to grow. A scent of burning ore and wet earth filled his nostrils. The strong smell of ozone hung over the area. Samuel sniffed. It smelled as though a thunderstorm might be brewing.

Samuel was too far away to have a clear view of the object that had come crashing through the still of the night and curiosity was beginning to nag at him. His heart was racing with anticipation of what he would find. He watched the other men quickening their paces as they neared the crater the meteor had dug.

Samuel estimated there were more than a hundred men gathered there, and he knew there would be hundreds more before much longer. The men who were close enough to view the meteor were shouting in their excitement. He wondered how far away people had been able to see the bright path cut through the sky. All of the Highlands had probably been lit up.

Rising from the boulder, Samuel began making his way to the crater. Keeping a wary eye for anyone who might pose a threat, he began weaving his way through the crowd, eyeing the men standing at the top of the knoll, their bodies black silhouettes against the glow.

A bagpiper began playing a tune, an exciting piece that encouraged men to gather. As Samuel was approaching the top of the crater edge, he slowed his pace while scanning the faces of the men around him. Most were intent on staring at the meteor and took no notice of him. He pushed his way through the last group and finally saw it. His eyes went wide. His jaw dropped in awe. He stood in stunned silence.

The crater was awesome in its own right. The earth surrounding the area had been charred black. A nearby oak tree was smoking, its limbs still being consumed by tiny flames trying to satisfy their hunger. Inside the crater was what looked like a mammoth rock that was white-hot from the heat generated by entering the Earth's atmosphere. There was a strange glow. It was different from anything Samuel had ever seen. It had what seemed like an electrical quality.

"What is this?" one of the men standing on the edge asked, his face white in the meteor's strange light. "I've never seen anything like this … and it's so hot."

Samuel extended a palm toward the object and felt the heat coming from it. He looked at the hundreds of men standing, gawking, wondering, questioning. And he was as much at a loss as any of them. As he watched, the object seemed to pulse, throbbing like a beating heart. It was beginning to change color now, seeming to cool.

Still, the men stood and watched. Most were silent, seeming almost afraid to voice their wonderment. A sudden flash of lightning lit up the area and men shouted. One man who had been standing too near the edge of the crater stumbled and slipped down inside it. His kilt burst into flames and he managed to scramble to safety where friends helped him extinguish the burning cloth.

Without warning, a sheet of rain blew in from the storm. The raindrops bounced and hissed as they hit the still glowing meteor. Another hour passed and the crater was surrounded by curious onlookers. The men were so engrossed in the strange object before them that they had temporarily forgotten about their enemy clansmen and lessened their normal vigilance. There was little talk among them, as they seemed enthralled by the strangeness of the occasion. They simply stood and watched the huge stone slowly cooling before them.

The eastern horizon began to brighten with the approaching sun, turning pink, then a misty blue. Still, the men stood and stared. "Maybe it's an egg and it's going to hatch a baby dragon," one said. The men near him laughed nervously and kept watch.

By noon, more than a thousand men had gathered around the crater. The huge stone was cooling ever so slowly, a cloud of steam rising above it. A group of women appeared from one of the villages, bringing food and water. Few of the men were willing to leave their favored positions to eat or drink.

Samuel was as hypnotized as the others were. This was truly one of the most spectacular and mystifying events of his life. He had seen the meteor hurtling to Earth and felt the tremor when it crashed into the ground. Now he stood, watching, waiting, with all the others. Wondering.

More hours passed and the sky darkened as another cloud approached. A steady, soaking shower began falling, speeding the cooling of the stone. Suddenly, a jet of steam escaped from the object, followed by another and another. Men yelled and moved back from the crater's rim. The fool who had spoken earlier cried, "See! Dragon! I told ye!"

God, what an army this would be! Samuel thought. Almost every man from the four regional clans seemed to be at the scene, some of them arriving on horses. The descent of the meteor had brought men from the four corners of the country. Even a group of Druids was there and they were chanting in Gaelic. The McDonalds had brought their banner. Several of the different clans seemed to remain grouped, but other men appeared to be alone. Where had these loners come from? Other than the women who had brought food and water, then disappeared, there were no females in the crowd.

By the time darkness had fallen, the stone had cooled to the point that it was no longer glowing and had become an almost incandescent red. The night was clear and a thousand stars twinkled above. Some of the men began making campfires, and the food that the women had brought was being passed around.

A murmuring growing from the crowd attracted Samuel's attention. "I'll do it!" someone shouted, and Samuel recognized the voice. It was Bruce McGuire, the chieftain of his clan, a strong man in his late forties with a face that was as weathered as a tree trunk. Bruce's strength was legendary and some described him as a walking oak tree.

Samuel worked his way through the knot of men to a place where he could see what was taking place. "I'll go down there," Bruce said. More men approached, but no one protested. Bruce knelt at the rim of the crater and scooped up a handful of the scorched earth. It was cool to his touch and he let the gravel slip through his fingers. Then he unsheathed his sword and began descending into the crater. He moved slowly and the men watching him almost appeared to be holding their breaths as he neared the rock. The piper quieted the wailing instrument in mid note, leaving it lingering in the air like the echo of a dying cat's final cry.

Bruce was only a few feet from the meteor when the men began cheering him on. Another step and he paused, extended his sword and inched the point of the blade forward. The cheering men fell quiet. Blade touched stone, just a simple touch of steel against the opaque red stone. A huge sigh escaped en masse from the men. Some of them slapped each other on the back. A few of the braver ones began moving to the rim to lower themselves into the crater.

Bruce suddenly screamed and his body began jerking like a man being electrically shocked. The men who had entered the crater stopped and drew their swords. A small bright light was emanating from the meteor, so bright that it cast Bruce's shadow upon the ground. The chieftain stiffened and his face reflected the horror he felt.

The light was coming from the area that had been touched by the point of the sword. A fragment of the huge stone detached itself and seemed to actually enter the tip of the sword. It began moving up the blade toward the chieftain, not along the blade, but inside it. Amazingly, the sword didn't split or break, the blade simply bulged as the small stone moved inside it, reminding Samuel of a snake swallowing a field mouse.

Bruce was close to panic. He tried to say something that turned into a low shriek. He was mumbling, mouthing words like a frightened child. Making no sense.

The electric-white bulge inside the blade continued its movement toward the hilt in Bruce's hand. The closer it crept, the louder the man's incoherent mumbling became. He tried to drop the sword but couldn't release it. He fell to his knees and furiously tried to pry his hands from the hilt. He couldn't get free and the stone inside the blade was almost to his hands. Bruce became quiet; watching the relentless approach of whatever had entered his blade.

The sword suddenly turned white hot and Bruce broke his short silence with a low moan. He still couldn't free himself from the sword, which began taking on a liquid form, much like mercury, and streamed into his clutching hands. The mercury-like substance was quickly absorbed by Bruce's flesh and within seconds, the entire melted sword was immersed. Bruce fell backward and began scooting away from the meteor on his haunches. He tore off his jerkin and began feeling his arms and chest, seeking to find the sword and stone that had entered him.

A loud cracking sound suddenly came from the meteor. Men yelled and tried to move away from the crater, pushing against the horde of onlookers around the rim. A crack began forming in the huge red stone and it split into two pieces. Those pieces cracked and became four and the process was continuing. Faster and faster. The huge red stone was reducing itself to large pebbles. Within twenty minutes, the meteor had rendered itself into thousands of tiny stones no more than two inches in diameter.

The men were mesmerized. They stood in shock, too stunned and awestruck to react. As they watched, there was a stirring among the tiny stones and they took on lives of their own. They began moving through the black earth, fanning out across the crater. They worked themselves up to the rim of the crater. A man leaned over the rim to get a closer look and one of the stones left the ground and leapt upwards, striking the man in the forehead and immediately burrowing beneath the skin. It was gone in an instant, leaving no trace of its entrance. The man cried out, began running and slapping at his forehead. The throng parted, making no effort to come to his aid.

The air was suddenly filled with the flying stones as they left the crater and found their hosts. Men were scrambling, screaming and knocking each other to the ground as they tried to escape. Bruce the chieftain stood where he had been, a forgotten man, his back pressed to the crater wall and his arms still outstretched before him. None of the stones seemed interested in him — he had been claimed — leaping over his statue-still form to pursue the other men.

A glow suddenly appeared in Bruce's hands and his sword began to take shape in front of him. It began oozing from his hands in the mercury-like form, but quickly solidified and became the weapon.

Samuel watched this happen in stunned silence. The sword Bruce was holding again was exactly as it had been the steel gleaming. However, before Bruce could sheath the sword, it began morphing again, glowing whitely and turning back into the odd liquid that again merged into his flesh.

A tapping on his right boot snapped Samuel out of his trance-like state and he looked down to see a small stone with a reddish streak in it bouncing up and down on his foot. Acting on reflex, Samuel kicked the stone back into the crater and quickly moved away from the huge pit.

Men were running, yelling and fighting to keep the stones from attaching themselves. Some escaped by riding away on the horses that had brought them. However, the coming days and weeks were a time of terror and nightmares for the populace as the stones hunted down their quarries. It seemed that each stone had pre-selected its host that day at the crater and was not to be denied in finding its home. The stones never stopped moving, rolling and searching until they were united with their designated carriers.

Men slept in their beds, thinking they were safe at home, and the stones found them. Some men hid in the forests and catnapped in trees and the stones found them and merged with their hosts.

Samuel had so far evaded his stone, but he knew it was coming. He had seen it a couple of times, recognizing it by the red streak, but he had managed to escape. He spent several days inside his room, tightly barricading the door at night and making sure there was no opening large enough for the stone to creep through. He hammered planks of wood and wet peat moss over the windows. He literally slept with one eye open and his sword in his hand.

It happened on the third night. Samuel woke when something small and light touched his cheek. He put his hand to his face and brought away a splinter of wood. He knew immediately what was happening and moved his eyes to the ceiling. His stone was busily working itself through a space between the mud and wood. It had burrowed through the roof and now was going to burrow into Samuel.

"Oh no you don't!" However, before the protest had been completely voiced, the stone dropped onto Samuel's chest and disappeared inside his flesh.

The Swordslinger jerked awake and sat upright in the Winnebago. He had been asleep for hours and his chest was afire with ribbons of pain. He realized that he must have been clawing at his chest during the dream

CHAPTER 4

THE COMING OF DEXTER

The Swordslinger slowly opened his eyes and looked down at his chest, a snarl crossing his lips. He was relieved to find no telltale redness. He lifted the blinds an inch and saw that it had grown dark outside. He moved to the table and switched the plasma ball on again. There were several dozen lines pointing the way to others like him but they were miles away. The lines were weak. He periodically checked for a strong, intense line that pointed upward. This signified a powerful one was in the vicinity. He was searching for Dexter Frasier.

The thought of his enemy in the opposite world moving freely through the Highlands of Scotland, mowing down men for their stones, sickened him. His sole purpose for existing was to be the executioner of Dexter. When he had passed through the Rippling, he was sure Dexter would be right behind but, apparently, he had been wrong. Instead, Dexter had sent one of his lackeys in hopes of finding a shocked Stranger lost in woe. But the only thing the lackey had gotten was a steel blade across his neck.

Opening the door of the rear closet in the Winnebago, Swordslinger selected black pants, a black tee shirt, black socks, black boots, and his long black London Fog coat. He began dressing, putting on each piece of clothing as if it were armor. When that was completed, he began shaving before a covered mirror. The only reflection the mirror would have revealed was a ghost of a man. A dead man walking. Vanity, ego and pride had all cooled white like burned-out charcoal. The only thing cooking on this ghost man's grill was the steak of vengeance, still raw, but ready to be served. Dexter had to come; it was his nature to follow the most suffering heart. "I know you followed me. I can feel it," the Swordslinger hissed.

He got behind the wheel of the Winnebago and drove to downtown Charlotte. As the Winnebago passed beneath the overpasses on North Tryon Street, the Swordslinger fought the creepy feeling that always possessed him in this area of the city. North Tryon was a street besieged with homeless persons, soulless men, women, and perverts who preyed on anything they could find that was weaker than they were. Shadows lurked in the shadows and the huge concrete columns supporting the overpasses were perfect hiding places for would-be assailants.

There were only a few blocks of this, though, and North Tryon turned into the main artery of Charlotte's heart. He was back in civilization. Normal people stood in clusters below the neon lights of nightclubs and a few shops that were hoping to catch some late traffic. The Omni-present bus stop booths with their sleeping homeless tenants and a few scraggly remnants of humanity sitting on the stoops of urban apartments revealed that this was just another typical night in Charlotte. The Queen City.

A thousand lights glimmered in the skyline as the Swordslinger wheeled his home on wheels through the city. His destination was the Bank of America Building, the tallest structure in Charlotte. The building could be seen for miles as one approached the city. Many travelers said it reminded them of the Empire State Building; it was so splendid in its stature. It was made to look even taller because of the squared platform that from bottom to the top grew smaller almost to a point. And atop that was a steel tower with lights extending to the tip.

The Swordslinger collected the ticket from the parking attendant and steered the Winnebago to the upper deck and into the over-sized section of the parking lot. He cut the engine and sat in the seat for a moment, his eyes scanning the area for anything that might seem out of place. Finally, satisfied that he was secure, he left the Winnebago and moved to the exit stairs. Instead of heading downward, he glanced around once more, then reached up and pulled down the steel ladder that led to the roof of the parking deck.

The parking deck was huge, but was only one-tenth the size of the Bank of America Building. Swordslinger had been here before and always enjoyed watching the steady stream of automobiles and people moving along the street below.

The Swordslinger closed his eyes and summoned his sword. "Draconis … come." The air before him began to stir like a heat wave rising from desert sand. The light was blinding bright in the darkness and he backed away from the ledge overlooking the street, hoping the glare had not been noticed by anyone below.

As the blade completed its formation before him, the Swordslinger grasped the hilt in his right hand. He pointed the sword at the folded iron fire escape on the side of bank and whispered, "Bring it down." He released his grip and Draconis began moving through the air. It traveled past the parking deck ledge and over the sidewalks four stories below, continuing to the folded ladder stairs, where it placed its point against the latch. The flight of stairs unfolded and dropped down beside the wall of the bank. There were three more floors before the fire escape reached the pavement below. However, the Swordslinger wasn't interested in what was below. He was going upward.

The Swordslinger opened his hand and gestured for the sword to return. Draconis obeyed without hesitation. As much as he had initially resented the sword for its uninvited entry of his body with the stone, the Swordslinger had to admit its presence did offer some advantages. The unlocking of the fire escape stairs was just one of them.

The "Rippling" was the most important function, of course, creating a portal between this world and his homeland of seven centuries ago. This magical event had been discovered by accident when one of his clansmen had flung his sword in frustration and opened a portal to a world of the future. That world had been entered near Charlotte, North Carolina, and since that memorable occasion, hundreds of the Swordslinger's otherworld friends had done the Rippling in order to escape the bloody clutches of the evil Dexter Frasier.

Regardless of which world the Rippling was taking the visitor to, it always placed him near the vicinity he had previously left. So when the pioneers of the early Ripplings returned to SkyeEden, they brought friends and loved ones back with them to Charlotte, a dream city of the future, a city with a million lights, astounding to those who had never experienced the magic of electricity. The sea of speeding automobiles, the zooming airplanes that landed and took off in endless streams from Douglas Airport were a source of amazement to the newcomers.

However, while the modern conveniences were magical to observe and experience, not everything was good for the visitors from the otherworld. They were aliens, illegal and without proper identification. The more intelligent and industrious were able to cope and make decent lives for themselves, but many became street people, blending in with the homeless on the bleak streets. Their Scottish accents went unnoticed among the land of the near dead. Others found low-end jobs that paid just enough for survival. But, they had escaped the dread of facing sword of the murderous Dexter Frasier.

Searching for a familiarity in the new world, many of the Rippling evacuees migrated to the nearby Blue Ridge Mountains. They felt more at home in the hills and rugged terrain. Moreover, they didn't stand out the way they did in the city. When these men returned to the otherworld for a brief visit, they spoke to the gathered members of the McGuire Clan about the wonders of their new home. They told of discovering the mountains that could rival those of Scotland. They boasted of having scaled Mount Mitchell, the highest point on the east coast of the new world.

The Swordslinger measured the distance between the parking deck ledge and the fire escape ladder extending down the Bank of America Building wall. Satisfied, he ran to the ledge and leaped across the opening, catching a rung of the ladder and clinging to it. He pulled himself up, hooking the heels of this boots on the rungs for balance, and began the ascent.

The wind was gusting, making the climb somewhat of an adventure, and the Swordslinger held tight to the railing as he climbed. After several minutes, he reached the top of the building and pulled himself up to the observation deck, then paused to catch his breath. His legs were shaky from the climb.

The city of Charlotte lay stretched out before him. Even though he had viewed the scene several times before, the Swordslinger found the myriad of lights below a wonder to behold. His visage clouded momentarily as he thought of Robert. He longed to see what his brother's expression might have been at such a sight. The scene was an insanity of movement with the automobiles moving along the streets resembling lines of ants with their eyes glowing in the dark.

From his viewpoint, the Swordslinger could see for miles. A plane moved along the east horizon, its lights flashing in the sky. The stars were visible tonight, much clearer from this height than from the street level, where the light layer of pollution hovering over the city diminished their brightness.

It was beautiful serene scene, but the Swordslinger had no more time to enjoy it. "All right, Dexter," he said through clenched teeth. "Come on. It's been twenty-four hours and I know you miss me." He stood on the roof, the long black coat billowing in the wind, one hand holding the black hat in place.

The Swordslinger waited, on edge, his nerves beginning to hum. However, two hours passed and there was no sign of his archenemy. He began to feel the pangs of hunger and the constant wind was becoming an irritant. Was he wrong about Dexter? Was the bastard too smart to allow himself to be engaged in a fair battle with someone who might be his equal? It sickened the Swordslinger to think of Dexter back in SkyeEden, perhaps even now dealing a horrible death to one of the McGuire clansmen.

Dexter was no doubt still gathering stones, strengthening himself with each new one. How many stones did the killer have by now? It took only eight stones in a sword for a man to create a Rippling. Dexter obviously had dozens and with each one his strength and powers grew. The Swordslinger was constantly amazed by the feats his sword was able to accomplish. Mercy of God, what could the sword of Dexter be capable of after having taken so many dead men's stones?

Tears suddenly welled in the Swordslinger's eyes as he recalled the way Robert had died. He could still see Dexter's sword swishing through the air, separating and shooting toward them like arrows. He relived the moment when he saw his brother's face contort with anguish as the spikes penetrated his body. He saw again the haunting look in the eyes of Robert, a look that screamed, "I can't believe I'm dying, my brother."

The Swordslinger shook his head vigorously, shaking the troubled memories from his mind. How could a ghost still feel such raw emotions? Yes, he was a ghost. A living ghost. Dexter had succeeded in killing the humanity that had once been inside him. Dexter had ripped out his heart, chewed it up, spit it out and stomped on it. Two words played over and over in his mind. A single thought that drove him, kept him moving. Kept him alive. Kill Dexter! It was an obsession. It was the air he breathed. It was the only reason he existed. There was no longer room for compassion, no room for kindness or love or even grief. He was one hundred percent vengeance. His sole reason for remaining alive was to kill Dexter. He fed on the thought. The hate nourished him, kept him functioning even when tired muscles and mind rebelled.

Impatient, the Swordslinger began pacing over the roof. There was a feeling of anxiety growing within his breast. Somewhere, Dexter was killing someone tonight. Perhaps some of his kin back in SkyeEden. "Come on, Dexter!" he shouted into the wind. "Come on!"

Then it happened. East of North Tryon, about a quarter of mile distant, the lights of half a city block began to flicker. The Swordslinger saw it and recognized it immediately for what it was. A Rippling!

"Ah, and it's about time," he said. "I thought you were going to stand me up, Dexter." He whirled, raced around the observation deck, reached the fire escape and began descending as quickly as possible. After the first few rungs, he placed his feet and hands on the outside rails and simply slid to the bottom. He caught the last rung, and then dropped to the pavement. He pushed his way past a couple of young lovers holding hands and sprinted for the entry to the parking deck. He raced to the elevator, punched the up button. Precious seconds passed as the elevator tediously climbed to the top level.

When the elevator door opened, the Swordslinger bolted through it like a bullet and ran to the rear of the Winnebago. He hurriedly unleashed the harness holding the Harley-Davidson motorcycle, let it drop to the pavement and was astride it before the tires had stopped bouncing. He hit the start button and the cycle roared to life. Keeping his head low, just barely above the handlebars, the Swordslinger sent the powerful machine into a flying start. The tires screamed as the bike circled the deck, missing the concrete wall by an inch.

The parking attendant heard the madman coming before he saw him and began frantically trying to get the barrier to rise. He was outside his booth with a hand clasped to his head and his mouth agape as the Harley zoomed past him, the barrier only just above the head of the crazy man in black with the coat streaming behind him. *A demon from hell*, the attendant thought. He didn't know how close he was to being right.

The Swordslinger bounced the bike into the street, skidding in front of a desperately braking Ford Taurus. The light at the intersection was red, but he didn't wait, instead veering onto the sidewalk, sideswiping a trash barrel and sending it spinning into the street, spewing its contents.

A late-night bar patron, trying to focus his eyes enough to see the "Walk" sign, saw only a black blur and heard a roar as the Harley rushed past him. The Swordslinger crossed North Tryon with the bike registering 80 miles-per-hour. A city cop approaching in the opposite direction almost gave himself whiplash trying to turn his patrol car around quickly enough to get a look at the speed-blurred image. He frantically grabbed for his radio.

Two blocks ahead on the left, the lights of a large building with a spacious walkway in front were flickering.

The Swordslinger steered the bike into the complex, put the kickstand down and ran past the store fronts toward the flickering lights. He could feel the presence of Dexter. He neared the building and saw that it was older than the others around it were. A door was swinging open on its hinges. The Swordslinger raced up the steps to the door and summoned his sword. "Draconis!" The sword formed instantly in his hands and its momentary glow was enough to reveal the interior of what he now realized was a warehouse. The building was filled with wooden crates and dusty, discarded restaurant equipment.

"Okay, you bastard! I know you're here, Dexter," the Swordslinger shouted. "Come on! Let's end this here and now! Show yourself, or are you really just a coward?"

From deep inside the building, the Swordslinger heard glass shattering. With a foolhardy fearlessness, he charged blindly in the direction of the noise. He could barely make out the crates and chunks of metal in the darkness as he ran.

"Where are you?" The Swordslinger had run completely across the floor of the building and was facing a wall. He had seen no one. A neon sign was shining through a window to his left and the blue-tinged light illuminated the sheetrock wall. The sheetrock had been scarred with a blade as someone had carved a message into it. The words tore into the very soul of the Swordslinger.

Your brother's stones were invigorating.

Now I go listen to some Rollin' Stones

Manny ... west highest peak soon dead.

Your devoted friend,

Dex

Manny? No! Manny McGuire had been the Swordslinger's father's best friend in SkyeEden and the father of Heather. Manny had made the Rippling shortly after his wife Martha's death and was living in the Blue Ridge Mountains. Manny had garnered many stones in his revenge against Dexter's men before exiting his homeland. Therefore, the avaricious Dexter was after them.

"Not if I can help it," the Swordslinger said. He melded Draconis back into himself and began retracing his steps to the Harley-Davidson. The highest peak was Mount Mitchell. That was at least a three-hour drive. It was going to be a long, hard night.

CHAPTER 5

TRAPS

As he hurried through the warehouse, the Swordslinger began formulating a plan in his mind. Dexter could not have too much of a lead. He wasn't sure exactly where Manny and his wife were, but Mount Mitchell seemed like the best guess. Dexter obviously knew and wanted him to follow. That's why he had taken time to leave the message carved into the sheetrock: West … highest peak.

At times, the world just seemed too big. The enormity sometimes momentarily overpowered the Swordslinger. This world and SkyeEden. For months, he had tracked the dastardly Dexter, but the killer was always a step ahead. Instead of Dexter, the Swordslinger found his aftermath. Charred bodies. De-stoned men. There were thousands of men in SkyeEden with stones and Dexter seemed driven to possess them all. To get the stones he must kill the owners, which he seemed to delight in doing. And with each stone possession, his immeasurable strength continued to grow. God only knew what magic Dexter's sword possessed even now.

The Swordslinger wondered if Dexter's clansmen, who blindly followed him and outnumbered the prey to assure easy kills, had considered what their mad leader might do after he had consumed all the stones except the ones they owned. If it reached that point, no one in either SkyeEden or this world would be able to stop him.

As he neared the warehouse door, the Swordslinger saw flashing blue lights and heard the trebled nasal twang of men speaking on police radios. Two police officers were standing by his Harley-Davidson One officer was reading the license tag number to the dispatcher. The other was shining his flashlight along the walls of the storefronts, searching for anything suspicious.

Great, the Swordslinger thought. *At least the plate numbers wouldn't raise any red flags.* The bike was clean, the registration

40

and insurance were in his name and there had been no prior incidents to make the bike a target. Still, he wanted no confrontation or interview with the police officers. He didn't have the time. He paused just inside the warehouse and watched the police at work. How long would they stay here? Would they have his bike taken in? Perhaps he should have Draconis do a dance for them and while they were being entertained, he could get to the Harley and escape. Would they shoot him? He doubted that, not for just riding away on the bike. They would probably chase him but their cruisers would be no match for the powerful Harley.

However, suppose they had made a connection between him and the body ashes that had been turning up around the city. That could complicate things. The Swordslinger tipped the black hat back on his head and closed his eyes. A drop of perspiration formed on his brow, trickled down his cheek and rested on his upper lip. The hair on the nape of his neck began to stiffen and rise. The Swordslinger stiffened and without thinking moved his hands into position to hold the sword when it solidified.

The familiar ozone-flesh-steel odor suddenly infiltrated the room. The electrical crackling of a Rippling filled the Swordslinger's ears. Fully alert and with Draconis gripped firmly in his right hand, he shot a quick glance toward the police still busily checking his bike. One of them looked up, attracted by the light coming from warehouse windows. The Swordslinger continued to face the entrance, his back to the sound of the Rippling. Nevertheless, his nerves were finely tuned. He and Draconis were ready for the fight.

"Donachee, that you?" The voice came from behind the Swordslinger. The light from the Rippling had faded and it was dark inside the warehouse where the smell of ozone was still strong in the air.

"Could be. Who's asking?" the Swordslinger responded.

"Three Frasier brothers. Cousins of Dexter."

"Great," the Swordslinger said to himself. "So Dexter knew I would be here and he had these guys come a few minutes after he made his Rippling. He knows me too well."

The sound of a blade slapping against a meaty palm interrupted the Swordslinger's thoughts. There were three of them, standing about 20 yards behind him. Three to one, eh. Good, that pretty much evened the odds.

"So, we gonna stand here all night or we going stoning?" one of the Frasiers asked.

"It's your choice when and how you want to die," the Swordslinger said, his back still to the trio. "You have an option — you can leave now and live or you can still be here when I turn around and die. I will kill you."

There was silence behind him. He could feel the doubts coursing through the three. They had been expecting to find an easy mark in this man, whoever he was, and instead had found a nightmare. Had either of the men been alone, he would have no doubt turned and walked away from this dark stranger of death. However, in the presence of their brothers, manly pride prevailed. One could not show cowardice before the others. So they made their choice. They stayed to fight.

Tension strained the air and the Swordslinger could hear the three men breathing. A snarl began at the corner of his mouth and he gathered himself to move. He let out an ear-shattering "AAAAAAAAHHHHHHH!" and whirled to his right, flinging Draconis at the man on the left side dressed in brown leather.

The sword sped parallel to the floor aimed just below the knees of its target. The man screamed in desperation, leaping into the air and making a downward thrust with his own blade. The swords struck, sending a scattering of sparks into the darkness, and the man fell to the floor with a grunt and a thud. Draconis held in place near the crippled foe.

The remaining two brothers had been taken by such surprise that they had not yet moved. Their heads swiveled to their injured brother on the floor and back to the Swordslinger, then to the beautiful but deadly sword that was hovering near the floor, seeming to emit a glow in the semi-darkness of the warehouse. Draconis seemed peaceful in its inert state, but they were all too aware of its awesome power. They turned in unison to look at the Swordslinger again and he was gone. Frantic, they moved closer together, hoping to draw courage and strength from each other. Back to back, they scanned the surroundings, the crates and the ugly hunks of stainless steel kitchen equipment, sinks, stoves, air vents and grease machines.

Where was the son of a bitch?

Suddenly their attention was drawn back to the sword. It began to lift from the hilt and stand on its point. The blade glowed white-hot for a moment, a trickle of jagged static electricity running along the steel. Then it began spinning … slowly spinning, then increasing its speed. The tip began to rise so that the blade was again parallel to the floor. The hilt raised a couple of inches and the spinning increased in velocity as the angle gave the sword a wobbling effect. As the speed of the spin increased, the sword formed a blurred figure eight in the air.

The brothers raised their swords to defensive positions and continued staring at the spinning blade. Suddenly, it stopped, and then began speeding across the room toward them. They jerked their swords in position to fend it off and Draconis stopped in mid-air. It whirled and streaked for the wall by the door, where it embedded itself deeply into the wood. A steely wood-cracking echo resonated though the warehouse.

From behind them came death in the form of the Swordslinger. His eyes were filled with rage as he charged the two, the long black coat flapping like wings behind him. He struck one of the men from behind, grabbing the startled man's hands and jerking them to the side, neatly slicing his throat with a dirk.

The other brother circled to his right and the Swordslinger dived toward him, his hat tumbling aside and revealing the long hair. The Frasier brother took a mighty swing with his sword, trimming some of the Swordslinger's hair as it passed. The Swordslinger grabbed for the sword that the man with the sliced throat had dropped and the brother drove his blade downward, attempting to pin the Swordslinger's hand to the floor. It was close, too close. The point of the blade struck between the middle and third finger, slicing through a quarter of inch of flesh. The Swordslinger released the sword and rolled into the man's legs.

The brother who had been wounded by Draconis had risen to his knees and recovered his dropped sword. The brother battling the Swordslinger had his sword raised and was starting a downward killing blow when his legs were cut out from beneath him by the rolling block. He toppled forward and his blade missed the Swordslinger and found his kneeling brother, piercing his back. The man screamed in agony and his brother drew back, horrified that he had just killed his own blood. He turned eyes filled with rage and bloodlust onto the Swordslinger, who was scrambling to his feet.

He yanked the sword from his brother's back and came at the man in black, his mouth wide open with a scream that split the night. The Swordslinger was still off-balance, scrabbling backward like a crab. He cast a quick glance at the still-embedded Draconis but was forced to defend himself against the madman coming at him. The last of the Frasier brothers hoisted his sword high and began a swooshing swing that ended in mid-air as the force of Draconis impaling him through the chest broke his forward impetus. The man's jaw dropped. His eyes went blank. He dropped his sword and grabbed at the blade protruding from his chest. He fell to his knees, and then toppled forward, dead before his head hit the floor.

The three swords of the fallen brothers began to glow. They slowly rose and stood on their hilts. The Swordslinger held his bleeding hand and watched the happening, knowing the ritual well. A ring of lightning-white light surrounded the Frasiers' swords and Draconis began pulling out of the dead man. The sword rose several feet in the air and began to blur. The two swords on the floor were crackling as lightning coursed through the steel. From the center of each blade, several dark stones emerged and the swords clanged to the floor. The released stones blazed white and red and drifted toward Draconis. One by one, they moved into the blur that was the sword, which brightened to an almost blinding light. When the final stone had been immersed, the sword twirled until its point was aimed at the floor, and then drove itself into the wooden planks with the force of Excalibur being driven into the stone.

"Hey! What's going on here?" The police officer sprayed his flashlight beam across the floor and it rested on one of the recently deceased Frazier brothers. "Holy Christ! Fred! Fred!" The police officers began clawing at his holster, trying to unsheathe his weapon.

The Swordslinger couched behind a crate in the darkness several feet from the door and watched the scene.

"Wha-?" The second officer had entered the warehouse and he was left mute by the sight of the three dead men on the floor, their bodies lying in what looked like a sea of blood.

"Man, oh man! We've walked into another Valentine's Day massacre," The older police officer named Fred said. "Give headquarters a call and get some people out here. I'm calling CSI."

While the cops were occupied with the dead, the Swordslinger slipped to the door and outside. He had found his hat and was holding it in his hand. Thank God, the police hadn't got around to doing anything with the Harley-Davidson. He saw it standing where he had left it and bounded astride; kick starting the engine into roaring life. The police officers heard the roar and the young cop ran to the door. He lifted his 9mm sidearm and fired off three rounds. The shots surprised the Swordslinger and made him realize how panicked the officer was from what he had just witnessed in the warehouse. The bullets missed, but the Swordslinger was sure he could hear them whiz past his head. He knew his days of moving freely around Charlotte were over. His life in this world would change from picnic status to blood fest. The city would be a shooting gallery and he would be the target.

Thanks, Dexter, you bloodthirsty devil from hell.

The super-charged bike leapt along the pavement, hitting Trade Street and heading west. Over the scream of the engine, the Swordslinger could hear sirens in the distance.

The rookie cop had just fired his final shot and turned to speak to Fred when the three corpses on the warehouse floor burst into flames.

Samuel had put some distance between himself and the warehouse, but he knew the squad cars with the sirens blasting had been given a description of the man in black on the big Harley. He had to use some strategy. As he crossed another intersection, he spotted a taxicab stopped idling in the parking lot of a Pantry convenience store. He slowed the bike, cut across the median and stowed the Harley behind a dumpster near the store. He tapped on the taxi window and the driver rolled the glass down. It was the same driver who had taken him to the junkyard the day before.

The driver felt his face go white when he saw the wild-looking figure in black standing by his cab. "Scare me next time, will ya!" he snarled. Then, getting a closer look at the Swordslinger, he noted the bedraggled appearance, the dusty clothing and the trickle of blood coming from the left hand. *Oh, God*, he thought. *What now?*

"You better getta in, buddy," the driver said. The Swordslinger mumbled a "Thank you" and slid into the back seat. He removed the black hat and brushed the tangled mass of hair with hand that wasn't bleeding.

"You getta into some kinda scrape?" the driver asked, peering at the man through the rear view mirror.

"Yeah, you could say that. Look, take me to the parking deck at the Bank of America Building."

"No problema." The driver wasn't about to give this guy any reason to have his hackles rise.

The Swordslinger leaned back in the seat and watched the scenery flash past. He needed a rest desperately, but knew that would not come soon. He had to get to Mount Mitchell. He had to reach Manny and his family before Dexter.

The cab passed the warehouse where the battle had ensued and the parking area was overflowing with squad cars as well as unmarked vehicles. The rookie cop was getting his tail chewed for discharging his firearm at the fleeing suspect.

A television news van was arriving as the taxicab drove by unnoticed. A police helicopter circled the area, hovering as low as safety allowed, lighting the surrounding area with its huge searchlight.

"Shit, man, you the cause of alla that?" the driver asked, his eyes flicking to the mirror.

"Just keep driving," the Swordslinger said wearily. "I'll make it worth your while."

When they had reached the Bank of America Building, the Swordslinger got out, took a fifty-dollar bill from his wallet, handed it the driver, and began walking away.

"Hey," the driver called after him, "you know the cops gonna trace you to me. Whadda you wanna me to tella them?"

The Swordslinger paused, shook his head tiredly, and then smiled. "Just tell then you picked up some lunatic who was laughing hysterically. In addition, the loony bin tells you he's just pulled the damnedest hoax ever on the Charlotte cops. He burned a couple of mannequins and lit up their lives."

"You gotta weird sense of humor, man," the driver said, and hurriedly pulled away from the walking nightmare.

"Yeah, I do," the Swordslinger, said to himself as he made his way to the Winnebago. He entered the motor home and went to the bathroom, running warm water over the cut on his hand. Leaning forward, he rested his head against the mirror. Tears suddenly came, running down his cheeks. His hands began to tremble.

Irritated, he wiped the tears away. Tears were for living people with emotions. He did not have that luxury. He was a dead man, inside and out. He went to the couch, laid down and used the remote to click on the television. The Live News story was just breaking.

"Here we are again, standing outside the yellow tape of a crime scene where the ashes of three human bodies have been found in a city that has been gripped by fear," the pretty blonde newscaster was saying. "Police say they have no ID, no DNA and can't even determine what race or sex the victims were.

"Only minutes ago two Charlotte police officers were in pursuit of a motorcyclist that they believed had been in this warehouse on Trade Street. As you can see, (the reporter pointed several times, then arched one of her lovely eyebrows at the cameraman who suddenly caught on and panned the camera in the direction she wanted) inside this warehouse are three piles of ashes. Police are sending out an all-points bulletin for the man on the motorcycle, believed to have been a Harley-Davidson, who was dressed in a black coat. The man is tall, probably just a little more than six feet. He was wearing a black hat, not a helmet, and was last seen speeding west on Trade Street. If you have seen this man or have any information, the police ask that you please call.

"I have just been informed that we have just interviewed a man that may have seen the murderer at the scene of the first murder off Third Street and North Tryon. Go head.

Swordslinger recognized the drunk from the alley.

"I saw him down that alley. I was looking for a quiet spot to finish off my booze when I saw him. He was grinning at something on the ground. That's when I saw the head on the ground. I mean that man was scary. What really, really spooked me; he didn't see me at first. Oh, nooooo, it was his sword, help me Jesus. That sword moved in his hands as if it saw me and turned my way. I had to walk two hours with stink in my pants till I got me another pair. Oh, yeah, what really pissed me off was when that sword looked at me, I dropped my bottle and was getting the hell out of there. Then I realized I only heard a clang, not a shatter. It was a shame to leave good booze. I turned around and that...that devil in a black hat said "Leave it. I told him it was his and waddled out of there with a pound of stink in my undies. And you officer, by the camera man, if you ever see me needing a drink bad enough to chop peoples' heads off, shoot me, will you officer? By the way, would you get my bottle if it's still down there? "

The Swordslinger clicked the TV off. He took a first-aid kit from the cabinet, wrapped his left hand in gauze and taped it. It wasn't serious, but the location of the wound made it extremely painful. Finishing the job, he turned his mind to the task at hand. It was time to get moving. The police weren't going to be looking for the Winnebago and Dexter was gaining precious time. Besides, if the cops had located the taxi driver, he knew they would be checking out the parking deck soon. Time to go.

He started for the front of the vehicle, and then stopped, a dazed expression on his face. The realization paralyzed him. He had left Draconis in the warehouse. His face drained white. This was the first time he had been without the blade since his stone had found him in bed that night and merged into his body. Could it be possible that he was rid of the stone and yet still lived? No. Something wasn't right. Even though he had detested what the stone represented, he found a sudden emptiness building inside him. The blade and he had been as one. Now he felt like a walking fragment of a being. A body without a spine. He felt weak and powerless.

Was it possible to just put the sword down and walk away from it? He had. Perhaps the sword knew not to merge back with him because outsiders were watching. Had the sword moved, it would have drawn the cops' attention upon him.

Had the sword sacrificed its merging for his safety? The Swordslinger was astounded by this revelation. But it had to be; Draconis had resisted its natural tendency to merge with its master in order that he could escape. This was something new. Yes, the sword followed his commands, but never before had it shown signs of decision-making for his interests.

The Swordslinger felt a sudden surge of love fill his heart for the blade. For the first time, he had a desperate longing to be united with his sword. He felt that he had been split into two parts and he yearned to be one again.

The Swordslinger took a quick shower and changed clothes, slipping into a pair of Wrangler blue jeans and red turtleneck. He started the Winnebago and left the parking deck, heading across North Tryon to Trade Street. As he neared the warehouse, he noticed that a crowd of onlookers had gathered. Dozens of cars were parked along the street and he parked almost a block away from the building. As he neared the scene, he saw a group of curious people gathered around the roped off area. There were three television camera crews fighting for the most advantageous position.

The crime scene investigators had arrived and taken charge, working quietly and efficiently as they processed the little evidence, they could find. The Swordslinger pondered his next move. He couldn't just walk up to the tape and summon Draconis to come to him. Obviously, the investigators would be transporting the sword to the laboratory, so maybe he could work some magic before it was taken away. *Just wait*, he thought. *Be patient.* He stuffed his bandaged hand into a pocket and watched.

It was almost three hours before the investigators were satisfied and began packing up their equipment. They moved the bags of ashes and other evidence from the warehouse to the van. The sword had been wrapped in plastic and one of the men carefully placed it in the back of the van.

The Swordslinger could feel the yearning of the sword to reunite with him. The ebb and flow of electricity and liquid steel surged through his fingers. His hands tingled with anticipation.

Two of the crime scene investigators climbed into the front seat of the white Ford van and the Swordslinger hurried to the Winnebago. He pulled away from the curb and fell in behind the van. Police headquarters had to be nearby. The van stopped for a red light and the Swordslinger pulled the nose of the Winnebago close up behind it. He had to come up with a plan. Time was running out and Draconis would be almost impossible to get to once it had been removed to the laboratory for testing. The light turned green and the white van pulled away, the Winnebago nosing behind it.

The Swordslinger sighed and closed his eyes, concentrating. "Okay … Now …" He braked the Winnebago and quickly got out and stood in the street in front of the vehicle. The red taillights of the van were steadily moving away. He lifted his arms high, closed, and opened his hands. As he did, a sudden image flashed across his mind, catching him totally off guard and unprepared for the emotion it evoked. This was the same gesture that Heather had made to him so many times. It was haunting to discover a similarity of yearning.

As the Swordslinger clenched his fists and then opened them, there was a stirring inside the back of the van. Heat waves began rising from the steel surface of Draconis and the plastic wrapping began melting. The sword rose in the air and pressed its tip against the glass of the van's rear door. The glass returned to its molten form and began running down the metal of the door. Draconis floated through the window and within seconds was with its master.

The teen-ager driving the Camaro passed the Winnebago just in time to see the sword floating in mid-air toward the figure in black. The kid stared at the blade, and then turned his eyes straight ahead. He reached into his shirt pocket, grabbed the half-smoked marijuana joint and flicked it out the window.

The Swordslinger felt like a man embracing his lover. Elation and sweet joy swept through him as the sword touched the tip of his fingers. Draconis glowed brightly, crackled, and then blurred. As the essence of the blade and stone coursed through his fingers, past his palms, his wrists and into his torso, he felt a warm healing throughout his body. A feeling of great relief came over him.

Swordslinger and Draconis were one again. Breathing a deep sigh, he climbed back into the Winnebago and drove to the convenience store where he had left his Harley-Davidson. He opened the back of the vehicle and removed a steel plank, placed it at an angle from the floor of the Winnebago to the ground. Then he started the bike and rode it up the plank and into the motorhome.

Finally, he was ready to head for the hills. Dexter had a huge lead now, but perhaps there was still time. He had to hurry. He turned the Winnebago west at the intersection. All he had to do now was get on Interstate 85 and follow that to

Highway 321. Another couple of hours and he would be on the Blue Ridge Parkway.

It was almost daylight. Only a few more minutes and the sun would be up. The Swordslinger reached for the lightning ball on the console and placed it in a black dome so that he could determine which way the single large beam was pointing.

West.

"Coming for you Dexter," he snarled

CHAPTER 6

A STOP ALONG THE WAY

He had been on the highway for almost an hour and the calming effect of the driving and the smooth ride of the Winnebago was proving relaxing. He drove with his right hand, resting the injured left hand on his leg. Traffic was beginning to grow heavier on the interstate as people headed into Charlotte for work. It was going to be another hot, humid day. He thought of his sword, Draconis, flowing through his veins and he smiled.

The blaring of the horn from the closely following tractor-trailer jolted the Swordslinger awake. He had nodded off for a second and the Winnebago was veering toward the median of the interstate. He quickly corrected the course, waved a sheepish "Thank you" to the driver of the semi and suddenly realized how exhausted he really was. This was ridiculous. He needed sleep but there was no time. He was already far behind Dexter. Maybe he could make a quick pit stop for some food and drink.

A few minutes after taking the exit onto Highway 321, he spotted a Bojangles Restaurant. *Good as any*, he thought, and pulled the Winnebago into the parking lot. Not wanting to try to negotiate the vehicle through the drive-thru, he parked it in two parking spaces and walked up to the take-out window. His stomach moaned quietly as it contemplated the food.

The teen-aged high school dropout at the window was busy playing with a zit on his face. When the Swordslinger tapped on the window, the teenager looked up, startled to see this strange looking man. He opened the service window, staring hard at the man in the large hat and black coat. What was this, trick or treat?

"Can I help you?" he finally asked.

"Aye, how about two sausage and egg biscuits and a cup of coffee, black."

"Ahh ... sir, this is a drive-through window, not a walk-through. If you're on your feet, you come inside to order."

The Swordslinger's lips curled in a sarcastic smile. "You always so cordial?"

"Huh?" The teenager's mouth hung open, revealing teeth that were pleading for some serious dental work.

"Never mind." The Swordslinger turned and walked to the restaurant entrance. He found a spot in line behind five people, and then decided he should take time to splash some water on his face and freshen up. He left the line and went to the restroom.

The stringent odors of the restroom washed the remaining cobwebs from the Swordslinger's brain. *This stench will probably attach itself to my clothing*, he thought, approaching the sink and taking the hat off. His image in the mirror startled him. No wonder the kid at the window had wanted him gone. His face was dark with beard stubble, his hair was tangled and looked unwashed, and the bandage on his left hand was dirty and added to the grunge look. The words to a song he had heard on one of the oldies radio stations came into his head: "It's been a hard day's night ... I've been working like a dog."

He turned water on and luxuriated in the coolness of it over his hands. God, if they could only have this kind of convenience in SkyeEden. He collected water in his palms and splashed it on his face. As he did, an electric shock surged through his chest and his heart began a panicked racing.

"Mackie, this is a miracle," an awed voice coming from inside one of the two-restroom stalls said as the toilet flushed. "Och! This is amazing! No more droppings in the woods and wiping ye arse with peat moss."

"Aye, cousin," a man in the other stall replied. "We'll have some fine stories to tell our friends when we return home."

More of Dexter's men. Had to be. Damn, they were everywhere. The shock in his chest made sense, now. Draconis was warning him. Glancing around the restroom, he spotted a mop leaning in the corner. He grabbed it and moved in front of the stall doors.

The door of the left stall began opening and the Swordslinger slammed it hard back into the man's face. The sudden impact sounded like a pistol shot and sent the enemy flying backward where he landed hard, his head cracking against the porcelain of the commode. The Swordslinger quickly thrust the mop handle through the steel handle of the stall door, locking the man inside. Draconis was forming from his hand even as he completed the action

The irony of the situation brought a wry smile to the Swordslinger's face. That he could have chosen a fast food restaurant in which two of Dexter's henchmen were taking a crap almost made him laugh. Fate was laughing its arse off at him, no doubt. Of all the Bojangles in the entire world, why …?

Movement from the second stall snapped the Swordslinger out of his brief reverie. The man had slithered underneath the bottom of the booth and emerged near the two urinals. He was rising to his feet, brandishing his still forming sword. The sword was an ugly claymore, small and rusty with a jagged edge on the blade. *Don't get a nick from this relic or you'll die of blood-poisoning*, the Swordslinger thought, stepping back and bending his knees slightly, assuming his fighting position.

As the two warriors faced off, the man with the bruised head slid underneath the booth and groggily gained his feet alongside his companion. His nose was crushed and his face bloodied. His eyes were wild with pain and rage. The Swordslinger knew this adversary would be unpredictable. The men were dressed alike, wearing jeans and flannel shirts. The man with the ruined face had a red bandana tied around his neck.

"Nice touch with the rag," the Swordslinger said, his tight smile grim. "Look, do we really have to do this?" He kept Draconis moving, pointing the tip at first one man, then the other.

"Well," sneered the man with the jagged claymore, "we could sit down on the floor and play marbles with our stones." The cousin snorted a laugh, spraying blood across the restroom.

The Swordslinger sighed. "You will die here today for no other reason but to seek my stones?"

"Something like that," the swordsman said, a macabre grin showing teeth that were as ragged as his blade. "Enough with the talk. Let's get to it."

"As you wish, fool." The Swordslinger moved a step to the left. There wasn't much space to swing a blade and these cousins moved like jackals surrounding their prey. They were dangerous animals. He could feel Draconis buzzing in his hands like a live electric wire.

The man with the jagged blade moved suddenly, throwing his sword at the Swordslinger. The Swordslinger brought Draconis up and over to block and when he did this, the man with the crushed face thrust his blade straight toward the Swordslinger's torso.

Despite the quickness of his defensive response, it was impossible for the Swordslinger to bring his sword around and down to block the thrusting weapon. He desperately twisted his body and felt the blade cut though his bloused shirt. There was a searing pain across his midriff. The movement drove his shoulder into a mirror above one of the sinks and the shattering glass crashed to the floor so loudly that a semi-deaf old lady who was getting out of her car in the parking lot heard it.

The Swordslinger made a move with Draconis that came so close to the bandana man that it clipped an ear. This guy was beginning to look like a one-man sideshow. A crushed nose and one ear. Blood spurting from him like twin fountains. The Bojangles cleanup crew was going to do some serious cursing.

The man's ear fell from his head like an orange peel. Before it had hit the floor, the Swordslinger used the sink to push off and put a heavy shoulder into the man who had thrown the ugly claymore. The man stumbled backward, struggling to free a long knife from his belt.

"Having trouble?" the Swordslinger said, his lips contorted by a sneer. He brought Draconis up in a 45-degree angle from left to right. The sword sliced through the man's thigh, continued to work upward across his chest, and left shoulder. The man's hands went limp and the knife clanged to ceramic floor. His dying eyes fixed on the Swordslinger with a stare of disbelief.

"It was your choice," the Swordslinger said, turning his attention to the profusely bleeding one-eared man. Both men raised their swords and faced off when the restroom door suddenly swung open.

"She gave me a booty call. My babee …" The singing stopped in mid verse and the black teen-ager wearing the red and yellow Bojangles shirt and hat froze.

What the …? Two white dudes having your everyday sword fight in the bathroom. There was blood everywhere and that looked like an ear on the floor. And that honky lying on the floor covered in broken glass was doing some serious oozing from some vital areas. Jawad Jenkins had come to the restroom for a needed bladder relief. The bladder voided when the two swordsmen turned toward him.

But it kept getting worse. The body on the floor was suddenly engulfed in flames. Jawad heard someone scream and realized it was coming from him. The scream was so shrill that it created a pain in the Swordslinger's head. Jawad suddenly quit screaming and set a world record for the backward sprint, exiting through the restroom door and streaking through the restaurant and into the parking lot. The little old half-deaf lady saw him coming but couldn't move out of the way quickly enough. Jawad barely brushed her, but it sent her frail body sprawling to the macadam.

Bandana Man, apparently deciding he would prefer to live to fight another day, made a break for the door. The Swordslinger started after him, but Draconis had other ideas. The sword froze in mid-air, bringing him to a halt. This had never happened before. He jerked at the blade, but it would not be moved.

Then the dead man's ugly claymore began to rise from the floor. It spun wildly, like a man in the throes of death, and then began to brighten, finally stopping to hang in the air. The Swordslinger shielded his eyes from the glare and watched as the stone in the blade began to solidify and separate from the steel. The stone was rust-colored and jagged like the blade. An electric-blue beam emerged from the stone and attached itself to Draconis, which immediately began to brighten, seeming to will the stone to come to it.

The union was chromatic, bright white in the center and rippling, waving rainbow colors around. Bands of light whipped around, undulated, spread, condensed, circled and spiraled. Filaments of purple plasma formed squirming tentacles. Their tips changed into neon pink where they touched the walls and fixtures of the room. The hair on the Swordslinger's arms and neck and top of his head began to lift.

He could actually feel the strengthening of Draconis. What other magical feats could it do? The one magic trick needed now was to get out of here. He took the sword into his hands, watching as it melded into an electric mercury liquid that coursed up his fingers and arms. The liquid was ice and fire. He could feel it spread and run through his arteries, pump through his heart, course along the veins and capillaries, seeping into every cell of his body. His mind became more alert. The world around him seemed to brighten. His thoughts moved quickly, yet had more analytical depth and reasoning power. His confidence surged. He felt whole again and sensed the blade within him had grown in power, as though the wattage had somehow risen.

This was a new experience. Until now, the essence of Draconis had not been so completely given. Before, while it was merged within him, it had been whole and unsharing. It had moved with his summons, but had never felt so truly a part of his flesh and blood as now. He realized that the sword had been as reluctant as he to truly merge into one being. But he knew it was even more than that. The sword took but would not give. It aided its host when it came to confronting enemies, but that was for its own selfish purpose of possessing another stone.

Could it be that the addition of the last stone had enabled Draconis to reach a new level of potency? Something had changed, but now was not the time to ponder it or attempt an experiment to discover what the sword could do with its added stones. Every second was vital now. He had to get out of this place and quick. Police were like gnats on a mule's arse. They came from nowhere and were a serious irritant. They would be trying to kill him now because they were convinced he was a threat to society. There was no way to convince them otherwise. No way and no time to try.

"I know how you felt, Nathan." It was just the way it was. He simply had to deal with it.

The Swordslinger came out of the restroom running. He burst through the glass doors that led outdoors ignoring the possibility that a policeman might have already been summoned. He steeled himself for a hail of bullets, but saw no one except for an old lady struggling to regain her feet near the entrance. He raced for the Winnebago, feeling for the ignition key as he ran. He bolted into the driver's seat and had the engine running in an instant. He shot out of the parking lot and headed for Highway 321. The tires of the powerful Winnebago threw up gravel as he entered the highway and headed west. The pungent odor of burnt rubber permeated the air as the huge vehicle lurched onto the roadway.

Surprisingly, he saw no police cars approaching and heard no wailing sirens. So far, so good. But what he saw next made him have to fight the reflex of hitting the brakes. A strong bright blue plasmic beam shot straight up from the lightning ball. The beam did not waver.

Bandana Man was on top of the Winnebago. The one-eared, broken-nosed bastard was coming along for the ride. He had not fled the scene after all and was obviously planning to decapitate the Swordslinger at the first opportunity.

And then he heard the sirens.

"Oh, yes, there they are," Stranger acknowledged. "Perfect!" The cops were on the way and he was sure someone from the Bojangles restaurant had informed them about the Winnebago. "Damn!" Now he would have to get rid of the motorhome. That would complicate his lifestyle in this foreign land even more. The thought of ditching the Winnebago saddened and angered him.

He was nearing the mountains now and to the left he saw the first of the foothills. Farther away against the western horizon he could see the first dark shape of the mountains. Blue-black in the distance with a slight haze covering the tip. Somewhere up there was Dexter. But first, he had to deal with the most current danger, the man on the roof that was being pointed out by the lightning ball. The beam from the ball pointed straight above. Then another beam appeared in the ball, this one pointing due west. Oh yes, Dexter was definitely there.

His mind occupied with a killer on top of the Winnebago and another dead ahead in the hills, the Swordslinger was mindless of the speed he was traveling. The highway had not taken on the turns and twists of a typical mountain road yet and was still four-lane. The speedometer was hovering on 90 miles per hour. *Wonder if I should have Draconis punch a few holes in the roof*, he thought. No, it would be better to wait and deal with the bandana man when he could find a suitable place to pull off the road and take care of business.

The Winnebago lumbered past a series of cars, its speed creating a wake of air that made some of the smaller vehicles shudder and almost veer off the road. The speed of the motorhome was what caught the highway patrolman's attention. Sergeant John Justin had just finished jotting down a description of the wanted vehicle from an all-points bulletin when he felt his cruiser vibrate and looked up to see the Winnebago whiz past.

"Shit!" Sgt. Justin muttered. "I almost missed the S.O.B." Had the Winnebago been traveling at a normal speed, he probably would never have even looked up from his pad. He punched the radio and reported in. "Winnebago suspect in sight. Speeding. Am in pursuit."

The patrol car had been headed east, but a tire-smoking U-turn had the Ford Crown Victoria on the trail in an instant. The Swordslinger hadn't even seen the patrol car when he passed it, but he had picked up the U-turn action in the rearview mirror. "Great! Now what?" The patrolman was rapidly gaining on the speeding Winnebago. He had to do something. Quickly.

Large pines and hardwood trees, making an exit impossible, lined the highway at this point. Immediately ahead were the mountains, where negotiating the Winnebago was going to be treacherous at a high rate of speed. The sign read "Table Rock" and the arrow pointed left.

Almost as a reflexive action, the Swordslinger hit the brake pedal with his black boot and the Winnebago went into a wild skid, finally coming to a brain-rattling stop. There was a shout from above accompanied by a couple of thumps and Bandana Man's right leg was dangling in front of the windshield. The Swordslinger chuckled and turned on the wipers, then floored the accelerator and sent the vehicle plunging across the pavement, over a shallow drainage ditch and onto a one-lane gravel road that disappeared into the woods.

Sergeant Justin, a 15-year veteran of the proud North Carolina Highway Patrol. nearly lost his new black and gray Crown Vic as he reacted to the move of the Winnebago. He relayed the new direction to headquarters and whipped the cruiser through the blue smoke left from the burning tires of the motorhome. The car went airborne as it jumped the ditch and came down hard on the gravel road. Justin fought the fishtailing until he had regained control and floored the chase car. He was burning now. This stupid son of a bitch was looking to die and the sergeant just prayed that he didn't take anyone else with him.

The Swordslinger was desperate, but not as totally stupid as the trooper had him figured to be. If only he didn't meet someone coming down the narrow road, he might be able to make it. Top speed now was 40 miles per hour and even that was a bumpy, metal-wrenching ride over the seldom used road. It was like driving through a tunnel as the trees created a canopy and the rays of morning sunlight breaking through the foliage made the interior of the Winnebago flicker like a disco joint with strobe lights. The motorhome hit a huge rut and lurched up and sideways, causing the Swordslinger's head to bang against the roof and bite his tongue.

Wonder how Bandana Man was enjoying this ride?

The road was becoming steeper as it climbed the foothills. It had become a snake now, winding to lessen the incline. There was a thud against the windshield and the Swordslinger saw a surprised flying squirrel bounce off the hood and hit the ground the running. Tough little nut.

The Swordslinger was freewheeling, ad-libbing. This road could come to an abrupt end at any moment, maybe around the next curve. But he didn't think so and he had to trust his instincts. Through the branches and waving limbs he caught glimpses of looming mountains ahead and he knew that only a few curves back, there was one mad highway patrolman coming. Fast. As the road climbed, the vegetation became sparser and the terrain was dotted with huge boulders. The pines grew so tall that he couldn't see the tops from the Winnebago driver's seat. The motorhome was having its paint removed by the overhanging branches and the engine was beginning to strain from the ever-steeper climb. The accelerator was on the floor and the speedometer was registering a grumbling 34 miles per hour. The patrol car had to be gaining now.

"Come on. You can make it. Come on!" The Swordslinger was squeezing the steering wheel so hard his knuckles had turned white.

The sign read:

Table Rock

Parking Area Ahead

The parking area was nothing more than a miniature plateau. It was surrounded by trees except for an opening on the south side where there was a sheer drop-off. The cliff, covered with scraggly trees growing at a 45-degree angle in their struggle to reach for the sunlight, ended several hundred yards down in a rock bottom. The Swordslinger nosed the Winnebago to the edge of the precipice and stared at the obstacle. It was as dead-end as a brick wall in the city.

The patrolman was still coming, the siren eerie and distant but getting closer.

The Swordslinger sized up his predicament, shrugged his muscular shoulders and reversed the Winnebago to the far side of the parking area. He shifted the motorhome into park, closed his eyes for a moment to gather his nerves, whispered "God save me," and crossed himself. "Brother," he said, "start preparing supper. I may be dining with you tonight."

When he exited the vehicle, the Swordslinger saw the bandana's man leg shift to conceal himself on the roof. *Fine, stay up there, chump.*

Opening the rear door, Stranger rolled the Harley to the ground. Time was short now. The police siren was rapidly approaching.

Returning to the front of the vehicle, the Swordslinger picked up the lightning ball and wedged it against the accelerator, pushing it to the floor. The roar of the powerful engine was deafening and the motorhome shuddered as the power surged through it. The Swordslinger wondered what his hitchhiker on the roof must have been thinking. Whatever it was, the thought wasn't going to last much longer.

"Stay up there just a moment longer, friend," he mumbled, glancing toward the roof. He reached for the gearshift and jerked it into drive. The Winnebago lurched forward, the tires screeching in protest. It was moving fast — too fast. The Swordslinger jumped back and raced for the idling bike.

The Winnebago was screaming across the parking area, gaining speed as it neared the drop-off. The speedometer registered 35 miles-per-hour as the nose cleared the precipice and the front wheels bounced over the asphalt curb and the bandana man was running to the rear of the roof and diving but his pants leg caught on the luggage rack. He was caught and taken with the plunging vehicle.

"Tough break, fella," the Swordslinger said. The siren was blaring now as the patrol car neared. The Swordslinger could hear the gravel beneath its tires. Any second the car was going to appear on the ascent of the road.

The Winnebago completed its swan dive from the cliff and struck the rock floor on its nose. The horrific sound of metal crunching and ripping was followed by a deafening explosion that sent shock waves through the Swordslinger's body. Almost buried in the other sounds was a blood-curdling scream from the man who had taken the death plunge on the roof. Parts of the exploding Winnebago flew through the air and embedded in the cliff. Burning pieces of wreck scorched the nearby vines and tree trunks and some small blazes sprang up in the brush.

"Go, go, go!" The Swordslinger whipped the bike around. He didn't have time to continue up the road. He couldn't go down. Go along the edge to the right, go downhill and cut around the cop. The tip of the blue light bubble appeared down the road.

The Swordslinger sent the bike flying to the right dangerously close to the edge and the tires lost traction as the bike slipped over the ledge. He had cut his margin of safety too thin. He wrenched the handlebar accelerator all the way to max and the machine lurched forward, burning rubber on rock. His heart sank. The bike wasn't going to make it. Its momentum wasn't enough to get them up the side. He was going to fall. He was going to die. Then, the wheels gained traction for a second and sent him rocketing upward. The bike went airborne then landed in a skid and a spray of gravel. The front wheel struck a boulder, swung around with its hind wheel airborne and slammed into the trunk of a tree.

The impact was so abrupt the Swordslinger blacked out. A moment later, he opened his eyes and found himself partially beneath his bike. He was bruised and bleeding, but his survival instincts were still functioning. He used every ounce of his strength to raise the crumpled Harley off his aching body and managed to pull himself free, hanging on to the ugly little trees that now seemed so beautiful to him.

The siren wailed to a halt as state trooper Justin screeched his car to a stop in the parking area. The sergeant climbed from his car, ran to the edge of the cliff and saw the smoke and flames emanating from the wreckage below. For just an instant, he thought he saw a man's leg before the flames engulfed it again.

Returning to his patrol car, Sgt. Justin told the waiting dispatcher, "Suspect's vehicle has gone over the cliff at Table Rock. Send emergency assistance, but survivors are unlikely. Send the fire department, too, because the flames are spreading from the impact area. Jesus!"

"Justin?" the voice on the radio crackled.

"I got my binoculars out," Justin said. "There's a shoe wedged in the luggage rack on the roof of the vehicle. Jesus!"

"What now?"

"It looks like a body down there but it's just ash," Blackburn said.

"Officer Justin, please switch to a secure channel."

The trooper was talking loud and fast and the Swordslinger was so close he could hear the radio conversation. *Maybe I'm getting a break*, he thought. "Maybe they'll think Bandana Man's body is me. Ahh, that would be sweet justice."

The Swordslinger suddenly flinched. Like an unborn child giving its mommy a swift kick, Draconis suddenly awakened inside him. The sword was coming out on its own accord.

It would not be denied a freed stone and blade. It somehow sensed Bandana Man's stone was free. Thank God, it was still light. Maybe the sword's glow would not draw attention.

The Swordslinger felt the electrical essence flow from his arms to his hands. He watched in utter fascination as Draconis began to form and solidify. It's metallic and flesh odor thick in the air. Yes, he loved this sword now, but in moments like this, he felt a twinge of terror. The sword moved on its own. It either thought or moved in a mindless instinct that would not be denied. One day, this would get him killed. In the midst of taking flight for survival, Draconis was simply going to stop and take a stone. Dread reared within the Swordslinger at the thought of the patrolman peering through his binoculars and spying a

65

sword suddenly floating in the air and then following it to where the Swordslinger lay now.

"Get the stone! Quickly!" the Swordslinger hissed. The sword began moving down the mountainside and met the other sword half way. Bandana Man's sword was beginning its stone-giving process.

Draconis floated stealthily though the air and buoyed itself near the giving blade. The flames from the burning vehicle masked the beams of bright light that accompanied the stone giving. This was the fifth stone for Draconis in the past 24 hours. Even from his perch, The Swordslinger could hear the crackling and whirling of energy.

"Come back to me, damn you" he whispered. "If that cop sees you, I'll break you in half!" It was like having a loved dog, letting him out to pee and he runs all over the neighborhood, ignoring your calls. He loved the sword, yes. But, it's indomitable will made him want to plunge it into a pool of acid. Now that the stone transfer was completed, Draconis obediently rose and floated to him, settling in his grasp.

"Do you think in there? Hello?" Stranger tapped the blade. "Or are you just a mindless magical programmed relic. My life depends on you," he pleaded as the blade merged with his hand.

Moving cautiously, but as quickly as he dared, The Swordslinger edged as far right along the wall as he could before beginning his strategic descent down into the ravine. After a few minutes of scrambling, he reached the bottom and, remaining concealed in the dense brush along the cliffside, made his way into the woods. He wanted to put as much distance between himself and the wreckage site as possible.

A badly bruised left leg forced the Swordslinger to move with a limp, but he knew he had to keep moving. He was without transportation with both the Winnebago and the Harley-Davidson being rendered into twisted metal. He limped along, covering ground as quickly as possible, until weariness and the searing pain in his leg forced him to halt.

He sat down with his back against a tree trunk and began assessing his injuries.

He lifted his shirt to check out the sword cut on his abdomen from the fracas in the Bojangles and grunted with satisfaction. There was plenty of blood, but the cut was only skin-deep. Lucky again. The blade had been shunted by the broad leather belt he was wearing, probably saving his life.

Drained mentally and physically, his nerves raw and his body aching in every joint and muscle, the Swordslinger realized he had to take a break and gather himself. "Draconis, come," he said, and the blade immediately formed in the cradle of his hands. "All is forgiven. Protect me while I rest. I place my complete trust in you, faithful companion. My life is yours." He brought the sword to his lips and kissed the steel blade.

The sword was all he had left. It was a connection with his beginning and the only protection for the future. He pressed his flushed face against the flat side of the sword and it felt cool against his flesh. He could almost feel the blade pulsing. The Swordslinger's lips formed a wry smile as he recalled how Draconis had become his. His eyelids closed and the memories began playing across them like images on a movie screen.

CHAPTER 7

THE SWORDSLINGER COMETH

"**O**uch! Robert, don't hit the hands," Samuel said to his brother, shaking off the sting in his fingers.

"It's your lousy blocking," Robert said, grinning.

"Right! You, four years younger than I, not two weeks of learning the blade, and you're telling me it is my fault?" Samuel lifted his pretend claymore — a three-foot branch from a tree — and brandished it in mock anger.

"Ahh, you are older, but I am quicker," Robert said, dancing out of reach. "This 10-year-old can best the 14-year-old." He was thrusting his "claymore" and bobbing from side to side.

"You're just a wee bug not worth the whacking," Samuel retorted. He mockingly turned his back on his brother and began walking toward the house.

WHACK!

"Hey!" Samuel cried. He rubbed his stinging buttocks and turned to see his brother grinning, tapping the branch in the palm of his hand. He decided to keep his mouth shut. He was tiring of the game and perhaps if he didn't respond, Robert would settle down.

Samuel entered the main room of the house and found his father hard at work mending a shirt. As Samuel watched, he held the shirt out at arm's length, his tongue protruding from a corner of his mouth as he concentrated. Stewart was a huge man who stood six-foot, one-inch and weighed 270 pounds. There was a bulge above the waistline of his trousers that had developed from the ever-increasing amount of mead that he consumed.

"Could you use some help?" Samuel offered.

His father turned bloodshot eyes to him and said, "Aye. Run this thread through the eye of the needle. I can sew good enough, but damned if I can run a thread through this flea hole."

"Why don't they just make the eye larger?" Samuel asked, reaching for the needle.

Stewart cast a surprised glance at his eldest son. "Och, and that's a good question," he said, his lips curling into a smile. "I thinks it's the women keeping them small so they can make the men feel inferior."

Samuel laughed as he ran the thread through the needle on the first try and handed it back to his father.

"Aye, laddie, "I've had my suspicions that you were a god. Now I know for sure."

Samuel chuckled and watched his father as he resumed his mending chore. "Father," he finally asked, "could you teach me the ways of the sword."

Stewart lowered the shirt and raised his eyes to look at his son. "I guess you're big enough to lift a claymore now," he said, "but I just don't have the time, Samuel. Since the death of your mother, my having to do all her chores and the blacksmithing work, the days are past before I know it."

Samuel lowered his head and mumbled, "You could teach me at night, father. You don't have to go out every night."

Stewart's large face grew red. Anger flashed in his eyes. "How dare you speak to in that manner?" he blared. "I work to feed us, keep a roof over our heads, whack on the anvil hour after hour. Don't you think I deserve a wee dram of whiskey at the end of the day?"

A surge of rebellion filled Samuel. "A dram?" he said. "Nae, father, a gallon." He realized what he had done and gasped, wondering how his father would react.

He didn't have to wait long to learn. Stewart rose from the chair and gathered his son's shirt collar in a fist. He twisted it so tight that Samuel found it difficult to breathe.

"How dare you!" Stewart shouted, and shoved his son backwards. Samuel fell backward over a chair, his feet and legs dangling in the air. Robert came running into the room, saw what was happening and broke into a laugh.

But when Samuel clambered to his feet, tears in his eyes and his face contorted in a grimace, Robert grew quiet and took a couple backward steps. What was going on? It was too early for father to be drunk. He retreated to the bedroom and curled up on the bed, waiting for the crash of objects being thrown against the walls.

But instead of attacking Samuel or going into one of his all too often rages, Stewart reached out his arms to his son and drew him close. "I'm so sorry, Samuel," he said, his voice heavy. "I know I've been drinking too much, but it's just that I miss your mother so much. She's been gone these 10 years and I still grieve for her. Can you forgive me?"

Samuel stepped back and looked at his father. Suddenly, he felt more like the father than the son. "I forgive you, father. I do," he said quietly. Then he reached out a hand and wiped a tear from the older man's face, turned and walked outside.

The sky was as always overcast. If it wasn't raining, it would be soon. The day was unusually warm with no wind. The air felt sticky. Samuel hunkered on the ground near the door of the house and let his mind roam. The house was on the main path to the village center and he enjoyed watching the people pass on their way to shop or attend to chores.

Sitting in the almost bare expanse of the yard, Samuel was able to view everything that was going on along the street. He watched wounded men stagger into the village for treatment and watched the bands of vigilantes who almost immediately formed and headed off in search of justice from the persons who had injured their friends. The entire world — the part of the world that Samuel was aware of — passed along the street in front of his home.

The village sat in a valley, protected from the elements by the surrounding mountains. In the hills above, frigid temperatures and strong winds discouraged settlers, forcing everyone to reside in the valley. An observation post was maintained, with at least one volunteer from the village standing duty to sound a warning of approaching enemies.

The village was the last of the Highland Frontier. Just across the mountains was the Northern Sea and Samuel had crossed the mountains many times during the summer months to fish in the ocean and track any game that might be come across during the trek such as elk, moose, mountain lions, deer, bear and the gulls. There were thousands of gulls that roosted in the cliffs along the seashore.

Samuel loved the ocean. It seemed so huge and seemed to go on forever until it disappeared on the horizon. He dreamed of other lands beyond that blue horizon, but sometimes also had terrifying nightmares of drifting to the edge of the world and falling off. There were many often repeated wild tales of Vikings and giant barbaric men who rowed ships around the island, daring to risk losing their lives by falling off the edge of the world.

Samuel shrugged and sighed. *My adventures end at the doorstep*, he mused. His eyes fell on the scruffy and worn boots on his feet. He and Robert could have better clothing if his father didn't spend all his money on his nightly outings at the pubs. There were times when there was no money for weeks and he and Robert ate leftovers supplied by the generous village women. Mostly it was bread and soup — all varieties of soup. Strange soups made of combinations of foods that Samuel didn't want to spend a great deal of time thinking about. He knew the villagers made the soup from some truly disgusting stuff such as haggis, chunks of felled birds, various vegetables and, worst of all, pig brains. Revolting! Sheep guts and pig brains! Just the thought of the soup made his hunger pangs disappear.

Samuel stretched and sighed again. It was nearing dusk and the only thing he had eaten was fist-sized piece of bread he had found on the floor beside his father's bunk. He had cleaned off the green mold and washed the bread down with a swig of cool water.

The boy's reverie was broken by a shout. "Hey, Samuel!" the girl shouted. It was Heather, a year younger than he was at 13. A slim girl with thick reddish hair and green eyes that always made him want to stare closer into them. They were such a light, brilliant green that they seemed almost transparent. She was with an older girl and they were passing along the street.

"Hi, Heather," Samuel said, giving her a limp-handed wave. He and Heather had been friends forever and often talked about what life would be like after they had married.

"My mother is making some pudding for supper," she said, knowing how to get his full attention. "If you like, I'll bring some to you after we have eaten."

That would be great, Samuel said, his eyes brightening at the thought of some real food. He sat up straighter and involuntarily licked his lips in anticipation of the tasty, spicy pudding assaulting his taste buds. "You're a good girl. Thanks."

Heather tossed her head, creating a swirling mass of red hair, and continued along the street, casting one final glance toward the boy in the desolate yard.

It was then that Samuel saw the lone figure dressed in all black coming down the graveled path on foot. The man wore a round-brimmed black hat and a long black coat that waved and fluttered when the wind blew. His boots were black. Even his hair was black. It was as though someone had taken a knife and carved a silhouette from the scene.

The man's hands were covered by black gloves and one hand rested on the hilt of a sword that was partially obscured by the black coat. The black hat was pulled low in front and the only parts of the face that Samuel could see were the nose, mouth and chin.

The boy was so intrigued by the figure in black that he wasn't aware he was staring, his mouth hanging agape. There was an aura of danger surrounding the man. The black hat resembled one that a Catholic priest might wear, but Samuel knew this creature was no man of God. No, this man was more of an anti-Christ. He was the doomsayer — a bringer of death.

The man was very near him now and Samuel could hear the heels of the black boots scraping on the gravel of the road. The man's eyes, themselves as black as coals, appeared below the brim of the hat. The eyes were squinted as in a hunter's intent gaze.

Samuel's stare fell to the hilt of the sword. He could make out the shape of a dragon on the hasp and he felt a cold chill beginning to engulf his body. He had never seen such a sword. The hasp appeared to be solid silver and the dragon's wings were folded, eyes squinting from the horrible head as ominous as those of its' master.

"Boo!" the man said, the black hole of a mouth moving under the shadow of his hat. Startled, Samuel fell backwards a second time that day. He leaped to his feet, his heart racing. He hadn't known the man was even aware of him.

"Peripheral, lad ... think peripheral," the man in black said. As he spoke, neither his head nor his eyes turned toward the scared boy. He continued his pace along the roadway, the boots crunching in the gravel, acknowledging no further awareness of Samuel, who stood and watched the back of the man as he moved toward the village.

"What language is that? Samuel asked. "Per....pet...you...roll? Och, like a game. You see someone's pet and ye roll?" Samuel stopped with a sudden horrid look on his face. "Please tell me, Mister, you're not talkin' of boogerin'?"

"What?" The Stranger stopped, turning around, put both hands on his hips and laughed hard.

"My brother says the reason our milk goes sour so quick is that old man Farrow gets drunk and rolls his cows for boogerin' before he milks them," Samuel said, exasperated now.

"What?" The stranger staggered back, holding his sides. "No more. Shhh, on the matter, boy, you're killing me. Peripheral means seeing" he laughed, "Hold on," he tried to catch a breath and wiped tears from his eyes. "It means seeing from the corner of your eye. Be facing straight but being aware of what is happening to the sides of ye."

"Oh," Samuel bushed.

"I'll never be able to drink a bottle of milk again," the Stranger said to himself as he continued walking toward town

As Samuel regained his composure, he realized that this dark stranger's arrival in the village was going to create a commotion. This was something he did not want to miss. He turned to the house, meaning to tell his father that he was going into the village, and then thought better of it. Maybe the old man was so intent on mending the shirt that he might forget his nightly ritual of visiting the village pub. No need to interrupt him while he was doing something with his hands other than lifting a tankard of ale.

Glancing around to make sure that Robert wasn't watching, Samuel began jogging down the road. He slowed after a few yards, though, not wanting to attract the attention of the man in black who was several yards ahead. The man had probably already seen him. Must have eyes in the back of his head as well as the side.

The reaction in the village was just as Samuel had imagined. The first woman who saw the strange figure in black jerked her head up and emitted a little yelp, dropping a basket of linen in the middle of the commons area.

"Oh, this is going to be good," Samuel, chortled to himself. Nothing exciting ever happened around this place outside of the occasional raid from intruders who were quickly vanquished. This creepy guy was going to cause the end of the world for the villagers. Few of them had ever dared venture far from their homes and knew little of the kind of people who lived outside their little domain.

There was a moving wave of awareness among the people as the black-clad stranger approached. Men arose from whatever tasks they were performing and stared. Many of them unconsciously fingered the hilts of their blades. Women hurried inside, hoping to gain safety in their mud brick, straw-thatched homes. Even the dogs were nervous, beginning a staccato of barking and yowling that brought the curious to the stoops of their homes. "There's a stranger among us," the dogs yelped.

Clan chieftain Bruce McGuire was seated on a rock in the front yard of his home when he saw the man coming. Bruce was a tall, broad-chested warrior of a man. His legs showing below the kilt looked as strong as oak trees. Samuel watched the leader of the village, wondering what his reaction would be.

Bruce glanced around him, wondering if anyone was thinking of approaching the Stranger, either to extend a welcome or a warning. He saw no one moving. There was a space around the Stranger that no one seemed eager to violate.

Samuel grinned as he watched the emotions move across Bruce's rugged face. *Looks like it's you, our fearless leader*, the boy thought. He edged closer, not wanting to miss any conversation that might take place.

With the sun behind him, the Stranger's menacing shadow preceded him. His gait was even and unhurried as he strolled the village's main street. His hand was no longer caressing the dragon on the hilt of the sword. *Maybe that's a good sign*, Samuel thought as he kept pace with the man. Maybe the confrontation would be a peaceful one.

Samuel was near enough to the Stranger to be able to see the thick coat of dust that covered the black coat. He could hear the flap of the coat as if whipped around the man's legs. He could even smell the man … a strange smell, not unpleasant, rather like that of dried rosebuds.

The man in black was an arm's length from Bruce when he paused. He said nothing, merely staring at the chieftain.

Finally, Bruce broke the silence. "You are the Swordslinger, aye? You got our message and you're going to help us, aye?" There was almost a pleading quality to Bruce's voice. "Is there anything we can get you? Come on, anything you want, my friend."

The man in black stared hard at the chieftain, the slitted eyes seeming to measure the man before him. "A hot meal, a warm bath and soft bed for a night's sleep should cover it for now," he said, the voice quiet and giving away nothing of the mood the man might be in.

"Och, and I think we can help you with those," Bruce said. "I'll make the arrangements and we will meet at my home tomorrow. I'm sure you'll be desiring to rest from your journey this evening. Take your time. There's no rush. We'll have several days to make our plans."

The man in black stared at Bruce for a moment longer, then said, "I'll see you tomorrow," and turned to walk away. But the chieftain wasn't quite ready to let him leave.

"Hey," he said, glancing at the curious onlookers, "there's not going to be any trouble until, you know, until they come. Right?"

The Swordslinger stopped and turned back to face Bruce. For the first time, he smiled. The teeth were white and even, a stark contrast to the blackness that shrouded the man. "Peace begets peace," he said. "Uninvited trouble begets my wrath."

The Chieftain thought for a second, his eyes studying the man's face beneath the hat brim. "Some say that you lived in the Frasier territory before you became a swordslinger. But you speak differently. Where have you been?"

The man in black tilted the hat back on his forehead and continued to stare at Bruce. "I come from one end and go to the other," he said. "You talk too much. Where will I find my room?"

"Follow me." Chieftain Bruce turned and began walking, his eyes never leaving the Swordslinger in black. Samuel giggled, expecting the chieftain to stumble over something and fall. Bruce walked to the two-story stone-faced building that was called Rock Inn and rapped his knuckles against the door. The door creaked open and the men entered, closing the door behind them.

This perplexed Samuel. He wanted to keep the man in black in his sight. He ran to the inn, circling the building until he found a window on the south side that offered a view of the interior. He could see the dark shape of a man inside but the room was on the second floor. The house next door to the Rock Inn had a low roof and by climbing up on the stack of firewood piled alongside, Samuel was able to pull himself up to the straw-thatched cover. He crawled around until he had a bird's eye view of the inn window.

The Swordslinger removed his coat and hung it on a wall hook. He tossed the black hat toward the hook and it hung there, just as Samuel had known it would. Then with a lightning-quick move that made Samuel blink, the Swordslinger unsheathed his sword. He bent slightly at the knees and settled into position. The blade was held in the right hand, parallel to the floor on a level with the dark eyes.

Moving slowly and gracefully, almost dance-like, the Swordslinger began swinging the sword through a routine of angles and arches. The sword moved in circles so swiftly that the blade was a silver blur in the dim afternoon light.

Just as quickly, the sword was returned to the sheath. Samuel's pulse raced and he was afraid he might lose his balance and fall from the roof. This was magic! He had never seen anything like this! The Swordslinger loosened his belt and removed the sheathed sword, placing it on the bed. Standing with his back to the window, he removed the black shirt, the strong muscles in his shoulders rippling from the movement. He moved to the night table and began bathing himself with water he poured from the ewer into the bowl.

Samuel had seen enough, He scrambled down from the roof and ran home. There, he found his makeshift sword and began trying to mimic the moves the Swordslinger had made. At first, he was awkward, several times losing his grip on the branch and dropping it. But after a dozen tries, he managed to twirl the "sword" in one hand. Elated, he screamed, "Yeah!" and ran to the room where he had left his father with his mending chores.

"Father," he cried proudly, "Look what …" The chair was empty. Robert sat on the floor, idly flicking small stones against the wall.

"Gone out again, is he?" Samuel asked.

"Aye, he's out."

Samuel shrugged and tossed the make-believe sword into a corner of the room where it clattered to the floor. The magic was gone. It was just a stick. He stood for a moment, his bottom lip forming a pout. Then he brightened and smiled. "Come on," he said to his brother. "Let's go over to Heather's house. Her mother's making pudding."

Heather's promise was valid. He and Robert stuffed themselves on creamy rice pudding that was sweet and served to stimulate the boys' deprived taste buds. Everyone had a laugh at Robert's expense as he somehow managed to smear his face with the yellow pudding. His portion gone, Robert covertly eyed Samuel's remaining morsels.

"No way, you barbaric beastie," Samuel laughed. "Ugh! Clean yourself. You look as if someone had used your head as a spoon to get pudding from the bowl." Heather and her parents laughed along with the feasting boys.

Heather's father Manny was a stonemason by trade and brought his profession home with him in the way of dust and calluses. But he was a proud man — proud of his ability to provide well for his beloved wife and four children. The wife was no longer the attractive young thing he had married, but she had given him two sons and two daughters and their life together was a good one. Besides, he often thought to himself, I am no longer a stripling myself.

The wife had beautiful eyes, but the rest of her was worn and used. The toll of caring for four children and a husband, cleaning and cooking and scouring, showed in many ways. Her short reddish-gray hair appeared to have been gnawed by a wolfhound.

Still, Samuel could see some of the mother in Heather. The girls had obviously inherited the best traits of each parent, including the red hair from the mother. It was a light auburn and in the sunlight, it sometimes seemed that Heather's head was surrounded by flame.

No one spoke of the boys' father, Stewart, or offered to send him any pudding. There was no need to dwell on the subject of a night-lost father. It was heart breaking; it was "low-being."

"Samuel, it's going to be cool tonight, do you have blankets to sleep under?" Heather's father, Manny, asked.

"Aye, we do, sir. No need to worry for us. If it gets cold this evening, the pudding in our stomachs will keep us warm."

Everyone laughed, but it was a laugh tinged with a hint of pity on the part of Heather's family. Manny seemed to want to say something else, but decided not to. He smiled at the boys and said, "Well, guess we should all get ready to retire soon. Goodnight, lads. It's always a pleasure having you visit."

"Aye, our stomachs feel the same," Samuel said. He reached for Robert's elbow and helped him to his feet. "Thank you, sir for your kindness."

Heather walked part way to the door. "Samuel, tomorrow I have to help wash clothes.'

"Sure, I'll come and protect ye from the barbarians and wild beasts," Samuel said, puffing out his chest. And again, everyone laughed.

As they left the house, Samuel cast an eye on the Swordslinger's room at the Rock Inn. It was dark now and the lamp was out. The Swordslinger was sleeping or, maybe,… Samuel turned to look farther along the street to row of pubs or…maybe he was there. Maybe in the same place as his father.

"Come on, Robert. Let's go home.

The smell of whiskey told Samuel that his father was at home. The boy woke from a deep sleep to find his father leaning over the bed, the stale breath harsh in his face. What time is it?

"Wake up, Samuel! The rough hands on his shoulders shook the drowsiness from Samuel and he sat up, rubbing his eyes. It was dark outside, the middle of the night. "What is it, father?" The boy knew there was disgust in his voice but he was too sleepy to care.

Stewart sat down on edge of the bed, the old mattress complaining under the weight, and ran a dirty sleeve over his lips. His eyes looked like two rotten eggs in a slop bucket. Samuel couldn't help giggling at the thought. "I just wanted to tell you something," Stewart said, increasing his grip on Samuel's shoulders and leaning closer. The stench of his putrid breath made the boy want to gag, but he tried to conceal the grimace on his face.

"I love ya, boy," Stewart said, slurring the words. "I really do love ya." He swatted Samuel on the back so hard the boy felt his skin burning beneath the thin nightshirt. "You're my first born, son," Stewart continued, pulling the boy to him and pressing his stubbly cheek against his face.

The stink of whiskey breath was worse than the prickly feeling of the beard, but Samuel didn't pull away.

"You know I love ya, boy. You know your father does, don't ya?

"Aye, father," Samuel said coolly.

"I know ... I know I spent me money. But it's okay. I have some work for this week, some swords to make and a skillet. We'll have food on the table, son. Piles of food. Food like you never seen before. And I will buy you and Robert some new shoes. I love ya, Samuel."

"I know father."

Suddenly, Stewart was sobbing. He held onto Samuel, his body jerking with emotion. "I miss your mother, Samuel. God, I miss her. Why did she have to die? Why? She's supposed to be here taking care of her boys. I'm a blacksmith with a warrior heart. I don't know nothin' about child rearing. I love you, Samuel."

Samuel held himself rigid in the man's grip. He wanted to feel pity for his father but he understood that it took whiskey for him to speak so openly. How could a man be so aware of his problems and yet do nothing about them? It was as though two people lived beneath his father's skin. There was the father that was sensitive and loving ... and there was this pathetic whiskey-drinking tinker who gave no thought to family or money — only the drink.

"Samuel, I think I have to go outside. I'm getting' sick."

"Yes, father," Samuel said, tears beginning to flow down his cheeks.

Stewart rose on unsteady feet and Samuel watched him stagger toward the door. As his father stumbled through the dim candle-lit room, Samuel wiped the mixture of whiskey sweat and tears from his cheeks.

Moments later, he heard the gagging and dry heaving coming from the yard. The mental image made Samuel feel sick himself. Half the neighbors were probably awake by now, looking out their windows and doors to see Stewart's magical trick of transforming money into liquor, then to whiskey-stinking mud.

Stewart was trying to say something through the gagging and vomiting. "I waaa ddrinnk..ing... be...cawse of ye mooooooother... I'm so sor(gag)ree."

"Sweet Jesus," Samuel swore to himself. He went outside and helped his father off his knees. "Come inside, father, I'll clean you up."

"I loo ahhh ye so-son."

"Aye, it shows in all ye do," Samuel said, hoisting his father up and guiding him toward the door.

"Waaaa...what did you say?"

"I said we better start to move."

"Och, aye! Thought ye wer-re trying to be witty on me."

"Come on before the neighbors see you," Samuel said.

Once Stewart was washed up and the puke wiped from between his fingers, Samuel walked outside to get some air. He had no other intention but that; however, he found himself walking toward the village, as if some invisible string was pulling him along.

The air was crisp and laden with cold. Puffs of mist came from Samuel's nostrils as he walked. His kilt of wool did a fair job of keeping him warm. It fell to below the knees but his legs were bare between the hem and the boots.

He quietly climbed up on the roof of the house next to the Rock Inn until he was eye level to the Swordslinger's room. The single candle flickered from the nightstand in the room. The shutters were still open, even on this cold of night. *A man like that is used to cold night air*, Samuel thought. *Or, cold simply don't bother him at all.*

The Swordslinger's silhouette filled the window. Samuel gasped, instinctively ducking down, and almost lost his balance and tumbled off the roof. Did he see me? Did he? Samuel panicked. He prayed to the Almighty he was not seen.

Peripheral, kid. Peripheral.

He did not know what that word meant, but thought it probably applied right now. After a long, tense moment, Samuel dared lift his head. The Swordslinger was no longer there. The candle was out. All Samuel could see was darkness.

Morning began for Samuel with a furious knocking on the door. He rose and pulled his kilt up around his waist. Half asleep, he mumbled, "We hear you. We hear you. Patience." The air in the room reeked of whiskey.

"Stewart," the man had who rapped on the door said, "you got a man waiting at your shop. I don't think he's the type who's accustomed to waiting. I have a feeling he'll pay good for any service ye render him."

"Uncle Mac," Samuel called out. He opened the door enough to stick his head out. Mac was his father's brother. The other villagers referred to him as the runt of the liter. He was no taller than five-foot-five inches and weighed about 20 drams of whiskey.

"Father went to the stream to clean some berries he bought for us last night," Samuel lied. "We'll be having a big breakfast, but I will tell him to hurry to the shop. He should be back any moment."

"He needs to be there now," Mac said, his voice testy. "Stewart needs the money for you kids, Samuel. You're getting skinny as me. I eat, but this is the way I am. You're half starving and I know it. Get him now. Go!"

Samuel blinked at the outburst. "I'm gone." He let the door slam behind him and crossed the road into the meadow that led to the stream. When he knew Uncle Mac could no longer see him, Samuel sneaked a peek from behind an oak. Uncle Mac had his ear pressed against the front door. Finally, he straightened, shook his head and began walking back toward the village.

Samuel ran back to the house and slid to his knees next to his father's bed. He worked his arms underneath his sleeping father to lift him up. "Come on, father, you got a customer. He has good money."

"Oh, me, Christ riding on a donkey upside down. Me head's a killin' me!" Stewart opened his eyes to peer through yellow crust. "Ah, what a wretched day this is. Get me some water. Uggghhh! What? What did you say?"

"There's a man that needs your work. He's waiting and Uncle Mac says he'll pay."

"Pay? You'd think I've never made a coin in me life the way you're blabbering," Stewart said, stretching one arm with one hand on the side of his head.

"I only meant he may pay ye well. And, we need the money this morning to buy some food. Robert and I have only had pieces of bread and pudding in two days."

"Pudding?"

"Heather's mother."

"Aye, Ohhhhhh," Stewart stretched again and placed both hands on the side of the bed before attempting to rise. "Be a good lad … get me a cloth and some water here. Guess I better hurry down there. I don't want my boys starving and having to take handouts."

Samuel had a secret motive in rushing his father to leave for the shop. He thought the chances were pretty good that the waiting customer might be the Swordslinger.

"Can I go with you, father? Maybe you could use my help today." There was a plea in Samuel's voice.

"That's fine, but what about your brother? He's still a wee young to be left alone."

"I'll drop him off at Heather's. She's washing clothes in the stream today. She won't mind and will be glad to have him keep her company."

"Okay … if you really want to."

"I do … I do." Samuel gave his father a bowl of water and a washcloth. He then turned toward Robert's bunk, where his younger brother was sleeping face down with his little buttocks poking in the air. "Wake up, me impish brother. The ghostly Haggis is coming to get ye."

Stewart left while Samuel was helping Robert to get dressed. He escorted Robert to Heather's house, telling them his father had a job to do and needed his help. He embellished the tale by saying they were going to make some money, buy some food and have the heartiest midday feast they had ever had.

Samuel ran the rest of the way into the village, casting an eye at the Swordslinger's room at the Inn as he passed. The shutters were drawn, what if the Swordslinger had simply decided to move on? The sudden thought made Samuel anxious. He quickened his pace and was winded by the time he reached the doorway to his father's shop.

His fears proved unfounded when he saw that the Swordslinger was there. Samuel had to fight the urge to let out a cry of relief. Holding his breath and walking softly, he approached until he was only a few feet behind the man in black.

"My …. oh, my. This is a beauty. The craftsmanship … the forge of its steel. There's not a sword of this quality in the Highlands. Where did you get her?" Stewart asked.

Samuel inched closer and turned the side of his head to get maximum hearing. He didn't want to miss a word that the Swordslinger said.

"The sword was made for payment of my services."

"Wha' did ye do? Win a country for a king?"

"Something like that. So, can you do it?" The Swordslinger asked.

"Aye, I can do it. She'll be the sharpest she's ever been. What is the hilt made of? Is this really silver?"

"Don't worry about the hilt. When will you be finished?"

"Give me a couple of hours. I want to do her right, oil her, and have her shining as crystal on a summer's day."

"You do her right and you'll have a week's worth of money coming to you."

"Aye, ye know how to woo the muscle of an ironsmith," Stewart said, holding the sword in both hands.

"Do you have a heavier blade I can carry until this one is finished?" the Swordslinger asked.

"You must be a very cautious man," Stewart said. "I've got a 12-pound claymore leaning in the corner if that will suit you."

"The heavier the better." The Swordslinger hefted the claymore and felt its weight. "This will do fine. I'll be back in a few hours. You'll have my sword for security."

"Aye, I understand. I'll begin work on this immediately," Stewart said as he moved to the wet stone wheel.

CHAPTER 8

BECOMING A STUDENT

The Swordslinger walked out of the shop and past Samuel without acknowledging the boy. He stopped in the street and looked around, seeming to ponder which direction to take. Finally, he turned to the north, adjusting his leather gloves while the claymore was in the crook of his arm.

Villagers did not shrink from the Swordslinger's presence now. They were becoming accustomed to seeing him and merely looked up to see where he was and where his sword was, then continued at their chores.

The Swordslinger reached the outskirts of the village and cut through a thicket of brush before pausing in a clearing among some giant oak trees, not seeming to notice the boy furtively trailing him He removed the black coat, laying it carefully across a boulder, and placed his hat on the heap. Stepping into the center of the clearing, he began a stretching routine while holding the claymore in an extended position.

Samuel watched from his hiding place behind one of the oaks as the Swordslinger began a repetition of various strokes. He repeated an overhead stroke over and over. The muscles in his arms bulged from the weight of the heavy claymore. The next stroke was a 45-degree slice from right upper shoulder that finished by the lower left thigh. Anything that came in the path of that blow would be devastated. The routine continued through eight different strokes that the Swordslinger repeated a dozen times each. His face and arms were glistening with perspiration in the morning sun.

The Swordslinger paused for a moment, closing his eyes and seeming to gather himself before resuming the workout. This series consisted of a continuous swing that created the figure eight before him. Seeing that advance had to be a terrifying feeling for a foe, Samuel thought. He was thankful that he was behind the man.

The Swordslinger moved into position near one of the old oak trees. Taking a fighting stance, he suddenly lunged at the tree and began a lightning assault. The blade, moving so quickly that it blurred in the sunlight, stopped centimeters from the bark of the oak. The moves were stunning, belief defying, and so deceptive that it would be impossible to predict where a blow was going to fall. When it appeared he was taking the sword back to swing around his head, it swooped downward just inches from his chest, then cut straight back across about where the imaginary enemy's neck might be.

With eyes still riveted on the oak, the Swordslinger suddenly swung the blade at a smaller tree nearby and a lopped off branch fell to the ground. "Pick it up, boy. Might as well swing something if you're going to stay here and gawk."

Samuel froze in fear. The Swordslinger knew he was here! Terror tingled brightly across Samuel's whole body. And yet, his heart beat excitedly at the prospect of learning some of the moves the Swordslinger had exhibited.

"Move, boy," the man said. "There won't be a second chance."

Samuel rose to his feet, keeping wary eyes on the Swordslinger. Not once had the man even glanced his way. Picking up the branch, Samuel moved directly before the man. Summoning all the courage he could muster, he raised his gaze into the Swordslinger's eyes.

The eyes were a mixture of ebony and brown that seemed as black as the Swordslinger's wardrobe. They appeared to be bottomless holes, except there was something lurking within them. They were dead, but haunted eyes.

"Who are ye?" Samuel asked.

"I have no name," the Swordslinger said evenly.

"Then, what are ye?" It was an odd question, but it certainly seemed appropriate to the awed Samuel.

"I'm a swordslinger."

A swordslinger! Samuel had heard tales of drifters who wandered the lands, selling their deadly talents with a sword to the highest bidder. Many were revered as heroes for having rid a village of murderers and thieves and bullies. But there were only a few remaining in the land. The way a swordslinger made his reputation was by proving that he was the better man by defeating other swordslingers in duels to the death. No wonder there were so few young blades. And no old ones. Until now, a swordslinger had only been a myth to Samuel.

"I know you've been watching me, lad. You like my sword, do you?" It was statement more than a question.

"Aye," was the only response Samuel could find.

"You want to know the ways of the sword?"

"Aye."

The Swordslinger held the claymore in the palms of his hands as though offering it to Samuel. "Swords — true swords — are not made solely of metal," he said. "They can be infused with your soul. They are like lightning rods. They become extensions of yourself. They represent you. Their steel is their constitution. Their straightness is your unbending courage and morals. Their sharpness is your wit."

Samuel's eyes were helplessly transfixed on the blade, roaming the length of the 52 inches of forged steel.

"A swordslinger lives and dies by the sword," the Swordslinger said. "She is your mistress. She is the spine of your soul. To bring dishonor to yourself brings dishonor to her. She never… NEVER… is allowed to touch the ground. That is a most grievous sin that reveals a lack of respect."

Samuel nodded. He had no idea such reverence was paid to the blade. It was almost fairytale romantic. He wished that he had a real sword. One made of steel instead of the wooden sticks that he pretended were his swords.

"Never show the full length of your blade unless you intend to draw blood," the Swordslinger continued. "Never let the sword stain or rust. Remember, the blade is a part of your soul. It is the most precious, most sacred part of your being." He gingerly moved his gloved hand along the length of the blade as a lover might stroke the leg of his mistress.

"What happens if it breaks?" Samuel suddenly asked.

The Swordslinger's eyes widened. "Your back breaks. You become a broken, worthless man not worth the air you breathe."

Was that true? Samuel wondered. He imagined his back snapping. That would have to hurt — would have to kill you. "Can you teach me how to fight?"

"To fight?" the Swordslinger growled. "Nae, boy, not to fight, but to harmonize."

Samuel cocked his head to the side, not comprehending.

"You become a living force with the blade. You become part of the balance of nature. And, it is your part to make the balances."

"You mean fight the bad men?"

"You will find the forces of disharmony seek out the swordslinger. All he has to do is wander the land. The purity of spirit and steel attracts anti-balance. You simply harmonize with your blade the forces around you. Peace, serenity and balance are restored."

"Will you teach me to be a swordslinger?" Samuel asked.

The Swordslinger paused, seeming to reflect for a moment. "There are so few left. And those that are have short lives. You are a boy, live as a boy, and grow to be a man, build a home and family. That is what you should do."

"But I don't want that. I want to be like you. I want a sword of my own," Samuel blurted.

The Swordslinger stared at Samuel and a deep sadness crossed his face. "I once dreamed a thousand nights those words would be spoken from my own son."

"You have a son?" Samuel was surprised. A swordslinger had no time for women.

"Before I became priest of the sword, I was a husband and father of a son. My wife was butchered after she was raped by a band of tinkers. It ignited a fire in my heart that has not gone out. I wandered for days, weeks, and months to track them down. I found them on a December night just outside a village on the eastern shores. I walked into their camp and I cut them to pieces with my dirk. My body was soaked in their blood."

A chill passed through Samuel's body. He was horrified. He felt the violence and horror in the Swordslinger's voice and sensed the emotion that fueled it.

"I gathered their swords and broke a piece from each blade. I carried these with me until days later when I got a man to row me to the mainland. From there, I wandered east. I walked the land, and as I walked, I made balance along the way to any criminals or bad men. I stayed for a while in a village; found the disharmonies, and made the balance. The villagers paid me for my services. Then, I moved on. I wandered and walked miles after miles, stopping at villages where the languages were strange.

"Months passed and I continued walking and harmonizing, laying a trail of blood behind me. Then, one day I wandered into a village of men with slanted eyes. Their customs were strange ... but they accepted me for what I was and invited me into their world. And it was there that I first saw the ocean. I had walked to the end of the earth.

"While in the village, I sought an ironsmith. I brought to him the pieces of blades from the swords of the butchers of my wife. He forged them into one blade and made a carving of the hilt into a dragon.

"With this magical blade, I began my journey back home. It was time to go. My trek home was quicker and less bloody than before. However, the villages I revisited carried my name in fables and legends. There were folk songs praising my exploits. Brave young men sought me out to prove they were the better swordsman. They sought me out and they died.

"After a passage of time, I'm not sure how long, I came back here to the Highlands. I thought often of my son. I wondered what kind of young man he had grown to be. I felt ashamed for leaving him as I had — abandoning him — but at that time, I was no longer a man. I was walking vengeance. I was blade and nothing else. The only reason I lived was to avenge my wife's death. After I fulfilled that quest, I just kept going until I could go no longer.

"It was there, when my next step would have sunk into the sea that a part of me awoke from this bloodlust dream I

89

lived. Finally, I knew that I had to return for my son. Perhaps there was something in me left untouched or unsoiled by the violence and sins of those tinkers. Maybe my son was a man of honor…. a man worthy of carrying the blade."

The Swordslinger sat down on the trunk of a fallen tree, resting the claymore across his knees. It seemed time had stopped. The world had stopped turning. Spellbound by the tale of the gunslinger, Samuel became only an ear that listened.

"I returned to my Frasier Clan. Yet, when I got there, for reasons I still don't understand, I concealed my identity. I kept my hat low to conceal the features of my face.

"It was the second day I was there when I discovered my son in the village square where the youth gathered each day for schooling. He was tall and stood straight. I was proud. I wanted to run to him, embrace him, and say your father has returned. Yet, I didn't. I don't know why.

"When the school day ended, he skittered off with several lads that were of the unseemly type. I followed, always within hearing distance. I heard them cursing and making obscene remarks to the women. I heard my son saying these things.

"When evening came, they went behind a pub. They talked a man into bringing them mead outdoors. They drank and told raunchy tales. My heart sank each time I heard my son's laughter.

"Eventually, they began walking along the outskirts of the village. They moved like a pack of wild wolves. I realized soon into their quest, that they were seeking a woman. It was not long before they caught this beautiful young lass alone. She was heading back to the village, when the pack surrounded her and forced her into the forest. They taunted her, circled her, and nipped like dogs at her heels to tear a piece of her clothing off.

"I cannot tell you the rage and shock I felt to see this happening. When I looked upon them, I did not see this lass, but my wife. It took all of my strength to hold back. I don't know why. It was not out of fear, but possibly shame . I don't know.

"But when I saw my son strike the girl down and began to lift his kilt, I saw black spots before my eyes. Black rage consumed me. I drew my blade and screamed. "Dexter! God damn you! Not my son! Not this!

"The lads scattered. There I was, suddenly, after years of wandering, standing before my only son with his kilt hiked up over his thighs and the most ridiculous look on his face. He was shocked. Dismayed. And, I imagine, terrified. For my sword point was pressing against the center of his spine.

" 'Father?' he snarled. 'My beloved cowardly father who ran away when mother was killed? My truly great heroic father who abandons his son?' He knocked my sword away from him. I was speechless.

"Then he spat on my boots and said in a cold voice that could freeze blood, "See what you have made me, Father, I am a mother's raper. Are ye proud of that, Father?

"I reached out to him, wanting to console him, wanting to ask for his forgiveness and tell him what had happened to me and why I had left. But, he did not give me a chance. It was his next words that broke my heart, making me realize he was damaged forever and had become a creature from my own loins that now had become my personal demon. He told me, 'I was only teasing her, but now that you are here, I want to rape her, father, and you pretend it is mother all over again. I want to put you there to witness what you so cowardly ran away from. I rape her in your name, father. Watch.'

"I grabbed him by the shoulder. He whirled and put his dirk against my throat. "If I ever find you again, I will bring the wrath of hell upon your cowardly flesh. Never! Never come within my gaze!' He turned and walked away. He left the girl lying on the ground, weeping. The other boys, lurking nearby, followed him. I've not seen him since."

Samuel swallowed dryly. This was not a specter or a mysterious swordslinger, but a tormented man, who had nothing else but his sword — a sword forged by the blades of the murderers of his wife.

The Swordslinger raised his eyes to meet Samuel. "You're a good lad. Run back home. Live."

Samuel remained unmoving. He slowly reached out and touched the claymore lying across the Swordslinger's lap. "I want to be a swordslinger. I want to right the world of wrong. I want to bring harmony and balance into being. I want to be the blade."

Tears came to the Swordslinger's eyes. "Perhaps you are the son I should have had."

"Then teach me. Teach me the way of the sword," Samuel insisted.

"It is a lonely, dangerous life, lad," the Swordslinger said.

"Then, that is my fate," Samuel said.

The Swordslinger studied Samuel's face. "A swordslinger ye shall be."

CHAPTER 9

THE WAY OF THE SWORD

"When will you teach me?" Samuel asked anxiously.

"Hmm, right now is as good as any. For your first preparation", the Swordslinger reached into a small pouch hanging off his belt and retrieved some coins "get us some bread and cheese from the baker. You must keep your teacher fed so he may teach." The man in black gave a short laugh.

Samuel darted for the village like an arrow. It seemed for the first time in his life, he had a mission, a purpose in life. Being a swordslinger was akin to being a knight, a protector of the people. His father's trade was respectable — he made the blades and sharpened them for warriors. But therein was the problem — he created them; he did not use them to make the balances, as the Swordslinger liked to say.

Several huts before the bakery was his father's ironsmith shop. Samuel jarred the side of the hut with his sudden entrance. "Father," he said, excitedly and out of breath, "The sword ..., I mean, the man whose sword you are sharpening is going to teach me to swordfight."

Stewart rose from his sitting position by the spinning whetstone and turned toward Samuel. He wiped sweat from his brow. "And why would he do that?"

Huh? The question caught Samuel off guard. What did that have to do with anything? He gathered his breath. "I don't know ... because he's lonely I guess, needs someone to spar with. Because I asked him ..."

"Och, you asked him to. We don't know this man. No one does. He could be a murderer and you ask him to teach you. Why don't ye just ask me?"

Samuel was confused. Why had he stopped here? How stupid was that? And the question he was just asked astounded him. "Father," he said carefully, "I have asked you."

Stewart's face reddened, either from the exertion of sharpening the blade or anger at the impudence of his son. Samuel braced himself. Had father been drinking? He glanced quickly around the shop for a mug of mead.

Stewart just stared at Samuel, his face emotionless. He started to speak; mouth opened, shut, and opened again. "Go, then. I have work to do," he said, turning his back to the boy.

Suddenly, Samuel felt guilt. All of his excitement had dissipated like a tiny flame under a stomping foot. Then, like bile, anger began to rise in his stomach. Why did his father do this? Why couldn't he for once have something to be happy about with being chastised? *No*, he thought. *No, I will not let you ruin this time for me.*

"I'll be north just left of the road about quarter of a mile," he said and literally fled from the shop so he could rekindle his fire of enthusiasm.

"Samuel," Stewart started to say something, but turned to find Samuel was gone. "God, help me. I am not a mother." He pulled off the leather apron and stepped outside his shop. He saw Samuel at the bakery and wondered what he was doing there. Maybe looking at the food they hoped to get after the Swordslinger paid him later this afternoon. He took a couple of steps toward the bakery and heard Samuel saying, "The Swordslinger's buying us food and he's going to teach me how to use the sword."

"Oh, is he now, young Samuel?" asked Fredrick the baker, as he handed the boy a loaf of bread and a slice of cheese large enough to feed a family of six.

Samuel paid the baker with the swordslinger's money and turned to sprint toward the road when his eyes locked on to his father. Never had he felt so caught in the act of some despicable deed. He was transformed from excited young boy to a standing stone. Somehow, his mouth began moving and words came out loud and clear as if everything was fine. "He asked me to pick up some food for him as payment for his teaching me the sword," Samuel said.

Stewart stood in the street with his hands on his hip. No opening or closing of the lips. It dawned on Samuel that perhaps his father was as stunned as he was.

"Better get going," Samuel said, and began jogging toward the northern road out of the village. He didn't look back, yet he felt his father's gaze upon him. "What was all that about?" he wondered. There was nothing harsh or mean in what his father had said, it was only concern. His anger toward his father for not being excited for him was unjustified. He was only acting the role as a father who cared for his child. But just now with the food ... what was all that about? He wondered as he hurried, but his worries faded with each step toward the Swordslinger.

Samuel thought of all the adventures and duels the Swordslinger had faced. The confrontation with his son was horrible. "Perhaps you are the son I should have had," the Swordslinger had said. *Maybe he was the father I should have had*, Samuel thought. All his father did was beat iron and drink. The Swordslinger was a living, walking, breathing legend. He was a hero to the people he helped and walking death to those who opposed him.

Oh, the cheese smells so good ... the thought popped into Samuel's mind, causing him to forget about everything else. He brought the wrapped cheese to his nose and inhaled. The aroma almost made him swoon. His side wasn't aching from jogging but from hunger. Just take the food and run, the devilish voice sounded in Samuel's mind. He laughed, and hurried on.

The Swordslinger was sitting against an oak tree, one hand resting on the hilt of the claymore. He raised his head at the sound of Samuel's approach. "Och, ye made good time." He arched an eyebrow. "Is it all there?"

"Aye, I only sniffed it once," Samuel said, smiling. He placed the food before the Swordslinger and watched like a starving pup by a pot of stirring stew.

Swordslinger unwrapped the cheese carefully. Agonizingly slowly, he removed his black gloves and carefully folded them on his lap. Next, he unwrapped the long, thick loaf of bread. He removed the dirk from his boot and methodically wiped the blade with the bread wrapping.

Samuel knew he was going to faint of starvation any second. He closed his eyes trying to blot out the sight of the cheese and bread.

The Swordslinger held the dirk before him, catching the light and making sure the blade was clean. He slowly began slicing the bread.

Samuel's tongue parted his lips.

"Never let a man know the intensity of your wants," Swordslinger said as he began cutting into the cheese. "A man knowing your wants is a man that has power over you."

Samuel's mouth was watering as he stared at the cheese.

"When you see something you want — really want — but cannot have, you can choose to torture yourself and grieve about it or turn your head from it and end your self-torturing," the Swordslinger said. "Which way would you choose, my young student?"

Samuel cleared his throat and pulled his tongue back from between his lips. "I turn my head. But what does this have to do with sword fighting?"

"Self-control," Swordslinger said, and took a bite of the bread and cheese. "Discipline," he continued, the cheese and bread showing in his mouth as he spoke.

Samuel felt like crying, but dared not.

"There is much more to be aware of than a swing of a blade," the Swordslinger said, taking another bite. "Ummm …," he wiped his lips. "Ever keen you must know the difference of what is right and what you desire. From town to town, you'll roam. You are a sword for hire. Yet, you must …," he swallowed and took another bite, "… decide as a judge what is the right and what is the wrong. You protect the weak, the meek, and the good from being trampled by the bad. You never … NEVER … succumb to temptation or desires of what ye want if it draws you to the side of bad. Once you cross that line," the Swordslinger closed his eyes and took a long, slow bite into a piece of the cheese, "ye break your oath, your honor, and yes, your blade."

"I don't want the cheese!" Samuel blurted the lie.

The Swordslinger burst into laughter, then tossed the hunk of cheese to Samuel. "Eat it and enjoy. It is no longer what you desire. Desired things always seem to have a price. If another knows your desires, they will make you pay a price. If they think you do not want it, you'll get it for free."

"I don't want this," Samuel said, chewing frantically at the deliciously tangy cheese, almost choking. "I don't."

They both laughed.

After their snack, the Swordslinger began the lessons. "There are eight swings to the blade," he said. "Watch as I execute each one. This is the overhead, the right 45-degree angle cut, the bottom left to right shoulder cut; the left shoulder down to the lower right; the lower right to upper left; the left shoulder behind the head to right; then the reverse, the back over the right shoulder, going over the left shoulder to make the head cut. Then, there is the forward thrust."

Samuel was lost. He had been confused since the second stroke. It was frightening seeing such a massive blade as the claymore slicing the air and sounding its steel swissshhh! The long, heavy claymore was meant to be held in both hands. The Swordslinger swung the claymore as he would have a much smaller sword.

"Now, let's go through it one swing at a time. We do one at a time many times every day. I do 50 cuts with each of the eight swings daily. Then, I practice the duel swings."

Duel swings sounded deadly and exotic. "Okay, I'm ready."

"Good, now, stand by my side and follow the moves I make. First, the overhead move." The boy copied the slow motion move. "When you bring the sword over your head, it should be parallel to the ground, not straight up. Like this," the Swordslinger displayed the motion.

For an hour, they practiced the first three moves. Once these were being performed properly, the Swordslinger began to call out the strokes by their numeric order. He switched their order to test Samuel's reaction,

"This must be done every day. You must constantly drill yourself with your moves so that they come without thought. They must be a reaction without thought. Hesitation kills you."

"How many fights have you been in?" Samuel asked.

"I don't keep count, I keep faces. Those haunt me. Their eyes that ask 'Am I really dying now?' or 'I've fought over nothing only to die. There are many other eye messages I have been given," said Swordslinger. "Some die in disbelief, having thought they were invincible. No one is invincible. There will always be someone better somewhere."

"No one's better than you," Samuel said.

"The day a man believes that, he will surely die in his next fight. There is always someone better than you are. All you can hope for is that today, it is not him," the Swordslinger said. He stopped the claymore's swing an inch from Samuel's throat. "Always be alert. Always be reactive. You will have only one chance."

The Swordslinger paused. "Now, I must practice my duel moves."

Samuel sat on the ground and watched, his rapt gaze never wavering, his makeshift sword lying across his lap not touching the ground. The Swordslinger was going through a stretching routine. Finally, he spoke. "Yesterday, when you came into town, Chieftain Bruce said it was good you came early so you could plan before they come. Who are they?"

"The Manteo Brothers," the Swordslinger said as he began doing a series of waist twists.

Samuel froze in disbelief. "The Manteo Brothers? There are five of them and all are a bunch of cutthroats. Everybody's afraid to stand up to them."

"Not everyone."

"They collect ransom from our clan or else they will burn our village," Samuel said.

"That's what they say," Swordslinger said. He now stood before the large oak tree and began a fake swing, dropping the blade, then bringing it up and cutting straight across as though he had just sliced an enemy's throat.

"You can't face them alone. Get some of the men to stand by you."

"If there were any around to do that, they wouldn't have needed my services," the Swordslinger said.

"But … but what if you die?" Samuel said, panic in his voice.

"I guess they go on collecting their ransom."

"No, I mean, if you die your life is destroyed. You're ended."

"Aye, that's right, my young friend. A brilliant deduction."

"You will die for people who don't have the courage to fend for themselves. You will sacrifice your life in an effort to do what they are too cowardly to do. You don't even know these people. You don't have to do this."

"Samuel, there is nothing in this world that ties me here. I have no family. My son is not my son. Most of me died the night my wife was butchered. The rest of me died when I encountered my son."

"But why die for these men who won't even fight for themselves?"

"Samuel," the Swordslinger placed a hand on the boy's shoulder and knelt so that they were at eye level, "it is not for the people I fight, but against the evil of men like the Manteo Brothers who find pleasure in killing and instilling terror among the people. They are evil. They are throwing off the balance. I must set the balance straight again. It is my destiny to be a swordslinger, to live as one, to die as one."

"I will stand by you when they come," Samuel said.

The Swordslinger smiled and felt something in his heart that he had thought he was no longer capable of feeling. "I tell you what, Samuel, when the time comes that I die, my sword will go to you. But first, you must only practice and live your life, my son. We are meant to be husbands and fathers and landowners. Live your life. My sword will be yours, but I pray you will never have to assume my role. I would rather you be a happily married man …"

"Yuck," Samuel interjected.

" … than a swordslinger"

"But I want to be a swordslinger. And I will be by your side when the Manteo Brothers come."

"No, you are too young and inexperienced with the sword. I won't be able to concentrate on the fight if I am worrying about you. You will be a distraction to me. Your presence could get me killed. If you want me to live through this, please don't come. Don't be anywhere near when it happens."

Tears welled in Samuel's eyes. "It's not fair!"

"Perhaps. And yet, this must be. They are not expected here for another three days, so I suggest to you, take advantage of me while you can. Learn all you can. You are helping me by doing this, helping me practice and refreshing the basic skills."

"I hope these next three days last forever," Samuel said.

"Well, these next three days will be in our hearts as long as we live. So, my young Samuel, stand before me and let me show you some moves that have never failed me."

For the next two hours, Samuel and the Swordslinger worked. The Swordslinger performed his duel swings. Samuel contributed by attempting to block the swings, but the swordslinger's blade would suddenly come from the opposite direction. It was like magic. The blade was a blur to the eye. When he moved in one direction, the Swordslinger came from another. When Samuel lunged ahead or swung, the Swordslinger simply melded into his motion, becoming a part of it, then misguiding it, and attacking.

Samuel was befuddled. It seemed that the Swordslinger was in more control of his actions than his own mind. "What ...??? You have invisible strings attached to my arms? You make me react one way and you come at me in another."

"It's called practice in execution of strokes."

"It's called yanking my strings," Samuel said. "Okay, try your number one duel move again." He assumed the sword stance, his eyes watching closely every limb of his teacher.

Swordslinger laughed. "You are an intense child aren't you? I think we have had enough for today. Let's return to the village. My sword should be ready by now."

CHAPTER 10

DOUBLE-EDGED SWORD

"Samuel, you remind me of a little sparrow flying around a hawk," the Swordslinger said, chuckling. The two walked along the road leading back to the village, the sun, low in the west, casting long shadows behind them.

"The day is almost gone. That means you have two days left before the Manteo Brothers," Samuel said.

"Yes, two days. Meet me tomorrow at the same place and we'll practice some more."

"I will," Samuel said, and then remembered that he had school tomorrow. Well, he considered being with the swordslinger as schooling, so it should be all right.

As they neared the village, Samuel began to pretend he was a swordslinger entering the town to get rid of the Manteo Brothers. It felt so good. He felt powerful. "I am the undefeated swordslinger who has been across the world aiding the defenseless, poor, and sick," he said to himself.

Once in the village, Samuel's fantasy quickly faded. He actually debated whether to go with the Swordslinger into the ironsmith shop or perhaps hang back a little. Why this became a dilemma in his mind, he was not sure. Then Charles, one of Samuel's young friends, saw him keeping stride with the Swordslinger. There was a look of wonderment in the boy's eyes. All of Samuel's concerns evaporated like dew under a hot sun. He held his head high and placed a hand over his brow to fill the place that lacked a hat. Every kid in the village would hear of him being with the Swordslinger. This was a huge moment.

They reached the ironsmith shop and when Samuel stepped through the doorway, he felt suddenly small and day-dreamingly lazy. His father was sitting by the anvil, pounding a glow-fire red sword. He stopped when he saw the Swordslinger, wiping his brow, then his hands, on his badly soiled and worn apron.

"Och, it must be a horror being a swordslinger without his blade," Stewart said. He continued to sit and appraise the Swordslinger. "There's a lot of talk around the village about you. Some doubt you will be able to stand against the Manteo Brothers. Others say you have a reputation that goes far beyond the island. They seem to have great confidence in you. What should I feel, Mr. Swordslinger?"

Samuel felt his face redden with embarrassment. Was his father really saying these things? It was the way his father weighed a man. He worked a man over like a blade. Pounding it here, pounding it there, searching for fissures and weak points.

"Feel that you'll have another day coming with your two sons. Is my sword ready?"

"Aye, it is," Stewart said, but there was more he wanted to say, more he wanted to pound. As long as he had the sword, the Swordslinger was a captive audience. "My wife died also, though not in the way yours did. You must be a very bitter man."

That was a good pound, father, Samuel thought, and clinched his eyes in shamed disbelief. He opened them and looked at the Swordslinger for any fissures in the stony facade.

The Swordslinger's eyes turned hard and narrowed to slits as he said, "The man in me died that day. My sword, please."

"Word has it you killed every one of those men at their camp. Is it true you cut off their heads, brought them back to your wife's grave and burnt them over it?"

"Myths have a tendency to exaggerate. My sword, please."

"Very well … all right. It is a blade of wonderful workmanship. It is also a blade with a lot of notches." Stewart lifted a cloth on the wooden table and presented the blade to the Swordslinger.

"I sharpened her so that she'll part a boar's hair," Stewart said with pride.

"Here's a quarter of your money," Swordslinger tossed a small bag of coins to the ironsmith.

"And where's the rest?" Stewart sounded exasperated.

"The rest was given to the baker before I gave you my sword. You have an account there for food. Take care of your sons." The Swordslinger turned to walk out the door.

"And who the hell do you think you are?" Stewart shouted. The Swordslinger continued walking. Samuel stood in shock. For the fourth time in two days, he felt frozen and unable to move. "I take care of my sons. What concern are they of yours? You walked away from your own family." People on the street were being attracted by the commotion.

The Swordslinger stopped and, without turning, said. "You are blessed with two fine sons." He appeared about to say more but decided against it and walked away.

"Samuel, go to the bakery and tell Frederick I want my money," Stewart said. Tell him if he don't give it to me, there'll be more burning in his oven than dough. Tell him!"

"Aye, father, I will." Samuel ran to the bakery and relayed the message to Frederick.

"Och, your father said that now, did he? You tell him that if he wants money, he'll have to come and ask for it. I'll give it to him, not you."

Samuel sighed then went back to the ironsmith shop to tell his father.

"He can kiss my hot anvil," Stewart said. "Come on, Samuel."

Stewart strode into the bakery and put his hands on his hips. "Frederick, I'll have me money now. You can give me a couple of loaves of bread, some Haggis if you have it, and stew, if there's any in the pot."

Frederick smiled, "Aye, I will Stewart. I'll even throw in some extra."

"That's all right. I didn't mean to lose my temper on you. I just don't like a stranger making accounts with my money."

"I understand, Stewart. Well, here you go, four loaves of bread, a pound of Haggis, and enough stew to last you and your boys for two days."

"Thank ye, Frederick. Now, give me the rest of the money."

"Here, that swordslinger paid you good, Stewart. You can buy enough food here for a month and still have some left over.

"I'll send Samuel to pick up more food in two days. Good day, Frederick."

"Aye, Stewart, in two days, we hope this town is celebrating. I do dread the thoughts of what will happen if the Swordslinger fails."

"He'll fail, Frederick. And, we will pay the price." Stewart gathered up the food on the table and gave the bag to Samuel. "Take this home. Feed yourself and your brother with the stew. I will be home soon."

"You think he'll really fail?" Frederick asked. The question went unanswered. "Better take my valuables home for the day," he mumbled to himself.

Samuel stirred the hodgepodge of stew and the vapor, laden with spices, rose from the cast iron pot over the fireplace. The smell was intoxicating. Young Robert sat at the table fighting to keep from drooling.

They ate too quickly, scorching their tongues. They jammed the fat squares of meat into their mouths and swallowed almost without chewing. The taste of the meat was delicious and it felt warm and solid in their deprived stomachs. They stuffed themselves like squirrels on the final day before hibernation. Samuel burped. The brothers laughed. Afterwards, they sat on the floor with Robert resting his head on Samuel's shoulder. They were stuffed, and within moments, they had fallen asleep.

When Samuel awakened, it was well past 10 o'clock. His father was still not home. He rose and gently placed his brother's head on the floor. Taking his makeshift sword, Samuel headed toward the village.

Something unusual was happening in the village square. The center fire was blazing and most of the men of the clan were gathered. Samuel eased into the surrounding group keeping a wary eye out for his father. Stewart was there, sitting in the first row of those gathered. His cheeks were flushed. That was a telltale sign he had been drinking. Nothing new there.

In the center of the group was Chieftain Bruce. "We have two days before the Manteo Brothers come," he was saying. "They'll be bringing their wagons to load with our crops and meats. As I'm sure most of you already know, I have hired the Swordslinger to rid us of the Manteo Brothers. He says he will do that, but all of us must prepare. Swordslinger ..." Bruce motioned with his hand.

A shadow rose from among the men and became the Swordslinger. He lit a short rolled fag of tobacco, the match lighting his face. "If they think it is only me, then they will think I am their only problem. They will think all of you are cowards and they will come the next harvest season and the next as they have been doing the past four years."

"What do you want us to do?" a man asked in the ground. "We've not swung our blades in years. There has been no need. The clans are not fighting and foreigners never reach this far north."

"And yet you have the Manteo Brothers taking your produce each year leaving your children and wives to survive on bird meal portions. Tonight, I will refresh your sword skills. All of us as one force will defeat the brothers. They will not return if they know your clan is ready to stand up to them.

"You have two days to get ready. I suggest you go home, get your weapons and meet here in the village in the morning. We will train and be ready when they arrive."

"What if we fail?" Frederick the baker asked. "They will be very angry and it will be worse. They will punish us."

"Then I suggest we don't fail. Go home, men. Sleep with your wives, eat a hearty breakfast and prepare for two days of training. I will make you into warriors again."

The men mumbled amongst themselves, then one-by-one they rose and departed to their homes. Samuel wanted to stay and talk with the Swordslinger but knew if his father caught him away from home this time of night it would be a week or two before he would be able to sit.

Samuel returned home, roused Robert and helped him to his own cot. An hour passed and still his father had not returned. With the extra money, he would probably be out until daybreak. Fear rushed into Samuel's heart. He was acutely aware of every passing moment. If the Swordslinger died now, it would bring him the greatest sadness since his mother's death. The thought of the Manteo Brother's wrath made him cringe. "They will burn this village down."

The last time Samuel heard a prayer had been from his mother just as her labor pains began with Robert. But he prayed now, hands clasped before him and eyes looking heavenward. "Please God, let the Swordslinger live and defeat the Manteo Brothers. Please. We have suffered enough. Make food aplenty for us, Lord. Never let my brother be hungry again. Protect Heather and her family. And Lord, please help my father to stop his drinking. It is destroying his soul, Lord. I want my father back. I'm scared." Samuel turned on his side and watched his brother sleeping until finally his own eyes closed and he dreamed of dancing among the oaks and swinging a mighty sword.

"Yeah, yeah, I'll be there. Getting my things now," Stewart said from the doorway of his home. The words woke Samuel and he rose in bed and shaded his eyes from the morning light.

"Morning, my little weasel," Stewart said, as he staggered inside, reaching out to grab a chair to keep his balance. He blinked his eyes, rubbed them till they were bloodshot, and wiped the back of his hand against his lips. "Did you eat?"

"Aye, we ate, father. It was good. I saved you some stew, but I'll have to heat it up for you."

"Nae, son. I am not hungry. I am sleepy and have a headache. I see two of everything and the world keeps swaying."

Samuel took the crook of his father's elbow and led him to his bed. The smell of whiskey, smoke and sweat made him nauseous. He lowered his father into bed and removed his boots, then undid his belt. Out of curiosity, Samuel opened his father's money pouch and found one coin. Only

106

one coin? He felt the wind had been knocked form him by the blunt end of a sword. There was two months of food now gone. "Oh, father, you didn't?" Samuel said looking up, but his father had passed out in a drunken stupor.

Samuel prepared a bowl of oatmeal for his brother, and then was out the door, carrying his makeshift sword over his shoulder. There were several clansmen walking toward the village, carrying blades that seemed too big and strange to be in their hands.

"Hmm, Chief, I am surprised. We have a fairly good turnout," the Swordslinger said. "All right, there is a small pot by the fire. It is blue face and body paint. I want you to put it on. It is warrior's paint. This will help get you into the mood. I want you wearing this as part of the welcome party we're going to hold for the Manteo Brothers."

Samuel felt shame that his father was not among his gathered men. Manny McGuire was there and Samuel could not help but laugh at this scrawny uncle with such an evil warrior blue face. "Aye, I feel so strong and mean," he said, making a grrr-ing sound. "Where's ye father?" he asked.

"Home sick. He has a touch of the flu. I come in his stead," Samuel said.

"Your father more than likely has the touch of a hangover. And you, you're too young to be here."

"I am big enough to swing a blade. I can hold my own. Besides, the Swordslinger has been training me."

"Oh, has he now. Well, I see no harm with us now, but when the time comes, I want you home to protect your brother and your sleeping father," Manny said.

"All right," Swordslinger said, "first, I want you men to line up in rows of four. There are about twenty of you. Stack your weapons along the rocks by the fire first. Okay. Good. Now, I want you to follow me through a series of exercises. You should do this every day."

The Swordslinger began doing leg stretches. He knew that there wasn't time to prepare the men physically for the battle they faced, but at least the exercises would keep their minds occupied. Samuel took a place on the end of the fourth row and couldn't help smirking as the men attempted to follow the directions. They moaned and grunted. Some lost their balance and fell to the ground.

"Hope the wind don't blow and knock us over," someone said. Laughter followed. The Swordslinger dropped to the ground and began doing pushups. The men joined him and after about a dozen, one man became sick and vomited.

Samuel caught a glimpse of Heather among the women gathered to watch and winked at her. She waved and smiled.

The grave concern on the faces of the women told the story. This rag-tag bunch of weaklings puking their guts out on the street after a few exercises was going to protect them from the Manteo Brothers? Their eyes turned to the Swordslinger, who was not even breathing heavily after the workout. It was obvious that this stranger they didn't even know was their only hope.

"All right, now collect your weapons, get back into formation but put more room between ye. We don't want gouged eyeballs and poked thighs," the Swordslinger said. "I am going to teach you a series of sword cuts. Afterwards, I want you to pair off with a partner and practice."

This is going to take a lot of work, Samuel thought. *Please, God, make these the two longest days in our history.*

After several hours of constant drilling over the eight major sword cuts, the men were given a lunch and tea break. The women carried the food to their husbands and sons. Their talk became more intimate and there seemed to be a closeness about everyone that had not been felt for a long time — longer than Samuel could remember. Robert appeared and brought Samuel a liver pudding sandwich.

"Aye, thank ye, brother. I needed this," Samuel said. "Is father still sleeping?"

"Aye, he sat up once and threw up over his boots and down the side of the bed. I tried to get him up so I could clean the mess, but I couldn't. I guess he'll do it when he wakes up."

"Thanks for sharing that vivid information with me, Robert."

"Young Robert, what a pleasant surprise to find you here," Chieftain Bruce said as he spied the boy. "I was just thinking we need a piper to rouse our spirits when the time comes. I've heard you play very nice. Would you like to be our piper during the duel with the Manteo Brothers?"

"Would I? I'll go get my pipes and be right back." Robert said, dashing away as fast as his legs could carry him

"No, Robert," Samuel warned, "wait until father is up and ask his permission. You don't want his wrath."

Robert stopped and closed his eyes in frustration. "Aye, whatever." He ran back to the house, head down in dejection.

"He's just a child," Samuel said to Chieftain Bruce. "Father's approval is needed for such a thing."

"No offense, Samuel, but your father is…. Oh, never mind." Bruce decided it best not to pursue that train of thought.

"No, go on, what were you going to say?" Samuel insisted.

"Very well," Chieftain Bruce lowered his voice, "Your father…well, his drinking … his not being here ... he's …" Chieftain Bruce straightened, closed his lips and simply walked away.

The Swordslinger divided the men into groups and had them go one on one, practicing defensive blocks to offensive attacks. There were yelps of struck fingers and whacks on arms. Many of these men moved as awkwardly as squeaky rusty armor. Their swings were choppy, hesitant, fearful, and less than graceful. Several of the men did show some promise, however. Samuel paired off with one of those and practiced the moves with him. Dugan McBane was a strong man with arms as thick as oak limbs and Samuel struggled to keep his balance as he fended the swings and whacks.

While the men were busy with their pretend bouts, the Swordslinger approached Chieftain Bruce. "I'll be back shortly, he said, and an alarmed look came upon the face of Bruce. He didn't want the Swordslinger leaving, not for a minute. They were lost without their protector and mentor.

"Ye want me to go with you?"

"Nae, tend to your men. I will return soon."

"Soon?"

"Before the shadow of your home reaches midway the street."

"Just don't want you disappearing before the Manteo's come," Bruce said, a sulking look on his face.

"Don't worry," the Swordslinger said, reassuringly. He shook the dust from the black coat and straightened his hat. "I just have to see someone. Keep the men practicing." He turned and began striding down the street.

When he reached the home he was looking for, he went to the door and rapped his knuckles against it. There was a shuffle of feet and a small boy appeared at the door.

"You must be Robert. Is your father in?"

Robert was clearly panicked. He stole a glance over his shoulder then back at the Swordslinger. "He's in bed. Not feeling well. Flu."

"Aye, I see, then I need to come inside and talk to him," the Swordslinger reached for the door above Robert's head and pushed it open. Robert was speechless as the man in black walked past him and into their home.

The reek of vomit permeated the air. The bed and floor had been wiped down, but the stench of stale whiskey lingered. "Stewart, wake up. I must speak with you."

Stewart stirred but didn't open his eyes.

"Stewart," the Swordslinger gently shook the drunken man's shoulder.

A few quick blinks, a snort, and Stewart was suddenly keenly aware of the dark figure standing above him. His hand thrust out from beneath his pillow to grab the sword that lay on the floor. The Swordslinger used his boot to push the sword farther out of the man's reach.

"There'll be no need of that. I come for talk only," the Swordslinger said.

"Well, then, say your piece, intruder. How'd you get in here anyway?" Stewart glanced toward Robert and knew the answer from his son's sudden cringe and whipped-puppy look.

"Robert, everything's okay," the Swordslinger said. "Would you step outside? Your father and I have something to discuss in private."

Robert looked at his father, not sure what to do. Stewart just stared at him, giving no hint as to what he should do. "Okay, I'll be outside." Robert left and closed the door behind him, then placed his ear against the wall hoping to hear the conversation.

"I just wanted you to know I lost a son because vengeance turned me away just as whiskey is turning you away from your sons," the Swordslinger said.

"This is cow dung!" Stewart protested.

"Shut up, fool!" The Swordslinger seized a fistful of Stewart's collar. "I lost my son because of the sickness of mind I had. Don't lose yours. They need you. You don't have to be a mother to them, just be yourself. And for God's sake, stop your grieving, man! Your wife is looking down upon ye. Don't ye know that after this life, ye will be with her again? I'm sure it kills her soul nightly to see you grieve yourself to death by drink. I know she wants you to raise your sons right. Feed them. Clothe them. Love them. Be their father!"

Stewart huffed and snatched the Swordslinger's hand away from his shirt.

"I come to you because of your wonderful sons and I see myself in you when I was sick. Don't make the mistake I made. One day you will wake up and see what you have lost and what a fool you appear to others."

Stewart rose to a sitting position with his back against the wall. He stared straight ahead, unblinking.

"I know you are a good man, Stewart. Your sons know you are and they love you. They need you now. Don't lose them as I did my own."

The Swordslinger stepped back. "That's all I wanted to say." He turned and started toward the door. Stewart made a move toward his sword, still in its scabbard leaning against the chair. "You touch that sword, you die. I didn't come to hurt you, but help you." And with those words, the

Swordslinger opened the door, the movement causing Robert to stumble to the side.

Stewart released his grip on the hilt of his sword. "What are ye gawking at?" he said to Robert. "Come in and shut the door."

The hours passed. The sun was on the setting side of the sky almost hidden in the ever-present blanket of clouds that covered the Highland country. The surrounding mountains were majestic in purple and black.

The Swordslinger directed the men to gather fire logs and place them in a pile in the village center. He planned to have a huge fiery greeting for the Manteo brothers when they came. The pile grew steadily higher with logs and peat moss and was soon the height of two men.

"All right, that is good for now. We have had time to rest our hands. Now, I want you to pair up and draw a square the width of two men. Draw a line to divide the square. After that, I want you to each step in a square and take turns making offensive moves. The idea is not to step out of the box. This will certainly sharpen up your defensive skills. If you step out of the square, you'll have to run around the village once shouting, "I will stay in! I will stay in!"

Several of the men laughed at what they considered a childish game, but they had learned to listen to the Swordslinger in black. They began drawing squares in the gravel of the street, casting sheepish grins at each other. Samuel and Manny paired off as sparring partners.

Suddenly the chattering of the men was silenced as the air was shattered by the piercing wail of bagpipes. Young Robert, his cheeks bulging and one arm flapping up and down with the air bag, entered the square along with Stewart, who bellowed out with a thunderous baritone voice:

"We are the mighty warriors of SkyeEden
When our foes fall, they are eaten
For no one is mightier nor so fierce
To withstand our claymore's pierce
We are the mighty warriors of SkyeEden
We make our enemies flee and screaming
For no one is as strong

And if they think so bring them on

For we are the warriors of SkyeEden ….

The screeching of the pipes silenced abruptly. The aroused men roared and thrust their blades in the air.

"That was as fine a song as I have ever heard," the Swordslinger said. "Glad you have joined us, Stewart."

Stewart straightened his vest and put his hands on his hips. "Aye, I had better join to help beat the Manteo Brothers, lest I'll be repairing your broken swords for the next 10 years. The men laughed and swatted Stewart on the back. It was obvious he had not fully recovered from his hangover, but Samuel was relieved that his father had made an effort and appearance before the clan.

"I will teach you, father," Samuel said.

"Oh, you will, aye? The day has come where ye will best your father. Well, then, warrior son of mine, let's begin."

Samuel drew his makeshift wooden sword and thrust it toward his father. His first two attempts were easily blocked and Stewart laughed, "Och, your old man is still the champion."

"Aye, ye are invincible, Father. Come humble your son one more time," Samuel said, a huge grin brightening his face.

"Ohhhhh, I will skin ye like a wet newborn weasel!" Stewart said, brandishing his sword.

Samuel loosed a warrior cry and brought his sword over his left shoulder, but instead of coming down with the blade, he circled it over his head, dropped it in front of him so that it was parallel to his body, letting it move to the left, then he brought the sword up and moved it straight across and, to his amazement, just stopped the wooden staff an inch from his father's throat.

Stewart was stunned. He thought the sword was coming down on his right side, so he moved his sword in that direction to block the blow … and suddenly the sword was at the left side of his throat. "What was that? What kind of magic or trickery was that?"

"It's not magic. It just a duel move, father."

"A what? No, that was more like luck. Come on, give me another."

"Father, are ye sure?" Samuel asked.

"Come on, I want to know if that was a boy's luck or a warrior's skill," Stewart snorted in laughter, rubbed his head, then moved into a defensive poster. "Come on, ye weasel."

Samuel sighed. He was delighted to find his father still in this playful mood and not actually seeming furious at being bested. Yet, he wondered what was still to come.

"All right, prepare for duel move number two," Samuel said, slightly flexing his knees and holding the sword handle toward the center of his body. "Arrrrgggghhh!" He stepped forward to his father's left and swung his blade in a roundhouse arc at his head. Stewart easily blocked the swing, but Samuel suddenly dropped to one knee, swung in the opposite direction around his head, and brought the wooden sword across his father's belly.

Stewart's mouth gaped open in surprise. He dropped his sword, reached down, and grabbed Samuel by the waist. Father and son rolled on the ground, trying to position themselves on top. It was no contest, of course, as the heavier, stronger Stewart quickly prevailed. Samuel would have had as much success attempting to crawl from beneath a two-ton rock.

"Who won that last bout? Who won?" Stewart bellowed.

"You did," Samuel gasped and laughed.

"What? I did not hear ye?"

"You won, Father, no question about it."

"Aye, now that is better," Stewart rose to his feet and offered Samuel a hand. Samuel took it and suddenly found himself embraced in his father's arms. He glanced over his father's shoulder and caught a wink from the Swordslinger.

When at last it became too dark to continue the sword drills, the Swordslinger told the men to go home and get some sleep. "We have only one more day. Let's meet here tomorrow morning for one more practice and make certain preparations that will have the Manteo Brothers thinking they took a wrong path that has led them to hell."

"Arrggghhh!" Several of the men grunted.

Samuel went to the Swordslinger. "I would like to stop by your place for a visit tonight if that's all right."

"Sure. But, go home first and tend to the needs there."

"Aye, I will." Samuel gave Swordslinger a mock bow and hurried to reach his father's side as they headed toward their home.

Once inside, Stewart said, "I'm hungry. Stoke the fire, Samuel, and let's warm up some potatoes and sausage."

"Aye, sounds good to me. Come on, Robert, you can help," Samuel said.

Samuel was having trouble remembering the last time the three of them had actually sat down together at the table to eat. He noticed that his father was having some problems with trembling hands and was trying to hide the tremor from his sons.

"I'll get our baths ready, father. Do you want a fresh shirt and kilt? Heather washed them for us yesterday."

"Nae, Samuel. I am not going anywhere tonight. I think I am going to stay right here. In fact, after we've washed up, I will tell you a tale about your grandfather when he fought the Frasier Clan and was captured."

"Och, that's good father," Samuel said, but failed to completely conceal the disappointment in his voice that his opportunity to visit the Swordslinger might be lost.

The fire blazed in the hearth. A sudden storm had moved in and rain pattered against the roof. Sheets of hail and rain battered the walls. Stewart gathered his sons around him and began to tell a fable of his grandfather that was part truth, part fiction. They all knew most of it was lies and the retold events were always different. But that was part of the allure of the stories … the mere creation of them. The boys stared at their father with wondrous eyes and hung on his every word.

In the Rock Inn, the Swordslinger was resting on one knee before his open window. He let the cold rainfall upon his face, freshening his spirit. There was no portent, no sign in the sky, no oracle. He simply had the feeling that something bad was going to happen. Why he had this feeling now was confusing to him. He certainly had been in more dire straits. Maybe it was only because he was feeling a little human again. Or perhaps this was a premonition of sorts. Either way, he just wanted to feel alive ... savor every emotion of the moment. Allowing the icy rain to run down his cheeks and over his chest was certainly one way to do that. He reached upward with his hands, cleansing them in the rain, visualizing the stains of blood washing away. He felt this was like a cleansing — a baptism in an odd mystical way. There was no longer the ire of vengeance burning his guts. The Manteo Brothers no longer represented a need of retribution for his wife's butchery. They were simply an unbalanced force thrust upon a village of good people.

For the first time in years, the Swordslinger felt at peace with himself. Perhaps when he had pleaded with Stewart about his sons, it was redemption for his own sin — and, at last, he was able to forgive himself for the loss of his son.

"Let it rain," he said quietly, "let it rain."

This inner peace was short-lived however. A short time later, Swordslinger awoke from a bad dream in which his son Dexter had been leering at him. "With every woman I rape, Father, I think of you. I think of you watching my mother. I think of you running away a coward into the night."

The Swordslinger wept like the rain, his face buried in his pillow, feeling alone, feeling the awful effects on his soul of irreparable damage and unforgiven sins.

CHAPTER 11

ONE DAY TO GO

The Swordslinger rose from a sleepless night, went to the open window and drew in a deep breath of the crisp morning air. The air felt moist in his throat and lungs. He inhaled the aromas of breakfasts floating with the smoke from chimneys, fires burning of peat moss. The sky was hazy as always. Across the village proper toward the woods where he had practiced with Samuel, a gray hawk circled above. Its wings spread as it glided upon a higher current of air.

The tall oaks swayed softly in the early breeze like the rocking of a mother with a babe in her arms. It was late summer and the leaves on the crowns of the trees were beginning to darken as they prepared for the change of seasons.

The Swordslinger dressed and went downstairs where he paid for a muffin and bowl of oatmeal from the Rock Inn's kitchen. He went outside, crossed the street and stepped into the small Catholic Church. A pair of worshipers rose and departed quickly when he entered. Probably feared the walls would fall, the Swordslinger humored himself. He made the cross with his fingers and touched his forehead with oil. He loosened the belt that sheathed his sword and leaned the weapon against the wall.

Not quite sure what to do next, he sat on the pew, and then moved forward so that his knees were on the kneeling board. He removed the black leather gloves and brought his palms together. He bowed his head, closed his eyes and began to pray.

"God, I've erred in many ways. I guess those are sins in thy book. I became your wrath upon the evil men of this world. In doing so, I lost my humanity. I guess you are pretty proud of your son, but I abandoned mine in my fury. I don't actually know how to do all this, but I heard that if a man asked for forgiveness that most likely you'll grant it. I've heard that our loved ones are up there with you and that if

117

we live good lives, we will be rewarded by uniting with them. It's a little too late for me living a good life, but, for the time that I have left, I will try.

"God, when this Manteo affair has ended, I promise to retire my sword and find a little spot in the mountains to live out the rest of my life. I guess that's all I have to say for now. Thank you for listening to a sinner. Well, I have work to do, so I'll be getting back with you later."

The smell of ham and eggs awakened Samuel. The boy opened his eyes and looked around, pleasantly startled, thinking he must have fallen asleep at Heather's house. But to his amazement, he was at home. And, lo and behold, his father was standing by the fire flipping a piece of ham on the skillet. Robert was already at the table. His jaws were bulging and his face showed he was experiencing a moment of pure ecstasy.

"Mornin', Weasel, come get your food," Stewart said with a hint of pride sounding in his voice.

"Aye, ye know I will," Samuel said. He sat at the table and turned the empty plate in circles on the table before him. His jaws ached with anticipation. He reached to take a nibble of ham from Robert's plate, and had his hand slapped by his hungry brother.

"Och, breakfast. This is so divine," Samuel said when two eggs and a thick slice of ham were placed in his plate.

"Divine is it?" Stewart laughed.

"Aren't ye going to eat?" Samuel asked.

"Why ye know, that is a good idea. I guess I'm not used to eating this early either. It would be a nice thing to get accustomed to, aye?"

"You got that right, father. Hmmm, this is good," Samuel closed his eyes and chewed slowly, savoring the juices. When the plates were empty and the three were relishing the feeling of stuffed bellies, Samuel asked, "Tomorrow, do you think everything will turn out okay? I mean it will, right?"

"It's what we hope for," Stewart said.

"Long as the Swordslinger is with us, we have to win. He's never lost," Samuel said.

"He's only a man, Samuel. He has much experience in this sort of thing, but he's still a man and a killer of men."

"He's a good man, Father. You know what happened to his wife. And, he takes time to teach me," Samuel said.

"I don't care for ye spending so much time with the man. I will teach you how to use the sword…," Stewart raised his voice, "and the ironsmith trade. It's about time you started working with me at the shop, let me pass along my ironsmith skills to you. You'll live longer."

"But…"

"No, buts, I've made my decision. If I am to be a father, by God, I will be a father."

Samuel straightened in the chair and crossed his arms in youthful defiance. "This isn't fair. He's a good man, Father. He's chancing his life to help us."

"He's doing it for pay, Samuel. Bruce has hired him with coin and cattle."

"Do you condemn a man for accepting food and living expenses for offering his life to give a village protection?"

"I'm just saying he ain't no saint. A man in his profession hires out to kill and enjoys it. He dresses in black and walks around like Mr. Death."

"He wears the black because he's grieving for his wife, just as you are," Samuel said.

"Shut up, boy! Shut up! Stewart slammed his fist on the table and knocked over their cups. "Never compare your mother to another woman. Don't you dare!"

Samuel rose from the chair and went to sit on his bed. Stewart raised his hands in frustration and noticed them trembling. Self-consciously, he stuffed his hands beneath his armpits. "Clean up this table, Samuel. When you're through, bring Robert with you to my shop. Robert, bring your pipes. Samuel, you can practice some with me and Manny and I don't want you talking to the Swordslinger anymore. Don't say another word about it or I'll keep you locked in this house until this affair is over."

The entire clan, women, children, men, all were gathered at the village center. The Swordslinger walked among the men and inspected their weapons. Overall, it was a sorry lot, more for scaring old women and children than doing battle with warriors of the sword. But they would have to do. At least the men were ignorant of their failings. It didn't matter anyway; he was planning to use the villagers more for show than for fighting.

The priest was seated on a chair with a bowl of anointed water in his lap to tap on the foreheads of those that desired to be blessed before their face-off with death. The men passed before him, their faces solemn in anticipation, appreciative of a touch of faith or the feeling that God was presiding over them.

When the last man had been blessed and mumbled his thanks to the priest, the Swordslinger addressed the rag-tag bunch. "I want each of you to take positions along the street. The Manteo brothers will be coming from the east and I want two of your best archers to get on the roofs of the huts at the end of the street. Frederick!"

"Aye."

"You will be in charge of the bonfire. We'll have … let's see," the Swordslinger scanned the people. "Och, Samuel, I want you to climb to the top of that tall oak tree and when you sight the brothers, give us a whistle. Robert, that's where you come in. I want you to blow those pipes so that it will be heard across the Highlands.

"Father," he said, addressing the priest, "I want you to ring that bell slowly but constantly when Samuel gives us the sign. Frederick, I want you to set fire to that pile of wood and moss and keep it blazing." The Swordslinger looked up at the sky. "Hopefully it won't be raining at that moment."

"As for the rest of you, I want you in a semi-circle along the huts so that when the brothers come, you'll have them surrounded. When they get past the bakery shop, I want every man to charge them at once. Kill them!"

The men cast startled looks at one another, and then back at the swordslinger. Chieftain Bruce spoke up, "Uh, where are you going to be during all of this?"

120

The Swordslinger allowed a thin smile on his lips. "Right in the thick of it, Chieftain. Now, I want all of you to assume positions. I'm going to take this wagon, for which as you can see I have made a straw dummy. Doesn't it resemble you, Chieftain Bruce? I am going to drive it into town and I want each of you to concentrate on performing your roles, except for you, Frederick. You stand by the pile of wood, but don't set it afire, all right? I want the archers to assume their places on the roof and to shoot at the dummy. I want the swordsmen from each side of the street to come charging inward and have each of you to engage the man you confront in battle. Make it realistic, but please don't draw blood. We're going to need every one of you for this to succeed."

"Remember, you want to look scary and mean. We want these intruders to feel our wrath before they feel our swords.

"Och, and one more thing," he said turning his eyes to the chosen archers. "I trust you can aim and shoot straight."

The archers nodded, but glanced nervously at each other, their confidence waning.

"It's okay, when the time comes you will be ready. Your instincts will take over." He only hoped those instincts weren't to run for the hills.

The Swordslinger mounted the wagon and steered the wary horse a short distance out of town to the east. He turned back to face the village and "whoaed" the horse, sitting on the board seat across the wagon and evaluating the scene before him. This was what he hoped would at least momentarily confuse the Manteo brothers. Taking a rolled paper of tobacco from his coat pocket, he lit it, closed his eyes and inhaled, savoring the tobacco, relishing in the sharp taste and the morning breeze upon his face.

"Yah!" He suddenly whipped the reins and the horse and wagon sped forward. The dummy tied in the back bounced and waggled from left to right.

When Samuel saw the horse begin moving, he put his fingers to pursed lips and issued a shrill whistle. "They're coming!" he shouted from his perch on the oak tree.

"The Manteo Brothers?"Robert cried.

121

"No, stupid, the Swordslinger and the dummy! Play the pipes!" Samuel shouted to his frightened brother below.

"Aye," Robert said, stomping his right foot to the rhythm in his head. He began moving his elbow in and out to pump air into the bagpipe. His lips found the mouthpiece and he began blowing. The shrill notes startled a group of nearby ravens into flight.

Frederick ran to the pile of wood and struck a match. He held it there, cupping his hands. "Och, I've done my deed."

"Here he comes," Samuel shouted. The Swordslinger had the horse moving at full speed, the old wagon groaning in protest. The archers' arms and hands moved in a frantic uncoordinated fashion. One of them accidentally sent an arrow flying, sticking in the ground within a few feet of Chieftain Bruce's boot.

The other men held their positions, swords and axes drawn. In the distance, they could hear the galloping of hooves on gravel. Samuel looked down at the men. Every face was tense with terror. It seemed this exercise was bringing home to them the reality of the situation.

What a fearful sight, Samuel thought, as he looked back to the road and saw the approaching Swordslinger. What a ghostly black sight as the man's black coat flitted and whipped its tail like raven wings.

The speed with which the Swordslinger covered the distance caught the archers unprepared. They hastily drew their bows taut and released arrows. But both missed their target, striking the graveled ground well wide of the speeding wagon.

The Swordslinger brought the horse to a skidding halt, making the wagon shudder on its wheels. The dummy bobbed and weaved, untouched by the errant arrows.

"Attack!" Swordslinger cried.

The men looked at one another first, and then in unison they converged on the wagon and raised their swords to meet their assailant from the opposite side of the street. One of the men tripped and fell. The others reached their adversary and swung carefully at them.

"No, no, no. This is not some kind of pretty sword dance. I want to hear steel clang. Just break the swing if it looks like you're going to actually strike the other. "And you guys," Swordslinger said to the archers. "What was that? You were late with your firing and missed by ten feet. If they are riding hard along the street, shoot a little before them. Aim a little over your intended target to compensate for the loss of momentum."

The Swordslinger sat on the wagon bench and began turning the horse. "All right. We do this again and again and again until we get it right."

The second run gained better results. It still wasn't anything to frighten the Manteo's, but at least the archers came closer to their target. The arrows struck the sidewalls of the wagon. No one tripped over their feet. Nice blade bell sounds peppered the air. "That's better."

After the fifth exercise, Swordslinger told the men to take a lunch break. The women appeared with very generous portions of food. The Swordslinger glanced at Robert and Samuel, saw they were busily eating and had smiles on their faces. When his eyes met with Stewart's, Stewart dropped his gaze, breaking eye contact immediately. *What's wrong now?*, the Swordslinger thought to himself. He made a mental note to inquire about Stewart's behavior.

While the men ate, the Swordslinger mingled with them, hoping to gauge their preparedness. He patted some on the shoulders and gave compliments to the women for the meals they provided. Since the death of his wife, it had been too painful to watch other couples together, causing a sharp pain in his heart. The sound of a young boy's laughter or one calling out, "Father," felt like a sword impaling his heart. But not today. Today, seeing the husbands and wives showing expressions of love toward one another actually made him feel good. He glanced skyward, smiled, and said to himself, "I know you're up there watching." For the first time, he had discovered enough faith to believe his wife awaited him in the afterlife. So what he saw today with the couples gave him happiness because he, too, still had a wife. She was not dead. She was awaiting him in the afterlife.

"Now don't go getting yourself killed, husband," Heather teased Samuel, brushing a bread crumb from his lip with a fingertip.

Samuel was mortified. "Don't call me that. And, I can wipe my own mouth."

Heather laughed. "Och, I forgot. You are a grown man now — a warrior — you don't play games anymore."

"There's just a time and a place for that," Samuel whispered embarrassedly

"I'm kidding with you, Samuel. Just you be careful and don't fall from the tree from excitement when you see those brothers coming."

"Aye, I won't."

Heather grabbed his hand. "I'm really scared, Samuel. What if … what if they …?"

"They won't, me darlin' Heather. I give you my oath no man will touch you tomorrow. You just leave the village with the children and make sure they are cared for."

"I can't do that, I'll be needed to help treat the wounds," Heather said.

Samuel stared deeply into the green eyes and his heartbeat quickened. Suddenly, he understood what the Swordslinger had meant about being distracted by caring so much for the safety of another. "Heather, you have to go. You are the reason I'm fighting. If I know that you are just behind me I'll be looking over my shoulder always checking to make sure you are all right. It is a dangerous thing to turn your head in battle with your enemy before you. Do you understand?"

A look of fright came over Heather's face and tears welled in her eyes. She reached out and cupped Samuel's face in her hands. "I can't bear the thought of losing you. If something happens to you, I will die. I will."

"Oh, Heather," Samuel gathered her up in his arms. He felt the hot tears against his throat and the heaving of her chest. Stroking her hair with his hand, he said for the first time, "I love ya, Heather."

She tightened her arms around his waist and there was anguish in her voice as she said, "I love you, too, Samuel."

Father O'Brian appeared, knelt and embraced the youngsters. "It breaks my heart that the evil of men have such an effect on our children … and … I guess, our lives, too. But be brave, my children. Say your prayers for tonight. God is listening. Here," he retrieved the bowl of anointed oil and drew the symbol of the cross on Heather's and Samuel's foreheads. He smiled at them and brushed the tears from Heather's cheek. "You know, I can't recall ever knowing the two of you being apart. I have a feeling one day you will be standing before me for a wee ceremony."

"Father …" Samuel blushed.

"He's still a coward with romance, Father. He'll grow out of it," Heather said.

"Aye, I am sure he will. God help us when he does."

"You will leave with the children tomorrow, won't you?" Samuel said, his voice almost pleading.

Heather sighed. She leaned over and pulled Samuel's dirk from the inside of his boot. Bringing the knife up to her hair, she began cutting off a braid that she had made earlier in the day on the right side of her head. "Here. Keep this with you. No matter where you go, I want to be there with you. And tomorrow, if you're …" She fought back tears…"if you're lying in the street dying, at least a part of me will be with ye, too."

"Oh, Heather," Samuel hugged her again. "I'm not going to die. My love for you is too strong to allow me to die."

They looked into each other's eyes, deeply, with soul-touching commitment. In that one moment, it seemed that all of their experiences together passed between them. Even at their tender age, they had experienced years of bonding and friendship, and the kind of love that will never allow a heart to have another.

"All right," Swordslinger announced to the crowd. "One by one, I challenge our 20. We will do the best of five bouts. This will keep you on your toes."

"You're speaking of wooden swords, right? Not steel blades?" Chieftain Bruce asked. Laughter rippled through the gathering of men.

"We will use the wooden tokens, just in case someone becomes too ambitious. But, remember," the Swordslinger's voice grew deadly serious, "tomorrow you will be fighting with live blades. Tomorrow, some of us may die. So, today, I want you to pretend it is real as far as your reactions are concerned. Give it your all today, men, because tomorrow your lives depend on it."

"I'd better let you go," Heather said to Samuel, and reached out and gently touched his lips with her fingertips. "I do love you."

"I'm blessed that you do." Samuel gave her a quick kiss and joined the men who were gathering in the village center. The would-be warriors formed a wide circle around the Swordslinger. "All right, who's first?"

"I am," Samuel said, arching his eyebrows. "Time to teach the teacher a lesson."

"Oh, is it now, my young student." The Swordslinger grinned and executed a few warm-up swings with the blade. "Come on, teach me my first lesson." Somewhere in the crowd, Samuel heard Heather squeal. The men laughed.

Samuel began circling the Swordslinger, taking slow cautious steps to the right. Swordslinger lunged to Samuel's right. This caught him off guard, causing him to trip and fall.

"Oh, yeah!" the men cheered. "That's showing him!"

Samuel continued to circle, planning his next move. He decided on his "duel swing number one." Bringing his sword up and over his right shoulder, he brought it back down parallel to his body to the left, and then brought it up to the height of the Swordslinger's throat.

WHACK!

Swordslinger had easily blocked the swing and their wooden swords were locked. "I taught you that move, remember," the Swordslinger said, grinning again. "That was two. Three more bouts."

Samuel lunged his sword forward aiming for the Swordslinger's midsection. The tip of Samuel's blade brushed against the Swordslinger's jerkin. Yet, he had dodged the strike. His sword came crashing down on top of Samuel's, causing the point to hit the ground. Just as suddenly, Samuel found Swordslinger's blade across his throat.

The Swordslinger smiled grimly. "That was number three."

They resumed sparring positions and began to cautiously circle one another. The Swordslinger gave out a cry, drawing his sword high overhead and bringing it downward. Samuel barely brought his sword up in time to block the blow. The downward force made his knees bend.

"Nice block, my young student. Very nice. There's just one thing you forgot," Swordslinger said.

"And what is that," Samuel said, looking his teacher in the eye.

"Notice that I am only holding the sword with one hand. You did a nice block. We're locked, but look down to your waist."

Samuel glanced down and groaned audibly when he saw the Swordslinger's left hand pressing a dirk into his side.

"That was number four," the Swordslinger said, and pushed Samuel back to disengage their swords.

The Swordslinger bared his teeth in a grimace and charged. He brought the sword high overhead and was going to swing it across to the right. His momentum stopped abruptly. "Ha, ha! Oh, my! That's a good one!"

When Swordslinger had made his charge, Samuel had dropped to one knee and thrust his sword forward. The point of the wooden sword caught Swordslinger in the belly button.

"Wooooo!"

"Did ye see that?"

"Stick 'im, Sam!"

"That was number five," Samuel said, bowing to his teacher.

"You'll have to teach me that one, young student."

"I will, during our next class after we're rid of the Manteo brothers."

"I can't wait," the Swordslinger said. "Who's next?"

Samuel returned to the other men, getting a few congratulatory swats on the back for having bested the teacher and trying not to strut. This was a new feeling, this sense of pride, accomplishment … and yes, honor. He was proud, yet humble, because he knew that whatever skill or talent he possessed with the blade had been bestowed upon him by the Swordslinger. He stood, heart pounding with emotion, and watched the other men have their turns with the master. Not one of them was able to get a stroke in against the impenetrable defense.

As man after man was dispatched by the Swordslinger, their respect for their teacher became almost reverent. Samuel noticed that even after having parried with the last of the men, the Swordslinger didn't even seem to be breathing heavily. His movements with the sword were so fluid and effortless that they apparently weren't taxing.

"All right," the Swordslinger said finally, "I want you to pair off and practice the eight basic strokes. Go through each routine 20 times with your partner blocking." He watched as the men paired off, then moved to the well and poured himself a cup of the cool water. Stewart took advantage of the lull to approach him.

"Can we talk??

The Swordslinger took another long drink from the cup and turned to face the man.

"Of course," he said. "What is it, Stewart?"

"It's about Samuel."

"Okay, let's sit." The two men moved to a nearby bench and the Swordslinger sat down. Stewart remained standing. There was a nervous tic below his right eye. He was obviously ill at ease.

"Don't take this personal," he said, "but I don't want Samuel spending time with you anymore."

The Swordslinger's face was puzzled. "May I ask why?"

Stewart's face reddened. "Because he's my son and he looks to you as a role model. And, well, pardon me for saying it, but a swordslinger is no model citizen. You kill people. That's what you're good at. It's what you enjoy.

"You don't know what I feel," the Swordslinger said, his eyes narrowing under the brim of the black hat.

"Nae, but I know how I feel. And you have forced me to wake up to my failings as a father to my sons. I've decided that I'm going to be father to them and I'm going to be a damn good one. And anybody who cares a fart's wind for his child is certainly going to keep him away from the likes of you."

The Swordslinger was taken aback by the passion in Stewart's voice. "You're serious, aren't you?"

Stewart was gaining confidence and his voice steadied. "I've already told Samuel to keep his distance from you. I heard him planning for another lesson with the sword and I won't have it. He is young and he won't listen to me, so as his father, I implore, I beg you, discourage any relationship with him. He is young and innocent and you are a walking bloodstain. He looks at you as some kind of god and he'll listen to you. Just do this. Keep him away. That's all I ask."

The Swordslinger closed his eyes for a second, mulling over what the man had said. Then he looked up into Stewart's face. "I'll respect the wishes of Samuel's father."

"Aye, and I thank you." Stewart's face softened. "There may be a bit of good in you after all, Bloodslinger. Anytime you need your blade honed, well, it's on the house."

"Aye," Swordslinger said, his face solemn, "all right."

The Swordslinger returned to the villagers and had the men go through three more practice runs with the dummy on the wagon. The archer on the roof to the left of the street planted an arrow in the center of his chest. The other bowman sent an arrow whizzing within an inch of the dummy's head.

The Swordslinger's lips turned up in something that could have been a smile. One more run and these villagers might actually become effective. But before the wagon could be turned, the storm cloud that had been forming began emptying its contents on the village.

The Swordslinger waved off the wagon run, but kept the men in the street in the driving rain. He had them pair off and begin going through the sword drills. It could be raining tomorrow when the bad guys came to town and this would be valuable experience. They were going to need all their newfound skills when the action began, and besides, some of them could use a little water on their reeking bodies.

Samuel was working hard, sparring with different men and one time even taking on two at once. He was feeling confident, maybe even a little arrogant, as he realized his skills were a cut above anyone else in the group. He tried to catch the Swordslinger's eye, but the man in black seemed to be avoiding him. Now what? Had he done something to irritate the master?

At last, the Swordslinger halted the drills. "You've done well today, mates," he said. "Now go home, rest and sleep well tonight for tomorrow will soon be today. First thing in the morning, you are to move your women and children out of the village into the hills where they will be safe. And don't forget: say your prayers, me lads."

Stewart approached Samuel and placed a hand on his arm. "Let's go, Samuel."

Samuel pulled his arm free. "I'll be with you in a moment. I have to speak to the Swordslinger."

The boy pushed through the mingling men and caught up with the Swordslinger. He tried to fall in stride with the man but was having trouble keeping up.

"Wait!" he said, and the man halted, the look on his face one that Samuel had not seen before. "I thought maybe we could talk for a minute." He felt himself blushing with embarrassment. "Is there something I can help you with in preparing for tomorrow?"

"Nae." The Swordslinger began walking.

"Is something wrong? Have I done something wrong?"

"Nae."

The Swordslinger stopped again and looked down at the boy, his face cold. "I don't want you around me anymore. You make me feel like I'm being nibbled to death by a duck. Just go. Get lost. Go home!" He turned and began walking away.

"But what have I done?"

"Nothing. Everything is fine. The only problem is you're bugging me."

"But ... I don't understand." The desperation sounded in Samuel's voice.

"Listen to me. Go! Run away now. Go home! And don't bother me again."

"But ... I thought we were friends ...? The boy reached out and placed a hand on the man's elbow.

The voice was loud, cold, and final. "Go away!"

Samuel cringed, the hurt reaching to his soul. "Okay," he mumbled, "if that's what you want." He stopped, watching the man in black move along the street until he reached the inn and entered. He turned and saw his father standing nearby, watching. He felt his face redden again.

The Swordslinger entered the inn, closed the door and leaned against the wall. Ribbons of grief unwound and flapped wildly within him. What an ironic twist of fate! Awaken a father only to have him forbid you of his son. Samuel was the son he should have had. They had bonded so quickly and completely. In only two days Samuel had restored to life places in his heart that he had thought were dead forever. There was something unique and special about the boy. He was a young man with compassion and innocence and no deceit. There was a strength within him that matched his own. He had immediately recognized the keen sense of justice and courage in the boy to right the wrongs around him, not in retribution or vengeance, but from concern for his fellow clansmen. The lad had such a powerful yearning to learn the sword, and his potential seemed unlimited.

Ah, a shame it is. But he's not my son and I mustn't come between him and his father.

The face of his own son, Dexter, rose from the black waters of his conscience and the emotion flickered over his face. "Every woman I rape, I will think of you watching my mother and how you ran like a coward in the night." The words were like daggers being thrust into his heart, sharp and with poison tips. And what had Stewart called him? A bloodslinger? His own son thought of him as a coward. And the father of the lad who could make him feel human again and whom he wished was his son would not allow him to even speak with the boy. This was the reward he reaped for attempting to be a good man against the force of evil in the world. Was this the justness he received from the God he had begun praying to again?

For the first time, doubt crept in. What was the point of his efforts? He was putting his life on the line so that these villagers could live without the threat of evil. This was just too much! Having to hurt that lad by pretending he couldn't stand him any longer. Just out of respect for the father. What was the point of surviving in a world where you were so misjudged and others hated and feared you? "I'm sorry, Samuel."

Perhaps the father was right. Maybe a burned out swordslinger was not the best of role models for a young boy. But damn it, he couldn't leave the boy thinking he despised him. He thought of the boy as his own son … he had learned to love the lad.

The conflict of emotions tore through the soul of the Swordslinger and he pushed himself away from the wall, flung the door open and stepped outside. He knew he should let it go, but it was just so wrong. "Samuel!" he called, but there was no answer. The street was empty except for the pile of wood and peat moss that waited to be burned tomorrow.

CHAPTER 12

THE QUEST

Samuel's mind was whirling with confusion. Why had the Swordslinger turned on him? Only minutes earlier, they had been laughing and talking about their training session. *Maybe he's preoccupied with* the *coming of the Manteo Brothers,* the boy thought. Whatever the reason, the sudden shift in attitude had been devastating.

Samuel opened his sporran and withdrew the braid Heather had given him. He removed it from the piece of cloth he had wrapped it in for protection and ran the braid of hair across his lips, savoring her smell that lingered in the hair. At least he knew that Heather would never turn on him. His lips curled into a smile as he recalled their declarations of love for each other. There was no doubt in his mind that they would one day be husband and wife. There was not, and had never been, anyone in his heart other than her.

Suddenly a dark thought entered his mind. Suppose I die in the battle? He visualized one of the Manteo Brothers taking aim with a bow and arrow and in his mind saw the arrow whizzing toward him. All around him, the town was on fire and bloodied heaps of villagers filled the street. The Manteo Brothers, crazed with the lust for blood, galloped along the street, searching for the hiding women and children.

"No!" The cry escaped Samuel before he realized it was happening. Robert stirred on the cot beside him but didn't awaken. His father was snoring loudly in the adjacent room. Good. He didn't want them to be aware of his fear. Where was the Swordslinger now? Probably sitting alone in his room at the inn, staring into the darkness and watching the ghosts of his sad life replay their tragic destinies.

The shout from outside made Samuel bolt upright in bed. He held his breath and listened. Someone was still shouting. The Manteo Brothers! Oh, God, they're here already! "Father, wake up! They're coming!" Samuel realized he was screaming the words.

"Wha ... — grab your sword, boy! Stewart sat on the side of the bed and struggled to get his boots on. He rose, straightened his kilt and prayed aloud. "God help us."

Samuel followed his father out the door and they ran to the town center. The church bell suddenly began tolling, calling to the villagers who were still in their homes. People were rushing out into the street, panic on their faces. The women gathered the children in a group and prepared to take them to shelter away from the village.

"Samuel?" It was Heather, her face white in the pale moonlight. She was holding hands with her two sisters, hurrying them along. "Samuel, be careful. Please!"

"I will, Heather. I will," Samuel shouted to her over his shoulder.

Samuel was prepared to see men entangled in battles to the death when he reached the village center. But to his surprise, there were no sword battles being waged, no huge men on horses wielding swords of death. The men of the village were gathered in a circle, standing quietly. The church bell stopped its tolling and for a few seconds their haunting sound echoed from the surrounding mountains. Samuel reached the group and began squeezing his way through them. When he reached the inner circle, he could hear Chieftain Bruce addressing the men.

"I just wanted to go over a few things about tomorrow," the Chieftain was saying. "I knocked on his door and there was no answer. I tried the door and it wasn't locked so I went inside. The room was empty and the bed was still made. I checked the closets and all his clothes were gone. The money I had paid him to protect us was in this bag on the table. And then I found this ..." Chieftain Bruce held up the Swordslinger's sword. I checked downstairs and the clerk said he had gone. He had just come down, settled his bill with the clerk, and left. I checked the stables and his horse is gone, too."

"He's gone?" someone in the crowd asked, his voice incredulous.

134

"Yes, he's gone. The big brave man in black has run off and left us here to die. He left his precious sword sticking in the dirt of the street and just rode away. There's no way we can stand up to the Manteo Brothers. If we try, we'll be like pigs led to slaughter."

Samuel was having trouble breathing. He glanced at his father and something in his face told the boy more than he wanted to know. He remembered seeing Stewart cornering the Swordslinger yesterday and it was shortly afterward that the man had treated him so coldly. What had his father said to him?

The brightness of a full moon made it appear almost daylight and Samuel broke from the group of men and ran to where he could see down the empty street. Nothing. He checked each direction, hoping to see the man in black on his horse. Nothing. He was gone. The boy thought for a second, then turned toward the east, the direction in which the Swordslinger had come from the day he entered the town, and began running.

Panic was spreading through the village. The Swordslinger, the man they had placed their faith and hopes for survival with, had disappeared without a trace. The men milled in the town center. Some prayed. Some cursed. Some had tears streaming down their cheeks. And there was panic written on every face.

Chieftain Bruce was being anything but the brave leader the villagers needed. "We can forget all this foolhardy fantasy of fighting off the Manteo's," he said. "We will just pay them, let them have what they want, and they'll let us live."

The words of the village leader infuriated Manny. "We can't do that!" he cried. "We can't back down and let these murdering thieves have what they want! Don't you understand? If we let them do as they like, rob us of everything, sure, they may leave us alive, but they'll be back again as soon as we have replenished our goods enough to make it worth their while. Look, we've practiced our defense and we got pretty good at it. The Swordslinger is only one man. We can do this! We can protect our village against these bloodthirsty bandits!"

"Practice drills are one thing, but hand-to-hand battle is something else altogether," Chieftain Bruce said. "If we go up against the Manteo Brothers, we'll all die. Then they'll still take what they want."

Samuel was still running eastward. He reached the crest of the first hill and paused, peering down the winding road. Still nothing. No man, no horse and no telltale trail of dust. Nothing.

Suddenly Samuel felt a hand on his shoulder. Swordslinger! He whirled as his face lit up with excitement. It was his father.

"He's gone, Samuel. He is not the man he pretended to be. Once again, he has proven to be a coward."

Samuel stared at his father in disbelief. "I don't believe that. What did you say to him yesterday? You made him leave, didn't you?"

Stewart's voice was a growl. "I did no such thing, you impudent little ass! In fact, I had even changed my mind about you learning from him. I asked him to continue working with you as a student. But he said he didn't want to have anything else to do with you. He said you were too much of a nice lad and would never make it as a swordslinger and he wasn't going to waste any more time with you. He said he was planning to tell you this himself, but now I could do it for him. He said he was tired of you bugging him."

"No! No! I don't believe you. We're friends. He said he felt I was the son he had never had. He was like a father," Samuel paused, realizing he had made a mistake.

"So, he's like a father to you, huh? Let's get something straight, boy; I am your father. Don't argue with me! Let's go back to the others before the Manteo Brothers catch us out here alone. When we get back, you get Robert and find Heather and her family and join them. And you protect your brother!"

Samuel took one last look down the road to the east but could see nothing. The road was as empty as his heart.

Somewhere out there the Manteo Brothers were coming and he felt helpless. His honor, his courage, had drained from his body. He no longer wanted to fight. It was as though his ambition to be a swordslinger had vanished along with the man in black.

Samuel made his way back to the center of the village and joined the gathering of townspeople listening to what Chieftain Bruce had to say.

"Well, as I see it, our main line of defense has walked away," Bruce said. "We can try and stand up against the brothers but if we lose, and we are almost certain to, the price will be too dear to pay."

Men grumbled and muttered amongst themselves.

"Well, we can do this the democratic way," Bruce continued. "Let's have a show of hands. Who wants to fight?"

The men looked at each other, waiting for the first to raise his hand. Samuel was so disheartened over the Swordslinger's departure he couldn't have lifted his hand if he had tried.

"Well then," Chieftain Bruce said, "That is that then. Everyone bring me your 20 percent in the morning. We'll put it by the pile of wood here. The sooner the Manteo's get their portions, the sooner they'll be leaving. Let's retrieve our women and children and go back to our homes now. We'll meet here in the morning."

There was an audible collective sigh from the men. A few of them felt shame. Samuel felt nothing. He returned to his home and laid down on the bed. A few more hours and the nightmare would begin. A burning anger began to rise in the breast of the boy. How could the Swordslinger abandon the town? And what was wrong with the men of the village? Not one of them was willing to raise a hand in defense of their homes. They would rather be trampled by a bunch of bullies than risk harm to themselves. This wasn't right! Even if the Swordslinger had turned out to be a coward, he had spoken the truth about honor and pride being necessary to maintain the balance.

Samuel suddenly sat up in bed. Something was calling him. It was a feeling within, not a sound from outside. Someone had to stand up the Manteo Brothers. He visualized Chieftain Bruce cringing behind the huge pile of wood and peat, telling the bandits to take what they wanted. Twenty percent of everything the villagers owned. The jewelry, food, clothing, chickens, sheep ... all of it would be waiting for the Manteo's to take. In his mind's eye, he could see the terrified villagers peeking out their windows, waiting for the outlaws to take their plunder and leave. Where was the courage that men should have? Was everyone a coward? No. No, he could not believe that the Swordslinger had run. Some people thought he had run away when his wife had been killed, but Samuel knew the opposite was true. He had gone after those men and had extracted justice. That wasn't being a coward.

Some things just aren't as they appear. That wasn't something the Swordslinger had imparted, it was an original thought of the boy. What had happened to bring this uncharacteristic reaction from the man that he had begun to idolize? Where was he? His sword was still standing upright in the middle of the village street where Chieftain Bruce had replaced it. The blade stood where the Swordslinger should have been standing when the Manteo Brothers came.

Samuel sighed deeply. It was going to be useless to try to get back to sleep. Stewart was sound asleep in his bed, apparently unconcerned about the perils of tomorrow. No courage needed when you weren't going to stand your ground. Samuel wanted to scream. He had listened to his father and the other men boast of how they were the wild men, untamed and free, and how no Englishmen or foreigners dared approach them. Well, look at the brave men now, cowered beneath their covers, waiting for daylight and a band of bullies to come in and take the things they had worked for so hard.

He knew that the Swordslinger had felt the same anger and frustration and that was why he had chosen to fight against the injustices. He couldn't have just walked away, not from the fight or from the boy he had accepted so warmly.

The man in black and the boy had bonded. The Swordslinger had confided things to Samuel that he had never revealed to anyone else. They had felt almost like father and son, perhaps not by blood, but by heart. Something had happened and Samuel felt compelled to learn what had transpired to change the Swordslinger so quickly. Why would he have turned on him so bitterly and told him to get lost? Well, okay, something had happened and he was going to learn just what. He would find the Swordslinger and stick to him like a burr on a mule's arse until he was given an explanation.

Samuel rose from the bed and wrapped his kilt around him. He went to the mantle above the fireplace and withdrew a red-hilted claymore and a long dirk. He slid the dirk down inside a boot and stealthily left the house.

Samuel stared at the sword sticking in the street for several minutes as he formulated a plan. He could not fathom why the Swordslinger would leave his blade here. A man's sword was part of his soul, his spine. That is what the man had told him. Samuel knelt by the blade and studied the steel. The blade had been forged from the seven broken blades of the men who had killed the Swordslinger's wife. He would no more have left this sword than he would have his soul. There was too much terrible history embedded in the weapon. The soul of the man had been forged into the blade along with the metal from his enemies' swords.

Samuel thrust his claymore into the dirt and pulled the Swordslinger's blade free. It was heavier than his own sword, but it possessed an incredible balance. He took a few trial swings with the blade and felt the comfort of the maneuvers. This sword would be deadly in a fight. The edge was razor sharp and the metal had been hammered and forged with great care and expertise. The silver hilt depicted a dragon with folded wings. The mouth of the dragon was open and snarling, ready to devour and ravage.

Samuel rose and strapped the sword across his back. He studied the roads that met to form the village center and shrugged. He had no way of knowing which direction the Swordslinger had gone, but he had a one-in-four chance of being right. Why not east? That's the direction in which the Manteo Brothers would be coming from. Great. He'd either find the swordslinger or meet the brothers head on. Instinct told him that the Swordslinger was not running away from, but toward the Manteo's.

Samuel walked quickly along the gravel road. The outline of the eastern mountains was visible in the light from the moon. Stars twinkled in the clear sky, outlining the Black Alps that were some 20 miles away. The Swordslinger had a huge head start on the boy, but he was undeterred. His mission was to find the man and he would do so. Logic told him that his friend would use the night cover for travel and probably await the Manteo Brothers from a hiding place in the woods.

Looking back over his shoulder, Samuel could still see the outlined silhouette of the village. His journey was just beginning, but his faith was strong. There was a feeling of dread that he might never see the village or his friends and family again. He had no idea what fate held in store for him, but he was certain that he was going to meet it head on. He would not be like the cowards hiding in their beds. He became so fixated on finding the Swordslinger that he temporarily forgot that he might also encounter the Manteo's along this trail.

Although the sky was still clear, Samuel knew that didn't mean much. The weather changed frequently and almost without warning. It was cool in the early morning and his breath left a vapor trail. The brush of the wool kilt against his legs was warming and the quick pace he was keeping kept him from being cold. The leather boots protected his feet and legs.

He had long been out of sight of the village now and the gravel road had become a path worn in the grass and peat moss. He passed through a thicket of oak trees and literally flinched when a large gray owl hooted. He was traveling up an incline now and he could feel the sharp stones beneath his boot soles. The terrain had a sleepy, eerie feel to it and mist was beginning to rise from the earth. A haze hovered above as the early morning light began trying to filter through.

The next village was on the other side of the mountains, but there was an occasional house near the path. Some hearty souls enjoyed the solitude and preferred living in the wilds. Samuel wondered how they protected themselves from the trespassers. Maybe they just gave freely of what they had. Or maybe some of the men were strong enough to make the outlaws wary and keep their distance.

Samuel had walked for the better part of an hour when a pang in his stomach reminded him that he had brought no food or water with him. *No food. No water. No smarts*, he thought. *What a great adventurer I am*, he scolded himself. He paused and thought for a second. He knew there was a small lake in the direction he was taking, so he wasn't too far from water if he became too thirsty to continue. And as for food, he could go all day without it if necessary. Okay, the thing to do was to continue in his quest to find the man he had come to idolize. He wouldn't detour for the water because that would mean a delay in his journey. But was he even headed in the right direction? How could he be sure? The Swordslinger could have traveled west. Samuel pondered the dilemma, and then shook his head stubbornly. No! He must keep his sense of purpose, no doubts now. Just keep heading east. He had to be right.

There were no signs on the road of recent travel. He had seen no fresh hoof prints. Nothing. The Swordslinger must be traveling off the path. Being smart. Keeping himself hidden until he had the drop on the Manteo Brothers. Aye.

Samuel's young legs were beginning to tire. He paused and bent over, running his fingers over the damp grass and transferring the moistness to his lips. The mist was becoming heavier, rising a couple of feet above the ground. But he knew that the sun would be rising soon and burn it off. He walked on, determined to complete his journey. *Fool.* How could he expect to catch up with the Swordslinger who was on horseback? *Fool. Dummy. Stupid!* He had left the village in a funk and now he was sunk. He stopped, dropped to his knees and pondered the futility of his search. He pounded a fist against the dirt and called himself more names.

Then his stubborn nature kicked in. "I can't quit now," he said out loud. "No, I will find you if I have to walk to the ends of the earth. This sword belongs to you as much as I …" He hesitated, suddenly aware of what he was saying, "… as much as I do."

He resumed walking, finding that the mist had now risen high enough to block his vision. He could only see a few feet in front of him. It was like walking in a dream along a road that never ended. He was concerned that he might wander from the path and lose his sense of direction. Plowing ahead, he drew the sword and began swinging it through the mist. He envisioned himself cutting down a wall of enemies.

The voice brought him from the reverie with a startling jolt.

"I think we should bed ourselves until daylight. This wet grass is for eels and silkies."

Samuel stopped dead. He didn't even breathe. Gradually he placed his left foot on the ground. He had halted in mid-step.

"I think I'll gather me some kilts and jerkins tomorrow. Keep me arse dry," a man said.

"Yeah, I'm looking to get some of them women, meself," another voice said. "They got some fine lasses in the village, aye?"

"Aye, but you mess with the women, you may piss off a grandpap. I can see him now, chasing after you with his crooked cane."

Then the other man dropped his voice to a whisper. "What about the others with us? We expected to split the loot with them? This is our territory. These are our people. I don't even know who the hell these outsiders are."

"Be careful, fool. There are twenty of them Vikings. We're lucky they didn't slit our throats when we ran into them. We're tough, but them bastards is bloodlusters. They're as wild as a bunch of boars turned onto a sow in heat. Hell, if they want all the loot I ain't arguing with them.

I'm just looking to get away from them with my arse in one piece."

"Och, and you are right, Charlie. They do have madness in their eyes. That's why I took night watch. Hell, I can't sleep with them wooly-bears within a mile of me."

Night watch. Samuel's mind was racing. These unseen men were standing guard while the others slept. *Dear God, did he say twenty Vikings? And the five Manteo Brothers? Jesus, this was terrible news. The villagers were so fearful of five brothers that they were willing to give up their property. How would they react when they learned the raiding party was now 25? A lot of grown men with soiled pants*, Samuel thought, almost smiling at the picture in his mind. He had heard tales of the Vikings and how they not only raided the villages for possessions but also raped the women and girls and then burned the towns to the grounds. The Manteo Brothers were bad news. The Vikings were a plague.

I have to warn the others, Samuel thought. *I have to turn back and let them know. If I don't, these savages will kill everyone.* His face paled as he thought of what might happen to Heather and her sisters.

He started to turn when a hand came out of the darkness and clamped over his mouth. He started struggling and then heard a familiar voice whisper, "Be quiet, Sam. Don't move and don't make a sound."

CHAPTER 13

DEAD AWAKENINGS

The Swordslinger led Samuel backwards about 30 yards, moving off the road and away from the men that they had heard talking. Finally, he motioned for the boy to lie down on the wet grass.

"God, you scared me to death! How did you find me?" Samuel asked in a hoarse whisper.

"Could've reached out and touched you in the oak grove you walked through a mile or so back."

Samuel suddenly put his arms around the man, his own body quivering with fear and excitement.

"It's okay, lad. The question is, what are you doing out here?"

"Seems you forgot something back at the village," Samuel said, pulling away and reaching for the sword on his back. He held the blade out to the man.

"I left that behind for a reason," Swordslinger said, making no move to take the sword.

Samuel pushed the blade closer to the man. But he still made no move to accept it.

"What's the point, Sam?" he asked. "If those men don't care enough to defend themselves, then why should I?"

"Because ... you're a swordslinger and that's what you're supposed to do. It's not about the village men. This is about you and what is right and wrong."

"I don't know what is right or wrong anymore, get it? I think I'm doing right, and then I'm treated wrong. What the hell sense does that make?"

"You know what is right. God knows, too. I know it. We have to help the village. They have no idea what they're up against. They'll be slaughtered tomorrow."

The sound of feet on gravel sounded and the man and boy pressed their bodies closer to the ground. The owner of the feet spat and moved away. "Thought I heard something," he said to his cohort. "Be glad when we get these Vikes away from us. I won't sleep till we do." The voice grew distant as he walked away.

The Swordslinger grumbled some unintelligible words, and then said, "Give me the sword."

"Yes!" Samuel exclaimed in an excited whisper. "Yes."

"There's at least 25 of them," Swordslinger said. "Their horses are farther to the right of the road. Stay put. I'm going back to my horse. I have to get something from my saddle."

"Aye," Samuel said, his heart racing. What were they going to do? Twenty-five wild men against one swordslinger and his puppy. As he lay still, he heard several huffs and neighs from the horses. The fog was still thick. He had seen no sign of a campfire, just a wall of white mist within an arm's distant. Samuel drew his dirk from the boot. He was trembling, and he wasn't sure if it was from excitement or fear. Maybe both.

Minutes passed. Samuel thought he was going to die of anticipation. The fog's going to lift and it might be daybreak before the Swordslinger returned. He suddenly had the urge to sneeze. He clamped both hands over his mouth and squinted, fighting to keep the sneeze from coming.

A wild-eyed leafy beast pushed its head through the fog. Samuel's mouth flew open, forming to make a scream. Having to sneeze and scream and keep them from happening was a brain buster. "Ahhh …"

The Swordslinger covered Samuel's mouth with his black-gloved hand. "It's my horse. Shhhh!" he whispered.

"I know I heard something," a voice said from nearby. The man was so close the two dark shadows on the ground could hear the sound of a sword being drawn.

"Who's there?"

"Joe, will ye get back. You go any farther you'll get lost in the fog," the other Manteo Brother said.

"Aye, maybe it was a deer. I'm coming back."

Swordslinger whispered to Samuel, "We can't handle all of them. The best we can do is put a few down and maybe scare off their horses. I want you to move to the left side of the road with my horse for about 200 yards. "Here, this is a

145

match, compliments of my eastern friends. Here's several of them. I also brought back what they call firecrackers. They make a fierce racket. I got them all linked to a fuse hanging over the horse. She's gonna be pretty pissed and a wee burnt when they go off, but I can't think of anything else at the moment. She's gonna buck and run when they start banging. You got to hang on, though, because if you fall off, those Vikings got ye."

"I won't fall. I'll tie my hands to the reins."

"Don't care how ye do it. Just stay in the saddle. Once she's finally calmed down, head back to the village. Run her fast as ye can go. Tell them what's coming. Tell them they have to fight, that this is a Viking raiding party and there are no rules."

"All right. But what about you?"

"I'm going to work myself around to their horses and try to set them loose when the fireworks go off. I'll try to cut down a few bandits while I'm at it."

"Will you be coming back?"

Swordslinger hesitated with the answer. He sighed. "Yeah, I'll go back. I'll finish this job, then I'm disappearing."

"Oh, no. Not without me."

"Sam … look, we'll talk about that later. Once you make 200 steps, I want you to count to a hundred. You can count, right?"

"Aye, I go to school."

"Good for you. Have the horse headed in the direction of the village. Try to keep her on the left side of the road. Remember hang on for dear life."

"Aye."

The Swordslinger started to move away.

"Wait! What's a firecracker?"

"You'll know it when you hear it. It will pop and spark and make a lot of noise. Och, I almost forgot the fuse. I wrapped it around the saddle horn. You light the end of it and let it burn. It will go quick and run toward the back of the horse. There's a lot of firecrackers hanging back there. And Samuel, keep low. Hug the horse. She's disguised as a monster. If they see anything, I want it to scare the holy haggis out of them."

"Aye." Samuel hugged the Swordslinger. "God, help us."

They parted and Samuel lifted himself into the saddle of the horse. He wished he knew the horse's name. He found the fuse wrapped around the horn and the matches were safe and dry in his sporran. The Swordslinger had also had given him a strip of rough leather to scratch the matches to life on. Samuel crossed himself and gingerly urged the horse forward.

This is about the dumbest tactic I have ever conceived, Swordslinger was thinking. He knew he was putting Samuel's life at risk. There must have been something else he could have done without the aid of the boy. Still, the Swordslinger knew that Samuel would be a part of this one way or the other. He was a stubborn lad. *He's like me*, Swordslinger thought.

Crouching, the Swordslinger ran across to the right side of the road. There was no sign of the camp the men had set up and the fog was as thick as ever. *You wouldn't know you were near a Viking until you stepped on him*, Swordslinger thought. He moved with stealth and used the length of his sword like a blind man as he moved forth. "What if Samuel falls from the horse? What if they kill the boy? Stewart will blame me. And why not, am I not accused of about every wrongdoing there is? Keep moving. Careful now."

Another step and the Swordslinger's foot would have been on the man's outstretched hand. He drew his foot back and veered a few feet to his right. The horses were close and their snorts grew louder. He could smell them.

He didn't have time to smell the Viking. They were face to face and the Swordslinger drew his blade back for a slash when he realized the man was sleeping. He was leaning against a tree, supposedly standing watch but asleep on his feet. Swordslinger quietly moved around the man and found the rope tied between the trees with the reins of the horse attached. He slipped beneath the rope, praying he wouldn't startle the horses. So far, so good. One of the horses snorted, a little louder than before, and the snoozing Viking stirred slightly against the tree trunk.

The Swordslinger reached up and held the rope with one hand, waiting for Samuel to get into position and light the fuse. A loud splat sounded. Then several more. Swordslinger jerked his hat off his head and felt the rain. He lowered his head in defeat. The fuse will be wet. Samuel is going to panic. "Great! Come on rain. Come on. Let's wake everybody up and we'll sit and have tea."

Samuel was at 192 paces when the first raindrops came. There was one thing he knew with living in a world where it rained every day; fire and water don't mix. He opened a blanket that was rolled on the back of the saddle, undid his kilt and wrapped it over the firecrackers hanging off the side of the horse. Then, he put one end of the blanket over his head and stuffed the other end beneath his wrapped kilt so that the water would hit the blanket and roll off, hopefully not wetting the firecrackers.

Samuel rode nude on the horse, his thighs squishing against the wet leather of the saddle. Two hundred! Okay, hmmm… count… One, two…" He continued to count. He wrapped the reins around his wrists and planned to hug the horse around the neck when the fuse started burning.

The rain continued at a steady fall, slightly slanted from west to east by the wind. Cold water soaked the blanket on Samuel's back. He could feel the water running down the blanket and hopefully off the side of the horse. *God, what a sight he must look*, he thought. Then fear ran through him like a shiver of cold. Seventy-eight … eighty-one … ninety-two … ninety-four … ninety-seven… He had lost the count! He continued to count and tried forcing himself to be able to count and think at the same time. It was impossible. Maybe it was better to just count and not think. He closed his eyes and shivered and counted.

It seemed like forever for Samuel. He tried to guess where he had lost the count but had no idea. Sighing, he picked up the count at eighty. It seemed an hour had passed before he was nearing the end. How many times had he lost the count? How far off was the timing? Ninety-three. *Oh,*

God, help me, help me. Ninety-three. Eighty-four. Please hurry. Hurry!
He quickened the count. One hundred... where was I? Okay. Enough
already. Samuel had a match in one hand and the rough
leather strip in the other. They both were dry. It was
awkward trying to strike the small stick with sulfur on the
end of it, when his hands were bound tight with the reins.

Samuel's tongue protruded from his lips. He squinted
his eyes. Even in the cold and all wet, sweat dripped from
his brow. He struck the leather strip with the match.
Nothing happened. "Huh?" No. No! Come on. Please! He
rubbed the match against the leather again and the stick
snapped. He held the broken match with his fingers almost
to the sulfur head and struck the strip of leather. The match
flared. Samuel jumped, his fingers stung and the startled
horse lurched forward. Samuel's chest banged against the
saddle horn. He almost cried out in pain and found that the
match was no longer in his hand. He reached into his
sporran and brought out another match. Then he realized he
had dropped the leather strip. Now Samuel really wanted to
scream. He was so messed up! The Swordslinger was
counting on his timing everything and he was totally
confused. He searched frantically along his thigh and saddle
but couldn't find the piece of leather. His mind raced now.
Every second counted. The whetstone! He always carried a
small whetstone in his sporran. It was something he had
picked up from his father. Never have to worry about a dull
blade if you carry a whetstone.

Nervously, Samuel gripped the whetstone in his left
hand. The horse began moving. His right hand held tight on
the matchstick but the dumb horse was turning in a circle.
Now Samuel was totally lost. He didn't know what was east,
west, south, or north.

The match scratched on the rough surface of the
whetstone and flared into flame. *All right. Now, the fuse. Where*
was it? He felt around on the saddle for the fuse but couldn't
find it. *Now what?* In his fumbling, he dropped the
whetstone. Okay, here it is. He seized the fuse and pulled it
up toward the flickering flame from the match. The flame
died, and along with it, the boy's spirit. *Don't give up. There* are

two more matches. You can do it. He pulled another match from the sporran and remembered he was no longer holding the whetstone. He gasped. *Where was it?* He frantically searched for the stone in his lap and on the saddle. Nothing. A feeling of helplessness began creeping over him. Tears of frustration formed. He had failed. He was soaked from the rain. The blanket from the horse was heavy from the wetness. He was ready to panic.

What could he use to strike the match? His mind raced. There was a string of leather that ran though his jerkin along the V in the front. Would it work? Maybe, if he could find a dry spot. He prayed as he stroked the match gently against the leather thong. Nothing. The leather wasn't rough enough to create friction. *Now what?* He ran his hands over the saddle, seeking a dry spot, and felt something rough just beneath the saddle horn, Maybe. He leaned forward, trying to protect the match from the wind and rain. He pulled the match across the rough patch of leather and it burst into flame.

Thank you, God! Thank you! Samuel put the burning match to the end of the fuse, but nothing happened. *Now what?* He was screaming in his mind. *Come on! Come on!* And the flame flickered and died.

Sobs of frustration wracked the boy's body. Tears mixed with the rain on his cheeks. He had failed the Swordslinger. It was probably already too late. Suddenly he had a thought. *The hair!* The braid of hair that Heather had given him. He had wrapped it in cloth and it would be dry inside the sporran. Maybe ... He quickly pulled the braid from his sporran. It was tied with a silk ribbon and it was dry. He reached for the last of the matches and scratched its head against the rough leather of the saddle. His heart was pounding. The last chance. He held the match to the ribbon-braided hair and it burst into flame. He held the flame to the end of the fuse and it suddenly sparked and began fizzing. The red glow from its end began traveling along the fuse toward the string of fireworks.

Samuel stood in the stirrups, allowing the burning fuse to move under his leg and toward the firecrackers. This was new to him. He had never seen fire travel a rope before. The firecrackers were attached to the fuse by their own fuses and he wondered how the horse was going to react when they started popping.

He leaned forward, clenching the reins tightly with his bare butt just above the seat of the saddle. The fire reached the first firecracker and the short fuse began spitting sparks. BANG! The first firecracker exploded. The startled horse reared on its hind legs and loosed a shrill nightmarish neigh.

Nearby, Joe Manteo shouted, "What the …!" And another BANG! rang out. Manteo hit the ground, covering his head with his arms. Other men began shouting. Some pulled their swords and their heads jerked around as they tied to pinpoint where the noise was coming from.

Another BANG! Joe Manteo rose to his knees and saw a dark blur moving past him. It was a creature from hell! It was as huge as a horse but it was covered with grass, weeds and gnarled branches. And ohmigod! *That looked like a* naked *boy riding it!* Another BANG! and the ghastly creature from hell was speeding past. Too fast for his numbed brain to register exactly what he had seen.

The men were milling around. Some of them were screaming in excitement and fear of the unknown. Amid the confusion, the Swordslinger was quietly carrying out his plan. He quickly cut the rope that held the horses and the frightened animals began scrambling in all directions. The Viking who had been sleeping upright against the tree woke up with a start and lost his balance. He scrambled to regain his feet and was drawing his sword when a blade impaled him from behind.

The Swordslinger placed his booted foot on the man and freed his sword. He leaned against the tree and waited as a ghostly figure materialized from the mist. It was another Viking, a huge man with a bushy beard and long hair concealing his facial features. He never knew how he died. He caught a glimpse of what appeared to be a winged phantom in a wide-brimmed hat rushing at him. But before he could bring his sword up or yell for help, he was dying

151

from the thrust of a blade to his midsection. He died with only a slight sigh coming from his lips.

Another Viking came out of the mist before the man in black had fully retrieved his blade from the body. Swordslinger felt him before he saw him as the huge man barreled into him. They crashed to the ground, the breath forced out of the Swordslinger and his sword knocked from his grasp. The two men rolled on the ground and the Viking's hands closed on the Swordslinger's throat.

"Here!" the man yelled. "I've got him!"

The pressure cut off his breath and Swordslinger knew he had only seconds to react. He reached into the waist of his trousers and pulled out the dirk. An instant later and the Vikings' hands relaxed their death grip as the dirk slammed into his belly. He grabbed futilely at the wound, trying to stem the gushing flow of blood. The Swordslinger shoved the dying man off him and began searching for his sword. He reached for the blade when a heavy foot slammed down on his hand. He felt the edge of a blade across the back of his neck.

"You move, you die!" the man said in a Highland accent.

One of the Manteo Brothers, the Swordslinger thought. All he could see were the man's leather boots.

CHAPTER 14

FOR WHOM THE BELL TOLLS

The horse and the nude boy galloped through the mist. The hard strides of the animal sent jolts through Samuel as he bounced in the saddle. He didn't know how far they had traveled and he had no idea where they were. He pulled on the reins and brought the frightened animal to a halt, jumped to the ground, found his kilt and wrapped it around him.

Samuel was trembling, both from fear and from the cold rain. His hands were shaking and he had trouble remounting the horse. The saddle was wet and cold. Everything was soaked. And the rain was still falling. He tried to gather his wits and discern where he might be. He cocked his head to one side, listening. But there was nothing but a deadly silence.

Samuel gave the horse what he hoped was a reassuring pat. "Don't be mad at me," he whispered. "I didn't like those firecrackers any more than you did." He dug his heels into the horses flanks and turned the animal back in the direction they had fled. The visibility was still dim and he could see only a few feet ahead on the narrow dirt road. He wanted to put the horse into a gallop, but knew that would be dangerous. He settled for a jarring trot.

Reaching down, Samuel felt the hilt of the dirk in his boot. If he had to, he could use it for protection. Yeah, that thought was some cold comfort. "Me and a little knife against the Manteo Brothers." He urged the horse to move a little faster. He wanted desperately to find the Swordslinger.

The bouncing against the hard saddle was beginning to take its toll on the boy. The horse was beginning to pant, too, and he knew they both needed a rest. The fear and excitement had drained him. He reined the horse in near a grove of oak trees and tried to gather himself. Where was he? Where were the Manteo's? Where was anyone?

Samuel's mind raced. Had the Swordslinger been killed? Should he try to find him or return to the village and warn the townspeople? Were the Vikings and the brothers lurking somewhere near? His heart pounded.

He tried to regain his bearings. He had no idea how near he might be to the outlaws' camp. He looked upward and rain pelted into his face. How much longer until daylight? It couldn't be much longer. He felt as though he had been in the dark for an eternity. Where was the Swordslinger? Was he dead? He pondered the situation. He really had only one option. If he tried to find the Swordslinger, he was much more likely to be captured by the rogues. Then he couldn't warn anyone.

"Okay," he whispered to the horse. "We go back to the village. God be with you, Swordslinger." He knew the man had risked his own life so that the villagers could be warned.

"Giddy up, Firecracker," he said to the horse, giggling at the nickname he had given the animal. "Let's go. I just hope we're heading in the right direction." The horse moved off in an easy canter, not nearly as jarring as the earlier trot had been. Good, because the skin on the inside of his thighs was burning raw.

It was getting lighter as dawn neared and the mist was lifting. Samuel tried to ignore the searing pain of his thighs and kept the tired horse moving. The life of those in the village depended on him getting there in time to warn them. He thought of Heather and his heart did a flutter beat. He pictured her being chased by a hairy Viking and shuddered. He urged the horse to move faster. What was going to happen? Life would never be the same, he knew. He sighed, and dug his heels into the wet horse.

Thank God for the horse, he thought. But what about the Swordslinger? How would he travel? Maybe he could use one of the outlaws' horses. If he was still alive. The boy shuddered again.

The rain had ceased and it was almost daylight. The only sound was that of the horse's hooves against the hard dirt and the squeaking of the wet saddle. Stars appeared in the brightening sky. Samuel realized he was hungry and felt in the saddlebag. He found some bread and a piece of cheese and began munching on it. There was water in a goat stomach bag and he drank deeply, feeling the water slosh in his belly as he rode.

Dawn was breaking and the rising sun announced itself with a deep purple band across the horizon. Samuel could see the outline of the village ahead, smoke coming from some of the chimneys. He urged the horse into a gallop and felt his heart begin pounding anew. Maybe he could warn the people in time for them to save themselves.

Samuel steered the panting horse to a stop in the street in front of the chapel and rushed inside. His thighs were on fire and his ribs ached from the pounding of the ride, but he raced to the small bell tower and began tugging frantically on the rope. The church bell rang out loudly in the still morning and the startled villagers rose from their beds and began streaming into the street, some of them still in their nightwear. Others appeared in doors and at windows, frightened and curious.

They were even more startled when the wet, bedraggled boy burst from the chapel's door and began shouting. "They're coming! Get your weapons. They're coming!"

Chieftain Bruce came on the run. He was holding his beltless pants around his waist. "What are you yelling about, boy? What?"

"The Manteo Brothers ... and a bunch of Vikings ... they're coming! We have to get ready to fight them! We have to arm ourselves and set fire to this." He pointed to the pile of wood and peat moss in the street.

"Are you daft, boy? We can't fight them. There are only about 20 of us and we can't fight them. Maybe if the Swordslinger was here, but he ran off, didn't he?"

"No, he didn't run! He's out there ... trying to slow them down. He may have already been killed. I don't know. I rode his horse here to warn you. But we have to hurry. There isn't much time!"

Chieftain Bruce glanced to the spot where the Swordslinger's blade had been stuck in the street. "He got his sword? He's fighting them now?"

"Yes," Samuel lied, "he came back for his sword and I saw him and followed him. When he found the outlaws he gave me his horse and told me to come back and warn you."

"How many Vikings are there," the chieftain asked.

"I don't know. Maybe twenty-five."

"Twenty-five Vikings and the Manteo Brothers? Chieftain Bruce's eyes widened in panic. "All right," he shouted to the gawking villagers. Get your families, your horses and anything you want to take with you. Now! We'll meet back here in five minutes and load the stuff onto the wagons. Move!"

Samuel stared at the chieftain, unbelieving. "Go? That won't help. They'll follow our tracks. They'll run us down!"

"Just shut up, boy. There are places we can hide in the hills. Let's go!" he shouted, and ran towards his home.

Samuel's shoulders slumped. What were they thinking? He had ridden this hard to warn them and they were just going to run? "Cowards!" he shouted. "You're all cowards!"

"Where the hell have you been, lad?" The shout made Samuel turn. His father was racing toward him Samuel said nothing; his heart was high in his throat, pounding fiercely.

"Come on, boy! Help me pack. When we get in the hills, you and me are going to have a little talk! Now, move it!"

CHAPTER 15

DEATH COMES CALLING

"I am already dead," Swordslinger hissed to his attacker. He thrust his dirk between his neck and the blade of the man above him. He pushed off to the left and in the same movement used his left hand to grab the man's ankle. He pulled forward as he pushed to the left and Bailey Manteo was thrown off balance and began falling, still holding the sword. His left knee drove into the Swordslinger's shoulder, paralyzing the upper arm with agonizing pain and causing him to drop the dirk. He lunged to his left again, pushing with all his strength at the man. Off balance, Manteo fell and his sword cut into his upper shoulder.

The man moaned and rolled onto his back. Swordslinger scrambled to retrieve his knife and even as his fingers were still closing on the hilt, thrust it into the man's neck, just below his chin.

Before he could regain his feet, one of the Vikings was upon him. The Swordslinger tried to roll away from the charge, but the blade of the man's sword nicked his left calf. The Viking raised his blade to take another swing and the Swordslinger rolled again. He tried to rise, but the wound in his left leg refused to bear the weight.

"Now you die!" the Viking cried, rushing forward, and then screamed as the hurled dirk buried in his chest.

Suddenly there were men everywhere, shouting and confused in the darkness; two of them attacked each other with their swords. Swordslinger rolled into one of the Vikings, taking him down. They rose to their knees and the Viking took his sword back for a strike. The Swordslinger dove into him, seizing the man's hands and they fell to the ground in a death struggle for the sword. The Viking sunk his teeth into the Swordslinger's neck and the searing pain gave him new strength. He wrestled the sword from the man and slashed the razor-sharp blade across his throat.

Once again, the Swordslinger struggled to get to his feet. But before he could manage it, he felt a sharp pain in his left shoulder. A Viking had taken a wild swing at him and the tip of the sword had sliced into the flesh. Swordslinger swung the dead Viking's sword blindly and felt it cut into the man's mid-section. He yanked the blade free and felt a stream of hot blood course over him as the man crumpled.

The other men were still trying to sort each other out and the Swordslinger took advantage of the confusion to crawl into the surrounding bushes. He was hurting and bleeding from wounds in his neck, shoulder and leg, but he was still alive and able to maneuver. He spotted one of the horses and dropped the sword to pull himself astride the animal. He kicked the panicking horse in the sides just as a hand grabbed at his foot.

The horse bolted, breaking the hand's grip, and the Swordslinger dug his boots hard into horse. The galloping steed pounded down the dirt path, with its rider leaning over against its neck. The white hair of the horse was being stained red.

CHAPTER 16

GHOST TOWN AND DEAD MEN

Somewhere between a nightmare in hell and a skipping stone upon the water was how Swordslinger felt. He was barely conscious. The horse had to be constantly pulled by its mane to keep it on the road. From his position sprawled across the horse's neck, all he saw were hooves and road. The steady rain now turned into a drizzle but the water was not enough to wash away the odor of blood — his blood. He was afraid to get off the horse to assess his wounds for fear the horse might run away. Or that he wouldn't have the strength to remount.

As the horse plodded along dirt trail, the Swordslinger found that the shoulder that had been kneed was more painful than the one that had been slashed by the sword. But he was afraid that the leg wound might be the more serious. He "whoaed" the horse to a stop, removed his belt and made a noose from it around the horse's neck. He guided the horse off the road and into a copse of trees nearby, and then slowly slipped to the ground. He raised his pants' leg and saw the gash in his calf was several inches long, but not seriously deep. It was still bleeding, but was beginning to coagulate around the edges. At least an artery hadn't been severed. He tore a piece from the tail of his black shirt and tied it above the wound.

The horse flinched, but the Swordslinger had a tight grip on the belt. "Steady, girl," he said, and returned to assessing his wounds. He couldn't see the gash in his shoulder, but it was about two inches long and laying open. He ran his fingers along the cut, intensifying the pain. He knew he was almost unable to defend himself with both shoulders practically immobile, but he had to keep moving. He used another piece of the shirt to tie under his arm and across the shoulder wound. At least it was covered.

The only weapon he had was a small deer horn knife that was wedged in his boot. His sword was somewhere back in the bandits' camp. He hoped he didn't have to face any of those men in the near future, but he knew that was probably just wishful thinking.

His musing was interrupted by the sound of horses coming fast down the road. He placed a hand on the horses' withers to keep her quiet, and watched as three riders galloped past. *Great*, he thought. Maybe he would be fighting again sooner than he had planned. But how? With what?

The rain had stopped and the rising sun would quickly burn off the fog. The trees he was hiding in weren't thick enough to give him cover in daylight. He was going to have to move. Okay, so what were his options? He knew that he had killed four of the Vikings and one of the Manteo Brothers. That left at least 20 more men that were hell bent on killing him. And he had one little knife to help him stand them off. Great odds.

He painfully pulled himself astride the horse and began moving down the road toward the village. He hoped he would be able to hear riders coming from behind before they were able to see him. A ribbon of purple light snaked along the eastern horizon. He had enjoyed such sunrises many times in life, but now he could only wonder what other horrors this new day might bring. A sudden urgency to reach the village made him dig his heels into the side of the horse, speeding her along. Despite himself, he felt a responsibility for the fate of the villagers. They were men, but not men such as the gang of bandits that would be invading. They would be like pieces of meat thrown to a pack of hungry wolves.

Five down ... twenty to go. And he had lost his precious sword. Maybe one of the bandits would pick it up and bring it into the village when they attacked. If so, and he saw it, he would find a way to get it back. But first, he had to find strength to get to the village. At least he had stopped the bleeding and he was feeling stronger. None of the wounds were fatal nor had severed a tendon. He had been lucky. *Lucky?* He laughed aloud.

More alert now, he focused on guiding the horse and planning a defense. If he could get the men in the village together and put their plan in action, it might still work. He

160

wondered if the boy had made it back safely. Maybe the men would be alert and ready when he arrived.

He clucked to the horse and kicked his heels into her flanks, urging her for more speed. The tired animal responded, moving into an easy lope. *Yeah, we can still cause a little trouble for the raiders*, he thought. Surely, he could find 20 good men willing to fight for their families and homes. Still, he wondered how effective he could be in a fight. He wasn't sure he could pick up a sword. Hell, standing would be a problem.

Swordslinger allowed the horse to have its rein, set its own pace, and the animal slowed to a walk again. He closed his eyes, trying to muster some strength. The blood he had lost had weakened him, but at least he wasn't dizzy anymore. He rested, and his mind wandered. He was in a small boat, riding choppy waves. He was being washed downriver, over the rapids, in slow motion. The crunching of the horse's hooves against the gravel road entering the village roused him. He opened his eyes and saw the buildings. But no people.

It was too quiet. The chapel bell should have been ringing if someone had spotted him riding in. If the villagers had been warned, why hadn't someone in the observation trees sounded an alarm?

The sound of galloping horses caused him to look back down the road. Three more horsemen were coming in. Riding fast. The raiders must have decided they could cover more ground in their search by separating into small groups.

"There he is!" one of the Vikings shouted. One of the riders placed the reins in his mouth and raised his bow, losing an arrow. The Swordslinger kicked his heels into the horse's side and jerked at her mane. He heard the sound of the arrow as it whizzed past. The Viking reloaded and fired off another shot. This time the arrow struck a stone to his left.

The Swordslinger guided the horse out of sight of the men and slid off, giving her a swat across the rear that sent her running off into the nearby trees. Wincing in pain, he stepped behind the tree that was supposed to have served as

161

an observation post. Now what? Was he going to tackle three men on horseback, all armed, with his little dagger? *This could be my last stand*, he thought.

Acting quickly, ignoring the pain coursing through his torn and slashed body, Swordslinger noticed a thick tree branch on the ground. The branch was about five feet long and seemed sturdy. He hefted the limb and waited as the men approached the tree. If only they hadn't spotted him …

His heart pounding, the Swordslinger waited … waited until the Vikings were almost at the tree. Then, gritting his teeth against the pain, he lunged from behind the tree and swung the heavy branch at the front legs of the first rider's horse. One of the front legs snapped like a twig and the horse somersaulted. The Viking went overhead first, the horned helmet flying from his head and going end over end. The horse screamed in pain.

The second rider, the archer, lost his balance when his horse shied, and fell awkwardly from the saddle. His left boot wedged in the stirrup and there was an audible snap as the tibia broke. He hit the hard ground chin first and the horse bolted and ran, dragging its unconscious rider along the road.

The third Viking escaped the entanglement and pulled his horse to a halt. He turned in the saddle and held his sword ready to strike.

It was an awkward eternity between the foes. The Swordslinger rose to his feet, trying to mask his injuries. The Viking sat on his horse, sword raised, poised for the killing blow. But he seemed momentarily frozen. One of his companions was sprawled in the road, moaning in pain, perhaps with a broken back. The other was being dragged into the village behind a frightened horse. And the bloody bastard who had caused it all was standing there staring at him.

The Viking looked like the barbarian that he was. His red hair was long and hung in ringlets held by gold. A full beard, a darker red than his hair, touched his chest. He wore a breastplate that appeared befitting a Celtic King. The breastplate was engraved with the image of a Viking ship. A huge dragon was carved into the ship's bow. The sword in the Viking's hands was massive. A single swipe with that blade could down a row of five men at once. But something seemed to puzzle the man. His mouth hung agape, revealing a gap where a couple of teeth had once been.

There was an odd, confused look on the face of the Viking. He stared at the bloodied man standing in the road with wonderment. Even the man's horse had a wild look in her eyes, strained and bulging with terror.

The Viking's mind was racing. Who was this man in black? His clothes were torn and filthy with dirt and dried blood. And he had killed seven men already. Five back in the camp and two just moments ago. The Viking's face, what could be seen above the beard, turned red with anger. His body began shaking with rage.

Then the Swordslinger in black went even further. He smiled at the man on horseback. A maddening smile that enraged the already angry Viking. Then the man in black moved, a lightning-quick maneuver that caught the Viking by surprise. He grabbed the sword from the fallen man's scabbard and turned to face the enemy.

Spurring his mount, the Viking's horse reared, clawing at the sky with its front legs and hooves at the sky, and then lunging straight for the man on foot.

The Swordslinger stumbled backwards over the dying horse of the archer and was defenseless for a moment. The Viking began a mighty swing of the sword from above his head, meaning to decapitate the foe. But the man was too quick, ducking beneath the blow by a fraction of an inch.

The Viking regained control of his horse and prepared to make another pass at his intended victim. But this time the man in black was ready. Although there was obviously something wrong with one of his legs, the man still presented a formidable presence. And there were those seven dead men ...

The Swordslinger peeled his lips back in a menacing smile. "Stop now and I might allow you to live," he said.

A mad laugh erupted from the Viking and he spurred his horse toward the man again. He brought the large sword down in a move strong enough to cleave a mountain. Swordslinger narrowly evaded the swing and slashed his newly acquired blade across the lower leg of the man in the saddle. The Viking screamed in pain and when the horse swerved to the side, came crashing to the ground. He tried to gain his feet but his left leg was useless. He still had his sword, though and rushed a swing at his tormentor. The Swordslinger easily sidestepped the sword and brought his own blade around in an arc so fast that it was a blur when it connected with the man's neck and almost severed the head.

The man's body jerked in the spasms of death as the Swordslinger stood above him. "I wasn't kidding," he said. "I might have let you live."

The Swordslinger dropped to the ground, his body aching from the wounds and fatigue. His heart was pounding and streaks of fire raced across his chest. He closed his eyes and gathered himself. Eight down, only seventeen to go. Could he survive another encounter? He doubted it. Without help, without some distraction or an intervention by God, he would die from one of the bandits' blades before the day was done. The image of his late wife passed before his eyes and he smiled. At least he might see his love again.

But not yet. There was still work to be done. As long as he was breathing, he would not allow those outlaws to rape and pillage. He had made a promise and he would keep it. He assessed his tortured body and found that the wounds, though painful, were mostly superficial. A few days and they would heal, leaving only scars from another battle. His joints were stiffening and the pain was extreme when he put weight on his left leg. He shook his head to clear it and almost blacked out. This wasn't going to be easy.

He went to the Viking's horse and pulled himself into the saddle. He might as well ride into the village square in style. Yeah, if style meant clothing that was crusted with blood and wounds that were like nipping dogs.

It suddenly dawned on the Swordslinger that he had forgotten about the three Vikings who had passed him earlier on the trail. They must already be in the village or waiting for their friends on the outskirts. He rode on, trying to blot out the pain caused by the jolting steps of the horse.

His thoughts were interrupted by a blur of movement from some bushes alongside the road. One of the Vikings stepped into the opening and leveled his bow. The arrow whizzed in, barely missing his thigh and burying its point in the saddle. Swordslinger crouched over the horse and kicked her hard in the sides, spurring her toward the village. Why wasn't the bell tolling? Where was the bonfire? Where were the people?

What was going on here? There was no one in sight. Doors of homes and shops stood ajar. He pulled the horse to a stop in front of Chieftain Bruce's home and noted that door was standing open and there was a sword and a dirk placed in the doorway. He continued on to the pile of wood and peat moss in the square and still no one had appeared. A huge mass of food, grain, smoked meat and even some furniture was piled in the street.

"They're gone," he said aloud. *They've panicked and run. They've left everything for the scavengers.*

The Swordslinger slid off the horse and limped to the well. He drew a bucket of water and poured some of the cold liquid over his head. Then he drank deeply and dropped the bucket. He turned and saw the three Vikings on their horses. They were coming into town. From high above, the cry of a gray hawk sounded. An omen? At least it wasn't a vulture.

A wry smile creased the Swordslinger's face. *I'm like that gray hawk*, he thought. *We both cry out and no one pays attention. We're both alone. He's circling and I'm perching.*

The irony of the situation amused the Swordslinger. He was preparing to fight to the death for a village whose occupants had fled to the hills. Samuel had warned him. The villagers were too cowardly to fight for their own homes. Why should he give a damn? But this was more than a fight for property. He was fighting for mankind. For principles. To kill the evil in men's hearts. *I could just limp away*, he thought, *and never think of this place again. But where would I limp? No, I must stand and fight. This is what I am. This is why I live and*

165

breathe. If I die, it will be for the right reasons. If I run, I won't be able to live with myself anyway. I will not allow myself to become a sheep.

This was bigger than the courage or cowardice of a bunch of villagers. It was bigger than him. This was about right and wrong. Good and evil. Yes, he would stand up against the insurmountable odds because it was the only way he knew. He would fight with faith. Faith that after this life he would be with his wife again. No, he didn't want to die, but if he did, at least there was no one to mourn. If God was keeping tally of the good and bad things men did, then perhaps he could pile up a few points in his favor. Fate had made him a loner, had shaped his destiny. And now destiny would decide his fate. He knew that the villagers, wherever they were, didn't care if he lived or died.

He thought of his sword and wondered where it might be. Would one of the raiders be carrying it? He would feel so much more potent if he had his own trusted blade. Samuel had thought he was being helpful when he brought the sword to him, but now he wished it had been left sticking in the dirt of the street. He suddenly wished that someone had stayed in the village. Perhaps it was just his ego, but he would have liked someone to witness his death. The villagers were meek, grown soft and fat from reaping their crops and they wanted no part of fighting. How could he blame them? They were peaceful men. Not like him. Not ready to slice man apart or be sliced. These were people who thought life was a precious commodity. Maybe it was, but for him it was life with no honor, no wife and no son. All had been taken from him.

He stood in the street and stared at the three men waiting outside the village. How much time did he have? Maybe an hour? It didn't really matter.

"Bring it on," he muttered. "Bring it on!"

CHAPTER 17

SAMUEL'S CAVE BEAR

They gathered in the mouth of the cave that was located on the backside of the foothill facing Loch Myst. The cave was only two miles from the village, but was well hidden and invisible to the naked eye from that distance. The loch was approximately three miles wide and offered easy access for water.

Approaching men, unless they knew exactly what to look for, would see nothing out of the ordinary. The space between the protruding hills appeared to be only water reaching to the sky. During the ebb of night, a thick mist rose above the body of water and only the soft lapping of the gentle waves hinted of its presence. At times, the fog grew so thick in the area that it felt like a walk through a curtain of wool.

It was quiet in the camp. The children played in silence or simply sat and watched their elders as they went about chores to make their new home comfortable. There were a few chickens pecking the ground, about a dozen sheep grazing and two huge oxen that chewed and swatted at insects with their sparse tails.

The villagers were a sorry looking lot. In total, there were about a hundred of them, forty men, a dozen lads, about twice as many lasses and 30 mature women. At least half of the men were well past their prime, old and beaten. They hobbled around on canes, their old joints aching with arthritis and other afflictions. A couple of them were unable to walk at all and were moved around in carts by family members. The younger children sensed that something was terribly wrong, but in the innocence of youthful bliss were chiefly unworried. The adults were worried, however, and it showed in the tense faces, the rapidly darting eyes that constantly scanned the surrounding area, and the terse conversations.

Samuel was familiar with the area as he and Heather had explored the cave on a number of occasions. Limestone

167

spikes were everywhere, frozen in place like lava drips. The interior carried a strong odor of ammonia. The tallest of the men had to stoop upon entering the frontal chamber, and were forced to walk in a bent over position when they ventured into one of the tunnels that branched off. The farther one advanced into those tunnels, the smaller they became, and after some 300 yards, one was forced to crawl. The feeling of claustrophobia was prevalent, as well as the terrifying sense that a wrong movement or sudden sound might loosen an avalanche of stones, turning the cave into a tomb.

Heather had waited as Samuel disappeared into one of the tunnels during one of their excursions, only to return minutes later soaked in perspiration and with scrapes on his knees and elbows. He had grinned sheepishly and followed the smirking Heather back to the village.

The young couple walked along the small beach of the lake, holding hands and watching the villagers going about their tasks. Samuel saw his father staring at him and averted his eyes. He didn't want to talk to him right now. He gripped Heather's hand a little too tightly.

"What's wrong, Samuel?" she asked. "What is troubling ye? Are you worrying about your friend?" Samuel had told her of the night's adventures.

The boy looked at her, the beautiful auburn hair shimmering in the morning sunlight. "Does it show? Well, yes, I am worried about him."

"Worrying won't do you or him any good. You'll make yourself sick."

"It's just that I feel I've abandoned him. I mean, if he's still alive, he's probably either fighting with those guys or he's hiding somewhere. Suppose he comes back to the village and finds us all gone?"

"He knew exactly what he was getting into, Samuel. There's nothing you can do now. Do you even think he expects you do anything alone?"

"I didn't think the men were such cowards, Heather. I'm ashamed of them."

It was Heather's turn to squeeze his hand. "So, what do you think you can do about it?"

"I can go back and help him fight those men."

"Oh, Samuel, you have a brave heart and I love you for it. But what can you do? It would be hopeless and you would only be killed."

"It wouldn't be hopeless if the men would go with me. There are enough of us that we could defeat them, or at least force them to leave." The boy's voice had grown louder during the last words and several of the men were staring at him. Stewart took a couple of steps in his direction and said sternly, "Samuel, you need to keep your mouth shut until you and I have a talk!"

"Aye, father," the boy answered, embarrassed. He began walking slowly toward his father. "I'll be back," he said to Heather, and followed Stewart, who was walking away from the camp.

Stewart found an outcropping from the hill and paused under it, well out of sound of the other villagers. "Where did you go last night, boy?" he asked, his voice gruff.

"I couldn't sleep and went for a walk," Samuel said. At least that wasn't a lie. "Then I saw the sword still in the street and I thought maybe I could find the Swordslinger and give it back to him. I guess I just kept walking longer than I thought and I caught up with him."

"What in heaven's name is wrong with you, boy? What is your fixation with this man? He's just a hired killer who's for sale to the highest bidder."

"I don't believe that. You don't know him the way I do. He's a good man."

"Look, you little piss ant; I've heard enough about this man. I know that when those men raped and killed his wife he just ran off and deserted his son. That tells me all I need to know about him! He sells death, son! He's just a swordslinger who will take a man's life for an ounce of gold. Is that what you want to be, Samuel? A killer?"

Samuel bit his lip and kept his eyes lowered. He didn't want his father to see the look in them right now. "Father, you just don't know him."

"I know a bad man when I see one. This man has no conscience, no morals, no feelings. He's a walking dead man!"

Samuel couldn't hold back any longer. "He has no conscience, but he's the one fighting for our village while all the cowards are up here hiding!"

Stewart's face paled. He grabbed Samuel's shoulders and forced the boy to look at him. Teeth bared in a semi-snarl, he berated his son. "Look at me," he hissed. "I'm trying to protect you. I'm like a bantam hen over her chicks. I'm doing the best I can, Samuel." He loosened his grip on Samuel and held out trembling hands.

"I'm dying for a drink, boy! But I'm not having one. I've given up the whiskey for you and your brother and I've got the shakes and I hurt inside. But I'm trying to be a father to ye. I work hard, son. I'm an ironsmith and that's an honorable trade, and I had a good wife — God bless you, Margaret — who gave me two fine sons. But now some stranger comes riding in and you've given him all your affection. Why, Samuel? Why?"

Stewart rubbed his shaking hands together and continued. "I know I'm probably wasting my time talking to you, boy. But that's all right. I won't have to worry about that son of a buck much longer because he'll be dead. You'd better know that his chances of living through this day are slim. And when he's dead, maybe you'll come to your senses and forget learning how to use a sword and let me train you to be an ironsmith. I know what you and Heather are planning and you'll need to make a decent life for her and your children."

Samuel felt his face redden. Yes, he loved Heather and he planned to make her his wife, but this talk about marrying and children ...

"There, I've said my piece," Stewart said, placing a gentle hand on his son's shoulder. "We've just had a father-son talk. Now, let's make the best out of this situation that we can and get our lives back to normal." He smiled and Samuel knew that what he saw in his father's eyes was love. He felt tears forming in his eyes.

"Aye, father."

Father and son left the depression in the rock and returned to the gathering of villagers.

CHAPTER 18

THE LAST SUPPER

The three horsemen stood like the Apocalypse on the road from the east. They were unmoving except for an occasional flinch by one of the horses. The mounted figures formed silhouettes against the morning sky. They were vultures, waiting for the wounded animal to die. The sun glinted on their weapons.

The Swordslinger knew he had to keep moving or the wounds would stiffen his abused body. He cast another glance toward the three men, knowing they were just awaiting the arrival of others. He managed a thin smile as he wondered how long it would take the three vultures to flock into the village if they knew he was the lone occupant. They must be wondering why things were so quiet. Maybe they thought the villagers were preparing an ambush. "Aye, right!" He looked around at the dead village and decided to pay a visit to one of the stores that sold clothing. The door was locked, but he kicked it open and went inside.

Wool kilts and coats were stacked on one table. A loom stood in one corner, strung with fresh clippings from a sheep. There was an array of hats and tams on another table. He picked up a hat, a brown felt with a hawk feather wedged in the band. He plucked the feather and placed it on the table. Not his style. The hat was slightly too big and the brim was not as wide as the one on the black hat that he had lost during the skirmish with the raiders, but it would do for the time being.

He found a pair of black leather boots and chose a pair of thick socks. His feet were wet and cold and he could use the change. Why not? The storeowner obviously was prepared to give up all his merchandise. The good guys might as well partake. He sat down to change socks and boots and winced in pain as he bent. Okay. Nothing but pain. Pain was something you learned to live with, both physical and mental. The dry socks felt warm on his feet and the boots were comfortable.

The Swordslinger relaxed in the chair and studied the shop. The owner had spent time making the interior attractive for his trade. A painting of a lone woman, her hands busily working with a loom as she sat at a window, hung on the wall. Too bad. All this would soon be destroyed by the raiders. The thought raised his ire. These villagers had done nothing to deserve this fate. They were a self-sufficient society, living at peace and taking care of their own needs. He shook his head sadly, rose from the chair and went back outside to the street.

The three horsemen were still in position. They appeared to be carrying on a conversation and his movement caught their attention. He stared at them for a moment, then reached into a pocket for some tobacco and rolled himself a smoke. He flicked a match with a thumbnail and lit the tobacco. Taking a long drag on the smoke, he lolled his head back and held the smoke deep in his lungs, reveling in its soothing effect for several seconds before exhaling.

Guess I'll just keep them wondering, he thought, and strolled across the street to the village pub. The shelves behind the bar were stocked with whiskey and rum, bringing a smile to the Swordslinger's face. Oh, some of those villagers were going to want to get back for a taste of this!

He found a bottle of 100-proof whiskey and poured the contents over the wound on the calf of his leg, grimacing as it entered the cut. He found a clean cloth behind the bar and used it to bandage the wound. The he picked up the bottle and raised it to his lips, taking a long swallow. The whiskey burned his throat, but he didn't care. Another deep pull on the bottle and he sat it on the counter. That was enough of the painkiller for now. He had to keep his reflexes sharp because he knew there would be fighting before this day was much older.

When he returned to the street, he almost wished he had drained the rest of the bottle. There were now six horsemen on the hill. "Right on cue," he muttered, and rolled himself another smoke. From the attire of the new arrivals, he knew they were part of the Manteo Brothers. As he watched, one

173

of them raised his hand to his brow to shield his eyes and scanned the village. They were no more than a quarter of a mile away and they must be wondering why he was the only person visible. Okay, six riders on the hill meant there were almost another dozen still unaccounted for. Oh yes, this was going to be one interesting day. Well, let's keep them guessing.

Swordslinger casually flipped the stub of his smoke away, sent one last look toward the watching men, and walked over the bakery. Smokes, drinks, and now food. Why not? This might be his last meal.

He gathered up some bread, smoked sausage, a couple of meat pies, a bowl of cold stew, several potatoes and an uncut loaf-shaped haggis. Taking the bounty outside, he walked to the well and deposited it on the bench alongside. He returned to the bakery and came out moments later lugging a huge cast-iron pot.

He glanced toward the group of horseman and smiled. They must be jabbering among themselves trying to figure out what this lunatic was doing. "Just going to have a little lunch," he said quietly, and began arranging a small pile of wood under the pot. He struck a match to the fuel and soon had a fire burning. He dumped the bowl of stew into the pot and while that was warming, went back to the pub and came out with a stool and a small table, as well as a new bottle of whiskey. "Might as well do this right."

The Swordslinger sat down on the stool and propped his feet on the table. He pushed the brim of the new hat down on his forehead and began spooning some of the haggis onto his plate. The spices, meats and oatmeal mix were never the same in haggis, he thought. Always left something to the imagination. But he knew it had been slowly boiled inside the stomach of a goat. He swallowed a mouthful of the haggis and rinsed it down with a swig from the bottle. Ahh! Fuel for the furnace. He held the bottle up, admiring it, so that the men on the hill could see him.

The stew was warm and he scooped it in to the bowl. He tore a couple of chunks from the bread loaf and dunked them into the bowl. Delicious! He took another look at the six horsemen. One of the Manteo Brothers kicked his horse forward as though to ride into the village, but a word from one of the Vikings brought him to a halt. "Good, Don't' want them interrupting the meal." He placed the sword he had taken from the dead Viking on the table, wishing for his own blade. This one felt heavy and clumsy. His own sword had felt like an extended part of his body. He wasn't looking forward to having to parry very many blows with this plowshare. Maybe there was something in the ironsmith's shop that he could use.

He wiped a sleeve across his mouth and rose, heading toward Stewart's shop. There were a few swords, several dirks and a couple of chained balls placed on one side of the building. Many weapons, but only one man to wield them.

As he stood inside the shop, the Swordslinger's mind wandered to the boy. He felt sadness and an empty feeling when he thought of Samuel. What was it about that young man? He knew, of course. The boy reminded him of himself as a youth. If only Samuel's father could be made to understand how special his son was. But that appeared hopeless. Stewart loved his son, but part of the man's brain was mush from too many nights with the demon rum. Stewart had called him a "bloodslinger" and ordered him to stay away from Samuel. Bitterness spread through his chest like a burp from stomach acid with the thought.

Don't do this! he scolded himself. *Don't spend the last moments of life regretting something that could never be.* Instead, he would borrow some of the man's handiwork for a weapon.

Swordslinger selected two claymores and strapped them across his back. He found another sword that he liked the heft of and put it into a sheath attached to his belt. He placed a dirk in the side of each of the new boots and imagined how he would look to the men on the hill. Fierce, maybe, but certainly not frightening. Not as long as they had him outnumbered more than a dozen to one. He paused before going outside and picked up an apron that Stewart wore in the shop. It was made of soft leather and the Swordslinger placed it to his face, sniffing the aroma of the old leather. *Maybe I should have been an ironsmith*, he thought,

175

smiling. No, Stewart's fate was to hone weapons. His was to use them.

Returning to his seat by the well, the Swordslinger sat down again and put his feet up. The men were still there. He rolled and lit another smoke, pulled the hat brim down and closed his eyes. The warmth of the midday sun and the food he had consumed made him drowsy and he actually dozed. He jerked awake moments later and looked in the direction of the men. There were nine now. Okay, about half of the survivors were there. Would they wait for the rest? Had they all been able to round up their scattered horses?

How much longer would they tarry? The sun, a bright ball of haze in the sky, had passed the midday point. Surely, they wouldn't wait until dark. Too many places wary villagers could hide for an ambush. Oh yeah. If only those men knew where the townspeople were really hiding. Obviously, they didn't know the village was empty. There was an uncertainty in their movements. The scumbags didn't know the meaning of fear, perhaps, but they did like to know what they were riding into. An empty village? One crazy man acting as though he was the only person in the world? Another hour and the rest of the band should arrive, even those who might still be on foot. Wait. There was time. And when they were at full strength, they would swoosh down on the village; either chase the men off or kill them, and spend the night partaking of the food and women in the deserted village.

The Swordslinger could almost read the thoughts of the enemy. Hopefully, they didn't know the extent of his injuries. Too bad he didn't have a couple of days to heal; he might still be able to give these outlaws a run for their money.

He picked up an apple from the food he had brought outside and turned so he was facing the men on the hill. He held the apple in his right hand, then tossed it in the air. His right hand was a blur as he reached across his body and drew the sword on his left side. He swished the blade once through the air, and then caught the halved apple with his left hand. Let them see that he wasn't going to be an easy piece. He sheathed the sword, and still facing the men, began eating the apple. He knew they had to be hungry, so let them watch him enjoy the food. Make them mad was probably more like it.

Something was happening. One of the Manteo Brothers kicked his horse into action and began moving toward the town in a slow gait. He held a sword in his hand with a white piece of cloth fluttering from it. Samuel stood and watched as the man approached to within about a hundred yards of the well. The Manteo Brother wasn't very tall, but his shoulders seemed about as broad as his height. This man would be hard to knock off his feet. Swordslinger took a few steps toward the rider.

"What is your name?" the rider asked.

"Swordslinger. What's yours?"

The rider seemed taken aback by either the answer or the question. "I'm John Manteo," he said. "You killed Bailey, my youngest brother, last night."

"Oh, too bad. Well, rest at ease, you'll be seeing him soon enough."

"Just who are you?"

"Oh, I'm the owner of this village. It's all mine. If you want it, you'll have to take it from me."

John Manteo rubbed a hand over the bristle on his chin, confusion showing in his eyes. "You know you're going to die."

"Maybe. But how many of you bastards have died since we met? Eight, nine? I've lost count. And I assure you that there will be more of you dead before this sun sets. You can tell the rest of your brothers and your scabby friends that I will not die alone. Some of you may survive, but will you be one of them? Is my village worth that to you?"

The man spat. "We no longer care about this village," he said, "we want you. And we want you to die a slow death."

"Well, here I am. Are you guys hungry? I would have invited you to dinner but I wasn't sure how many places to set."

The confusion in Manteo's eyes grew deeper. What was going on with this madman? Was he indeed insane? He opened his mouth to say something, and then thought better

177

of it. He pulled the reins of the horse and rode back toward the clump of men on the hill.

The Swordslinger watched with amusement as John Manteo rejoined the others and a heated conversation ensued. The man stabbed a finger in his direction several times during the animated talk.

The Swordslinger turned his back on the horsemen and walked to the well. He leaned against the structure, removed his new brown hat and ran his finger through his hair. He turned his eyes to the sky and watched some clouds drift lazily past. The gray hawk suddenly made another appearance, soaring high above, wings widespread, riding on the air currents. A gentle breeze was stirring, cooling the air, and the peaks of the mountains to the west were a heart-aching purplish. It was a beautiful, peaceful setting, belying the storm that was brewing among the men gathered on the hill.

A place like this should have been my home, the Swordslinger thought. What a wonderful place to raise a family, a small garden, maybe some sheep. Yeah. Come home from grazing the sheep and find Shelley making dinner while little Dexter played in the yard. No angry bandits on a hill, no scared villagers hiding who knows where. Just a quiet spot in the valley with Loch Myst lying below.

"This is what I wanted, Shelley." Time seemed so precious now. Every second that ticked away brought the confrontation nearer. Why did men hold such malice toward one another? Wouldn't those men on the hill have been happier with loved ones to return home to after a day in the saddle? Did bandits have wives and children waiting somewhere for them? If so, there were going to be some widows and orphans before this day was done.

He thought of his wife, Shelley, and how happy they had been. *If I had only known that our time together was going to be so short, I would have milked every precious second of it. You were my world, the only thing I needed.* You and our strong young son. *I was happy as a farmer although some of the men I met last night might have trouble believing that. I'll probably be with you again soon, Shelley. And we'll have a home near a mountain and a lake, just* like *here. I'll build the house of stone with a large tower and many windows. We can watch the setting of the sun and the stars at night. Holding each other. Making love. Sleeping in each other's arms. God, I miss you, my darling.*

Tears stung Swordslinger's eyes. It would soon be his turn to die. He faced the church and stared at the cross on the steeple. "Give me the strength, Almighty Father, to fight the good fight. I know I am nothing special, Lord, just one of your soldiers defending the cause we believe in. If I die today, I ask that you bless these people, especially the boy, Samuel, and the lass he loves and their families. These are simple people who only want to live life as thou meant us to do. Forgive my bitterness toward Stewart because I know he wants only the best for his sons. I don't want to hate anymore, Lord, so I ask forgiveness for the men who murdered my Shelley. I only want serenity and peace in thy name. Amen."

When he looked up, the group of horsemen on the ridge had been reduced to seven. Where had the other two gone? Wherever they were, they were planning no good.

As he watched, the men dismounted and began gathering wood for a small fire. They were preparing to warm some food and eat. One of the Vikings suddenly rose from his haunches and shaded his eyes with a hand to look down the road away from the village. He shouted something and began waving. A few moments later a group of men appeared over the crest of the hill. The Swordslinger counted 10 of them, two on horseback and eight walking and carrying their weapons. Great. The enemy was massing. It wouldn't be long now. He felt like a tragic hero, waiting for the last act of the play. The men were gesturing, talking loud, swearing. It was a lively debate between one of the new arrivals — a Manteo Brother — and the others.

This Manteo shared the same body shape as his brother John. But this one was bald, whether from a natural loss of hair or shaving, the Swordslinger couldn't tell from the distance. But he was definitely a take-charge kind of person. He gestured to some of the men, then towards the village. He was obviously planning an attack.

Finally, the conversation ended and the men gathered around the campfire, preparing to eat. A couple of them availed themselves of the opportunity to take a nap. It had been a long night for them, too. Some of the Vikings finished eating and began working on the edges of their swords with whetstones. They seemed prepared to wait for dark before making their move on the village.

The Swordslinger couldn't help smiling. If they only knew, they were making all these preparations for one man.

CHAPTER 19

THE MANTEO BROTHERS

"We'll wait until dark," said Max Manteo, "they will be tired and their nerves will be frayed." Max was the oldest of the brothers and strongest — maybe not the strongest physically — but the maddest in an insane-lose-your-temper way. He had never lost a fight and no one challenged him anymore; therefore, he was the boss. The most distinguishable trademark between him and his brothers was the baldhead. He could have had scraggly hair like his brothers, but he felt shaving his head added to the image he wanted to create. A smart man, just crazy enough to be unpredictable. He loved the image, loved seeing the fear of uncertainty when he faced off with other men in arguments or fights. It gave him an edge and he made the most of it.

Despite the madman appearance, Max had a sharp and devious mind when it came to tactics. It wasn't his style or polished technique of sword fighting that made him fierce, it was the fierceness itself. In battle, he became an undeniable, unstoppable 250-pound block of a man that had scream in his eyes. He simply ran you over and stomped you down whether by boot or sword, and most of the time by both.

The one skill Max had totally mastered was the art of intimidation. He enjoyed psyching opponents out, making them feel they were going to lose before the fight began. Today, however he appeared calm and poised. There was a coolness about him that brothers John, Angus, and Max had rarely seen. There was no joking, no vivid descriptions of what they were going to do to their next victim. Perhaps the calmness was the result of Bailey having been killed by the bastard in black. They were seething with hatred and revenge and they knew that Max was, too. But he was hiding his anger under a cloak of cool. The Vikings were a pissed group, too. They had lost several of their warriors to the man in black and had sworn vengeance. Who the hell was this man?

"He's been mocking us all day," John Manteo said. "Look at the bastard, the way he sits there with his feet propped up, smoking, eating, drinking, and going in and out of the buildings just as if we weren't anywhere near."

"Oh, he figures he's some kind of bad arse," Max said. "Probably a swordslinger the villagers hired to scare us off." The others laughed at the suggestion of their being scared. Still, there was some trepidation.

"Maybe he's some kind of sorcerer," Angus suggested, glancing to see the reaction of Max. "I'll swear that when all that fuss was going on last night I saw a naked boy on a horse galloping through the mist. There is something unnatural about this man. We know we put our blades in him and he's still alive and well."

Max laughed, slapped his brother on the shoulder and said, "We all heard the noise last night, Angus, but you were the only one who saw this beast with the naked lad on its back. What's wrong with you, man? You been on the hunt so long you're fantasizing about buggering boys? Maybe we better get you on down to that village and find you a woman!"

Angus didn't find his brother funny. "Look, I saw what I saw," he said. "Whatever it was it was big as a horse and it looked like something straight outta hell. It moved like a horse but it looked like a big bush and it was shooting fire out its arse!"

All the men roared with laughter and Angus's face reddened.

"Look, Angus," Max said, turning serious, "despite your secret desires, you are the best archer among us. Take your bow and sneak through the woods to the village. When you get there, work your way in behind this fellow and climb up on a roof. We'll start coming down the hill to get his attention and when you're ready, put a shaft in his back."

"Aye, I can do that. But are you sure this isn't a trap the villagers have set for us, brother."

A rumble of laughter emerged from Max. "A trap! Are you kidding? Remember their leader, Chieftain Bruce? He's a spineless coward and so are the other men. No. There's no trap. They've hired this swordslinger and they're hiding behind the skirts of the women. Well, when we get down there we'll raise a few of those skirts, eh men? And to show them how we feel about them hiring a swordslinger to protect them, we'll skin him and string him up, then burn the damn town! Yeah. They'll rebuild it after we're gone, but that's good. We'll visit them again next year. Some of their younger daughters will be a year older then, too."

The men raised their fists and shouted in anticipation.

Max turned to Mortala, the leader of the Vikings. Mortala was at least a foot taller than Max, but not nearly as thick. His body was lean and muscled, however, and the blond hair topped blue eyes that flashed with intensity. His face was covered with a brown scraggly beard that completely concealed his mouth and lips. "We'll take our share and you men can have the leftovers," Max said to him. Do whatever ye want. Me, I just want to take a small portion and then have some fun with this man who thinks he is some kind of ghost."

Mortala nodded and spoke to his men in their language. The men laughed, then grew silent. They were remembering the comrades they had left dead in the fog. They were itching to get on with the kill, and had hesitated this long only in deference to the Manteo Brothers. After all, this was their homeland.

Mortala turned back to Max. "We have no quarrel with your plan," he said, "except that we, too, want a piece of this man in black. He has slain our brethren also, and we would like to cut off his head and leave it on a pole as a warning to the villagers for their defiance."

"Good idea," Max said, his heavy lips curling. "We all owe this bastard something. We will wait a couple more hours until darkness begins to fall. That will give our men a while to rest and sharpen their weapons. As soon as we take care of the swordslinger, the town is yours. Me, I'm going to find one of those young lasses that are hiding indoors. When we were here last summer, there were a couple who were just beginning to blossom. They should be ripe now."

183

"Blossoms, aye," Mortala said, wiggling his bushy eyebrows.

CHAPTER 20

SUNDOWN

Several small fires burned in the villagers' makeshift camp on the side of the mountain facing Loch Myst. The men rigged up poles and lines and fished, soon having more than 50 pulled ashore. The women busied themselves with cleaning the scaly creatures and soon the smell of cooking fish over the open fires had mouths watering. The hungry children wasted little time loading their plates with the fresh food.

Samuel, Manny, Stewart, and Robert continued to fish, using a rowboat that Manny had stowed near the lake during happier days. The weather was perfect, one of those blue-sky, no-cloud days that Highlanders dream of but seldom see. The foursome found a new school of perch and was kept busy baiting hooks and removing the fish.

The troubles of the moment were put aside while on the rowboat. If one did happen to make mention of the raiders or the impending danger, Stewart quickly changed the subject to another topic. Young Robert was enjoying the outing, whooping every time a fish took his bait. The others laughed at the youngster's exuberance.

But Samuel's mind kept returning to the Swordslinger. It would soon be approaching dusk and his new friend was very likely lying dead or wounded somewhere. He pictured vultures circling over the corpse. He moaned, not realizing the sound was loud enough for the others to hear.

"Sudden pain?" Manny asked, glancing at the boy.

"It's nothing, just thinking out loud," Samuel said, grinning sheepishly. He checked his line and found the bait was missing. Wonder how long? His thoughts returned to the Swordslinger. He had risked his life opposing the raiding party and the villagers had abandoned him. It wasn't fair!

Samuel raised his pole, taking the line from the water and beginning to wrap it around the cane pole.

"Giving up?" Stewart asked.

Samuel faced his father, willing himself to face the man's wrath. "I can't just sit here any longer. I'm going to find him."

"Find who? Oh, the swordslinger? Stewart's countenance darkened.

"Aye. I'm going back to the village and see what's happening."

"Me., too," Robert chimed in.

"Nae, you're not. Neither of you," Stewart said, his voice a growl. "It's too dangerous. If you're seen, they'll kill you."

"I have to go, father."

Stewart clamped a rough hand on his son's shoulder. "I'm warning you. Don't go!"

"I have to," Samuel said, breaking free from his father's grip and diving into the water."

"Samuel!"

"Got to go," Robert suddenly said and followed his older brother into the water.

"Get your arses back in the boat!" Stewart yelled, but his sons paid no heed. He rose in the boat, seeming ready to jump overboard. Manny took his arm and said, "Let them go, Stewart."

"That damned swordslinger! Samuel is possessed with that devil!"

"Samuel's a good lad, Stewart. "He's becoming a man and he's doing what he thinks is right. This is an act from the heart."

"Then he needs to cut his heart out. It's going to get him killed!" Stewart made another attempt to jump into the water.

"Don't do it," Manny said. "Remember, you can't swim. You'll sink like one of your anvils."

Stewart stood in the boat, cursing. "I swear to God, Samuel, if anything happens to your brother you'll pay!"

He watched in futile frustration as his sons neared the bank.

CHAPTER 21

CONFRONTATION

The last of the golden light was beginning to fade into a bruised purple. A bank of low clouds was moving in from the east. Along the crest in the road outside of the village, men remounted their horses as the Swordslinger stood in the street and watched. He was surprised when they turned and disappeared over the hill.

"All right," he said to himself, lips forming a thin smile. "The show is about to begin." He wondered if it would come in the form of a sneak attack or an all-out charge. Moving to the pile of peat moss and wood in the street, he struck a match and lit it. The moss began smoking, and then burst into a yellow tongue of flame. The pile was soon blazing.

The shouts turned his attention back to the road. Three horsemen were galloping toward the village, spurring their mounts and screaming. Swordslinger removed the tobacco stick from his lips and tossed it to the ground, snuffing it out with a heel. He moved into position so that he was outlined against the flames and assumed a fighting crouch, the Viking's sword held at ready.

The charging trio was Vikings, their long swords held in front of them as they approached. Their appearance and the war cries they were screaming gave a terrifying appearance. The Swordslinger was wearing the thin smile again. The horsemen were nearing, the hooves spraying gravel from the road as they thundered into the village.

Swordslinger's muscles grew taut. His nerves were steeled. The galloping horses were almost on top of him and the Viking in the center leaned low, thrusting his sword forward with the intent of impaling the fool standing in the street.

The Viking was only 10 yards away and charging, when the Swordslinger screamed his own war cry. The Viking lowered his sword, coming in with the weapon aimed at his target's chest. Just as the sword seemed on the verge of

187

penetrating his chest, the Swordslinger fell backward, swinging the borrowed claymore at the horse's front legs. The impact yanked the sword from his hands and the Viking's own blade missed him by a fraction of an inch. The crippled horse fell forward and the Viking — half thrown and half jumping — came out of the saddle, his sword flying several feet away. He rose to his knees and began scurrying after his weapon. His companions were several yards down the street, fighting to turn their mounts and re-enter the fray.

The Swordslinger, still on his back, drew the other sword from the sheath at his waist and was ready for the Viking's charge. The huge bearded man brought his blade down hard, but the Swordslinger managed to parry the blow. The Viking kept the pressure on, using his weight to force the blades down. The point was an inch away from entering the stomach of the Swordslinger.

Swordslinger turned his blade so that the Viking's sword slid down and away from his body, then lunged upward and across the man's wrists. The Viking loosed a scream from hell as his sword clattered to the ground, hands still attached in a death grip. Still screaming, he staggered backwards and stumbled into the raging bonfire. Flames engulfed the shaggy beard and hair and blood spurted from the stumps of his arms. He broke free from the flames, everything on him burning, and Swordslinger mercifully sunk his blade into the middle of the human bonfire.

The dying Viking fell face forward into the street, life leaving him in a gushing sound of air. Curls of flames leapt from his still burning clothes and the acrid smell of burnt flesh and hair was nauseating. Nine down.

"Run" yelled one of the other two horsemen. But instead of attacking, they galloped back down the street to join their comrades on the hill.

"Another one bites the dust," Swordslinger muttered grimly, the tight smile still in place. Adrenaline made his heart pound. The battle had been joined and he was no longer aching and tired. "Bring it on!" he shouted after the riders.

He didn't have to wait long. Torches, formed from limbs and brush were being passed out to the riders. They quickly lit them and came charging back down the hill. The rage showed in their angry faces. They were no longer concerned about an ambush. They were tasting blood.

The Swordslinger's mind raced as he watched the enemy near. He spun a figure eight with his sword, a move that had always helped him relax. Time was fleeting and certain death was approaching at a full gallop. Life was only as long as the yards between him and the advancing men. And those yards were being eaten up in long strides. He really didn't want to die, not like this, but he had been preparing himself for death since the night before. His spirit could live in the mountains and perhaps find the peace he had been denied during life.

It was time to die. There would be no surrender, even if he had thought the raiders should give him the opportunity. No, there was to be no quarter given today. He had killed too many of their crew to expect lenience. Six of the approaching horde were on horseback, with the others running behind. How many now? It didn't matter how many. There were too many.

For the first time that he could remember, the Swordslinger felt fear. Not fear of dying, but fear of losing the battle. He reached within himself to draw from the Samurai philosophy — never consider defeat. Think win. Use the age-old strategies and take as many of them with you to the other world as was possible. Leave the survivors with some bitter memories.

I've already killed nine of them, he thought. *I'll take a few more. Maybe a lot more. Kick their arses! I can do this. If nothing else, find the man who has my sword and put a blade in him!*

The riders were slowing, allowing the walkers to catch up with them. "Cowards!" Okay, come on. First man in is first man dead. Swordslinger flexed his fingers. Stay loose. His heart pounded. A pulse hammered at his temple. "I'll fight with honor! I will die with honor!"

"Swordslinger!" the voice of Max Manteo rang out loudly in the dusk. The horsemen had reined to a halt. Now what? "You have been a naughty lad, my friend, so we're going to put you down. You have killed my brothers and my friends and for that you are going to die!"

The Swordslinger was about to retort when a movement to the left rear of the raiders caught his eye. What? It was just a shadow. A weird, misshapen shadow that somehow resembled a horse. There was a rider on its back, maybe, and another smaller figure behind that. What? Could this be hope? Grab the initiative.

"I give you one last chance to live!" the Swordslinger shouted. "Turn your horses and leave now or you're all going to die. You're surrounded!"

"Ha!" Max shouted back, "Brother John is right! You are a madman! There is going to be death, all right. Yours!"

The sudden plaintive wail of bagpipes sounded from the left of the raiders. The piercing notes resounded through every nook and cranny, every ear. Hearts raced. Fear was roused.

Swordslinger smiled, hoping the raiders could see it in the growing dark. "Leave or die!" he shouted. He made a fearsome figure, outlined against the flames of the bonfire. The raiders were nervous, looking about, trying to locate the mysterious bagpipes. The shrill, haunting notes seemed to be echoing in all directions.

From his vantage point, the swordslinger could see his horse, still camouflaged with the branches. And damned if that boy Samuel wasn't naked in the saddle!

"Leave!" he yelled at the men. "Leave now or I will cast the spell of God Eeshebob upon you!"

There was an unrest growing among the ranks of the raiders. They were unnerved and not ready to challenge the unknown. A shift in the wind was blowing the smoke from the fire toward the raiders. As it engulfed them, they became even more restless.

"Go now!" the Swordslinger yelled, not wanting to give the men a chance to gather their nerves. Doubt showed in their faces. They were still not able to locate the shrilling of the bagpipes.

"I've seen this God Eeshebob," John said to Max. "I told you about him last night! Let's get out of here!"

"Shut up!" Max shouted, attempting to regain control.

The Swordslinger raised his face to the sky and intoned, "God of Eeshebob, I command ye to bring down your fury on these intruders!"

Max had started to say something when his mind shut down. From out of the drifting smoke to their left came a beast from hell. If this was a god, it was a terrible one. The beast had wild, rolling eyes and had the shape of a huge scraggly bush. It was moving fast and on its back was a nude boy.

"I told you!" John screamed, and spurred his horse, jerking the reins hard to turn him about. The other raiders followed horses and men running away from the village. Some of the fleeing men dropped their torches, the others held onto theirs, as they raced into the night looking like fireflies jiggling in the darkness.

The Swordslinger collapsed into the chair and doubled over with laughter. The release of tension flooded through him as the sight of the ferocious men fleeing into the darkness from a nude boy on horseback struck him as hilarious.

It was over, at least temporarily. He had survived, thanks to the ingenuity of two young boys. He managed to quiet the laughter and prepared to rise to greet Samuel and Robert.

That's when the archer on the roof of the bakery fired the arrow that struck Swordslinger in the back.

CHAPTER 22

RETRIEVAL

"NOOOOOOOOOOOOOOOO!" Samuel screamed in protest when he saw the arrow strike his friend. The Swordslinger's body arched and he had a surprised look on his face

Samuel jumped from the back of the horse and ran to the kneeling Swordslinger, who was trying to reach the shaft in his back. As he reached him, the Swordslinger's head fell forward almost to his chest.

The boy grabbed his kilt from the saddle and wrapped it around his lean body, then reached for his dirk and began running for the bakery. He had seen nothing but a blur, but he knew the arrow had to come from this direction.

Disregarding his own safety, Samuel dashed for the bakery. He had no plan, just a burning desire to find the archer. As he neared the bakery, he heard a familiar sound — the rustling of a body sliding down a thatched roof. Heart pounding, blood pulsing, body trembling, he raced around the side of the building, his eyes blurred with tears.

As he rounded the building, he glimpsed a blur of movement to the left and saw Angus Manteo fleeing into the thicket that surrounded the wooded area. "Run, you bastard!" he screamed. "Damn you!" Tears streamed down his face. He turned and ran back to the Swordslinger, still slumped over in the chair.

Kneeling, Samuel lifted the man's head and stroked his face. "Don't die," he whispered. "Please don't die now."

"Ahhh … I'm afraid to move," the Swordslinger said.

"Oh, thank God, you're alive!" The boy said, hugging the head to him.

"Take a look at this thing and see how bad it is," Swordslinger said, teeth bared in pain.

"It's not too deep," Samuel said. "I can see the arrowhead. It isn't even all the way in. It went through one of the slats in the back of the chair before it hit you."

"All right, that's good. Now help me get it out. Just take hold of the shaft and pull it straight out."

"Aye." Samuel was feeling nauseous. "Are you ready?"

The Swordslinger winced from the pain. "Not yet. I think I got lucky," he said. "But we need to find a cloth to bandage it and stop the bleeding when we remove the arrow."

Robert had joined them, the bagpipes silent and placed beside the chair. "I'll find something," he said, eyes as big as two moons in his face, and ran to the nearby fabric shop.

"Thank God you're alive," Samuel said. "I thought you were dead. Don't you die on me!"

"With the kind of will you have, lad, I think you'd raise me from the coffin."

"Aye, that I would. But I really thought you were … God, I've never been so scared."

The Swordslinger took a deep breath. "Do it."

Samuel gripped the wooden shaft and slowly pulled at it while the Swordslinger leaned forward. The steel head of the arrow brought a gush of fresh blood with it, but came out leaving a clean wound.

Robert reappeared with a stack of white linen table napkins. "Perfect," Samuel said. "Robert, keep a lookout while I do this. Make sure no one is sneaking up on us."

Robert grabbed a knife from the ground and walked a few yards down the street, facing the way the raiders had gone.

The Swordslinger stood up, then thought better of it and laid face down on the street. Samuel's face was white. The sight of the arrowhead emerging from the man's back had almost made him pass out. He released the shaft, leaving the arrow sticking in the wooden slat on the back of the chair.

"My back, Samuel. How does it look?"

Samuel worked the shirt loose and pulled it down to the waist. "I don't think it's too bad. It's not bleeding very much now."

"Good, press the cloth against the wound and find something to bind it."

Samuel ripped a couple of strips of cloth from the linen and tied the cloth tightly into place.

"Good. Now let's see if I can sit up." Swordslinger rose slowly to his knees, and then stood. "Okay, I'm mobile," he said.

"We need to get you to Heather's mother. She's good with wounds. She can stitch it shut."

The Swordslinger sighed. Not right now," he said. "Take those branches and the grass off my horse. I have some unfinished business."

"You're going after the raiders? But you're hurt."

"I'm going to get my sword." The voice was tinged with determination. The boy knew there was no point in arguing.

"Where is it? I'll get it for you."

"No, you can't do this. One of those men has it. Besides, as soon as they realize there's no monster chasing them and when that back-shooting archer tells them he shot me, they'll be coming back."

"You think?"

"I know. These are evil men and they will do bad things to you — very bad things. Samuel, you and Robert are the sons I should have had. You have made me alive again on the inside. Don't worry about me. I will return. I want you to go back to the camp and wait with the villagers."

"No," Samuel protested. "We will wait here for you. If you are coming back, I will be here."

"Okay, but find a hiding place and don't come out until you see me or some of the villagers. Now, come on, let's undress this Eeshebob monster."

When the horse had been stripped of the camouflage, the Swordslinger painfully pulled himself into the saddle. He stared down at the boys, compassion in his eyes. He knew that they, especially Samuel, loved him and he felt a need to impart some words of warning.

"Samuel," he said, "don't grow up to be like me. Do not be fooled into thinking I lead a glamorous life that you would like to copy. I have nothing to look forward to after this day. You are young and you have Heather. Love her and protect her. Love her as if each day could be the last with

194

her. As I have learned, that can be so true. Life is meant to be lived, men are meant to give life, not death. Now, find a hiding place. I love you boys and want to find you alive and well when I get back."

Samuel moved to the horse and wrapped his arms around the mounted man's leg. "I love you too," he said. "You come back. We'll wait."

"Just be here," the Swordslinger said, trying to put a stern look on his face. "When I get back, I want you to help me lay stone for my mountain home."

"Aye, God Eeshebob, and we'll move the mountain nearer to the lake if you want."

Swordslinger laughed and kicked a heel into the horse's side.

"You come back!" Samuel yelled. "You promised!"

"Aye, you did!" Robert echoed.

The boys watched as the man in black rode down the trail. Within minutes, horse and man had disappeared over the crest.

Robert walked over to the Viking sprawled near the well. "Is this man dead?" he asked.

Samuel didn't answer. Instead, he took his brother by the arm and began leading him to the chapel in search of a hiding place. Surely, even a barbarian would not enter there.

CHAPTER 23

THE SWORD

The Swordslinger's horse settled into a leisurely trot along the road. The full moon had risen above the tree line and cast a long shadow of horse and rider. The peaceful scene ended abruptly as they topped the crest of the hill and spotted the sniper archer riding several hundred yards ahead of them.

Drawing his "borrowed" sword from the sheath, the Swordslinger snapped the reins and his horse broke into a gallop. The wind rushed past and the horse's white mane flapped and whipped in the air. The rushing wind in his face was refreshing to the Swordslinger and his mind cleared as he formulated a plan of action. The many bruises and cuts were sent to a far place in his psyche and he mentally prepared to go into battle.

He spurred the horse, urging more speed, and the gap between him and the archer narrowed perceptibly. He raised the sword and stifled a desire to emit a battle cry.

The archer, Angus Manteo, was unaware of his pursuer. His horse moved along at an easy lope and the hood of his cape was pulled over his head. The arrows in the quiver slung over his shoulder bounced and rattled. He didn't hear the clatter of hooves behind until it was too late. The Swordslinger's blade made a "swooshing" sound and clipped the archer along the side of his neck. The startled horse lunged, throwing the wounded man to the ground; and, he laid there, one hand pressed to the bloody wound in his neck, staring at the black boots of the man who had attacked him.

"Shall I finish you with an arrow in the back?" Swordslinger asked with a cold smile on his lips.

"No ... please ... no," the archer managed, blood gurgling from the wound.

"So die slowly," the man in black said. "Your blood is leaving you as quickly as your comrades did. You are dying, backstabber; and, with all the evil deeds you must pay for, it

196

might serve you well to begin praying. I will leave you to your fate."

The Swordslinger remounted and put his horse into the gentle trot again. The beast was tired and he didn't want to overwork her. The ride was a short one as he rounded a curve and saw a group of men resting along the road. He reined the horse to a walk and pulled the hood of his coat over his head, concealing his face in the dark.

"Hey!" one of the Vikings yelled. "Who goes there?"

Swordslinger pulled the horse to halt.

Max Manteo stood and yelled, "Angus, is that you?"

"Aye." mumbled the Swordslinger.

"Did you kill the bastard?"

"Aye."

Well? Christ, Angus, a little detail would be nice. Did you bring his head?"

Nae."

"He IS dead?"

"Aye."

There was cheer among the men. "All right, Angus. Let us mount up and we'll ride back to the village. Some god that was protecting him, huh? Nothing but a hoax we fell for. Let's sack that village and burn it. And I'm going to have a final word with that black bastard. I'm going to cut his head off with his own blade."

There was another cheer.

Underneath the hood, Swordslinger was once again wearing the thin smile. Max had moved only a few steps toward him when he realized the figure on the horse wasn't his brother.

The Swordslinger saw the flash of recognition in the eyes of Max and reacted quickly, drawing his dirk and throwing it at the man's huge chest. The knife struck tip first and buried itself to the hilt. The other men were too startled to react immediately and watched dumfounded as the man dug his heels into the horse's flank and charged directly at them. They were too shaken to fight and frantically turned their horses and fled the scene.

The Swordslinger's first move was to pull alongside Max, still sitting in the saddle, his eyes wide in death and both hands clutching at the hasp of the dirk protruding from his chest. He snatched his sword from the sheath strapped around Max and said, "Fair trade, the dagger for my sword!"

Manteo knew he was dying but couldn't accept it. No man had ever bested him. He was immortal. He killed. He didn't die! But despite the denial, he could feel life draining from his body. His sightless eyes stared at the man in black.

Swordslinger sighed and watched the fleeing bandits disappearing down the road away from the village. Eleven dead. The odds were getting better. He considered chasing them and killing them one by one. But that was pointless now. They were as disheartened now as they were heartless and would have no desire to stage another attack soon.

He turned his horse back toward the village and urged her into the effortless trot.

CHAPTER 24

SAFE HAVEN?

With each jolting step by the horse, the Swordslinger could feel the adrenaline seeping from his battered and cut body. He was exhausted, physically and mentally and allowed himself to be absorbed in a cloak of serenity.

Was it really over? Were the years of wandering from hamlet to hamlet, slaying evildoers who preyed on others finally ended? It seemed a century ago that he had left his home in search of his wife's molesters. They were years lived in a foggy dream world. He had not felt human since returning home to find Shelley's body. From that moment, he had been a heartless avenging monster, as bad in some ways as the men he pursued. How many men had he killed? Seventy? Eighty? He had killed a dozen in the last two days. How had he survived against such odds? Feeling the aches and searing pain from some of his fresh wounds, he almost wondered if he really had survived.

It IS over and I am retired, he thought. *No more fighting. No more killing. I'll find me a nice quite place in the mountains and plant a garden. I'll raise some sheep.* He laughed at the image of himself herding some wooly ewes with a crooked staff in hand and sandals on his feet. *Okay, let's not get carried away.* But he was going to lead a new life. One filled with peace and tranquility instead of flashing steel and gushing blood. He was going to have a home.

When he crested the hill, he spotted Samuel and Robert standing in the village street, straining their eyes for him. He felt a tug at his heart. He was returning home and his sons awaited. He wished! The boys saw him and began running to meet him. His eyes misted.

The Swordslinger halted the horse and dismounted. "Easy now," he cautioned as the boys threw their arms around him. "I'm wounded you know." He put his arms around the lads. "I think it's over," he said.

"Did you get your sword?" Samuel asked, having already spotted the long blade strapped to his waist.

"Aye. I have everything I started out with other than being minus a few drams of blood and me hat."

"Should I return to the camp and tell everyone that it's safe to return? Samuel asked.

"Nae, not at this hour, son. Chieftain Bruce might suffer a heart attack at being wakened so abruptly. Let them come back when they're ready. They'll see the village quiet in the morning and they'll return. I'm sure Bruce will send some brave man out to scout the situation."

"You got rid of the raiders! I can't believe you did that!"

"He can't believe you did it," Robert repeated.

"Not me, but we. It was Robert playing the pipes and ye being God Eeshebob. What a performance you two gave."

"Did you see them running?" Samuel said, giggling. "They were falling all over themselves."

"I believe they're still running," Swordslinger said.

"Och, are they related to Chieftain Bruce?" Robert asked. The Swordslinger and Samuel laughed at the youngster's wit.

The dead Viking was still lying near the well, the moonlight reflecting from the whites of his staring eyes. The Swordslinger kneeled and closed the eyelids. "Guess we should bury him," he mumbled, his aching body rebelling at the thought.

"There's a coffin in the basement of the church," Samuel said, and the three brought it out and placed the dead man inside, then closed the lid.

"That's good enough for now," the Swordslinger said. "We'll take care of the rest tomorrow. They aren't going anywhere."

"I have no problem with that," Samuel said, hoping he sounded like a seasoned veteran of such occasions.

"Me either," Robert echoed.

The Swordslinger smiled. Well, let's adjourn to my room at the inn and have a wee nap."

"I have no problem with that."

"Me either."

"Enough!"

Within minutes after entering the room, Swordslinger was snoring in his bed. Samuel was restless, afraid to go to sleep lest the Swordslinger might awaken and leave without him. He removed the leather cord from his sporran and, lying down on the floor beside the man's bad, attached the string to the sleeping man's wrist. If he decided to go somewhere, the boy was going with him. Beside him on the floor, Robert was sleeping soundly.

Waking early, Samuel brought water to the room and was waiting beside the bed when the Swordslinger roused himself from the much-needed sleep. The man cleaned his wounds and tore strips from the bed sheet to bandage them. He could feel his body being renewed.

With all the bandages finally in place, Swordslinger turned his attention to the sword. He carefully cleaned it of the dried blood and dirt that had accumulated. "Remind me to oil her later today," he said to the wide-eyed boys who were watching his every move.

"Aye, I will." Samuel said, beaming at the prospect of Swordslinger planning to be around for the afternoon.

Having dressed and cleaned themselves, the three victorious warriors retired to the square, where the boys rounded up some eggs and pork strips and the Swordslinger prepared a meal over an open fire by the well. They sat at the table and dined as their bodies soaked up the warming rays of the new sun.

The Swordslinger finished eating, leaned back in the chair from which the arrow had been removed, and propped his feet up against the well. Samuel and Robert were cleaning the last of the egg from their plates when the voice startled them.

"Are they gone?"

Swordslinger tapped the brim of his hat back and peered toward the shadows of the nearby building. "Chieftain Bruce! Welcome back! Aye, you can tell the others that it's safe now. They can bring the women and children into town. Everything's intact except for a few missing muffins and a dram or so of whiskey."

"Is it really over?" Chieftain Bruce wasn't entirely convinced.

"It's over. You don't have to hide anymore." The sarcasm in his voice went undetected by the wary Bruce. "There is some burying to do, but we'll leave that to the brave men when they get back home."

Chieftain Bruce came out of the building's shadow and several other men began appearing from behind the walls. Stewart came out into the street and scowled when he saw his sons sitting at the swordslinger's feet.

Samuel wasn't ready to confront his father. He got to his feet and approached the chieftain. "You should have seen him," he said proudly. "He killed all of them who would fight and the rest of them ran away!"

Chieftain Bruce wasn't quite sure how to react, so he called on his official status as a bailout. "That's great,' he proclaimed in a suddenly louder and braver voice. "Well, he has done what I hired him to do. Now that we have our village back, we will bring the women and children in and hold a glorious celebration of our triumph tonight." He walked to the still sitting Swordslinger and offered his hand.

The Swordslinger considered the hand for a moment, and then took it without taking his feet from the well curb.

"Thank you," the chieftain said. "We had no doubt that you would take care of the situation," he said, still trying to gather himself in the man's presence. "That's why we decided to take the women and children and clear the way for you."

Swordslinger didn't try to conceal the thin smile. Chieftain Bruce shuffled his feet embarrassedly and dropped his eyes. Then he turned to the men and pointed to the coffin. "Take this coffin inside, then gather up the other bodies and bury them," he said.

Stewart motioned for Robert to come to him and they moved a few steps over to Samuel. The father knelt and placed his arms around his sons. "Are you all right?" he asked Robert.

"Oh, I'm fine the youngster said. "I was just the piper." Stewart then turned his attention to his eldest son.

"You disobeyed me. You have dishonored your father. We'll talk after the burying is done."

Samuel stared silently after the men as they gathered shovels and began walking along the road to where the corpses were scattered.

CHAPTER 25

THE CELEBRATION

Heather ran to Samuel and they embraced. "I didn't think I would ever see you again," she said.

"Thanks for the confidence."

"Your poor father was a nervous wreck after you and Robert left. He didn't sleep at all last night, I'm sure."

"I'm sure I'll hear about that."

The villagers were elated to find their homes intact and immediately set about retrieving their personal belongings from the heap in the village street.

The owner of the pub showed a generous nature and contributed to the upcoming celebration by donating some bottles of whiskey. The bakery owner heated up his oven and began turning out an array of goodies ranging from cookies to meat pies. The woman who owned the linen shop supplied the children with bolts of colorful cloth to create a May Pole around one of the ancient oaks.

The Swordslinger appeared in front of the inn and leaned against a post on the front porch, watching the villagers rejoice. These same men and women had been in mourning a few hours earlier, sure, that everything they had worked so hard for would be stolen and burned by the raiders. Now they seemed carefree, intent only on having a good time. They had no idea how close their worst nightmares had been to becoming true.

Swordslinger had to admit that his own attitude had changed. For the first time in years, he was outside without his sword strapped on. He felt somewhat naked, but it was a good feeling. This was the first day of the rest of his life. And it was going to be a different life. A happy life. A life with meaning once again.

Some of the villagers obviously recognized and appreciated what their benefactor had accomplished in turning the savages away from their doors.

"Thank ye, Mister," one elderly lady said, approaching him on the inn porch. "God bless ye for saving our homes.

"And our lives," her husband added.

The Swordslinger left the inn and began strolling down the street. A young girl, perhaps six or seven years of age, presented him with a purple thistle. He took the flower, smelled its aroma, and then stuck it into the band of his trousers. A flower where the sword once was. Appropriate.

The girl curtsied. "Thank you, Mr. Swordslinger."

The man in black with the flower in his waistband knelt on the street and took the little girl's hands in his. "Thank you for the flower, child," he said. "My name is Nathan."

The girl smiled and placed a kiss on his cheek. Bliss. He was moved almost to tears. He watched the child run back to her friends and touched his freshly kissed cheek with his fingers. He smiled.

The party atmosphere was spreading. Mandolins, a dulcimer, a fiddle, three pipers, and a dozen people beating flat drums, all added to the joyous music that rang through the air. The children played around the May Pole, having to duck from stripes of ribbons lower and lower as they wound the Oak Tree. Several of the young women, Heather included, danced.

Chieftain Bruce came forward attired in fresh clothes and wearing an air of officialdom. He spread his arms and hushed the musicians and merrymakers. "Mr.... Ah... Mr. Swordslinger," he said, "No one knows your real name around here." His voice rang loud in the sudden silence.

"My name is Nathan."

Chieftain Bruce was in his element. "On behalf of our village, our clan would like you to have a gift, Nathan" he said. "Anything you desire," he paused and smiled at the crowd, "as long as it's within reason, of course."

Nathan returned the smile. "If I took your money and food, I would be no better than the Manteo Brothers," he said. "But if you're serious, I do have a request." He pointed to the mountainside. "I would like to have a small piece of land on that plateau that no one is working. I'd like to build a home there and become a gentleman farmer."

The crowd roared its approval and Chieftain Bruce seemed puzzled. "You want a plot of ground on the mountain side?" He already felt safer from the thought of having the Swordslinger for a neighbor. This was good news. "That sounds like a reasonable request, me friend. Aye, that property is not deeded to anyone and we can give it to you. That seems to be very little in my eyes."

A warm feeling enveloped Nathan and he stepped back, shading his eyes and staring at the ground that he had just been granted. He was a landowner again. He could almost picture the house he would build with a view overlooking the village.

"I am retiring from the sword," he said, still staring at the mountain. I am hanging up the sword and I intend to live the rest of my life as a peaceful man."

Chieftain Bruce was taken aback. "Never thought I'd hear that from you," he said. "But the property is yours. We'll do the paperwork tomorrow. Now, let's continue the celebration. Let's rejoice in the return to our homes!"

The musicians attacked their instruments with renewed vigor and the drinking resumed. Some of the men were already beginning to feel the effects from the free whiskey and were singing raucously. The youngsters were excited, playing, yelling and running about happily. Nathan looked for Samuel but didn't spot him. He saw the lovely Heather, her red hair fanning as she danced to lively tune. The girl was full of life, happy and beautiful. She reminded him of a young Shelley. He gently moved the sad thoughts of his dead wife to a corner of his mind. Today he would be happy.

"Nathan!" a woman called out, and brought to him a plate piled high with fried chicken, potatoes, green vegetables, bread and pudding. The use of his name made him feel good inside.

"Thank ye, ma'am." Nathan sank his teeth into a chicken breast and savored the warm juices. He turned to find a seat, when someone called out, "Swordslinger!" He instinctively reached for the hilt of his sword and his fingers brushed the thistle in his waistband. He turned and saw the crowd parting.

It was the boy, Samuel. He was standing atop a wagon loaded with chiseled stone and mud bricks. The grin on his face was ear to ear. "If you're going to become a neighbor, you'll need some building materials," he said, still beaming. Manny wants you to use this for the foundation!"

Nathan was speechless. Again. He forgot the chicken and set the plate down, walking to Samuel and putting his arms around the boy. "You amaze me, laddie. I don't know what to say."

"Say nothing. Just enjoy. Tomorrow we begin building your home, aye?"

"Samuel ..." Nathan couldn't find words. "Tomorrow is going to be a fine day. Manny, what can I say? Thank you. I can only repay you by being a good neighbor."

"Nae, it is we who owe you, me friend," Manny said, hopping off the wagon and giving Nathan a hearty slap on the back. "You have saved our homes. It is only fitting that we should help you build one."

"You'll be among my first guests for dinner," Nathan said, laughing.

"A deal, my friend Nathan. I like that name. Nathan is a good man's name."

Nathan smiled.

The feasting was at last completed and some of the men became involved in a caber-tossing contest while others playfully wrestled. The girls were holding a dance contest. They were all in a festive mood. Many had feared that they might die on this day and instead they were having a party. Times were good. Robert was busily playing the bagpipes along with several other wannabe musicians. The wails of the pipes rang through the valley. The sweet sounds soothed the souls.

Samuel singled out Heather and they began an impromptu dance. Nathan watched them and his heart filled with happiness. This was what he had always wanted, not the lonely life of a swordslinger. He wanted to be loved, not feared. He stole another glance at his future home site on the mountainside.

The day grew late and the men were getting drunk. Their voices grew louder with each fresh fill of tumblers. But it was all in good spirits. No one was spoiling for a fight on this day of days.

As the sun sank behind the mountains and it became dark, Nathan gave the crowd a special treat, setting off the remainder of his cache of firecrackers in a dazzling fireworks display that had the children screaming in delight. For the finale, he tied 12 of the bangers together and set them off in rapid succession. Pop! Pop! Pop! The kids whooped in excitement and Nathan laughed a nice easy laugh that he didn't know he still possessed.

Samuel appeared at his side with two steins of ale and Robert in tow. "Drink a toast to yourself, Nathan," he said.

"Aren't you a little young to be drinking toasts?" Nathan asked.

"I've grown up a lot in the past couple of days," the young man said. "I think a drink might put some wind in the bagpipe, if you know what I mean."

"Are you sure this is your first drink?" Nathan asked, suspiciously. "But I guess it's okay." He tapped his mug against the boy's and said, "Thank you, Samuel, for giving me my life back. Cheers!"

Samuel wasn't quite sure what his friend meant. "Well, I'm just happy you're alive."

"Aye, and myself. Tomorrow I will begin building a house. My home — Eeshebob on the Mountain! Now I think you should be finding your father and be getting on to your home."

"I haven't seen him in a while," Samuel said, "but I guess he'll come home when he's ready. But it has been a long day and I'm tired." He put a headlock on his brother. "Think I'll go home and put this runt to bed. See you tomorrow, Nathan."

"Right, tomorrow." Nathan turned and walked back to the inn. He paused for moment on the porch and watched the villagers, who appeared to be running out of energy. The revelry wouldn't last much longer. Home. He was home!

What a glorious feeling! No getting up in the morning and beginning another trek to nowhere.

Reaching his room, he undressed and lay on the bed, but couldn't fall asleep. His mind was racing with thoughts of the morrow and plans for building his home. He finally rose and paced the room. It was beginning to appear that he would not sleep despite the exhausting day and night he had spent. He dressed and reached for the sword. No. He didn't need that any longer. He would just go for a peaceful walk and perhaps he could come back and get some sleep. He put on his hat and walked outside.

A shooting star streaked across the night sky. The moon was full and there was a silver ring around it. A beautiful, peaceful night, perfect for cleansing the soul and starting a new life. *A good omen*, he thought. He crossed the street and walked to the stable where Manny had left the wagon loaded with stones and bricks for his new home.

"Bloodslinger!" Nathan froze. He had hoped never to hear words like this again. He turned and saw Stewart standing at the rear of the wagon. The man was obviously drunk, swaying on his feet as he held a nearly empty bottle of whiskey in one hand.

"Stewart," Nathan said quietly, "what are you doing here?"

"Looking for you, killer."

"What do you want?"

"I want you, you bastard! You have stolen my son and I won't allow it!"

"Oh, Stewart, go home and get some sleep. Things will be better in the morning."

Stewart shifted the bottle to his left hand drew his sword from the sheath with the right. "You think you are good with a blade, huh? Well let's see who is better!"

"Go home, Stewart. You're drunk. We don't want to do this."

"You think you're so good, don't you? Well, I'm a better father than you were. I haven't run away and left my sons." He jabbed the sword at Nathan, nicking him in the side and drawing blood.

"All right, Stewart, that's enough!" Nathan moved quickly, grabbing the drunken man's hands and bringing them down to his sides. The bottle of whiskey dropped to the ground and the brown liquid spilled. Nathan put pressure on the man's right arm and he dropped the sword. "Now go home! Your sons are waiting for you!"

Nathan turned and began walking away. A mistake. The drunken Stewart lunged for him and threw a punch to the kidney. Nathan fell forward and slammed against the wagon wheel. Stewart's momentum carried him sprawling to the ground.

Nathan turned and stood over him, feeling the wounds in his back beginning to throb. He bent over and picked up his hat. "Go home," he repeated, "we're finished here."

Stewart was past reasoning, however. He rose to his feet and made another staggering lunge toward his foe. Nathan easily sidestepped the staggering man again and pleaded, "Stop it, Stewart! Go home!"

"You're a god damned murderer!" Stewart raged. "You've tried to steal my son, but he loves me, not you! I'm going to kill you, you bastard!" He threw himself toward Nathan and they fell against the wagon wheel.

"Enough!" Nathan shouted, feeling his temper beginning to rise. He shoved Stewart in the chest and the man staggered backwards. He tried to regain his balance, but his drunken legs failed him. He flailed his arms, tried to grab the wagon and fell heavily, his head crashing against the wagon wheel hub with a sickening thud.

Nathan bent over to help the man up. "Come on," he said. "On your feet, Stewart. You and whiskey don't mix well, man. Get up."

Stewart's body was limp and he didn't respond. "Okay, I'll help you home. Wake up, man!" He placed his hands underneath Stewart to help him up and felt the warm wetness of blood. He pulled him into sitting position and the head fell forward. Nathan placed a hand to the back of Stewart's head and felt a loose flap of scalp. "Oh great," he said. "Now you've done it, man. You've hurt yourself. Okay, let's get you comfortable here and I'll see what I can do.

Hang on." He lifted Stewart's wrist and felt for a pulse. Nothing. He placed his fingers on the man's throat. Nothing!

"Oh no, Stewart, what have you done?" Nathan placed Stewart's limp body back on the ground and stood. He had to find somebody to help move the man out of the street. He paused. What was he going to tell Samuel and Robert? Did they have to know that their father had died in a drunken stupor? "Stewart," he whispered, "why did you have to do this? What will happen to your sons? What can I tell them?"

Nathan thought for a moment, a plan forming in his mind. Stewart kept a horse in the stable, maybe … That's it. The man had gone for a ride and after drinking too much and fallen from his horse. That would be a story the boys could live with. After all, everyone had been drinking too much that evening.

He went to the stable and found Stewart's horse in a stall. He saddled the horse, leaving the cinch loose so that it would slip and walked the horse outside to the body. He wrapped the loose reins around one of Stewart's dead hands. "There, you fell off your horse. That's how it happened."

"The hell it is!" The voice came from the darkness of the hayloft above the stable. "You killed ol' Stewart and you think you can cover it up!"

The old man emerged from the loft, but Nathan didn't recognize him. "It didn't happen like that," he protested.

The old man began running up the street, screaming, "Murderer! Murderer!"

Nathan leaned against the wagon and dropped his head. What next?

A crowd began to form including many of the villagers who were half-drunk and tired from the long day of first fear and then celebration They streamed into the street in answer to the old man's yelling. What was happening? Were the Manteo Brothers returning?

Samuel was among those awakened by the shouting. He pulled on his kilt and boots and rushed outside. Robert was still soundly asleep. "What' going on," he asked one of the men running down the street.

"There's been a murder," the man yelled over his shoulder.

Samuel's blood suddenly ran cold. Nathan! The Manteo Brothers have come back and caught him asleep. Nathan was dead! He raced along the street, heart pounding, and pushed his way through the crowd gathered at the stable. What he saw sent him to his knees.

CHAPTER 26

JAILED

Chieftain Bruce took charge. "Everyone back," he ordered in his strictest mayoral tone. "Now, Bailey, tell us what happened here."

"I heard Stewart cry out, 'Murderer,' and I looked down from the loft and saw the two of them fighting. Then Stewart was dead, and this one (pointing at Nathan) tries to make it look like an accident with the horse."

Nathan listened to the accusation with wonderment. How could this be happening? He glanced at Samuel and saw a look of shock on the boy's face. Surely, the boy could not believe that he had killed his father. The happiness and feeling of well-being that Nathan had felt for the past few hours dissipated into one of irony and disbelief. He had been a fool to think that his life could finally be free of death and blackness.

"Murderer!" a woman cried out.

"Burn in hell, Swordslinger!

"Got to keep killin', don't ya?"

The voices rang out in the night air. An old woman stepped forward and slapped him in the face. At that moment, the Nathan in the man in black died. The slap was like a handful of dirt tossed upon the casket. Where once only hours ago these same people hailed him as a hero, they now cursed him as a murderer. The Swordslinger dropped his head and waited for the scene to play out.

"McDonald," Chieftain Bruce called, "take this man to the guardhouse and hold him until we can ask him some questions. The burly McDonald took the unresisting Nathan by the arm and led him away. A few minutes later, Chieftain Bruce and two other men entered the guardhouse. They all sat down at a small table and began to question the man they had revered hours earlier and were now ready to hang.

Nathan told his story once, and then shut up. The men peppered him with questions but he remained silent. He

213

knew what was going to happen, so why bother? And maybe he was guilty. *I did kill him,"* he thought. *"I did push him and cause him to fall. All I had to do was walk away. I didn't have to fight the man.*

"If you're not going to defend yourself, we might as well lock you up," Chieftain Bruce said. McDonald escorted Nathan to the small cell in the back of the building and slammed the barred door shut. Someone outside threw a stone that clanged on the barred window.

Nathan sat on the small cot and waited for the next stone to clang. Several were thrown before the men tired of the sport. They were getting no reaction from the killer inside.

Nathan closed his eyes and let his mind drift. He saw Samuel's stricken face and remembered the pain showing in the eyes. Bloodslinger! Maybe Stewart was right. Maybe that's all he was. Maybe he was cursed to sling blood on everything and everyone he touched.

Muffled voices from the other room broke into Nathan's reverie. He rose from the cot when he recognized one of the voices as that of Samuel. How could he face the boy?

"I don't know about that," McDonald said. "Your father was a good man who had a lot of friends, son. And half of them are out throwing stones at the jail right now. They're angry and I'm not sure it's a good idea for you to see this man."

"I need to see him. Please!"

McDonald was an imposing figure, a large man who was big framed and overweight, close to 300 pounds. The excitement of the night had been exerting for him and he was breathing through his mouth and sweating profusely. Sweat droplets dangled from the short-cut shafts of red hair. "He ain't talking, son. He just sits there, staring at his hands."

"He'll talk to me."

"Oh, will he, huh?" McDonald sucked in a rasping breath. "Okay, seeing as how you're Stewart's son, I guess you should be allowed to see his killer. But," he pointed a sausage of a finger at the boy, "don't get too close. You don't have a weapon, do you?"

"Only this," Samuel said, removing his dirk from a boot and handing it to the sweating hulk.

"You can't stay long." He opened a wooden door and led Samuel to the cell. "You got a visitor, Swordslinger, and if you show disrespect, he'll be your last visitor."

Nathan stood a few feet from the cell door, unmoving, waiting for the boy's reaction. Samuel turned to McDonald and asked, "Can we be alone?" The man nodded and left, closing the heavy wooden door behind him.

The two looked at each other for a moment. "What happened?" Samuel asked.

"Your father fell."

"You didn't kill him?"

"I pushed him."

"What? Why?"

He didn't want to leave this boy with the image of his father as slovenly drunk picking fight. A son should honor his father's memory. "He wanted to talk and I didn't feel like it. I pushed and he struck his head. I was going to try to make it look like an accident."

Samuel scoffed. "That's not the way it happened. My father was drunk, wasn't he?"

"I don't know."

"I know he was. He had been drinking at the pub since he and the other men buried those dead men."

"I don't know."

"Well, the men he was drinking with know. This is crazy. Everyone loved you. We were going to build your house. Everything was great. Now what happens? You have to tell Chieftain Bruce what really happened."

"I told you."

"Nooo! I don't believe you. I want to know the truth!"

"That is the truth!" Nathan moved to the door and gripped the bars. His knuckles grew white from the pressure.

Samuel was breathing rapidly, trying hard to keep from crying. He stepped back from the cell door and stared hard at Nathan. "These people think you are a monster! They

215

think all you can do is kill! I know you're not like that. You're a good man. I know that! And I know you didn't just shove my father! Tell me the truth!"

"Samuel…that is the …"

"Nooo!" Samuel shouted.

The wooden door opened and McDonald shoved his neckless head into the room. "Everything all right here?"

"Yes, everything's fine. A minute more, please." Samuel said. The head disappeared and the door was closed. Another stone banged off the cell window.

"You'll burn in hell!" someone shouted.

Samuel made another effort to reach the man. "I can't believe that the person you showed to me was a lie. All those things you spoke of — honor and dignity, the conscience of a Samurai warrior — was all that a lie? Was it?"

Nathan couldn't stand seeing his young friend suffering in this manner. He hit the cell bars with his hands in frustration. "Samuel … Oh God, Samuel. Yes! Your father was drunk! He challenged me and even nicked me in the side with his sword. I tried to reason with him, but he wouldn't listen. I pushed him and he lost his balance. When he tried to come at me again, he slipped and his head hit the wagon wheel hub. That's the story, son. That's all of it."

The knowledge lit Samuel's eyes. "You wanted people to believe he fell off his horse rather than how he was a drunk who attacked you!"

"Your father was a good man, Samuel. Let him be buried with honor."

"That's fine, but what about you? You didn't kill him. He fell! Why do you have to be in jail?"

"Listen to those people out there, son. Do you think they will believe my story?"

"They have to, it's the truth!"

Nathan sighed and his lips curled in a sad smile. "This is nothing new for me. People have misunderstood me for a long time. I am tired and ready for it to end. No, I didn't kill your father, but I've done things that are hellish and I've made my penance with God. My life is complete, Samuel.

Your father will be buried with dignity and I will be at peace."

"No! This can't happen. You're talking crazy! We're going to build your house and we're going fishing!"

"Samuel, all your father has left now is his honor. I won't take that."

"What about your honor?"

"I have killed men." Nathan lifted his hands from the bars and held them before his face. "These hands are bloodied. My dream now is to be reunited with my wife and I'm afraid that just asking for forgiveness isn't enough. Perhaps if I allow your father's name to remain untainted, that act will help my atonement and insure my being with Shelley again."

"You're talking crazy talk! I'm going to tell Chieftain Bruce the truth. They'll set you free. They have to if the dead man's son speaks for you!"

"No, Samuel. That is not the nature of these people. They will scorn you for siding with the man who killed your father. Remember, they have a witness who claims he saw me kill him. No. Let him be buried with honor and I'll rejoin my wife. Even if you told my story, do you think they will believe it? No. Leave things as they are. I don't want you getting yourself involved."

Samuel had run out of words. There was no way he could get through to his friend. He seemed determined to face the gallows for a crime he didn't commit. He reached through the bars and took Nathan's hand. A lone tear ran down his cheek.

Nathan leaned his head against the bars. "We had one day," he said in a soft voice. "That day is in my heart and no one can take it away. It's okay, Samuel. I am at peace. It's okay."

Samuel released Nathan's hand and stepped back. "I've never known a man as good as you. You're willing to sacrifice your life for the honor of a man who tried to kill you." The boy shook his head in wonder.

"It's the best way," Nathan said.

The tears came freely now and Samuel had trouble talking. "I love you, Nathan. There is no man on this earth whose heart is as gentle as yours."

"Hey, time's up," Nathan said, forcing a smile. "The natives are getting restless. Go home and take care of your brother, Samuel. You are going to be a fine man."

Samuel walked to the door and turned back for a last look. He closed his eyes as if taking a snapshot, and went out.

"You okay, boy? McDonald asked.

Samuel didn't reply.

"There's a judge from the Frasier Clan coming to town tomorrow, so we won't have to wait long. We'll hold court and after he's found guilty, we'll hang the hooligan."

Samuel kept his eyes averted. He knew McDonald thought his words were solace to a grieving son. There was nothing he could say. He left the building and ran all the way home. He went to his bed and laid down, trying not to think of his father's empty room. Robert was sound asleep in a fetal position, hugging the pillow. Beside the bed lay one of his father's ironsmithing hammers.

After a few minutes of tossing and turning, Samuel rose and went to his father's bed. He picked up the pillow and held it to his face. An odor of stale whiskey permeated the air.

"I hate you!" he vented in a silent scream. Oh, Father! I love you! Why did you have to die? I hate you for what you're doing to Nathan!" He sobbed, body-racking sobs that seemed to tear from his throat. Finally, he collapsed onto his father's bed and clutched the pillow to him until he fell asleep.

The knock on the door awakened Samuel. Heather was there with a covered bowl. "I brought you some food," she said. "If you'd like, I'll stay with you."

Samuel put his arms around the angel and pulled her close. He felt the anger, grief and frustration draining from his tortured mind. Robert came into the room, yawning, and joined them in a hug that lasted for a long time.

218

Samuel and Robert shared the bowl of warm food and Heather sat at the table with them. "You're the man of the house now, Samuel," she said, watching his face for a reaction. "What are you doing to do?"

Confusion and broken heart made it hard for Samuel to reply. Finally, he took Heather's hand and asked, "Will you stay with Robert so that I can go to the trial?"

"I can do that, but I'd prefer to leave him with my mother and go to the trial with you."

"No, this is something I have to do alone."

"I know this hard on you. I can't believe that the Swordslinger killed your father and tried to cover it up. I had judged him so wrong."

For the first time that he could recall, Samuel snapped at the girl he loved. "Shut up! Just shut up, Heather! You don't know what you're saying!"

"I'm sorry, Samuel. I know you loved Nathan, too. This must be killing you."

"No, it's just hurting me. But it's killing Nathan. No one knows the real story, Heather. And I'm sworn not to tell. Not even you. Please forgive me for yelling at you …"

"It's okay, my love. I understand."

CHAPTER 27

THE SENTENCING

The men from the Frasier Clan rode into the village early that morning. Judge Morton Frasier wore a black suit and quickly retired to the makeshift courtroom where he slipped into a black robe and white wig. He was accompanied by two other court officials, a clerk and a bailiff. There were several other men in the group, and a couple of boys who appeared to be about Samuel's age.

Samuel stood in the doorway of his home and watched the procession pass. One of the village women had placed a wreath on the door and the judge had nodded in respect as he rode past.

"They'll be starting the trial soon," he said to Heather. "Robert, I'll tell you all about it when I get back. You listen to Heather and don't give her any problems.

Robert didn't feel up to giving anyone any problems. He was feeling very much like an orphan. "Father ... he's not coming back, Samuel."

"No, he's not coming back, little brother. But I am. We'll be all right. We'll bury father tomorrow."

"Heather, I know that I have only aged a day, but I feel much older. I want you to know how much I love you. And I hope to make you my wife one day."

"I love you too, husband to be."

"Eccch!" said Robert.

Samuel kissed Heather on the cheek and left. He looked at the ground as he walked, wondering if he could detect his father's footprints. He hadn't lied to Heather; he did feel much older. But he was also feeling very frightened. He was the man of the house now. He and Robert were alone. And his feeling of loss was doubled, because he had lost Nathan as well.

People were milling around outside the courtroom, set up in the village meeting hall, which meant that the trial was not yet under way. Samuel walked past the hall to his father's ironsmith shop and went inside. Stewart's presence in the shop was almost overpowering. The boy walked around, touching the tools laid out on the worktable. He picked up a sword and ran his finger along the edge. He could hear the clanging of hammer against steel as his father had forged the blade.

Samuel went to the wall and took down a leather apron hanging on a peg. The smell of his father was strong as he pulled the apron strap around his neck. The hem of the apron fell to his knees and it was heavy from the pocketful of nails and various scraps of metal. He felt something in the small middle pocket and pulled it out. It was his mother's gold wedding ring. He raised the ring to his lips and kissed it. "I pray that you and mother are together again, father," he murmured. "I promise you that I will take care of Robert. I will be his mother, father and brother."

Scattered raindrops were falling as Samuel left the shop. He lifted his face skyward, letting the rainfall on his face, hoping it would clear his troubled mind. The crowd at the meeting hall was larger and people were filing in. Samuel found a seat near the back of the room and tried to gather himself for what was about to happen.

The judge, looking stern in the back robe, called the room to order. "Chieftain Bruce, please state your case."

"Yes, my lord," the chieftain was trying hard to be formal. "We accuse this man, Nathan Frasier, of murder. He killed Stewart Donachee in cold blood and we are asking that he be hung for his crime."

"Tell us in your own words what happened, Chieftain."

"Well, sir, I do feel that part of the blame is mine. We were being threatened by the Manteo Brothers who we knew were going to raid our village and I hired the swordslinger, er, Frasier, to discourage them. Frankly, he did a good job at that, too. He drove them off, along with several of their Viking friends, and several of them won't be bothering anyone else, me Lord.

"So we were doing some celebrating, with everybody having a good time and sharing a few drinks. Everything was peaceful when we finally called it a night until old man

McGregor woke us up hollering about a murder. He says he saw Nathan Frasier strike Stewart Donachee. From the best we can make of it, Donachee struck his head on the wagon wheel hub and it cracked his skull. McGregor says that he saw Frasier then try to rig it so that it would look like an accident, with Donachee falling off his horse.

"That's our case, my lord."

"Is the witness present?"

"Aye, me lord. That would be me, Bailey McGregor. Born and reared here."

"Well, Mr. McGregor, you have heard Chieftain Bruce. Did he speak correctly and do you have anything to add?"

"He told it just like I seen it, me lord. The man killed ol' Stewart and then tried to hide it."

"That will be all, Mr. McGregor. Chieftain Bruce, have you discovered a motive for this murder?"

"Yes, my lord. We know that Stewart … Mr. Donachee … had done some sword work for Frasier a few days ago and we think they had an argument over the payment for that work."

There was a buzz around the room and the judge pounded his gavel for quiet. Nathan stared at Chieftain Bruce, a quizzical half-smile on his lips. He shook his head slowly. Samuel's mouth was agape in disbelief.

"Very well. Mr. Frasier, do you have anything to say in your behalf?"

Nathan stood and turned to look over the courtroom. His eyes suddenly went wide in recognition and he stared hard at the group of young men who had ridden in with the judge. His eyes fixed on one of them and the man smiled. Nathan turned back to face the judge and said, "Nothing, your lord. I am guilty as charged."

The young man who had drawn Nathan's attention erupted with a loud "Yes!"

"Silence or I will have you removed," the judge warned.

Judge Frasier leaned forward and dabbed a handkerchief at the beads of perspiration forming on his forehead. "I am ashamed that you were once a member of the Frasier Clan," he said. "You have received a fair and just trial by your peers, Nathan Frasier and you are judged to be guilty of murder. The sentence is death by hanging. The execution will take place tomorrow as soon as a gallows can be prepared. Justice has been served! This court is adjourned!

Samuel sat in stunned silence as the courtroom erupted with noise. The men huddled in groups. The women busied themselves in discussing the kinds of food they would prepare for the after-hanging party.

Chieftain Bruce strutted around pompously, making the most of his moment in the sun. He selected a group of men to build the gallows in the village center. "Get on it quickly," he said. "The hanging is in the morning."

Samuel remained sitting. His mind was numb. Men and women approached him, patted him on the back and extended condolences for his father's death and congratulations for the guilty verdict. When the room had emptied, he rose and went outside, making his way slowly back to the ironsmith shop. He felt like a zombie. Tomorrow he was going to witness the execution of a man he had learned to love and then bury his father. His hands trembled. He wanted to cry but the lump in his throat hardly allowed him to breathe.

He was devoid of hope. There was nothing he could do. The trial had been a sham, but it was legal and all that the villagers needed to hold a lynching. What was wrong with men who could turn on a benefactor so quickly? Even if Nathan had done what they claimed, didn't he deserve some consideration for saving the village and perhaps their lives?

Anger seethed within his young breast. He was powerless to intervene but even screaming the truth would do no good. He should have insisted on speaking at the trial. But it had ended so quickly he hadn't even had time to think about it. And now an innocent man was going to die!

It was no secret that he and his father often clashed, so it was doubtful that anyone would have believed him if he had tried to side with Nathan. In fact, as Nathan had worried, some may have even tried to suggest that the two of them had conspired to murder Stewart, with the boy's testifying in Nathan's defense. This was all so crazy. It couldn't be happening. He would awaken soon and discover he had been dreaming. His father would be snoring in the next room, sleeping off another drunk. No! This could not be happening!

Samuel used the bellows to start a fire in the furnace and soon had a strip of metal red-hot. He placed it on the anvil and began banging it with the hammer. Hard.

Later that evening Samuel stood across the street from the jail and stared at the barred window. He envisioned Nathan inside the cell, pacing back and forth, his brow knitted in a frown.

Inside the cell, Nathan was lying on the cot, eyes closed, reliving the short time that he had spent with Shelley. "Soon, my love."

The image of his tortured friend brought tears to Samuel's eyes and he was overcome with a desire to talk to Nathan. He walked slowly across the street and approached the back of the jail, moving below the barred window that was some eight feet above ground. He stood on his tiptoes and called softly, "Nathan, can you hear me?"

Nathan rose from the cot and came to the window. "I hear you, Samuel. What do you want?"

"I want to help you. What can I do?"

"Nothing. It's all right. I'm fine."

"No, it is not all right. You didn't kill my father."

"It doesn't matter anymore, Samuel. "I am at peace."

"But they're going to hang you!" The boy's voice broke and a sob escaped.

"Cut out the crying, Samuel. You're a man now. Be strong. If I only have hours left I want to spend them in peace."

"No. No. No. I'll tell them I did it. You're just trying to protect me."

Nathan laughed. "Samuel, stop this. No one is going to believe that. There is a witness, you know."

"But what will I do? I've lost everyone, mother, father and now you?"

"Samuel, there are many people here who will help you, especially Heather's family. The villagers are really decent

224

people. They just think they're avenging one of their own. They are right to do that. Listen to me. In my saddlebag, there is a black pouch with gold coins in it. I want you to have them. Use the money to help you survive and get a start in life. It helps me to think of you and Heather together."

"Great, and what about you?" Samuel asked.

"They're going to hang me."

"No, I mean after you die. What's going to happen to you?"

"I'm going to a mountain that will have a stone house with a garden. And waiting there for me will be Shelley. I will be happy again."

"Tell me about your wife. What was she like?

"Shelley was the sweetest woman I've ever known. She had long blond hair that the rain would curl. I called her my little lamb. She had huge blue eyes and a wonderful smile that pushed the darkness away. She was an artist and people were always begging her do their portraits. But most of all, she loved doing paintings of her horse.

"You lived on a farm?"

"Aye," Nathan laughed. "I was a farmer. I had pigs and sheep and a cow and we loved riding our horses together. We were happy."

Samuel forgot his sadness for a moment and giggled. "You with pigs? That I would love to see!" Then reality returned. "I don't want you to die."

"We all have to at some time. I have lived my life, Samuel. I want to be with Shelley again."

"Aren't you afraid?"

"No, I am not afraid. I have asked God for forgiveness for my many sins and I am at peace. My atonement is complete. Someday, many years from now, when your life has been lived, Shelly and I will greet you and Heather and we will spend eternity together."

"You believe that?"

"I do. I have faith and it gives me peace of mind."

Both were silent for a moment, then Nathan spoke. "Look at that star, Samuel," he said, pointing to the bright speck in the night sky. I gave that star to Shelley and when I see it, I think of her. You should give a star to your Heather."

Samuel stared at the star and was silent for a moment. "Will you sleep tonight, Nathan?"

"No, I won't sleep again, son. I'm going to stand here at this window and stare at Shelley's star and then watch the sun rise."

"Do you mind if I sit out here and watch it with you?"

"That would be a nice thing for you to do, son."

The two friends, one's life about to end and another's about to begin, talked through the night, the subjects of their conversation rambling. Nathan explained to Samuel how to plant potatoes and what he needed to know about building a chicken coop. Samuel asked Nathan about his childhood. Nathan had been an only child and when he was 16, his father had died from a severe case of influenza. His mother died two years later of a broken heart. Nathan, then 18, remained on the farm, working the fields. He met Shelley when he was 20, while in the village to sell produce. He was stricken immediately and she fell in love with him a few weeks later. Two months later they were married and two months after that, Shelley was with child.

"My son was at the meeting hall today," Nathan said.

"No!" Samuel scanned the faces in his mind.

"He was sitting in the back row, the tall lanky one with black hair."

Samuel's eyes widened. "The one who shouted out?"

"Yes."

"How did he know about the trial?"

"I'm sure when word of the murder spread through the Frasier Clan he heard it was me."

"He must really hate you."

"Aye, and I guess in his mind, he thinks he has every right to."

"But you didn't run away. You went after those men who killed your wife."

"Aye, and if I had returned home after finding them, perhaps it would have been different. But I was not thinking

226

right then. I became the 'Great Avenger' and I just kept going, hunting down and killing men like them. I earned good wages hiring myself out for jobs like the one here."

"But I don't understand. Why am I the only one who knows the truth about what you did?"

"Because you are the only one who has ever listened."

"I just isn't fair, Nathan. In my mind, you are a man of the greatest honor. You gave up the life you had to avenge your wife and now you're going to die to protect my father's honor. You saved this village from being destroyed and the people here from being murdered. How can they forget that?"

"It's human nature, my son. Men can have selective memories. But it really is all right, Samuel. I am ready to go. I will ask you for one favor, however. When they bury me tomorrow, please place my sword in the coffin with me. We have bonded over the years, that blade and I."

"I will," Samuel whispered. "Is there anything else I can do?"

There was no answer. The last conversation was over.

CHAPTER 28

THE GALLOWS RISE

Samuel walked home slowly, his heart heavy. He barely noticed the homes as he passed, smoke already rising from the chimneys of early risers. Some of the women had done their laundry late the day before and left it hanging on the lines in the back yards where the clothes would dry in the early morning sun. The ribbons flapped around the May Pole in the public square where the villagers had celebrated. That all seemed so long ago now.

The echoes of the children playing and shouting rang in the boy's mind as he trudged along the gravel road. The crunch of his feet on the small pebbles seemed loud.

Nathan would never walk this street again. This would be his last sunrise. He would never feel the rain on his face again.

Samuel raised his head to look at the home site Nathan had chosen on the hill and it was shrouded in mist. He felt a lump in his throat and his eyes stung with tears. He and Manny had spent more than an hour loading stones for the house on the wagon and now they would never be delivered.

Samuel blinked back the tears and continued walking toward home. Some of the houses he passed were decorated with flowers and curtains made by the women who lived in them and they stirred in the morning breeze. A few chickens pecked away in the dirt of the yards. He thought about his life and what it would be like. No father. No Nathan. All he had left was Robert, the house and the ironsmith shop. He felt young and helpless and overburdened. He shook his head, trying to clear it of the doubts. Perhaps it might have been better if the arrow from the raider that struck Nathan had killed him. At least the swordslinger would have died a hero's death and been buried with dignity. And his father would still be alive, probably home snoring in his cot.

He wiped a sleeve across his eyes and continued walking. Life made its own turns and he could only follow the path laid before him.

When Samuel entered the house, he found Heather asleep in his bed and her mother lying on a pallet at the foot of his late father's bed. Robert was curled up on his bed, also sound asleep.

Samuel moved quietly to the bedside and carefully removed the strands of hair from Heather's face, then knelt and kissed her on the cheek. After a moment, he rose and went outside. He was tired, but too emotionally aroused to be sleepy. He sat on the stoop at the front of the house and watched the horizon turn from black to purple and then blue as the sun rose and sent its golden rays fanning out.

The last sunrise, Samuel thought. He watched as large white clouds formed over the horizon, their bottoms tinged with gold. He heard the gentle breeze stirring the leaves of the giant oak trees. Nathan would never experience any of this again.

Unless there is a Heaven.

The door opened and Heather joined him on the stoop. She leaned her head against his shoulder, her beautiful auburn hair glistening in the early light of the sun.

"Heather, do you believe there is a Heaven with a God?"

"Aye," she answered without a pause. Her eyes noted the beauty of the sunrise and the peaks of the mountains appearing. "I believe God put a little of Heaven right here in the Highlands."

Samuel lifted her head and stared into the soft blue eyes. "I believe, too," he said. "There has to be a Heaven because I'm looking at an angel right now." He put his arm around the girl and pulled her close against him.

The village was stirring now as the sun signaled time for the citizens to prepare for work. Several men passed along the street on their way to jobs. But Samuel knew that today's major job was the building of a gallows. A wagon rumbled past loaded with planks. A few minutes later, the sound of hammering could be heard.

"How ironic," Samuel whispered into the red-gold hair, "only a couple of days ago, these same men were going to be building a house for Nathan."

"Are you going to watch?" Heather asked.

"Aye. I have to."

"You love him, don't you?"

"Aye, I do. The people just don't know him. He is a good man with a good heart. And he saved this village from being destroyed."

"But he killed your father."

"No, that's not the way it happened. Nathan didn't kill my father, Heather. Father was drunk and he challenged Nathan to a fight. He even drew his sword and threatened him. Nathan tried to talk to him and kept pushing him away, but when father attacked him, Nathan shoved him aside and he got back up and fell. His head hit the wheel hub and that's what killed him."

"Oh, no! Then he's innocent? But he's going to die anyway!"

"Yes, and there's nothing we can do about it."

"You have to tell them! Speak to Chieftain Bruce!"

"Heather, these men have created their own truths. They're not going to choose an outsider over one of their own. They believe what they want to believe. And Nathan is afraid that if I try to help him, they will think that he and I conspired to kill father. They know I had become as close to him as a son. And old McGregor is claiming he saw everything, which is a lie. But it makes him feel important and he isn't going to change his story. Frankly, I don't think he could see his own hand at arm's length."

"But this is horrible! We can't just …"

"It's the way Nathan wants it, Heather. He says this way my father dies with dignity. And he knows that if he did protest the charge, the people would just hate him even more. He doesn't want to go through that. He's found an inner peace and he wants to join his wife in the next life. He's lonely and he's tired of this world and its cruelties. He said he would not defend himself and for me not to because it will ruin me and our lives … and our children's lives."

"I don't care! We can't just stand by and do nothing!"

"What would you have me do?" Samuel said, his voice rising. "I don't know what to do! I'm sorry; I didn't mean to yell at you. It's just that I feel so helpless. I'll protest, but what good it will do. Are you prepared for this?"

"You have to, Samuel, Nathan is a good man," Heather said.

Samuel stood up and stretched, then rubbed his eyes. "I have to wash up and change clothes," he said. "I'll talk but I know how this day will turn out. I will bury both of my fathers."

CHAPTER 29

THE EXECUTION

The building of the gallows took longer than expected. Even with more than a dozen men working, it was almost noon when it was finished. The platform was firm and the bag of dirt weighing almost 200 pounds had served as a test hanging, proving the rope and noose to be more than capable of carrying out the grisly task of hanging a man. As a curious throng watched with morbid fascination, the rope swung gently in the breeze, the noose formed and ready.

Samuel watched the test hanging, his heart almost bursting with grief as the heavy bag dropped through the opening. A couple of the men standing nearby gave him consoling pats on the shoulder.

"Don't you worry, son,' one of them said. "That bastard won't kill anyone else. God bless you, me lad."

Chieftain Bruce made his obligatory appearance. "Well, she finished, boys?"

"Aye, it's done."

The chieftain turned to the village priest. "Well, Reverend, you can ring the bell. Let everyone know it's about to happen. I'll get the prisoner and we can have this thing out of the way in time for lunch."

Manny appeared at Samuel's side. "I had nothing to do with building that," he said. "Didn't have the heart. One minute we're praising the man and the next we're hanging him. Something's wrong with that." He put a hand on Samuel's shoulder. "You really think it was an accident?"

"Yes. I think my father got drunk and went to Nathan for a fight. Nathan refused and pushed my father aside. When he started back at Nathan, he was so drunk and mad he tripped over his own foot."

"Samuel, that's the problem ... was it a push or a trip? There's McGregor too. He claims that's what happened."

"He lies."

"But the horse was out of the stable. Your father's body was next to the horse. Even Nathan admits trying to make it look like a fall from the horse. Why would he do that? What was he covering up? His actions tell of a guilty man."

"He just wanted to keep my father's memory honorable for my sake," Samuel said.

"Och, I see, there's more dignity being drunk and falling off ye horse than dying in a street brawl."

"No. By tripping over his own feet, Manny! He was my father! If I thought that Nathan had killed my father, I would have slain him before he reached the jail. I know what Nathan says is true. If the son of Stewart says the man is innocent, why cannot anyone else believe it? Manny, you knew my father. What if you're wrong? What if Nathan is innocent? He just risked his life to save our village and our very lives. This is his reward? Doesn't what he's done for us carry any weight?

"He is a swordslinger. He makes his living killing men."

"He made his living putting his life on the line to protect the weak and people like us ... cowards!"

Manny took Samuel by the elbow. "All right, lad. All right."

"Why can't we just exile him?"

"Samuel," Manny led him away from others that could hear. "All right. Your father was a good man. He worked hard. He loved you and Robert. Aye, he drank hard, too. And yes, I can see him challenging this swordslinger, and yes ... yes ... I see him tripping over his own feet. I've seen him do that a hundred times before."

"You believe me then! Stop this! Please! Stop it!"

Manny grabbed Samuel's arm and led him to the side. "Sam, listen to me. Here's the truth of it. Your father was one of us. This man — this hired killer — is an outsider. Maybe he didn't kill your father, but he was there and he was in a fight with him. We are weaklings, scared sheep. A man of death in our presence reminds of that fact. He reminds us of how ruined we are because he's brave enough to stand up for what is right. He's got heart enough to die for those he

233

loves and even for those he doesn't. There's probably no man in this village better than he."

"So, we let him die? What if I shout more Vikings are coming? They would set him free, right?"

"Damn it, boy! All right. You're worse than a nipping duck. All right. I'll go before the others and tell them what we discussed."

"Thank you! Thank you, Manny!"

"Don't get excited. They are set in their minds as solid as that standing gallows. He's dying, Sam. But they'll know your protest. Quiet yourself now. You start crying out and raising a ruckus and it will only make them quicken the hanging.

Samuel nodded. "Go, do what you can."

Manny muttered, "For whatever it's worth."

The church bell began to toll. People scurried out of their homes and the surrounding fields. Manny gathered the elders of the village to the side of the gallows. He made sweeping motions with his hands. Samuel couldn't hear what he was saying, but the expressions were those of pleading. Heads shook negatively. One man burst out laughing. Another just threw his hands in the air and walked away. Another left. Then another. Manny grabbed one man that was turning away, but the man yanked his arm from him.

Samuel's heart pounded so loud it drowned out the church bells ringing. He felt he was going to faint. This couldn't be happening.

The tolling of the church bell quickly gathered a crowd. Some brought small tables and chairs and began preparing for a picnic lunch in the square. Mothers shushed their whimpering babies. A couple of the village elders began a game of chess. Samuel felt someone staring at him and saw the little girl who had given Nathan the Hero the thistle. The girl appeared to be about five years old, yet her eyes seemed piercing and all knowing. *She's just a baby, but she knows*, Samuel thought, and gave the girl a sad smile. She patted his hand then ran back to her mother, who was preparing a table of food.

Tears began to well in Samuel's eyes. How could his people hang an innocent man? He felt faint again and reached to take Manny's arm for support.

"Oh laddie, they wouldn't listen. Try to be strong."

"He can't die. No," Samuel murmured, and wiped a sleeve across his tearing eyes.

Someone in the crowd suddenly yelled, "Murderer!"

McDonald led Nathan from the jail, his hands and feet bound in chains. The walk to the gallows steps was slow and tedious with the chains clanking with each step.

Samuel could barely catch a breath. He looked around frantically, hoping desperately to see someone or something that could be used to stop this. Everyone was here, more than a hundred people, men, women, children, dogs and even a couple of chickens ready to peck up the table scraps.

"Take the prisoner up," Chieftain Bruce said in his most officious voice.

Samuel thought he might black out. He felt as though the blood had been sucked from his body. He felt a pressure on his arm and saw Heather beside him. "I had to be here for you," she said, slipping her arm beneath his.

Nathan reached the platform and stared down at the people he had saved only a few hours earlier. They had praised him and blessed him and offered him anything he desired then. Now they wanted only to see him die. The eyes that had looked at him with gratitude and adoration were now filled with loathing and hatred. His lips curled in a smile of irony.

Judge Frasier climbed the steps and joined Nathan and the jailer McDonald, two of the men who had ridden in with him were now wearing black hoods over their heads.

"Kill him!"

"Hang the murderer!"

"Swordslinger of the innocent!"

Judge Frasier raised his right hand. "Hold it down," he said. "Settle down, folks, we have some legal stuff to get out of the way here."

He turned to Nathan. "By the finding of this court, Nathan Frasier, ye have been found guilty of murder and sentenced to be hanged by the neck until you are dead. Is there anything you would like to say in your behalf?"

Nathan seemed to ponder the words, his eyes turned in the direction of where his home would have been on the mountainside. "I do have a request," he said. "I would ask that I be allowed to take my own life with my sword."

The words shattered the shell that Samuel had tried to build around himself.

"NO!" he shouted. "You can't do this! He's innocent. He didn't kill my father!! It was an accident! He tripped and fell! You have to believe him and stop this!"

A rumble swept through the crowd. What was this?

"Silence!" Judge Frasier roared, and old man McGregor pushed his way to the front row.

"He's guilty, me Lord. I saw it with me own eyes. He struck ol' Stewart on the head and he went down like an ox. Just before he was hit, Stewart called him a murderer. And he is a murderer! I saw it!"

"You can't even see!" Samuel shouted. "You're blind as a bat, old man!"

"That's enough, boy," the judge said, anger in his voice. "This man has been tried and found guilty. If you don't be quiet, I'll have you removed."

"It's all right, Samuel," Nathan said in a voice just above a whisper.

"Kill him now!" someone from the crowd shouted, and the people took up the chant. "Now! Now! Now!"

"Eviscerate him!"

"Yeah, gut him!"

"Stretch him first!"

The judge raised his hands and the crowd grew silent. "He's dying folks. We're not barbarians. We're ready to proceed with the court's orders," he said. "McDonald, will you fetch this man's sword?"

"Aye, Judge," McDonald said and climbed down from the gallows to return to the jail.

"All right men, unbind him," the judge ordered, and the two men with the black hoods removed the chains from Nathan.

236

Samuel was a ghostly white as though the blood had drained from his body. Heather and Manny gripped his arms, supporting him. Everything that was happening was surreal for the boy. He wondered if he was dreaming.

McDonald returned with the sword and climbed the gallows steps. Nathan followed the orders of the two men holding him and dropped to his knees. McDonald raised the glistening sword high above his head, brandishing it for the crowd and drawing a cheer.

Judge Frasier took the sword from the grinning McDonald and held it before the kneeling prisoner. "Is this your blade, Nathan Frasier?"

Nathan nodded, strands of his unbound long hair falling across his face. Someone from the crowd threw a half-eaten apple and it struck the kneeling man just below his right ear.

"All right, so be it," Judge Frasier said. He motioned to the two men in the black hoods. "Draw your weapons and stand behind the prisoner. If he makes any move other than to execute himself, kill him."

The men took their positions and the judge held the sword out for Nathan to take.

"No!"

The judge held the sword and turned to see who had spoken from the crowd. Samuel recognized him as the young man with the mane of black hair who had ridden into town with the judge's group.

"Wait! My life has been a living hell because of this murderer," the man said. "I am his son and I demand the right to satisfaction by executing him myself."

There were audible gasps from the crowd. This execution was going to become a legend in the village. Nathan appeared stunned by the development.

The crowd suddenly erupted in an out roar. "Aye! Let him do it! Let his son kill him! Cut his head off! Eviscerate him!"

Judge Frasier wanted this over with quick. These people scented blood. They were barely under control.

"I have already granted the prisoner his request," he said, staring at Dexter.

"Granting the request of a victim should take precedence over the request of a murderer!" Dexter yelled.

"I'm sorry, but how are you a victim?" Judge Frazier said. "If there was a victim it would be the son of the murdered father, I would think."

"It is said he fled while my mother was being raped and he abandoned me. He has killed dozens of men. A hundred ... maybe more ... I avenge my mother. As her son, I act in her stead."

The crowd screamed its agreement.

Judge Frasier frowned, seeming taken aback by the rabid response from the people. What kind of man was Nathan to bring on such hostility? He shook his head, and then shrugged. "The court bows to your wishes," he said. "I will allow the son of Nathan Frasier to carry out the execution."

Samuel gasped. The crowd cheered. Heather buried her face in Samuel's chest. Dexter Frasier smiled and ran up the steps of the gallows. He stopped before his kneeling father and, face contorted in hatred, said, "At last my dream is coming true." He spat in his father's face. "Give me the sword!"

The crowd grew silent, fascinated by the scene playing out before them. How could a son hate a father so much?

Dexter raised the sword high in the air and drove the point into one of the platform planks. "This sword will slay no other man!" he shouted. A woman among the onlookers cried out. Dexter made a sudden movement with his hand and the blade of the sword snapped, making a ringing sound as the metal parted.

"No more, father!"

Samuel was dismayed. Nathan had told him that breaking your blade was like the breaking of your own spine and your honor. "NO!" he screamed. "Not the sword!"

Dexter whirled, his mad eyes searching out Samuel. Then holding the stare with the boy, he raised the broken sword and plunged it into the plank again, snapping off another piece. Then he repeated the act. The once magnificent blade was now in four pieces. Nathan remained on his knees, eyes on the planks.

Dexter gathered the pieces of the sword and turned back to Samuel. "You are a strange son," he said. "This man killed your father, so here, take his blade." He threw the pieces of the broken sword toward Samuel.

Dexter turned back to Nathan and drew his own sword. "Look up, dear father, he said, hatred in his voice. "Look at your son, father. Look at the son you betrayed, the son of the mother you deserted in her death. You have been condemned by this court for murder. I now condemn you for abandonment." He reached out his left hand and grabbed a fistful of hair, forcing Nathan's head back. "With the knife I gut pigs with, I now taint with a viler blood! It's time to die, father!"

Dexter brought his sword down and across, but instead of slashing his father across the throat, he brought the blade arcing across the abdomen. Nathan's eyes went wide. A wave of blood surged from the gaping wound. "Not one cut, but a dozen I'll do. Maybe a dozen more."

Dexter slashed Nathan's arm.

Nathan gasped.

"Now a leg," Nathan made a slash.

A woman fainted.

"NO!" Samuel dove toward Nathan, but hands snatched him and drew him back.

"A cut for each man that raped my mother!" Dexter made another slash. He stepped behind Nathan and jerked off his boot. "I knife you through the foot for running away." He drove the blade home. Nathan cried out, arching upward, off his knees, and then falling forward. His face turned to the side. "How about an ear for the screams you heard from my mother." Dexter sliced off an ear.

"For God's sake! Stop it! Stop it! Samuel screamed."

Samuel broke free. He lunged for the platform and Dexter's boot heel caught him in the face.

"Now one slice on the throat like I do the pigs. Die now." Dexter cut Nathan's throat.

The crowd let out a collective cheer, and then just as suddenly grew silent, as though they had awakened from a frenzied trance. Expressions of excitement suddenly turned to horror. Several women gasped.

Dexter stepped back and dropped the sword to his side. He sat on the edge of the platform like a young boy fishing from a pier. He leaned on an elbow and watched his dying father.

Nathan's lips were drawn taut over his teeth and the body was tense. He began to gasp, bubbles of blood frothing on his lips. A tear appeared in the corner of one eye and trickled down his cheek. His eyes moved across the crowd and found Samuel. He moved his head slightly as if wanting to say something. Then an expression of calm came over his face and he smiled at the boy. There was love in his eyes when they closed for the last time.

"Oh, God," Samuel whispered, trying to rise from the ground. His head was in Heather's lap. He was seeing double and he couldn't breathe through his nose. "Oh, God, why did this happen? Let me up! Let me up!" Samuel wailed.

Heather and Manny eased him back down to the ground.

"No, Sam. No. It's over. There's nothing you can do," Heather whispered in his ear.

Samuel heard something fall and land against his leg. He tried to see but his eyes were swollen shut.

"There's the knife. You keep it," Dexter said. "Justice served." He walked away.

Samuel rose to his feet. He climbed on the platform and went to Nathan's body. He placed his head against Nathan's and cried.

"Priest... priest are you here?" Samuel asked.

"Aye, lad."

"Prepare a coffin for Nathan. Put him on a wagon tomorrow morning for me. I will pay."

"If that is your wish, son. The wagon will be behind the church."

"Aye." Samuel ran his hand through Nathan's hair and pressed his swollen face against that of his slain friend.

Heather placed her arms around him, trying to comfort him, and forced him to turn away from the platform. The crowd had dispersed. Some of the men were heading for the pub, talking among themselves about the way Dexter had killed his own father. The tables were heavy with food left untouched. Only the flies feasted.

The three began walking away, but Samuel suddenly stopped and pulled away from the others. "Wait." He ran to the platform where the priest was watching as two men placed Nathan's bloody corpse into a wooden coffin. He approached the priest and showed him a handful of gold coins. "I want to bury the body," he said. The priest looked into the boy's eyes and said, "I understand." He took the coins and pocketed them.

"I'll be back for him later today."

"Very well, my son, I'll have the coffin placed behind the church."

Samuel mumbled, "Thank you," and rejoined Heather and Manny.

"Samuel," Manny said, "you stay at our home tonight. Let's take care of your face. You have your father's funeral in the morning."

"My father is dead. Nathan is dead?

"Aye. Both are," Heather answered.

"I'm dead inside," Samuel muttered.

CHAPTER 30

THE FUNERALS

The next morning the villagers were gathered again, this time in the vestibule of the church for the funeral of one of their own, Stewart Donachee. The Reverend McFarley said a few words, praising the life of the man who had been the village ironsmith. He made no mention of the man's drinking. All the while, Nathan's body was wrapped in cloth on a wagon waiting behind the church.

"Stewart was a good man who suffered a terrible loss in the untimely death of his wife," the Reverend said. "He was a good father to his two sons and he was the finest ironsmith in the Highlands. Our prayers today are for the sons he leaves with us. God bless ye, Stewart Donachee. May ye live in peace in the Heaven above. Amen.

"Samuel, as the eldest son, you may speak."

Samuel stood behind the podium. His hands trembled. Before him was yesterday's lynch mob. The whole village was here. Robert, Heather and her parents sat on the front row with both of his grandmothers.

"My father gave his all to his trade as a blacksmith. He loved my mother dearly and when she died, I think part of him died too. It was hard on him to raise Robert and me and to keep a business going too. But, somehow, he did it. We all know he had a problem, but I think it was all related to being lonely. And when I look at myself and my brother, well, we turned out okay. I hope when my father opens his eyes again, my mother will be standing before him. That will be his heaven. We will miss him."

Samuel cleared his throat and swallowed dryly. "Now...," he stopped to force back the tears. His voice trembled. "Maybe this isn't the proper place or time to say this, but I have to. Yesterday we executed an innocent man. A man I had briefly known but had loved as I loved my own father. When my father drank, he fell down. He fell down a lot and I know, I know with all my heart that Nathan, the

Swordslinger, would never have struck out against my father. He was not that kind of man. He put his life on the line for this village and us when not one of us cared enough to defend it for ourselves. And now he is dead ... cut down by a ruffian son in the most hideous, dishonorable way imaginable. I've never witnessed such evil. I know all of you felt the same. That's why the tables of food were left untouched.

"So, think what you will about the Swordslinger, but God knows the truth. So do I. If I were you, I'd hang my head low. For what we did yesterday was as great a sin as the first in Eden. All will be forever changed here. It has for me."

He walked from the podium and stopped beside Heather. She took his hand and patted it. Robert took his other hand.

They walked to the casket and viewed their father for the final time. Stewart appeared to be sleeping and Samuel reached out a hand to touch his face. He stood with bowed head, his weeping brother beside him, and said his goodbyes.

"We miss you, father, but we know you'll still be looking out for us. We weren't very good in our roles as father and son, but we loved each other. A good man gave his life today that you might be remembered in honor. I hope now that you can understand how things really were. Goodbye, father."

Samuel turned and started to walk away.

"Wait!" Robert pulled his hand free and returned to the casket. He took a small hammer from his pocket and placed it on his father's chest. "You should always have your hammer, father."

The six pallbearers carried the casket from the church to the wagon out front and a stream of villagers formed a procession to the cemetery on the western outskirts of the town. Dexter Frasier and some of his friends were grouped beside the road and watched the funeral procession pass. The eyes of Samuel and Dexter met as they passed, but there was no communication between the two sons who had become fatherless within a few hours of each other. Dexter said something; and, the others laughed loudly as the wagon rolled past the group.

The Reverend McFarley offered a short prayer over the grave. Then a woman from the church choir sang one of Stewart's favorite hymns. Another short prayer followed and a chorus of "amens" finalized the ceremony. The casket was lowered into the freshly dug grave and the Reverend McFarley handed a shovel to Samuel. The boy drove the spade into the heap of reddish dirt and tossed it onto the top of the casket. He passed the shovel to Robert and the youngster repeated the act, tears running down his face. After each of the pallbearers threw a shovel of dirt into the grave, people began drifting away.

Moments later, only Samuel, Robert and Heather remained. They stood silently for a few moments until the gravedigger began filling the hole, then turned and walked back to the village.

The boys' home was filled with people when they arrived. The first thing Samuel did was go to his room and sit on the edge of the mattress. He opened his sporran and held the broken pieces of Nathan's sword.

Some of the visitors had brought flowers, but most had brought food. Samuel had not eaten since the afternoon before, but he still had no appetite. A neighbor woman volunteered to come over later and clean the house. Another offered to teach Samuel to cook some simple meals. He didn't tell her that he had been preparing most of his meals for years.

Samuel heard all the well wishes and the kind offers of aid and comfort. None spoke of Nathan. He was functioning in a daze. Everything was blurred; out of focus. He was still trying to sort through everything that had happened in the past couple of days and find some normalcy. He couldn't help thinking that these people who were making all these kind and generous offers were the same ones who had cheered as Nathan was being executed.

One by one, the people took their leave until only Manny and Heather remained. Manny put an arm around Samuel's shoulders and pulled the boy to him. "It's been a long, hard day," he said. "Heather and I will go with you to bury Nathan. The wife is having trouble with her legs today and asks if ye will forgive her for not going."

"I understand. Thank you for being here."

Manny nodded and patted the boy on the back. Heather leaned over and kissed his cheek. "You two ride the wagon. Heather and I will follow behind. Right now, we'll give the two of you some time to yourselves."

When they were alone, Samuel sliced two apples and gave Robert one, along with a chunk of cheese. They sat quietly, eating and lost in their own thoughts.

"It doesn't seem right without father," Robert finally said, breaking the silence.

"I know. It's going to take a while for us, Robert. But we'll be okay. We can manage. Look, it's dark outside with the clouds. You coming with me to bury Nathan?"

"Where you going to bury him?"

"We're going to take Nathan to his homestead on the mountainside and bury him there."

Father McFarley loaned the boys the funeral wagon and helped them load the coffin.

"This is a kind and decent thing you do, lad," the Reverend said. "And what you said at the funeral, I pray that God knows this man is innocent and will allow him through the gates of Heaven. God knows the truth. He will make the judgment."

"Then I have reason to be happy," Samuel said. "Thank ye, Father."

"Samuel," Father McFarley whispered, "You understand I can't go. He was convicted. My presiding over his funeral I'm afraid would cause a riot. I am with you in prayer. And though I am not at the gravesite, I will be here and I will perform the ceremony in my heart and to God."

"Nathan will appreciate that, Father." Samuel clucked to the horse and guided the animal to the livery stable. He pulled the horse to a stop, Then he and Robert dismounted and transferred a dozen stones from the wagonload that was to have built Nathan's house.

This time they proceeded without stopping to the home site Nathan had selected. Some of the villagers watched them. When they approached, they lowered their heads.

Within minutes, the wagon was traveling up the side of the mountain. The air was damp. Dark, brooding clouds piled upon themselves. The breeze smelled of rain and fresh peat. The horse strained under the load a couple of times during the climb, but less than an hour later, they had reached their destination.

"Okay," Samuel said. "Now we get to work." Samuel began unloading the stones set around the casket. When he reached the bottom of one pile of stones, he found a small standing stone. Words were carved into its face.

Nathan Frasier

Husband to Shelley

Defender of us all.

"Father McFarley must have done this last night," Samuel said, his eyes tearing. It took more than an hour for the boys to dig a suitable hole in the hard mountain earth. Samuel wiped his brow and walked over to Manny and Heather. "Take the wagon back to town. We will be a while still and the sun is setting."

"God bless you, Samuel," Manny said. "You have grown to be a fine man."

"I love you, Samuel," Heather said and gave him a hug.

Samuel glanced at the sky. Since they had been working, the wind had picked up and had moved the clouds eastward. The sun was setting in the west. Golden streams of light made paths across the sky and illuminated the purple undersides of the clouds.

"Och, a proper setting if ever they be one," Robert said, following Samuel's gaze.

"Peace in the valley," Samuel whispered. "Take a deep breath. The air is so fresh."

Robert inhaled deeply. "It is."

"What a beautiful night it will be," Samuel said, almost seeming to be talking to himself. "Look at the moon behind the clouds."

"I see it."

"I wish Nathan could see this. This is what he wanted and he was so close. Well, let's get started."

The casket was too heavy for them to lift, so they both got on one end and pulled it to the opening in the ground. They paused and Samuel opened the lid of the coffin. He went to the wagon and brought back the pieces of the broken sword. With tears in his eyes, he placed the sword on Nathan's chest and bowed his head. "Honor restored," he whispered. A moment later, he closed the lid. They used ropes to lower the casket into the hole.

"That's good," Samuel said to his brother. "Sit down. I can do the rest." He shoveled the dirt back into the hole and rounded the top off with a slight mound. Then he placed the stones on the mound. He made one last trip to the wagon and brought back the small headstone that the Reverend McFarley had provided. He dug a small hole at the head of the grave and placed the stone in it. He sat on the ground and put his arms around the headstone. Robert sat on the wagon seat, watching him.

"You're home now," Samuel said to the grave. "You have your sword and you're with your beloved wife. Tell Shelley I said hello, and tell her about God Eeshebob and how we scared the Manteo Brothers and the Vikings away. And tell her that you did have one son who loved you. As long as I shall live, you will be remembered and loved (his voice broke and tears began flowing) and you will be honored. And one day, I promise to find the ground where Shelley's dust lies. I will bring it here and make a grave for her by you where she is meant to be."

Samuel lost track of the time as he sat at the gravesite. Robert curled up against a boulder behind him. "Hey, see that star there, Samuel pointed.

"Aye."

"Swordslinger said that was the Shelley star. He swore he had never seen it before in his life until the night he buried her. He said that was her spirit shining for him, letting him know she was all right. And if he was ever lost, she was the direction to the south."

"Does father have a star?" Robert asked.

"Aye, I imagine he has. You just have to look up there and find it."

"I'm scared, Samuel. I'm scared you will be taken away somehow and I'll be all alone." Samuel put his hand against Robert's cheek and began to recite in a singsong voice:

"Such a fair man was he...
a man of honor, a man that was free
he married a good wife, they had a son
and though his life was with strife
he was a hero to the young
For many a battle he stood and fought
defending the weak, he never balked
He was the Swordslinger, his life be praised
he was the law-bringer, a savior in his day
And though he was slain and wrongly judged
God above will give him love
May he rest in peace, his sword intact
may god give him heaven for each of his acts
He was the Swordslinger, his life be praised
There's a place in heaven where his soul will be raised
And though we will miss him, our hearts filled with tears
We will meet him in heaven and give him great cheer"

Samuel wiped tears away with his sleeve and looked over the valley to the peaceful setting of the village, whose fires twinkled like earthly stars

.

CHAPTER 31

SHANE AND THE WILD RIDE

The Swordslinger groped for reality as he struggled to rouse himself from sleep. Images of Nathan, Heather, Robert, his father flickered through his subconscious. The grief from losing his family and loved ones was still fresh, the images vivid. He shook his head and rubbed his face to rid himself of the thoughts. He was in another place and another time, but no distance was far enough from SkyeEden to free him from the haunting memories.

It was almost dawn so he reasoned he must have slept for several hours. He glanced around, surveying the area. It appeared that he was in a valley, thick with trees and undergrowth. He couldn't see a road, just trees. Was he back in SkyeEden? He wasn't aware places like this existed in America.

He regained his bearings slowly and began formulating a plan. Mount Mitchell was due west. Okay. That was still many miles away and it could be hours before he could get there if he was unable to find transportation. It was probably too late anyway. Dexter seemed to always be a step ahead of him and the bastard had probably already taken Manny's stone. God, was it never going to end? The Swordslinger lowered his head, his shoulders sagging in defeat. All of his loved ones were dead because of this man and he was still killing. It was doubtful that Dexter even killed for the stones anymore, but probably just because it was something he enjoyed. The man had killed his own father. Was there anyone he wouldn't kill?

Samuel stretched his right arm out and looked at his hand. "Come out, Draconis," he said, and the flow of mercury oozed from his fingertips and formed the trusty blade. "I'll be needing you today, old and faithful friend." He rose to his feet and faced west. Time to go. He slashed the blade at some vines barring his path and began moving.

The way Samuel figured it, his only hope for finding Manny alive was if he was away from home and Dexter had been unable to find him as of yet, or that Dexter might be so confident in his quest that he was taking some down time. He quickened his pace, almost trotting through the wooded vale. His boots caught ivy and thorn vines, but he refused to slow the pace. It was already near 80 degrees in the warm Carolina morning and his shirt was beginning to dampen with perspiration. A huge spider web blocked his path and he destroyed it with an impatient sweep of his hand, sending a long-legged spider scurrying through the brush. The ground was uneven, dotted with fist-sized rocks. A long black snake looking for some early sun slithered off through the rocks.

Too late! He had spent too much time evading the police. And losing his Winnebago and Harley could have been avoided. Why hadn't he parked the motor home and ridden the motorcycle? Bad decisions. It must be at least 50 miles to Mount Mitchell. He had to find a road and some transportation. Just keep moving. The road had to be near. … What was that sound? Running water? A few more steps and he saw it, a huge stream bubbling merrily on its way. Great. Now what was he going to do?

The stream was flowing rapidly downhill, curling as far as he could see in both directions. How deep is it? "Well, at least it's no Loch Myst." He should be able to find a way across it. He followed the stream in a northwest direction for almost an hour. Then he heard it, the rumble of a diesel straining to climb an upgrade. A few more yards and he could see a blur of movement through the wall of trees. Cars! A highway! Transportation!

A chance.

Running, he broke through the last of the trees and found himself on a curve in the highway. He rounded the curve and saw cars parked a alongside the road a few hundred yards ahead. The first sign read "Apples." The second said "Pure Mountain Apple Cider." The third one said "Watermelons." People were gathered around the stand, sorting through the fruit and vegetables. No one even looked toward the Swordslinger as he approached.

He tried to gather himself, imagining how bedraggled he must look after his rush through the woods. He straightened his shirt and brushed a hand though the long black hair.

The middle-aged couple was looking at a watermelon, the man thumping the rind in an effort to learn if it was ripe.

"Forgive me, sir. Sorry about my appearance, but I've had an automobile accident and I'm a mess. I'm meeting some friends at Mount Mitchell and wonder if you could give me a lift."

The man looked up, his eyes narrowing. His wife threw him a cautioning glance. "Get lost, bud," the man said, and thumped the melon again.

"Hey, man." Samuel turned and saw a young fellow in his late twenties motioning to him. The man was wearing a light blue work shirt with the name Shane stitched over the left pocket and a pair of blue jeans. His face was covered with a thick, shaggy beard and his hair hung several inches down his back.

"You need a lift, buddy? I need some bread. I wasn't going that way, but I'll run you to Mount Mitchell for 50 bucks."

Samuel wasn't about to argue. "Deal," he said.

Okay, right over here." The man pointed to antique faded-orange Volkswagen van. "C'mon, let's get moving. Let's see the moola."

"Moola?"

The bearded man laughed, showing tobacco-stained teeth. "You're not from around here, huh, buddy? Okay, just hand over the fifty bucks unless you're jivin' my ass. If you are, then go back and help that old fart pick out a watermelon."

"Hold on," the Swordslinger pulled out his wallet and handed the man a crisp $50 bill.

"Cool, Dude. You all right. Name's Shane. Peace." He gave the V sign, then held out his hand.

Samuel smiled and raised his hand; fingers spread in a V, and then shook the grease-stained hand. "Peace."

Shane started the van and pulled onto the road. "Man, don't see your type around here much. You look like something out of the fifties, man."

"More like out of this world," Samuel murmured.

"Yeah, I could almost believe that, man. Well, hang on here, the clutch in this old piece of shit is a little sensitive and she lurches sometimes. But she'll make it to Mount Mitchell. I think. If she don't, we'll be close anyway."

"Fine. Don't mean to rush you, but I'm meeting someone there and I'm already late. I ran my car over ledge a few miles back."

"Wow! Over a ledge, huh? That's a bitch, man."

Samuel gave the driver a quizzical look. Shane laughed. "Dude, I know what your (lurch) problem is." He fumbled with clutch and gearshift, finally getting into the lower gear.

"There. Sometimes she's a little stubborn. Hey, open the glove compartment and hand me that plastic bag. You want a tote of du-be-wa?"

"A what of what?"

"Oh, man, you really are like off the planet. Mary ja wana. Mary J. Pot."

"Smoke a pot? All right." Samuel reached into the glove compartment and took out the small bag. Sorry. No pot here, just these fags."

"Whoa, Dude! Hope you ain't tryin' to tell me something 'cause I got a serious phobia against fags!"

"It's okay. I won't light one up."

"This?" Samuel held out a rolled joint.

"Yeah, man. Whoo-wee! Ha, ha. I think you're just naturally stoned, Dude."

"Stoned?" Samuel's eyes lit up. He cast a quick glance down at his chest.

"High. Dizzy. Drunk. Wasted," Shane continued. "What country are (lurch) you from?"

"SkyeEden," Samuel said, exasperated.

"Aaaah, I know that place. That's somewhere in the Middle East. Adam and Eve. Eden."

"Highlands."

"Oh, yeah, Dude. Highlands … yeah, Scotland, the wee leprechaun country. Wales, Braveheart and Rob Roy. Yeah, I got you there."

Samuel opened his mouth to say something, then shut it again and stared out the window trying to stabilize the dizziness this Shane character was causing him.

Lurch.

"Sorry, man."

They had been driving for almost exactly an hour when Samuel saw the sign:

Mount Mitchell

2 miles

In the distance, he could see the black mountain's peak, partially blanketed in fog. The temperature was 10 degrees lower than it had been at Table Rock and the road was now a steep grade.

Lurch.

Gears grinding.

"C'mon, baby, baby. You can-can little train can up this hill," Shane said, patting the console of his van. The speedometer needle jiggled around 15 miles an hour. Samuel could see Shane's foot pressing the accelerator to the floor.

Lurch.

"C'mon, sweetie-pie in my eye. Make this hill!" Shane had the van in second gear. Grind. Grind. Speedometer was heading left fast. "Woo-wee, man, I think that's about as far as she's going. I'll try holding the brake down long enough for you to jump out. Ain't got no emergency brakes."

"Swell. Thanks, Shane. Pleasure talking; with you."

"Hey, I hang out by the stand there. It's my parent's place. You ever want to do a toke of smoke, bloke, I'll be at the poke."

"Yeah, right. See ya," Samuel opened the door and almost fell as the van began rolling backwards.

"Slip sliding away, Dude. Gotta turn Missy around."

"Good luck!" Samuel waved and began walking up the grade. "Poke? Toke? Mary J?" Stopping, he let out a deep breath and looked around, gathering his bearings. Up ahead on the right was a trooper building; and, just up the hill from

253

that, a narrow road led into the woods with a sign reading, CAMPGROUND. Either Manny was there or had found a little niche in the woods to call his own. How did he survive up here? Food wasn't exactly hanging off the trees. Okay, take the road. It's still heading up the mountain.

Oh, Manny, please. Please be okay.

CHAPTER 32

THESE STONES HAVE EYES

Dexter Frasier stood on the lookout tower of Mount Mitchell, his long jet-black hair blowing in the wind, and surveyed the area. On a clear day, a view of 30 miles was not uncommon and he cursed the weather that limited his vision. He was on the tower with half a dozen tourists, who were oohing and aahing over the view, as limited as it was. *Silly asses*, he thought.

Despite the patches of fog obscuring the view, Dexter was still able to see the winding road that led to the summit. Impatient by nature, he fretted as he watched and waited for something that would arouse his senses. "Where are you?" he muttered to himself. "What's taking you so long?" The anxiety was building inside of him as he paced around the small viewing area.

Then he caught a glimpse of an orange van between some trees and the hair on the back of his neck stood up. He watched the old van laboring to climb the hill until it disappeared behind more trees. A few moments later, the van reappeared, this time coasting backwards down the hill. Now what? Had his senses been wrong? Something was awry.

No, his senses for this kind of thing were too sharply honed to be wrong. His cruel lips formed a sneering smile as he glanced at the tourists around him. They were huddled together, studying the display maps and trying to decide which mountain was which. Fat slobs! A waste. Worthless. Stoneless. He spat in contempt and moved to the stairs, walking quickly to the bottom of the tower, and found himself somewhat winded when he reached the ground level. Was he getting soft, too? Hah!

Dexter moved to a small copse of trees near the tower and, making sure he was out of sight of the tourists, raised his right arm and summoned his sword. The long blade spewed from his fingers in liquid metal and formed in his hand. The solid steel felt reassuring and he swished it through the air.

"Ahh," he murmured. "Good to have you back, Stone Reaper." He stroked the blade with his fingers. I need your eyes, my faithful servant. Send your stones aloft and seek out our enemy Samuel Donachee. Show him to me!"

Dexter opened his hand and the sword remained floating in the air. "Become my eyes!" The blade of the sword suddenly disintegrated into a dozen stones and the hilt liquefied and melded back into his hand. The stones floated above, each with an open eye scouring the surrounding terrain. Dexter moved to one of the trees and leaned against it for support. He closed his eyes and concentrated, waiting for the vision that he knew would be forthcoming.

The stones rose higher and began moving away in different directions.

"Find him," Dexter said. "I will wait."

CHAPTER 33

MANNY'S HOME

Samuel walked along the graveled road cut through the woods on the side of the mountain and marveled at how much this place reminded him of SkyeEden. The mountains appeared as suspended dark oceanic waves reflecting purplish on the storm clouds overhead.

Dexter was near; he could feel the evil. In a way that was good, because the longer the murderer was away from SkyeEden, the fewer of those good people he could slay. But the concern now was for Manny, the father of his bride and the man who had become his guardian after the death of his own father.

Manny had reluctantly done a Rippling a few months earlier and escaped to Mount Mitchell. He hoped that Dexter's nightmarish quest for stones would end one day so he would be able to return to his homeland safely.

Samuel's mind returned to the day of the execution of Nathan and he vividly relived the moment as Dexter snapped his father's sword into pieces and slashed him to death with his own blade. How could any man be so cold and cruel? What drove Dexter to be so evil and to kill another man with such contempt merely to possess their stones? Although some men bravely tried to defend themselves, none had been a match for the black-haired madman and his bloody blade. He seemed intent on seeing every man in the McGuire clan dead.

Manny had helped Samuel build a stone home on the site that Nathan had chosen the day before his death. He and Heather had planned to move into the stone home as husband and wife. That act alone had been enough to place Manny on the death-list of Dexter. Now it was time to repay some of the favors Manny had bestowed upon him over the years. He had to find Dexter and stop him before he killed again. "Please, God."

Samuel entered a cleared area that was being used as a parking and camping ground. A huge Winnebago was parked to one side. Someone had dug a hole in the earth and built a primitive grill, an iron grate keeping the meat from the fire below it. Wisps of smoke still came from the embers. A narrow path led from the site into the woods.

Three one-man pup tents stood on the other side of the clearing and outside each was a cooler. Several crushed beer cans littered the area around a large trash barrel. Someone's aim was a little off. Over to one side stood a larger tent, its opening facing the road. A man's foot protruded from the door flap, tapping the ground to the beat of country music emanating from a radio. The bluegrass song featured fiddles and banjos. Someone inside the tent issued a hearty "Yee-Haw!"

Samuel smiled and followed the path into the trees. He was sure he would recognize Manny's home when he saw it. He had walked only a few hundred yards when he found it. A stack of stones was piled alongside the trail. "Ah, Manny, always the stone mason." He hurried his step, making another turn through the thick spruces and the small stone hut came into view. The roof was slanted and covered with a layer of branches. A few yards away from the house was an outdoor grill also built of stone.

The scene was peaceful, but something troubled Samuel. He raised his arm and summoned the sword. "Draconis!" The blade solidified in his hands and he cautiously approached the hut. His skin felt cold. He reached the hut and shoved the door open. There was no sound. No movement. Then he heard a low buzzing.

"Manny!" No answer. "Manny, it's Samuel." No answer. The buzzing was louder. He stepped inside and froze. Had it not been for a small section of gray hair remaining on the scalp, Samuel would not have recognized the fly-covered mass on the floor as being a man. The charred remains on the floor were spread eagled, although the arms and legs had been burned into twisted remnants.

The walls of the hut were covered in blood splatters. It was obvious that Manny had been slaughtered like an animal. Several fist-sized chunks of burned flesh were scattered over the floor. The killer had opened Manny up like a gutted pig and allowed him to live while his organs were being removed. As Manny had been living in this country for months, his body had adapted to the environment and had not incinerated like the others Samuel wondered how long it would take. Maybe never.

Samuel felt himself becoming sick. He leaned against the doorframe and slowly slid to a sitting position on the floor. He was numb. Damn! He had failed again. Dexter always won. Would it never end? Poor Manny. He had been like a father to Samuel and now he was gone, too. First Heather and now her father. "Must I always be too late?"

What kind of monster would disembowel a man while he was still alive? Dexter, of course. The man was evil. He had no conscience, no feeling for his fellow men. He had killed Manny in this brutal fashion to evoke the worst possible emotions in Samuel when he found the body. This was a gift to Samuel from Dexter — the father killer.

A red rage rose in Samuel. He felt the familiar blinding anger building against Dexter. The bastard was killing everyone he had ever loved. The only way it would end would be with the death of Dexter. Or his own death.

"I'm sorry, Heather," Samuel moaned. "I swore to you that I would protect your father and I have failed. I'm so sorry." He rose to his feet, tears running down his cheeks, and raised his sword. "DEXTER! You are a dead man!"

He turned to the charred corpse on the floor of the hut and said, "I'll bury you, Manny. Then I'm going hunting." Swordslinger turned back to the door; and, then for the first time saw the bloody scrawl on the wall. Written in blood, it read:

Come to the tower

Dex.

"Don't worry, 'Dex'," he said. "I'll be there." He took off his long coat and rolled what was left of Manny's charred body onto it, then collected the scattered body parts and added them to the bundle. He went outside and found a shovel in the bed of Manny's old Ford pickup among several other tools of the stonemason's trade. He took the shovel and a chisel and went grave digging.

Almost an hour later, he had dug the hole deep enough. He lowered the bundle that had been Manny into the grave. Then he placed the chisel on top of the bundle. "I'm sure you'll find a use for this," he said, then bowed his head and stood silently over the grave for a moment.

"I'll come back for you," he promised. I'll take you to be with your wife and daughter, Manny. You will rest in SkyeEden."

It took the better part of another hour for Samuel to shovel the dirt back into the grave. It was tiring work and his shirt was plastered to his back with perspiration. He finally finished, smoothed off the surface into a small mound, wiped the sweat from his brow and sat down to think. From where he was sitting, he could see the peak of Mount Mitchell and the lookout tower. He sighed, gathered himself and went back into the stone hut. He found the keys to the Ford pickup and within moments was behind the wheel, heading in the direction of the tower.

If Samuel had looked up, he could have seen the two stones floating along, one on either side of the pickup as it climbed the mountain. The eyes were unblinking as they conveyed the image back to their master.

CHAPTER 34

THE TOWER

Dexter was having trouble controlling his emotions. He had watched through the eyes of the stones as Samuel had buried the old man's remains and now the stupid clod was driving right into the trap. He rubbed his hands gleefully and summoned his sword again. The "Stone Reaper" flowed from his fingers and formed into the gleaming blade that he worshipped. Dexter hefted the solid weight in his hands and shifted the sword from hand-to-hand as he waited. This was going to be good. He was going to enjoy spilling the blood of this old foe.

"I know where you are," Dexter said aloud. "Keep coming." He held the blade aloft and the stones returned, melding into the gleaming blade. When the last stone had returned, he slipped the sword beneath his coat and returned to the tower. There were eight flights of stairs to reach the top, but a cool breeze was blowing and he made it up without even breathing hard.

"Sorry folks," he said loudly. "Tower closes at five."

One of the tourists who was pointing out the sights to his wife and young son looked up in irritation.

"The sign says it's open till seven."

"Yes, normally it is, but we're closing early today for maintenance." Dexter flashed an apologetic smile at the man.

"Well, okay. But somebody should have warned us. We just got here."

"Sorry, sir, but we'll be open regular hours again tomorrow."

"Yeah, always tomorrow." The disgruntled tourists began descending the stairs and Dexter turned his attention to the road leading up the mountain. The white Ford pickup was almost to the top.

"This is too easy," Dexter said, laughing.

Samuel steered the pickup into the parking lot as a new mini-van pulled out. The man driving was mouthing something to his wife, while the boy in the back seat was looking bored. Only two vehicles remained in the parking lot, a red Mustang convertible and a white Chevrolet Silverado pickup with a green National Park Ranger decal on the door. The ranger was probably making himself comfortable behind a desk, sipping a last cup of coffee and waiting for closing time.

Samuel stopped the battered pickup in one of the parking spaces near the tower steps and began walking toward them when he spotted Dexter far above on the viewing deck.

Got you now! he thought, and quickened his pace. Dexter was standing at the top, staring down at him, a mocking smile on his face. Samuel wanted to run up the stairs, but decided he had better save his strength. He didn't want to reach the top and be winded. He summoned his sword and held it at the ready. His heart pounded with excitement. His shoes hitting the metal stairs emitted a hollow metallic sound. Everything was magnified and moving in slow motion. This was the moment he had dreamed of. There was no way for Dexter to escape. The only exit from the tower was down these steps. The killing was going to end today.

Only the metal door that closed the stairs off from the observation deck stood between the two old enemies. Samuel placed his hand on the door handle and yelled "DEXTER!" as he yanked it open. It was already too late when he saw the booted foot coming, catching him in the chest and sending him staggering backwards. He landed on his back on the stair landing and realized he had dropped his sword. He could see Draconis several feet above him on one of the steps.

"You called?" Dexter was gloating. A mirthless grin covered his face. He stood at the top of the stairs, his sword held casually before him. "How does it feel to know you are moments from death, Donachee? Frankly, I thought you would be more of a challenge. This is so easy that I'm disappointed. Tell you what; to make it a little more interesting, why don't you kneel before me as your good friend Nathan did and let me carve your guts out?"

Samuel regained his feet and retrieved his sword from the stairs. He was surprised that Dexter hadn't charged him while he was down. Maybe the bastard was feeling just a little too cocky.

"Oh, I'll come to you," he said, climbing the stairs again. Dexter laughed aloud and returned to the deck, slamming the metal door behind him.

"Let's do it right, then," Dexter yelled. "Let's do it on top of the world! Come on up, my bleeding heart of a woman!"

Once again, Samuel clutched the door handle. This time he took no chances of catching a boot and quickly moved onto the deck. The quick movement saved his life as Dexter's sword clanged against the wall only inches from his head.

There was a narrow catwalk that circled the deck and Dexter was on it, waiting with the demented smile still on his face. Samuel stepped onto the catwalk and Dexter took a couple of steps toward him, lifting his sword with both hands, holding it over his shoulder like a baseball player awaiting a pitch.

"I can't wait to add your stones to my collection," Dexter said. "You may even enjoy it. I'm sure it will be like a family reunion for you."

Samuel assumed a fighting pose and muttered between clenched teeth, "You want me, bring it on." His long hair was fluttering in the stiff breeze.

"Aye, that I will." Dexter took a slow step forward, and then lunged, making a pass with his blade from bottom left to high right. Samuel easily countered the strike, the swords clanging as they met. "Lucky," Dexter said, laughing.

"Do you dream of me, Donachee? I would think you might. You know, I've lost count of your family members that I've killed. But each one has been a pleasure. I've been wanting to spill your blood since the day on the gallows when I gutted Nathan the Coward.

263

Samuel lunged, making a shoulder level swing, but Dexter nonchalantly blocked the blow. Their swords pressed against each other. Their faces were only inches apart as they strained for an advantage.

"How does it feel to know that inside me is your brother Robert, your Nathan, and your Heather?"

Samuel grunted and lunged, shoving Dexter off balance, but the man was quick on his feet and quickly squared up again. That's when the shout from below echoed through the tower.

"Hey, you two! Stop that! Now!" The woman's voice reverberated through the building.

Dexter ignored the shout. "Ahh, I see you're a little sensitive …" Dexter dropped to his knees and swung his blade at Samuel's ankles, who avoided the slash by leaping into the air. When he landed, Dexter shouldered him in the knees. The force sent him reeling backwards and for a second, Samuel thought he was going over the rails. He regained his balance, brought his sword up and blocked Dexter's chopping blade.

The woman's voice was louder and more authoritative this time. "FREEZE NOW! PUT DOWN YOUR WEAPONS OR I'LL SHOOT!"

Dexter pushed himself back from Samuel and moved to a position where he could see the woman. It was a park ranger and she was holding a pistol with both hands, pointing in their direction. Dexter laughed, then whirled and ran to the center of the tower, out of the ranger's view.

Samuel rose to his feet and checked his position. Dexter was somewhere on the tower and the ranger was on the ground, making threatening noises and gestures. He cocked his head to one side, listening for Dexter's movements. The ranger had a pistol pointed in his direction, but Dexter was the one to fear. But where was he? Nothing. Not a sound from his adversary. Moments passed.

Samuel glanced at the woman, who seemed uncertain what to do next. He slowly began working his way around the tower balcony, tensing for an attack from the lurking Dexter. He heard a sound and looked up, just in time to see

Dexter in mid leap. The momentum forced both men to the concrete flooring and Samuel was temporarily stunned. The weight of Dexter and the concrete floor had forced the breath from his body in one huge "whoosh." Everything went black for a moment. He reached for his sword and Dexter kicked it out of his reach. He was still down and Dexter was standing above him, the point of his sword stinging as it was pressed against Samuel's left shoulder blade.

"Think about your death," Dexter said, a maniacal grin on his face. "I'm going to press this blade into your body until it punctures a lung. Then as you're beginning to drown on your own blood, I'll do the other lung. Think about how that's going to feel, Samuel. You'll have plenty of time to think because I'm going to it slowly, the way I did with Manny.

Samuel felt the point of the blade begin to penetrate his skin. "Go to hell," he said.

"Aye, that I will," Dexter said, laughing. "And when I do, I will use your stone as a token. He increased the pressure on the blade.

Samuel's face went ghostly white as the pain swept over him. He could feel the point against the bone of the shoulder blade.

"Just a little more pressure to let you feel the blade against bone," Dexter said, "then I'll take it into the lung. You're going …"

The tower door suddenly flew open and the young park ranger burst through, her weapon leveled at Dexter's chest. "Drop it!" she said. "Drop the weapon or you're a dead man."

Dexter issued a demonic laugh. "Oh, lassie, you have such rotten timing!" He lowered the sword and backed away from Samuel, who rose to his hands and knees and reached for his sword.

"Oh, no you don't!" The ranger stopped Samuel with a steely glare.

Dexter took advantage of the ranger's focus on Samuel and spun around to face the tower rails. "See you!" he yelled and threw his sword into the air, jumped to the top railing and leapt from the tower. "Another day, Samuel!"

The park ranger ran to the railing in time to see a flash of light below. The man had disappeared. What was going on here? "Did you see that?" she said, staring at Samuel.

Samuel wasn't talking, he was groaning. The wound in his back was bleeding profusely and the searing pain was getting worse.

"Relax, mister, and let me take a look at that."

Samuel sat on the floor and the woman bent over him. "Sorry," she said, placing a pair of handcuffs on his wrists, "but I don't trust you."

Samuel looked up at his benefactor and tried to smile. It was more of an ugly wince. The ranger unbuttoned his shirt and pulled it down around his waist. Samuel noticed from the park ranger badge she was wearing that her name was Tammy Swain. She dabbed at the wound with a piece of his torn shirt and he flinched.

"Sorry," she said. "What was going on here? You guys having a duel or something?"

"Something."

"Well, you shouldn't have picked my tower. Hey, you're going to need some stitches for this. It's pretty nasty. The bleeding's stopped, but we need to get you to a doctor. Can you climb down the stairs to my truck?"

When Samuel nodded, Ranger Swain continued, "I'll take you to the hospital and then we're going to play some question and answer stuff, okay? Like for example, what were you two guys doing on my tower? And why you were trying to kill each other. And where the hell did that guy go? Nobody just vanishes into thin air."

When they reached the bottom of the stairs, Ranger Swain silently motioned for Samuel to wait and she drew her gun and stepped outside. No sign of the other guy. She circled the tower and saw nothing. No blood. No body. No nothing. "No way," she muttered, and motioned for Samuel to come outside.

"You gotta tell me how he did that disappearing act," she said to Samuel. "How in the heck am I supposed to

266

write this incident up? Did he have a rope already there? Did he use some kind of bungee cord?"

Samuel shrugged.

"That's a lot of help. What's your name, buster?"

"Donachee. Samuel Donachee."

"That sounds Scottish."

"Yeah, it is. Look, this was no big deal and I'm not going to press charges. So let's just forget it happened and I'll walk away."

"Not yet you won't." Ranger Swain raised Samuel's sword that she had been carrying and stared at it. Hmmmm. Deadly weapon ... assault ... public nuisance. Listen, fella, I want to know what is going on here. And I want to know where the hell your buddy went."

Samuel forced a smile. "I don't know where he went. But I do know that he'll be back."

Ranger Swain stared at her prisoner and shook her head. "Come on," she said, opening the passenger door of the truck. "Get in. There's an emergency outlet a couple of miles from here."

"No."

"No? Listen, you're in custody. You're in cuffs. You're going to do what I tell you."

"Thank you, but ..."

"All right, you want me to charge you with resisting arrest? Look, I don't really want to arrest you, but you have to fill me in about what's going on. And you really do need to get that cut taken care of. Come on, let's get that done and then we'll talk."

"Another time," Samuel said. "I have to go now. Things are happening. And I need for you to give my sword."

"Look, I'm not asking. I'm telling you to get in the truck now. If you take one more step I will officially arrest you." She placed her hand on the butt of the holstered pistol.

Samuel decided he might as well appease the woman. She wasn't going to let him walk away. He got into her truck, leaning forward to keep the blood from his wound from messing up the upholstery.

Ranger Swain closed the door behind him and placed his sword in the bed of the pickup. She started the engine of the truck and asked again, "Where did he go?"

"Sorry, but I haven't a clue."

"Look, you guys knew each other. You don't just meet someone in a public place and have a swordfight break out. Now how did he disappear? And what was that flash of light?"

"Maybe the sun reflecting off his sword?"

Ranger Swain slammed on the brakes and the truck rocked to halt. "Don't be a smart ass! You're going to tell me what happened or I swear to God I'll have the magistrate hold you in jail until you do."

Samuel forced a pained smile. "You're cute when you're mad."

"Oh, man, pleasssseeee! Don't even go there!"

Well, she was kind of cute, Samuel thought. He had never seen a woman warrior and this one was about 5-foot-8, athletically built and filled out her starched uniform nicely in the right places. Her sandy blonde hair was cut short, just long enough that the strands lay over, and her eyes were a lovely greenish-yellow. What he really liked about her was her authoritative demeanor. Maybe the gun had something to do with that.

"Don't stare at me, okay? Look, you seem like a decent guy; for my sanity's sake, tell me how that guy jumped off the tower and vanished."

Samuel's lips twisted in a half-smile. "Guess he had a rope or something attached to his sword. Maybe he stuck the sword into the side of the tower, jumped, and then yanked the sword free and took off."

The ranger gave him an incredulous look and shook her head. Then she slapped her forehead with her palm. "Oh, damn! We have to go back. I can't believe I forgot to call that car in."

She made a U-turn and drove back to the parking area, pulling the truck in behind the Mustang and picking up the radio mike. "Ranger Swain to station."

"Go ahead, Swain."

"Run a make on a red Ford Mustang convertible, N.C. LZB-5552, please."

"Roger that."

She replaced the microphone and looked at Samuel. You stay put. Don't move. I'll be right back." She removed the keys from the truck's ignition, got out, and went to the Mustang. The door was unlocked and she checked inside. A North Carolina state map was partially open on the passenger seat. The ashtray was clean. There was a towel on the floor mat in the rear, stained with something red. Blood?

The ranger returned to the truck and reached for the radio mike again. "Ranger Swain to station."

"Go ahead, Swain."

"Better send someone to the tower parking deck. We need to secure the scene, including the Mustang."

"Roger that. Hold one. Ranger Pate wants to speak with you."

"Pate here. What's going on up there, Swain?"

Ranger Swain seemed to weigh her reply for a second. She was never comfortable with Chief Ranger Gerald Pate. *A jerk, high on himself*, she thought. "Uh, two guys were fighting on the tower, sir. Using swords, sir. I have one in custody, minor cut on his back that may require stitches. I was on my way to the ER outlet."

"And the other man?" His voice was impatient.

"Uh, he fled when I broke up the fight, sir."

"OK, you got a description? If he still has that sword, he's armed and dangerous."

Yes sir. He's about six-feet-two, black hair, brown eyes, no facial hair, wearing a long black coat, blue jeans and brown boots."

"Age?"

"Maybe mid-20s, I guess."

"All right. I'm coming up for a look. Be there in 15. Think you can handle the prisoner okay till I get there?"

"I think so. He isn't bleeding too badly and I can give him some first-aid."

"Okay. On my way. Hang tight and don't do anything silly."

Ranger Swain glanced at Samuel and rolled her eyes. She really didn't like Pate, whom she considered a pompous ass most of the time. He was full of himself and his uniform. Pate made it quite obvious that he didn't consider a woman to be ranger material.

She turned to Samuel and said, "Okay, stay right where you are while I get my first-aid kit out of the back. I'm going to patch you up till another ranger gets here." The radio interrupted her.

"Station to Ranger Swain."

"Ranger Swain."

"We have a problem here. DMV reports LZB-5552 is registered to a 2002 Nissan. Owner is a Beverly Albright of Charlotte."

"Swain." Pate had been monitoring the call and broke in. "Check the tag number again and make sure you got it right."

Swain cringed and made a face, but checked the plate on the Mustang again. "It's still LZB-5552," she said, trying to keep the sarcasm out of her voice.

"Okay," Pate said to the dispatcher, "check to see if that Nissan or the plate has been stolen."

"That's a Rog. Station out."

"Swain, how do you know the Mustang belongs to the missing man?"

"There are only two vehicles here, sir, the Mustang and a Ford pickup."

"So how do you know the man wasn't driving the truck?"

Ranger Swain's heart skipped a beat. She had assumed the Mustang had belonged to the other guy simply because of his appearance. He was dressed much better than the man she was holding in her truck.

"I was going to call in the plates from the truck next, sir." She turned to Samuel. "Is that your truck?"

"No."

"What? You're driving the Mustang?" The exasperation sounded in her voice.

"No."

"Look, quit jacking me around. Are you driving the truck or what?"

"Truck belonged to a friend."

"Let me guess ... your friend stole the truck."

"Don't know."

"Is there anything you do know?"

"Yeah, you're kind of cute when you get mad."

"It's stolen, isn't it?"

Ranger Swain glared at him and doused a small gauze pad with alcohol and a touch of peroxide. She patted the wound until the blood was cleaned off, and then taped a piece of gauze over the cut in his back.

Finished, she returned to the radio. "Ranger Swain to station."

"Go ahead."

"Another plate to check ... N.C. JL ... wait. Disregard. Over and out."

She left her truck and moved alongside the old pickup. She opened the door on the driver's side, then looked over at Samuel.

"I know this truck. It belongs to Manny McGuire. Where is he?"

Samuel pondered the question for a second. "He's in Charlotte. Took my bike. Said he wanted to spend the weekend in town."

"Oh, really." She slammed the old truck door and returned to her vehicle, staring hard at Samuel. "Yeah, that sounds just like something Manny would do."

A black Chevrolet Tahoe with a park emblem on the door drove into the parking lot. Ranger Pate stepped out, straightened his shirt and adjusted his tie. Mister spit-shine. He removed his hat, ran a hand through his air and approached Ranger Swain's truck.

"Swain. This one of the guys? Who is he?"

"He didn't say, sir."

Pate gave the woman a quizzical look. Smart assing? "You mean you didn't ask," little lady?"

Oh, please.

Pate walked around the truck and opened the passenger door. He squinted at Samuel, noticing the bloody shirt and the bandage on the shoulder. Samuel stared back, saying nothing.

"Boy looks a little frayed around the edges, don't he? What's your name, boy?"

Stranger turned his head away and stared straight ahead.

Pate reached inside the truck and seized Samuel by the neck of the shirt. "Boy, I'm talking to you. What's your name?"

Samuel turned, looked at Ranger Pate and smiled.

"Yeah. All right. Another smart ass, huh? Swain, take this jerk in to the station, fingerprint him and turn him over to a magistrate. We'll find out who our mystery man is. Photograph him, too, and put it on the Internet. Smart ass."

Ranger Swain mumbled under her breath, "Yeah, and I'll clip his nails while I'm at it." She moved underneath the steering wheel and gave Ranger Pate her best honey grin. Under her breath she mumbled, "Bastard!" She put the truck in gear and started forward.

"Hey, hey, hey!" Ranger Pate was waving for her to stop. *The bastard had heard her!*

"Has the smart-ass been drinking?"

"I haven't detected any alcohol, sir," she said.

"Well give him a test anyway. Maybe we'll get lucky." He chuckled. "And while you're at it, run a urine test. This smart ass has to be on something illegal."

"Yes sir. Would you like a feces test, too?"

Ranger Pate stared hard at her. "Nah, urine is good enough. 'Course if he gives you a hard time, you might want to do an anal probe."

Ranger Swain's face turned red. She bit her lip, rolled the window up and pulled away. When they reached the base of the mountain, she turned the truck west, leaving the Blue Ridge Parkway.

She glanced at the man beside her, apparently at ease now. "Well, how did he do it?"

"Where are we going?"

272

"I'm taking you to the police station, getting you fingerprinted and photographed."

"Am I under arrest?"

Ranger Swain looked at him, then back to the road. "That depends on what we learn. Your sparring partner was driving a stolen car. You say you borrowed Manny's truck. Hold on! You know what? We're only a couple of miles from Manny's place. Why don't we stop by there and see if he's around. Once I hear him say he loaned you his truck, I might start believing something you say." She braked the truck, made a three-point turn and headed back toward Mount Mitchell.

"He's not at his hut," Samuel said.

"Oh, well, let's take a look anyway."

"You don't trust people much do you?" Samuel asked.

"I've learned to trust that about everything said to me by a suspect is usually a lie."

"Oh, I see."

Ranger Swain guided the truck onto the gravel road and Manny's hut soon came into view.

"I told you he's not home. You're wasting your time," Samuel said.

Swain braked the truck to a stop near the front door of the hut and rolled the window down. "Manny! You there?"

There was no answer. The only sound was the rustle of wind through the spruces. Ranger Swain looked over to Stranger, "Stay in the truck." She drew her 9mm handgun and crept to the front door. "Manny, this is Ranger Swain, I'm coming in." She turned the knob of the door; opened it a crack; then, then shoved it the rest of the way open with her booted foot.

The odor of blood almost made her gag. A swarm of flies was startled from their blood fest. Ranger Swain scanned the room and her eyes found the wall that told a grisly story with flung droplets of blood crisscrossing and forming large loops on the rough-hewn interior. Someone had died violently here. And the man sitting in her truck had been driving Manny's vehicle. He also possessed a sword that he obviously knew how to use.

The ranger returned to the truck and approached the passenger side. She opened the door and stepped back, keeping a safe distance between her and the suspect as he got out.

"Okay, where's the body?"

Samuel said nothing, staring at her, waiting for her next move. She made that move suddenly, shoving him against the side of the truck and forcing him to stand spread-eagled as she patted him down.

"You're under arrest on the suspicion of murder," she said, breathing hard. She pulled his arms behind him and placed handcuffs on his wrists. "You going to tell me where the body is or do I have to get a search party and some dogs up here?"

Samuel straightened up and faced her. "Listen to me." His long hair was disarrayed and covered half his face, giving him a sinister look. "I did NOT kill Manny. The other guy did that."

"Right. What else would you say? And who is the other man?"

Samuel's lips curled into a thin smile. "Dexter Frasier."

"All right, that's better. Now we're getting somewhere. Get back against the truck and place your hands on the roof. Don't move."

Ranger Swain went back to the radio. "I have a possible 10-50 at the Mount Mitchell Campground. Suspect in custody. Please send backup and a crime scene unit."

She signed off and turned to Samuel. "This is not turning out to be my favorite day. Now, where is the body?"

"Over there."

Samuel's quick response startled her. He was going to take her to the body? Jesus! He must be the killer. This thing was getting bigger by the second. She wiped a sleeve across her brow to get rid of the perspiration and looked across the yard to where the man was pointing. Damn, she should have seen that. The mound certainly looked like a rough grave.

"Oh, my God," she muttered. "Up against the truck! Do NOT move or I WILL shoot you!"

Samuel pressed his body against the truck and saw his sword lying in the bed. His eyes widened. "You won't find a body," he said. "There were only parts left when I got here. I buried them in my coat. Check out the wall and you'll see a note from Dexter about meeting him on top of Mount Mitchell."

Ranger Swain was confused, but determined to learn what had happened here. "Don't you move," she said, then went to bed of the pickup and got a shovel, moved to the grave and began digging.

Samuel turned his attention to the sword, mentally summoning Draconis. The sword rose from the pickup bed and drifted upward, above Samuel's head, then began to slowly descend.

A glint from the metal caught Ranger Swain's eye and she dropped the shovel and pulled her weapon. "What ...?" There was another flash of light. She was out of position to see the sword, which had lowered itself between Samuel and the truck. But there was another flash of light. She pulled the hammer back on the 9mm and approached the man.

The handcuffs were still in place. What was going on? She moved closer and noted that the sword was no longer in the pickup. "Where's the sword?"

Samuel shrugged.

"Damn it!" The ranger's patience and nerves were wearing thin. "Back away from the truck! She was almost shouting now. "Back away!" She dropped to her knees and peered beneath the truck. No sign of the sword. "Where the hell is it?"

Samuel shrugged.

"You're really beginning to piss me off," she said, her voice angry and stressed. Where the hell was Pate and the backup? "Move over by that tree and sit down. If you so much as swat a fly, I'll shoot you. Understand? Now, where's the damn sword?"

"Maybe it fell out of the truck ...?"

Ranger Swain grimaced. "Don't hand me that crap, I saw it floating in the air between you and the truck. Now it's gone. What are you ... a sword swallower?"

Samuel shrugged.

Frustrated, confused, angry and ready to hurt something or somebody, Ranger Swain moved closer to the man. "Open your mouth. Wide!" She grabbed his jaw and stared down his throat. "Jesus! This is crazy! Okay, stand up."

Samuel stood.

"Turn around and put your head against the tree." When he did so, she frisked him again. She patted every inch of his body. To hell with niceties, this was business. Nothing. She backed away and stared at him.

"You're going to come straight with me," she warned, her voice harsh. "First, I see your sparring partner jump off the tower and disappear. Now, your frickin' sword rises from the back of my truck and just vanishes in thin air. Oh, no. What kind of gag is this? This is a joke, right?" She took a furtive glance around, half expecting to find a "Smile, You're On Candid Camera" crew filming. "You know what, buddy? You're really pissing me off."

Samuel stared.

"Stop looking at me." Her cheeks were flushed and her nostrils were literally flaring. "Come on, come on! Where the hell is backup?" She holstered her pistol, glanced at her watch, and started pacing.

"There probably won't be any evidence by the time your crime scene unit gets here," Samuel said.

"Oh, really? Is that all going to go poof! too?"

"Something like that."

"Now what are you talking about? You said that guy Dexter killed Manny and you buried him."

"I was a little pissed off at you and I made that up," Samuel said.

Ranger Swain looked at him, then back at the grave. "Mr. whatever your frickin' name is, you can kiss my -." She checked herself and closed her mouth. She looked at the grave, then at Samuel, then to the truck. "Jesus." Ranger Swain opened the toolbox in the bed of the truck and took out a Polaroid camera. She snapped off four shots around each direction of the grave, letting the photos fall to the ground. She kept glancing back at Samuel. "If that poor man is down there ....." She put the camera up, retrieved the shovel and began digging at the grave again.

Samuel closed his eyes and visualized Draconis forming behind him and cutting through the chain of the handcuffs. He turned his head to look at the ranger and smiled when she glanced up from her digging. She resumed her grisly task and a bright light began forming behind him. He could feel the liquid metal seeping from his fingertips. He straightened a bit and mentally commanded Draconis to cut the chain. The sword, fully formed, made a swing at the cuffs that was so quick it was blur to the eye. "Clink!" The handcuffs were separated and Samuel's hands were free.

The sound startled Ranger Swain and she left her digging to check on the prisoner. "What was that?" She drew her pistol and stopped a few feet from him.

Samuel shrugged. "That noise? Must have been an acorn hitting the truck."

She gave him a glare and holstered the pistol, picked up the shovel and resumed digging.

Draconis hovered beside the tree trunk, awaiting further orders. Samuel thought for a second, then smiled and mentally commanded, "Draconis, float toward the mountain and wait there." The sword lifted into the air and moved toward the mountain, passing directly over the ranger's head. When it was a few hundred feet away, it stopped, remaining suspended in midair.

"Ranger, there's the sword," Samuel said, pointing.

Ranger Swain followed his pointing finger and saw the sword, hanging in the air with the mountain in the background.

Startled, she grabbed for her weapon and aimed it toward the floating blade. Her mind short-circuited. She stared at the shining sword, just hanging there, her pistol pointing at it.

The sirens shattered the trance she had entered and she turned to look at the man. The smile on his face maddened her and she whirled back toward the suspended sword. She was going to fire off a couple of rounds, see if she could hit the damned thing.

Samuel took advantage of her distraction and scuttled to the truck, crawling underneath it. Swain fired twice but the sword was untouched, still shimmering in the sunlight. The sirens were louder. She turned and saw that her prisoner was missing.

"Damn! Where are you? You bastard, you can't be gone!" She turned to check on the sword and it was no longer there. She ran to the tree where Samuel had been sitting and found nothing. Not a trace. On the other side of the narrow gravel road were trees that revealed nothing.

Ranger Pate brought his Chevrolet Tahoe screeching to halt in the clearing and two sheriff's patrol units skidded in beside him. Things were happening too fast. Ranger Swain shook her head, trying to clear it. What was she going to tell that bastard Pate? She felt light-headed, out of control of her emotions. The suspect was gone. The sword was gone. And her job would surely soon be gone. But wait. The grave was still here. And the bloody cabin. They would just have to believe her story. There was evidence.

Chief Ranger Gerald Pate stepped out of the huge SUV with the park ranger emblem on the door and straightened his hat. He stared at the pale woman standing before him and summoned a condescending smile.

"Where's the suspect?"

Ranger Swain shrugged. "He escaped."

"He what?" Chief Ranger Pate's eyes widened. Turning to the two sheriff's deputies, he shouted. "Come on, guys! Take a look around. Which way did he go?"

Ranger Swain envisioned her career in ruins. Pate had never liked her anyway. "I don't know," she said, her voice quavering as she fought back tears of frustration. "He was handcuffed underneath the tree and I was digging in the grave over there."

Pate snorted.

"Okay, pull yourself together, Swain. Can you give us a description? You did see him, didn't you?" He turned to the deputies. "Get the K-9 unit out here. Then take a look in the woods over there. Maybe he's just sitting there waiting on us." He glowered at Ranger Swain.

"The suspect said Manny could be buried there," Ranger Swain murmured, her voice so low that Pate had to strain to hear her. He was surprised. He had never approved of the woman, but he had never seen her rattled before. Just proved he was right all along.

"Okay. Let's dig, then." He went to the grave, picked up the shovel and began moving dirt.

Another car wheeled into the clearing and a small man in his early fifties got out. He stretched, pulled at his tie, and said, "Dr. Stephen Jones. Where's the crime scene?"

Ranger Swain motioned toward the hut. "Lot of blood, doctor. Everywhere. All over the walls."

The doctor picked up a small black bag from the car seat and went inside the cabin.

"Hey!" Chief Ranger Pate yelled from the gravesite. "Found something!" He stared down at a dirt-smudged coat from the hole. "Doc, better get a picture of this before we move it."

"Okay," the doctor said, emerging from the cabin. He gave Ranger Swain a funny stare. "Uh, Ranger, where's the blood?"

"What?" Are you blind? It's everywhere; all over the walls on both sides of the door."

"I didn't see any blood."

Ranger Swain's head was spinning. Now what? She ran to the cabin door and stepped inside.

Dr. Jones followed her inside and flashed his light over the walls. Ranger Swain felt her face turning pale as the blood drained from it. This couldn't be! There were some dark smudges on the walls but nothing that resembled the fired blood she had seen only a short time ago.

"I don't believe this," she muttered. "This place was covered in blood just a few minutes ago. You could even smell it."

The doctor moved to the ranger and placed a hand on her shoulder. "Don't feel badly," he said in a condescending tone as if he was talking to patient, "I'm sure that these smudges must have looked like blood in the dim interior.

279

But look," he flashed the light over the walls again, "do you see any blood now?"

Ranger Swain stared at the walls, speechless.

"Well, let's check out the grave," Dr. Jones said. He went outside and shot several pictures of the opening in the ground and the bunched coat with a digital camera.

"Okay, that's enough. You can have the coat."

Chief Ranger Pate did the honors, removing the black coat and laying it on the ground beside the grave. He carefully began unfolding the material with gloved hands. Then he looked up at Ranger Swain and smiled.

"Wow! One DOA coat. Guess you'll have to do an autopsy on this thing, Doc." The other men laughed.

Ranger Pate stood and moved to Ranger Swain, who appeared to be in state of shock. "What's going on, Swain? Come on over to my truck and let's have a chat. They walked to the Chevy Tahoe, and he opened a door for her. The engine was still running and the cold air conditioning felt refreshing to the befuddled woman.

Pate got in beside her on the front seat and pulled out a pack of Marlboro cigarettes. He held the pack toward her. "Want a smoke?" he asked.

"I don't really smoke, but yeah, I think I will have one." She took a cigarette and noticed that her hands were shaking.

"Okay, Ranger, what's this all about?"

Swain told the story as best she could, knowing that parts of it must sound ridiculous to her boss. She related how she had seen the two men fighting on the tower; how one of them had jumped off and simply vanished; how she had decided to check on Manny and how the suspect's sword had floated in the air; and how the suspect had disappeared while she was distracted by the sword. *God, I don't even believe what I'm saying!*

Chief Ranger Pate shook his head, a sad look on his face. "You know what, Swain? You're in serious trouble here. You understand? You write this shit up in a report and your ass is history. This is the damnedest story I've ever heard!"

Ranger Swain dropped her head, feeling her face burning even with the flow of cold air from the SUV's air conditioning vents. "Yes sir." She tried to swallow. There was nothing else to say. Her story even sounded ridiculous to herself.

Chief Ranger Pate picked up the radio mike. "Station, this is Pate. Cancel the K-9 order and notify the state troopers to call off the roadblocks. We've been had. Send a couple of wreckers out to the observation tower and have those two reported vehicles towed in. Contact the owners and let them pick them up. Just looks like a stolen auto recovery from here."

Pate leaned across the seat and pulled the cigarette from Ranger Swain's fingers. "You go home," he said. "I don't want to see your face for a few days. When you get your head straight, come in and we'll talk about your future. If you have one."

"But, sir, I'm on duty this week."

"Damn it, Swain, listen to me. You're in serious trouble here. Filing a false report is a firing offense and you may never wear a badge again. I'm going in and try to salvage anything I can. If I can, I'll save your ass. At the very least, you're going to get some counseling. And if I were you, I wouldn't mention any of this to anyone. What's going on with you? I thought you had the makings to be pretty good ranger, but this is … Is it your time of month or something? Your hormones screwed up? Tell you what; just get out of my face. I'll see you next Wednesday in my office."

Ranger Swain's face was ashen, Tears gathered in her eyes. She knew she had no argument. Everyone on the scene was convinced she was a fool. They were all snickering, and truth be told, if the shoe was on the other foot, she would probably be doing the same. Nothing made any sense. Jesus! This was a story for UFO Magazine or Fantasy Realms. And the worst part was the loss of her credibility. She had never been questioned before. But, hell, she had never even heard of anything like this mess before. This stuff didn't happen. Maybe it was all a bad dream. Maybe she had fallen asleep in her truck at the tower. She shook her head. No, she was awake. Painfully so.

She got out of the Chevy Tahoe and glanced at the men. They avoided her eyes. She tried to ignore them. Oh, they would have some fun when she was gone. Her face burned. She went to her truck and started it, then dropped her head onto the steering wheel and tried to let it clear. As she lifted her head, Swain felt the tears ready to begin and angrily shoved the truck into gear, made a sharp turn and headed for the road. Seconds later, tears of frustration and anger were streaming down her cheeks. She would go home, find a bottle and maybe get drunk. She had never been blackout drunk, but maybe this was the time for it.

In the bed of the pickup, lying flat beside the toolbox, Samuel was being jolted by the bumps in the road. He had heard most of the conversation during the woman's humiliation and felt sorry for her. He remembered how confident and levelheaded she had been at the beginning of the encounter. And now she was a bewildered, sobbing woman who wasn't even sure if she was totally sane.

As Samuel bounced in the back of the truck, Ranger Swain began getting her emotions under control. She angrily swiped a sleeve at the tears on her cheeks and hit the play button on the truck tape deck. The cab was soon rocking with the sounds of Creedence Clearwater Revivals old hit "Run Through the Jungle."

Samuel reviewed his position. He felt utterly alone and almost as helpless as the dazed woman driving the truck. He was curled in a fetal position, much the same as his little brother had been the night their father had died. The wound in his back had opened and he could feel the fresh blood seeping from it. The woman had tried to help him and he had done everything in his power to thwart and confuse her. Guilt pangs joined the surge of thoughts that were overloading his mind.

Manny was gone, thanks to the bloodthirsty Dexter, and there was an all-points bulletin out on Samuel. His Winnebago was a heap of twisted metal and the Harley was destroyed. He had no transportation and no contacts in this world. Dexter had made a Rippling and returned to the homeland. Knowing that bastard was back in SkyeEden placed a feeling of dread over Samuel. He should return and do what he could to save his clan. Dexter had an enormous army compared to the McGuire Clan. He could easily sweep through the countryside and sack the small villages and outlying farms. There was little to stop him now.

Dexter had gained enormous strength from the acquisition of so many stones. He made his position even stronger by demanding his warriors to only wound their captives. Then later he would kill them so that he could receive their stones. The man must be approaching god status with all the stones he had collected. No one would be able to oppose him. Even the skills the Swordslinger had taught Samuel were nowhere near enough to survive his power.

Dexter's sword took on more magical qualities with each stone and its boundaries were unknown. For the first time in his life, Samuel knew fear. Dexter had won the fight at the tower, Samuel acknowledged. His sword had been in the right places to block Draconis. The throbbing pain in his back was proof that except for the interference of Ranger Swain, Dexter would have been taking Samuel's stones back to SkyeEden.

They had reached the main highway and Swain brought the truck to a stop at a traffic light. There was a squealing of brakes in the adjoining lane and Samuel could see the cab and sides of a huge truck alongside. The truck body was covered with Food Lion logos and Samuel could see the driver's head through the cab window. The driver saw him, too.

The driver rolled down the window and gave a shrill whistle to get the ranger's attention. When she looked his way, he motioned for her to roll the window down. "Hey, lady, you got a man in the back."

Samuel remained still. Maybe she would think the guy was trying to make a pass and ignore him. He could hear the music coming from her tape deck, where Creedence

Clearwater was now belting out "Heard it Through the Grapevine."

But the truck driver wasn't giving up. He shouted again and when he still got no response, opened the truck door and began getting out. Just as his foot hit the step, the light changed and Ranger Swain gunned the pickup. The frustrated truck driver got back into his rig and followed her down the road.

Swain was fuming. *What a stupid!* How could she have mistaken those smudges in the cabin for blood? And how could she have let the suspect escape. Four-day suspension? She had never had a black mark in her file before. Would that make a difference? God, that Pate was a real A-hole. It was almost a half-mile to the next light, and she prepared to make a left turn. The tape deck was loud as the lead guitar was jamming with the grapevines. She glanced to her right and noticed a truck driver waving at her. Now what? Did she have a flat? Probably, that would fit right in with the rest of this day. The truck driver was yelling something. She pushed the button to lower the window on the passenger side and reached to turn down the tape deck volume. The driver was still yelling.

"You got a man in your bed!" he yelled. But Ranger Swain heard, "Hot man in your bed."

Great! What she needed was a pass from a lousy truck driver. Just another perfect moment in a perfect day. "No thanks, jerk," she mouthed and hit the close button for the window. The light was changing and she had the truck moving when the green came on. At least she was turning off the main highway and wouldn't have to deal with the horny truck driver again. Jeez! First Pate had mouthed off about her "time of the month" and now some perverted truck driver was hitting on her. God! She was in uniform, driving an official truck with the Park Ranger seal on it. Women get no respect. Two more turns and she wheeled the truck into her driveway. Home. That first drink was going to be very good. The second one even better. This just might be a three-drink night.

Swain collected her briefcase and purse from the truck seat and went inside. She was proud of her of her house, a five-room log house that had survived two previous owners before she had purchased it almost a year ago. The house was on the mountainside and from the porch, she had a magnificent view of the black mountains. And best of all, there were no nosy neighbors.

Suspended! God! She couldn't believe it. Didn't a six-year perfect record mean anything? Okay, let's have that first drink. A vodka tonic with a twist of lime should do the trick. God! She had gone through the police academy and spent a full year with the sheriff's department as an auxiliary deputy before landing the job with the rangers. She sipped on the cold drink and tried to relax. She still had to write up a report of the day's incidents, even if she was suspended. That would be fun, explaining people, weapons and blood that simply vanished into thin air. *God!* This could be the end of her career.

She removed her holstered pistol, hung it over the back of a kitchen chair, carried her drink to the den and sank down in the recliner. Another sip of the drink and she rested her head on the back of the chair. Someone knocked on the door.

Now what! Irritated, she rose from the chair. Who could it be? She hadn't heard a car pull into the driveway. Great timing! She didn't need a visitor; she needed to finish that first drink so she could build a second one. She pulled a curtain aside and peeked into the yard. Her truck stood alone in the drive. Okay, now I'm having auditory hallucinations. She went to the door and pulled it open.

The man she had handcuffed moved too quickly for her to react defensively. He clamped a hand over her mouth and held his sword as though ready to slash her.

"I'm not going to hurt you," he said in a calm voice. "I just want to talk, that's all." She could hear pain in his voice. He pushed the door open with a bloodstained hand and motioned. "Let's go inside." He saw the fresh drink on the table near the recliner and steered her in that direction. "Sit down and put your hands under your legs," he ordered. His voice was weak and the wound in his back was bleeding. A drop of blood spattered on the off-white carpet.

Swain remained standing. She was too angry to be afraid. "Look, I don't know who you are or what you want, but will you please quit bleeding on my carpet? Let's go into the kitchen. Who the hell are you, anyway?" Her cheeks were flushed and her eyes flashed with anger.

""I'm going to explain things to you because I need your help," he said as they moved onto the tiled floor. "You've seen things today that no one else in your world has ever seen." His eyes squinted from the pain in his back. He pulled two stools from the counter and motioned for her to sit down.

"I can believe that," she said. "Only problem is, I'm not sure what I've seen and what I've imagined."

"What you have seen is a Rippling and a sword merge."

"What?" Thanks a lot. Guess that's all I needed to know." She wanted that drink she had left in the den.

"The man on the tower and I ... we're not from here. We come from a different world of many years ago."

Ranger Swain laughed. Where the hell was that drink? "Oh, this is getting curiouser and curiouser. "Can you get my drink, please?"

Samuel ignored the request. "You saw the man jump off the tower, right? Remember the flash of light?"

"Just another illusion," Swain said.

"No, it was real. If you recall, he threw his sword first. That creates the Rippling, a portal that leads from our land in the past to this time and area."

"Oh, God! No wonder I'm quoting Alice in Wonderland. You've been spending too much time watching the Sci-Fi channel."

"All right. I understand your reluctance to believe me so I'll demonstrate. Don't be frightened, I'm going to show you a sword merger. You saw this at Manny's place but you didn't understand it."

Swain stared at this stranger in her house, ordering her around. The 9mm was hanging on the kitchen chair that was only a few feet away. Maybe ...

"Look. Before you get into your magic acts, would you please let me get my drink? Believe me, I need it."

"Okay, go ahead. But be careful. Don't try anything foolish. I can reach you a lot quicker than you can reach that pistol."

Swain rose from the stool and went into the den as the man followed her closely. She picked up the chilled vodka tonic and took a slow sip. "Would you like a drink?"

Samuel nodded his head from side to side. "No. I want you to see this. Maybe it will help you to understand."

"Yeah, I'll bet." She took another sip of the drink.

"The sword becomes one with me. Watch." Samuel lifted Draconis, grimacing from the pain the movement caused to the wound in his back, and held it up in front of him.

"Draconis, merge."

The sword began to brighten like lava steel. A prismatic aura formed around the blade and it floated free from his hands. He dropped his arms to his side.

Ranger Swain felt her head becoming light. *Too much to drink too quickly?* The sword began to melt into two liquid snakes of metal but remained buoyed. The man raised his hands and the liquid snakes flowed to them, disappearing into his palms.

"That was a merger."

Swain was speechless. Eyes blinking, she asked, "That really happened?"

"Yes. Now watch. I'll call it back."

"Oh, I really want to see that," she said, her voice laced with sarcasm.

Samuel smiled. "Draconis, come!" His hands were held out as if he was holding the sword. A brilliant light flashed before him.

Swain flinched, and then lunged for her weapon hanging on the chair. She pointed it at the man, who was still standing with hands outstretched. The liquid snakes oozed from his palms and solidified into the sword.

She was still pointing the pistol at Samuel, but seemed to have forgotten it. She took a step back, mesmerized. "Jesus! How did you do that?"

"It's the way of the sword. It's a long story. Just believe it."

"Okay, mister. So you can do a sword trick. But this talk of Ripplings and portals and other worlds ... that's gotta be one hell of a trick."

"I can create the portal as the man on the tower did, if you would like to see it."

"Oh, I'd like to see it. Just remember," she said, and gave added emphasis by bringing the aim of her gun to his head. "I have the 9mm. Only a fool brings a sword to a gunfight."

Samuel smiled, "I understand. I'll need a little room. I've not tried this at such close range. You may want to stand back and be prepared for the bright flash."

"You make one suspicious move and you're going to see a bright flash, pal. I'm cocked and ready to fire."

"I understand. I'll throw the sword toward your fireplace."

"You mess up my wall, and I'll shoot you for that."

Samuel ignored the last remark, although it sounded almost like a joke. He lifted the sword over his head, his face turning pale with pain from the effort. "Draconis!" He threw the sword at the fireplace.

Ranger Swain held her finger on the trigger, ready to fire. The sword went end over end once and a blinding light filled the room. She gasped and brought a hand over her brow to protect her eyes. The light was bright white. In the center, the color was prismatic and it swirled into itself like a black hole or a whirlpool.

"I can step through that portal and return to the Highlands," Samuel said. "Only the sword bearers can do this and the portal lasts only about 30 seconds."

Swain lowered her weapon and reached for a vase on the countertop. She flung the vase into the whirlpool and it disappeared. The light suddenly dimmed and disappeared.

The sword remained floating in the air. There was no sign of the flowered vase.

"Samuel raised his hands. "Draconis, return." The sword moved to him, began to liquefy and flowed into his palms.

"Okay, that was impressive," Swain said. She raised the pistol to point at him again, "but what about Manny and the man on the tower?"

"The man on the tower was Dexter … Dexter Frasier. He's from a rival clan in the Highlands and he's a murderer. He hates me because of a connection I had with his father and he's sworn to kill every member of the McGuire Clan. He came to Mount Mitchell to kill Manny and succeeded before I could get there. You read the note on the wall asking me to meet him at the tower. You saw what the inside of the cabin looked like."

"Okay, but that doesn't explain what happened to Manny's body or the blood on the walls."

"When one of us dies, our blood and bodies burn until nothing is left but ashes. I guess it's or way of returning to our homeland. Manny's remains lasted longer because he has been living in your world for a time."

"Oh, for God's sake! I don't know what to believe." She pressed her fingers against a throbbing temple. "Okay, you're going to have to explain all of this to me. I don't know why, but I'm going to trust you. Let me fix us a drink and I'll try to do something for that wound on your back while you tell the story."

"Thanks, I can use the drink and the TLC."

"All right, let's don't get carried away." She went to the refrigerator and filled two glasses with ice. "I'm drinking vodka and tonic. That okay with you?"

"Sounds great." He took a long sip of the drink and sighed.

"Be right back. I'll get some bandages." She disappeared into the bathroom and emerged with a bottle of peroxide, iodine and gauze bandages. "Take your shirt off and straddle that chair. This isn't going to feel too good at first."

Samuel did as she said and she started cleaning the wound. "You're lucky," she said. "It's not too serious, just ugly. It would be better if we could use some stitches, but I don't do that. You'll have to wait for a doctor. Okay, go ahead with your story. I'm listening.

"This is the strange part," Samuel said, smiling as he thought of what her reaction was going to be.

"Oh, and all this other stuff is just normal?"

"All right, here goes — the condensed version. My people live in the Highlands but there it is several hundred years earlier than this time. We are a simple people and live on the northern part of the land. Few strangers venture there and we have formed clans for protection against raiders from other villages. A few summers ago — our time — a huge asteroid fell from the sky and attracted the attention of everyone in the land. We all gathered to look at it and when someone touched it with his sword, a small stone broke off and moved down the blade. It melted the steel as it passed and the steel merged behind it. Once the stone had moved into the hilt of the sword, it started to glow and brighten, then it melted and flowed into the man's hands.

"We were amazed by the happening, yet were not prepared for what happened next. The huge boulder began shaking and breaking into thousands of small stones. The stones began searching out the men nearby and melding with them. It did no good to try to run or hide, because the stone found you. It burned itself into you and when you pick up your sword, the stone liquefies and flows from your hands and melts into the blade. From that point on, the sword will merge into and out of you upon command. I know nothing of the origin, only the results.

"We have learned that when one stone-possessed man kills another, the stone of the dead man leaves him and merges into the sword of the victor. The more stones a man gathers, the more magical qualities his sword performs. Once the sword contains half a dozen stones, the owner can perform a Rippling.

"Dexter was a killer long before the stones appeared, and he has killed hundreds since then. He's taken control of the Frasier Clan and convinced them that they should gather all the stones and therefore have all the power. Each time he makes a killing, his powers grow stronger."

"So, Dexter killed Manny to get his stone?"

"That's right, among other reasons. He especially wanted to kill Manny because he knew how close Manny and I were. He can never forgive me for being closer to his father than he ever was. He has vowed to kill every member of my family and all our friends. So far, he's making good on that promise."

"And you were trying to get to Manny before this Dexter bad guy did?"

"Aye, you got it, lass."

Swain had completed cleaning and bandaging the cut. She used a piece of the gauze to wipe the sweat from Samuel's forehead. His face was pale. Swain massaged her temples again. "Mister, you have given me one heck of a headache, not to mention a four-day suspension."

"But, do you believe me?"

"I don't know. I want to, but this whole thing is so crazy."

Samuel's head dropped and he seemed to fall asleep. Ranger Tammy Swain rolled her eyes and fixed that third drink she had promised herself.

When Samuel awoke, he was lying on his stomach in a strange bed. The room was dark, lit only by a small night light plugged into an electrical outlet. He let his eyes adjust to the dimness then surveyed the room; a dresser with a huge mirror and an unlit lamp, a computer desk and chair, a closet, and Ranger Tammy Swain sitting in the computer desk chair.

"How long was I out?" he asked, yawning.

"About six hours," the ranger answered. She had changed out of her uniform and was wearing a pair of faded blue jeans and an Appalachian State University T-shirt. The 9mm was on the arm of the chair. Her hand rested on the pistol.

"Are you still going to arrest me?"

"You're under house arrest. I went through your pockets and I found coins that I don't recognize, a lock of hair and a clan badge. I checked the badge out on the net and it's an original one. Your sword is dated back to the same time period as the coins and badge. If what you say is true, you're 600 years old. Hey, did you know William Wallace?"

Samuel arched an eyebrow. "No, sorry."

"We'll have to get a video of Braveheart," she said.

Samuel wasn't sure if the woman was just being or sarcastic or was serious. Maybe somewhere in the middle.

He tried to sit up, but pain from the wound was a flame across his back. "Ouch! Hurts."

"Yeah, you've got a nasty cut there. The bleeding has stopped, but you're going to need stitches."

"I can't go to a hospital."

"Oh, I see. Don't have any medical history or background, right?"

Samuel was suddenly angry. It had been a trying couple of days and the woman's sarcasm was becoming tiring. "Look, cut the crap," he said. "I've been straight up with you. I felt bad for you because of the trouble I caused with your boss and I decided to be honest. You had already seen the Rippling and sword merger anyway, so I took a chance with you. I could have just walked away, but I didn't."

He moved his hand to grip the edge of the bed and realized he was shirtless. She hadn't …!

"I changed your clothes," Swain said, chuckling at the look on his face. You're wearing a pair of sweats. You know you're asking a lot of someone to believe these stories you're telling — time portals and magical swords and evil stones. This stuff doesn't happen except in movies. What does happen is people killing other people and making up wild tales to cover their asses."

"You must believe me , at least a little, or I would be in jail, not here in your bedroom."

Tammy Swain shrugged. "Hey, I'm already on suspension, probably as good as fired. What do I have to lose?"

"I know. I'm sorry about getting you in trouble. I just didn't know what else to do. Look, I've got as many questions as you do. I don't blame you for not believing. If I hadn't made the journey myself, I wouldn't believe it either."

"I'm so screwed up right now that I don't know whether to shoot you or hug you. I've seen you create the portal and I've watched the sword merge. So I have to believe that something is going on here. But the logical portion of my mind is kicking my butt. I can't separate the real from the unreal.

"I hope you don't mind, but while you were sleeping I took a picture of your sword and e-mailed it to a Scottish sword expert in Edinborough. If what you're saying is true, maybe he can back some of it up. But I swear to God, if you're pulling my G-string I'm going to shoot you and spend the rest of my life in prison with a smile on my face."

Samuel didn't smile. "I need your help, Ranger Swain."

Swain leaned back in her chair and shook her head from side to side in attempt help the pieces of the puzzle fall into place. She sighed deeply. "Your name is Samuel, right?"

"Yes."

"Well, I'm Tammy. Now that we know each other, what do you want?"

Samuel smiled this time. He was beginning to think this woman was a special breed. "When Dexter learns that I haven't followed him back to SkyeEden, he'll come back here and start hunting me. I need a few things that can help me find him first."

"Okay, come with me to the police station. Tell them who you are, convince them, and they'll help you," she said.

Samuel stared at the ranger. Maybe he had overestimated her. She certainly didn't seem interested in helping him beyond patching up his wounds.

"You say you knew Manny. Well, if you knew him at all, you know that he was a good and decent man. He came here hoping that Dexter would follow him and spare his wife. But knowing Dexter, he'll kill Manny's wife just for the pleasure of it. He enjoys massacring entire families. Manny is just one of the good men that Dexter has killed and will kill unless I stop him."

Tammy Swain wanted to believe the earnest young man lying in her bed. She really did. But how could she?

"I'm sorry, Sam. I have two choices here — I can believe you're telling me the truth or I can believe you're insane. And since nothing like you're telling me has ever happened, I'm going with insane." She picked up her pistol and pointed it at him. "Okay, the bathroom is right over there. You get washed up and dressed and I'll take you to the emergency room and get some stitches in that back. Then it's lock-up time."

Samuel raised a hand as if asking her to stop. "Look. Before you do this, give me one more chance to convince you I'm telling the truth."

"Enough is enough, okay?" Get dressed."

"Please, just this one thing. If you aren't convinced then I'll go with you, no more arguing. I'll even go with you to the station and talk with your boss."

"Oh, really?" The sarcasm was thick. "And I suppose you'll show Chief Ranger Pate your little sword trick?"

"Yes."

"Yes? You got a deal. Let me help you up," she said, offering a hand.

Samuel rose to his feet and examined the gray sweats he was wearing. "These are different." He cleared his throat and tried to straighten without causing too much pain. "Stand over here beside me so you can see."

"Remember, I have my pistol pointed at your head," she warned.

"All right." Samuel moved to the end of the room and faced the opposite wall. "Come, stand by me."

When the cautious ranger had joined him, Samuel summoned Draconis and the sword floated across the room to him. "Rippling," he said softly and hurled the sword across the room. Before it reached the wall, Draconis burst into a brilliant light that made Swain flinch.

"Look deep into the center of the light."

Ranger Swain leaned forward. Stranger shoved her into the vortex.

"AHHHHHHHHHHHH!" Ranger Swain was screaming when her feet touched the ground. She lost her balance and fell. Samuel fell beside her.

"Where am I?" Swain jumped to her feet and whirled around, eyes searching for something familiar. She was standing on rolling green terrain with mountains encircling. The sky was a rich blue that she hadn't seen since her childhood, bulbous white clouds floating overhead. The air was chilly, but fresh and cleaner than any she had ever breathed. "Where am I?"

"You're okay, just settle down. You went through the portal with me and you're in the Highlands."

"Bullshit. I don't know what you're pulling, but this is enough. Get me back! Get me back now!"

"Do you believe me?"

"I don't believe anything. Get me back! Just get me back!" She aimed the gun at him. "Do it now or I swear to God I'll shoot you!"

"No need for that." Samuel summoned Draconis and hurled it. A portal reopened. "Let me take your arm."

Ranger Swain was far from convinced. "Where's this taking me now? Where?"

"It's all right. We'll be back in your bedroom. You always go back to the place of your last Ripple."

She holstered the 9mm, moved beside him and her hands clamped on his arm like vice grips.

"Ready? Come on." Stranger moved her along with him and they stepped through the portal.

This time Tammy Swain stayed on her feet. She spun around the familiar room, then hugged Samuel in gratitude.

He could smell her shampoo and feel the tickle of her short hair. The top of her head fit nicely under his chin.

"It IS real! We just….just…"

"Rippled."

"We were in the…"

"Highlands," he said.

She pulled away from him. "Oh, my God, this is true. I think I'm going to faint." She reached behind her, felt the arm of her chair and sat.

Samuel sat on the end of the bed and stretched his back. "You have any sutures around here?"

Tammy's eyes widened. "No. But… I have a friend who can do it. Come on, Sam, let's get you taken care of."

"Where are you taking me?" he asked.

"To the vet. An animal doctor."

Samuel arched an eyebrow. "Wait a minute," she said, and went to the closet, reappearing a moment later with a plaid shirt. "Put this on while I make a call. The office is closed at night."

CHAPTER 35

SUTURES AT THE POUND

This time Samuel rode in the cab of the truck. Tammy had put a pillow behind him and applied a pack of ice on the back of his neck.

"Sam, when this is over, we have to talk. I have ten thousand questions. This is just amazing."

"Ranger Swain, eyes on the road," Samuel said.

"Oops. Sorry." She pulled the truck back into correct lane. "And don't call me Ranger Swain. Call me Tammy or Tam. Nickname is Tamalamb."

Samuel laughed. "Oh, that's cute. Tamalamb, huh. It's been a long time since anyone called me Samuel, much less Sam".

"Well, I like Sam, okay? Now back to this Manny-killer business." She kept her eyes straight ahead as she spoke. "You are hunting him, right?"

"Yes."

"Do you think he'll be coming back or staying in the other place?"

Samuel smiled. "It's called SkyeEden. He'll probably be coming back here, though. He has unfinished business with me and there's more to this than him just wanting my stone."

"What is it?" She gave him a quick glance.

"Our fathers died because of an incident between them. Dexter holds a special anger for me because of the relationship his father and I shared. I don't know if he's jealous or just insane, but he's determined that I am to suffer as much as possible before I die. He wants me to live long enough to see everyone I love die. After that, I'm sure he means to kill me."

"What could have happened to make him hate you so much?"

"It's complicated." Samuel closed his eyes and drew a deep breath.

He began talking and the words spilled from his mouth, each syllable layered with emotion. Only he and his brother Robert knew the truth about what had happened between Nathan and their father, Stewart. His voice broke as he related the story and he was still talking when they reached the vet's office. Tammy parked the truck and reached across to pat his hand. When he had finished, she didn't know what to say. She held his hand, tears running down her cheeks as she shared his grief from the needless acts of violence and death orchestrated by the devil called Dexter. She pulled him to her and hugged him.

A white Lexus pulled into the parking lot, its headlights sweeping across the Chevy pickup. Dr. Cristine Carter was wearing blue jeans and a long-sleeve pullover shirt. Her hair was held up in the back by a mother pearl chopstick. "Hi, Tammy. Bring him on in."

Dr. Carter asked no questions. Obviously Tammy had told her some story over the phone. She gave Samuel a local anesthetic and said, "The stitches I'll give you will just fall out after a week or two so you won't have to come back. From the looks of this, it's going to take about 15."

"I owe you big-time, Crissie," Tammy said.

"Yeah, at least a six pack of beer, a bag of buttered popcorn and an Antonio Banderas movie."

"You got it. I'll even snag a poster of him from Blockbusters," Tammy said with a beaming smile.

"Oh, girl, you do that and your debt will be paid in full."

When the suturing had been completed, Cristine motioned for Tammy to join her in the doctor's office.

"So, want to tell me about this?" Cristine said. "He's cute in that tough-guy, bad-boy, kind of way."

"Don't even go there," Tammy said. "I'm really not sure what happened. He was sword-fighting with a friend and accidentally got stuck."

"Hmm. Some friend. Where's he from?"

"Uh… Charlotte."

"Staying overnight with you?"

"Okay, that's all you need to know," Tammy said, smiling at her inquisitive friend. "I'll call you in a couple of days to plan our night out together. Sounds like fun."

"Okay. Let me give Sammy Boy a few words about caring for that cut," the doctor said.

CHAPTER 36

BACK TO THE TOWER

Tammy's mind was racing and her mouth was trying to keep up with it. "God, you lived way back then, but that means you don't even know the history of your country, doesn't it? Did you know that in the thirteen hundreds or so you guys beat England, King Long Shanks or something? Then the Brits gradually regained control and in 1745 there's this big war and you guys lose again. Jeez, it hasn't even been that long since England returned the Stone of Scion."

"Aye. That is the stone our kings are made upon."

"Wow, the possibilities here are mind-boggling. You know, we give you texts on how to make electricity, gun powder, cell phones." She laughed. "Yeah, and cars and planes. You guys are sitting on a load of oil, too. Don't even know what that is, do you? Man, you can go back and change the course of history! God! Was I really there? I was in the Highlands?"

It was Samuel's turn to laugh. "I wouldn't dare do such a thing. I only hope Dexter doesn't think about this changing history thing."

Tammy started to say something, and then stopped. "I'm sorry. I shouldn't be running on like this. I know you've got some serious problems that need to be taken care of. We'll go back to my place and settle down, okay? I'm beginning to realize that this Dexter guy is someone who has to be stopped."

"Yes, he is. And to do that, I'm going to need your help."

"But what can I do? I just wish I had shot him when I had the chance."

Samuel chuckled. "So do I. But then you might just as quickly have shot me. Look, the first thing I need to do is pick up a lightning ball. There is a novelty shop called Spencer's that sells them.

300

"A lightning ball? What's that?"

"You'll see. When one of my countrymen is anywhere nearby, the ball will start doing some strange things. And we can follow it to Dexter or any of his men."

"Jeez, how did you learn about that?"

"By accident. I was picking up some batteries in a Radio Shack and they had one of the balls there. It started flashing its little bolts of lightning in my direction and they followed me all over the store. Drove the sales clerk crazy. I bought it, but it was lost along with everything else I had."

"There's a radio shack a couple of blocks from here. I'll have to turn around." As she pulled into a side parking lot and entered the highway heading back to town she asked, "You got any money?"

"Yes, a little."

Tammy laughed. "Oh yeah? And how did you get that, rob a Seven-Eleven?

"I've been here many times and I've learned that you have dealers who will pay large sums for items from my culture."

"Yeah, I guess so. You're learned a lot of tricks in a short time, haven't you? Tell me something, wasn't all this a little mind-blowing for you?" She waved a hand at the four lanes of speeding traffic and the assortment of businesses lining the road.

"It was a little scary at first."

"Do you drive? Do you have a license?"

"Yes, to both."

"Okay, I want to hear this. How did you get a license?"

Samuel shrugged. "It was easy. One of your, uh, street people? … helped me. Fixed me up with a parking lot attendant who taught me how to drive and then found a friend who fixed me up with a social security card and a birth certificate. It didn't cost as much as I had made from one old sword. I just went to the driver's license bureau and …"

"All right, that's more than I need to know. Good grief, no wonder we have so many illegal aliens running around with the same names."

301

Samuel bought the lightning ball and a few minutes later, they were back at Tammy's home. Samuel placed the ball on a table and plugged it into an outlet. The ball lit up immediately and began flashing dozens of jagged lines, several of which were dazzling bright and pointed west.

Samuel's face darkened. "I have to return to Mount Mitchell soon."

"Not until you get some food in you," Tammy said. "I've already got a steak and some fries ready to cook. You'll eat that before you leave. Besides, what's going on at Mount Mitchell? It was pretty quiet except for you and your Dexter friend."

Samuel's look made her feel dumb. "When you do a Rippling, you always go back to where you Rippled from. Dexter is in SkyeEden right now, but when he comes back, he will be at the tower."

"Well, good. He'll break his freakin' neck because he Rippled in mid-air."

Samuel's look made her feel even dumber. "No. It doesn't work that way. He'll be on the ground when he arrives. As far as I know, no one has ever Rippled into a tree or a brick wall or in the middle of a busy highway."

"Of course not." Tammy was ready to accept anything. Nothing was too crazy to believe now.

"Where are my things," Samuel asked.

"On the chair in the bedroom." She nodded in the direction.

Samuel rummaged through his clothes until he found a rumpled pack of smokes and then lit up a tobacco stick. He returned to the kitchen and watched Tammy busy herself with the meal.

"Dexter will be back soon. He likes to skip back and forth a lot."

Tammy looked up, saw the smoke and barked, "Hey, you can't do that. No smoking in my home. Don't you even have the manners to ask?"

Samuel chuckled. "Okay, I'll go outside." He went out and leaned against the wall.

Tammy joined him. "Dinner will be ready in a couple of minutes. So, Dexter is coming back, huh?"

"Yes, he knows I'm still here so he'll be back."

"He must really hate you."

"The feeling's mutual. My sole mission in life is to kill him."

"Jeez, don't you guys have any kind of justice system to take care of people like him?"

"No, and especially not in the northern Highlands. There are bands of thieves and killers who roam the country and there's no one powerful enough to stop them. That's why clans are so strongly bonded … so we can protect each other. We were at peace, basically, and then the stone came. After that, Dexter went on a rampage. And every time he takes a stone, he becomes stronger." Samuel fretted for a moment, teeth pressed against his bottom lip. "Had you not been at the tower, he would have won today."

Tammy reached out and took his hand. "Hey, all that matters now is that you're alive. And you're safe with me. Remember, I have a gun."

Samuel laughed and squeezed her hand.

"Come on inside, it's time for your feeding," Ranger Swain said.

The meal was from heaven. The steak was slightly spiced and cooked medium rare, so tender that it almost melted in his mouth. Tammy had lighted two red candles on the table and the glasses of Merlot were perfect.

"Umm. This is delicious. I'm becoming heavily indebted to you, though, I fear."

"Just relax and enjoy. You've had a rough day. When do you think this Dexter character will be coming back?"

"Probably within a day or two. It won't be long. He always comes."

"Have the two of you fought before?"

"Yes."

"And yet you're both still alive?"

Samuel reached for the glass of Merlot. There was tremor in the wine from his shaking hand. "We've fought three times and he's won each time."

303

"So why are you not dead?"

"It's Dexter's private torture chamber. He wants me to be around to grieve for my loved ones as he kills them."

"He must be a real bastard. But if he's beaten you, why are you still hunting him?"

Samuel drained the wine and sat the glass down on the table. "As long as I am breathing, I will try to kill him. If he continues to make the mistake of allowing me to live, I will kill him one day. He's killed too many people close to me and there is no way to predict what he will do if he continues to collect stones from those he murders. When he kills me, he will inherit many stones from me, also, and his power will be even more awesome. He'll be able to conquer the Highlands and possibly even England."

"When he kills you? That's not a very positive attitude. Maybe I can help you."

Samuel looked at her quizzically. "Maybe you can," he said. "In fact, you've already helped me a great deal. But I need to get back to Mount Mitchell so that I can protect some of my clansmen who are there. Dexter sometimes sends others to do the killing and collect the stones for him. Sometimes they'll take the victims back to SkyeEden and Dexter will execute them there himself."

"Whoa! Hold on a minute! You're saying there are more people like you here in North Carolina? This is incredible. Where are they?"

"Oh there are a couple of dozen up in the mountains and in the Charlotte area. They tend to find places where they can blend in without being noticed too much. I don't know exactly where they are, but I can find them with the lightning ball."

"So how do you know if the person you find is one of your people or one of Dexter's?"

"I don't. Most of them I've never seen before."

Tammy gave him her best raised eyebrow look. "Hold on," she said, rising from the table, "I may have an idea. She crossed the room to her desk, opened a drawer and removed an object. She held it up, peering closely at it. "Oh, wow, it works! I think it does. Wait!" She ran to the door and went outside. Samuel saw her dash past the window. A second later, she was back inside, breathless, holding the object toward him.

"Look! This is a compass. The needle always points to the north. However, look, when it gets near you, it goes crazy! It's gotta be that stone inside you that you were talking about. Oh, wow!"

Tammy was so excited that she was bouncing on her toes. Samuel didn't even try to suppress the smile as he watched her. "Let me see," he said, reaching for the compass. The needle spun around the dial as he took it. Maybe you're on to something. You sure this thing isn't broken?"

"No, it worked just fine outside. Isn't that cool?"

"You're a bright girl, lass."

"Oh, I'm a real genius, buster. You ain't seen nothing yet."

Samuel reached a hand out and squeezed the ranger's arm. "Thanks," he said. "This could be a lifesaver. But I have to get back to Mount Mitchell. Dexter will be there sooner or later and I have to confront him."

"What if he doesn't go back there?" Tammy asked. "He has to know that you're looking for him. Why wouldn't he just stay in SkyeEden and rack up some more stones?"

"I figure I may have two days before his return. If he hasn't shown by then, I will go looking for him."

"Samuel, I want to help you. What can I do?"

"When there's a Rippling, there's usually a short power outage in the vicinity. You're an officer of the law … do you have access to this kind of information?"

"Well, you know, I'm not like a Texas Ranger, Samuel. I'm a park ranger and my only jurisdiction is on Mount Mitchell." She paused, her brow furrowed in thought. "What areas are you interested in?"

"The Charlotte area and your park."

"Oh … okay. I can make a call to the power companies and ask them to report any failures to me." She laughed. "Don't think it would work if I told them I was doing a study on nocturnal animals, but maybe I can give them some kind of line about a study on crime incidents during blackouts. Yeah, I can come up with something. I'll tell them I'm working on a thesis for my masters."

Tammy noticed the confused look on Samuel's face and grimaced. "Oh, that's right, you don't know about masters. Never mind; I can do it."

"Good," Samuel said, pushing his chair back and rising. "That was a most delicious meal. Thank you."

"Well, thank you, my lad." Tammy curtsied.

Samuel laughed and she moved across the room to a wall cabinet. "Something I think we might need to take with us," she explained. The shotgun was a .16 gauge and she picked up a box of shells. "Just in case somebody comes at me with one of those blades," she said, smiling.

She disappeared into the next room and emerged seconds later with a hunting vest. "Just want to look the part, you know? You ever used a cell phone?"

"Used a what?"

"Here" She tossed the tiny phone to Samuel and he caught it, stared at it.

"Jeez! For a smart guy you sure are dumb about some things! It's okay; I'll teach you how to use it and you can stay in touch with me after we get back to Mount Mitchell."

"Okay, that sounds fine, but I do have a favor I'd like to ask of you. Would it be proper for me to use your bath? I desperately need to rid my body of the stench of the past couple of days."

"Thank goodness! I thought you'd never ask! Of course, you can take a bath. In fact, I would much appreciate it.!"

Samuel threw the ranger a mock hurt look and they both laughed.

"I'll even let you use my razor," Tammy said laughing. "And if it won't hurt your male ego, you can use some of my Secret deodorant. It's made for a woman but strong enough for a man."

"That's very kind of you, I'm sure, my lass, but why is it a secret?"

"Oh never mind! Take your shower!"

While Samuel showered, Tammy sat in her recliner, leaned her head back, closed her eyes and reflected on the events of the past 24 hours. God! None of this was believable! She opened her eyes and stared into space. It had to be happening. She wasn't dreaming. The portal had been real because no matter how good a magician he might be, there was no way to fake transporting her to another country and time. And Samuel ... the guy was no dummy and certainly didn't appear to be trying to pull some kind of scam. Jeez! Imagine living in the 14th century and suddenly being set down in the 21st! Her eyes widened at the thought. Everything would be so different ... so strange ... so frightening.

The reverie was interrupted by Samuel emerging form the bathroom, towel wrapped around his waist. Tammy hoped her emotions didn't register on her face as she stared at the semi-nude man. God! He was a hunk! Check out that chest! Oh, mama! Look at those broad, strong shoulders. She imagined herself nestling against those rippling muscles. *Not many of today's women have made love to a 14th century guy,* she thought, smiling.

Samuel had shaved and his cheeks were smooth and tanned. His long hair was still damp and she realized he probably had never used a hair dryer. Oh well, don't want to overload that beautiful mind now, do we? The hair would dry quickly. She went into the bathroom and got a brush from a drawer.

"Come here and let me brush your hair," she said. Samuel came to her, still clutching the towel around his waist. She began brushing the dark hair, her heart beating furiously. She wondered if her face was red. It was definitely hot. "Okay," she murmured, "check that out in the mirror."

"I can't," Samuel said softly.

"You can't what? You can't look in a mirror? What are you, a vampire? Are you some kind of Dracula?"

"I can't look in mirrors," he said, his voice sober. "I am a dead man."

"Oh yeah? Well you don't look so dead to me. And you don't feel dead. What do you mean?"

"I'm talking about my heart. Dexter killed my heart years ago. I'm no longer a man. I'm a hunter; hunting for Dexter. I breathe and eat with the sole purpose of someday slaying that monster!"

Tammy was taken aback by the passion in his voice. His eyes were blazing with hatred.

"Oh, Samuel, I'm so sorry. Look at me …" Tammy reached up and cupped his face with her hands. "It's sad to see you so consumed with hatred for that man. You have to clear your head and think of yourself and your people. If you continue this way, Dexter has already won. You can't let that happen. Your people are counting on you."

Tears suddenly appeared in Samuel's eyes and one trickled down his freshly shaven cheek. "You don't understand all that Dexter has done," he said, his voice raspy. "His deeds are so horrible that I have difficulty speaking of them. He killed my younger brother only a few days ago and I was denied the opportunity of even burying him. When I get back, I'm not even sure I'll be able to find his burial place and erect a headstone."

Tammy put her arms around the strong, bare chest and laid her face against it. "Samuel," she whispered. She could feel his heart beating against her face. She wished she could melt into him the way his sword had done. She raised her head and moved her lips close to his.

Samuel drew away. "I'm sorry," he said. "I can't. Not now."

Tammy felt her face redden with embarrassment. "I … I'm sorry," she stammered and pulled away from him. "I don't know what I was thinking. Forgive me." She turned and fled from the bathroom.

"Tammy, don't think it's your fault. It's me. I just can't feel anything right now. My heart and soul are in shock. I … I …" He couldn't finish the sentence.

Tammy recovered her wits and donned her park ranger persona. "Hey, it's almost seven o'clock. Get dressed and let's get out of here." She mentally kicked herself for temporarily forgetting their relationship. He was a stranger, maybe even a murder suspect. Was she crazy?"

Samuel quickly donned his clothes and followed Tammy outside. She went to the garage and motioned for him. "Help me put the camper top on the pickup," she said. "One of us may need some privacy or a place to sleep."

Tammy drove in silence, focusing on the road in the beam of the headlights. She wasn't sharing her thoughts and Samuel seemed preoccupied. She scolded herself once again for her lapse in the bathroom. What on earth could she have been thinking? From the corner of her eye, she saw Samuel remove something from a pocket. It looked like lock of hair. *A woman's hair? Oh my God, was he married? Double stupid!*

"Do you mind if I play some music," she asked, and when he nodded, she punched in a CD of the soundtrack from the movie, Lord of the Rings.

After several minutes, Samuel turned to her. "When we get to the tower, I want you to just leave me," he said. "This fight is between Dexter and me. I don't want you getting involved."

"Excuse me!" Ranger Swain said, her face now red with anger instead of embarrassment. "I'm definitely involved here! This is my park and what happens here is my responsibility! Besides, I'd like to just do a little deed for mankind here and help stop this monster!"

"You could be hurt or killed," he said. "I don't want that."

"Believe me, neither do I, Sir Galahad. However, I'm no pushover. I'm trained in martial arts and weaponry. Trust me. I can handle myself. In fact, based on what I saw at the tower yesterday, maybe better than you."

Samuel stared at her for second, a smile in his eyes. "My, you are a spirited lass, aren't ye?

"Look, laddie, this isn't the 1300s. I'm a 21st century woman and I can hold my own. Besides, like it or not, you're my case now. You've belonged to me since the moment I saw you two trying to kill each other. Seriously, Samuel, this guy has to be stopped and you obviously need all the help you can get. So, like it or not, partner, I'm with you."

"Aye, you are a stubborn wench!"

"Aye, I'm stubborn and I've got a gun. Double trouble, buster."

They reached the turnoff on the Blue Ridge Parkway and took the road that led up to Mount Mitchell. When they reached the locked gate, Tammy stopped the pickup. "I've got a key," she said. "When I open the gate, pull the truck through. You can drive, right?"

Samuel gave her a quick glance. The woman was still a little angry with him. He drove the truck through the gate and slid back into the passenger's seat.

The mountain was blanketed in a dense fog. The headlights enabled them to see only a few feet ahead. The night was eerily silent except for the sounds of the truck's engine.

"We're not going to see anything tonight," Tammy said.

"We'll see the flash if there's a Rippling," Samuel answered. "We'll know."

They drove past the campground turnoff and Samuel thought of Manny. His heart felt twisted and wrung out. A deadly rage began building in his chest. How could one man have destroyed his life by killing everything he loved? Why had fate entwined their lives like a pair of enemy serpents? He knew that Dexter was demented by the hatred for his father and the hand fate had dealt him. The man hated everyone and found life detestable. He even hated God and had cursed Him for taking his mother and giving him a coward for a father.

But as much hate as Dexter held within his dark soul, Samuel knew that he hated Dexter equally as much. Did that make them alike? No! They weren't alike. He had to disassociate himself from that image. There would be no hate in his life if it were not for Dexter. Therefore, he must rid the world of the madman. I am a walking death machine, he told himself. *I am a swordslinger!*

He remembered the day when he had first practiced with Nathan and how he had pleaded with the man to teach him to be a swordslinger. *Well, look at me now! I have become you, Nathan!* It was if Nathan's sword has been forged into his soul and that steel was within him, they were one. At the

310

thought of the sword, a stab of pain slashed through his heart. The sword was linked to when ... no ... no ... no ... don't go there. Don't think of that. You are a dead man and the dead don't grieve.

The pickup braked to a halt and Samuel returned to the present.

"We're here," Ranger Swain said, staring out into the wall of fog. "Looks like we're in the middle of cotton ball, huh?" She glanced at the silent Samuel. "Hey, are you okay? What's wrong?"

"Nothing. Never mind ... I was just thinking. Let's go."

Tammy tuned off the headlights and used the beam of her flashlight to guide them to the tower stairs. The soft breeze stirred fog particles in a pattern that almost resembled a snowstorm. The mountain night air was chilly. The metal stair rails were wet and slippery. The steps were steep and Samuel knew that he had been dumb to try to run up them before engaging Dexter. No wonder he had been so winded.

Tammy seemed to read his thoughts. "I know. I climb them ten times a week and it still gets me," she said. "Where do you want to set up?"

Samuel placed his hand on the stonewall of the tower. This was the place where he had almost died. If the park ranger hadn't arrived when she did ... He stepped back and peered upward. The thick fog shrouded everything after a few feet.

"Let's wait by the tomb down there. If Dexter comes, we'll see the light and have a few seconds to get ready for him."

They left the stairs and sat down, leaning against the tomb of the man for whom the mountain had been named. It seemed fitting that this was a place of the dead.

"This is going to be a long night," Tammy said. "Come on Dexter, we're ready for you." She patted the shotgun in her lap and glanced at the sword Samuel was wearing. As she watched, he unstrapped another blade that she hadn't even known he was carrying. This was a much shorter weapon, with a handle made of six-inch buckhorn. There was a silver cap on one end of the buckhorn and an eight-inch blade wedged into the other end. A leather thong hung from the hasp.

Time passed slowly and the ground they sat on was hard. They rose from time to time and stretched, paced back and forth. Both were quiet, reflecting.

"Reminds me of the Highlands," Samuel said, moving his arms vigorously to keep the blood flowing. "But at least it isn't raining."

"Yet," Tammy said. "That can change very quickly in the mountains, you know." She reached out a hand and placed it on his wrist. "Samuel, how dangerous is this Dexter? I mean, he's not superhuman. A bullet or your sword will stop him … right?"

"Honestly, I'm not sure," Samuel replied. "He has amazing reflexes, much quicker than mine. He's very strong physically and is more agile than anyone I've ever encountered. I'm not sure what effect the stones have had on him, but they have increased his stamina, strength and even his intelligence. I can't begin to know how many stones he has possessed; therefore I can only speculate as to his powers."

Tammy felt an involuntary shiver convulse her body. "What if we can't stop him, Samuel? What if he's so powerful that he kills us, and when there's nothing left to ravage in your Highlands, he comes here with his men and tries to conquer our country?"

"Your soldiers have weapons that are too advanced for that to happen," Samuel assured.

"Maybe so, but if Dexter is as smart as you say and he keeps collecting those crazy stones, he may figure out a way to integrate his people here and pull something off. After all, no one here knows about these guys. God! This is scary!"

"There are many reasons we must stop him," Samuel said.

Tammy's imagination was working overtime. "Suppose he gets so strong that his people conquer England?" she asked. "It's the 1400s back there, right? So he could change the course of history, right? America might never exist as we know it, right?"

Samuel stared at her. "I wish I could tell you," he said.

"Well, this whole thing scares the hell out of me," Tammy said. "We're going to stop him right here. Look, if we're here now, it must mean we kill him because if he had lived we wouldn't exist. Right?"

Samuel laughed. "The ranger's mind wanders," he said kindly. "I really don't' know how it works, Tammy, but I think it's the present here and there at the same time."

"Okay, well do you believe that things are preordained? You know, like fate. Like us meeting and coming back here to wait for him. Are we living in the past, Samuel?" She laughed nervously. "God! This is getting me all confused." She paused, shuddered, and changed the subject. "How's your back?"

Samuel grinned and shrugged. "It's okay unless I move. The stitches are beginning to itch, though. And it's …"

He was interrupted by a brilliant flash of light to the left of the tower. Tammy gasped and grabbed the shotgun, pointing it out into the fog.

Another light suddenly flashed farther to the right. "Samuel …?"

"He's bringing company," Samuel whispered.

Another light flashed. Samuel unsheathed Draconis. "We'll stand back to back and wait," he said quietly.

Three more flashes appeared almost simultaneously to the left of the tower.

"What do we do?" Tammy whispered.

"Shoot the first thing you see moving," he answered.

Five almost simultaneous new flashes momentarily blinded Tammy.

"Don't look directly at the lights," Samuel warned. "Get ready. As soon as you see something, shoot! Get ready!" Their backs touched each other. Tammy held the shotgun poised, ready to fire. Samuel was holding Draconis straight out in front, ready to strike in any direction.

"Jesus, Samuel, I've counted 15 of those flashes," Tammy said, her voice taut with strain. *Why the hell was she holding a shotgun with two shells in it?* She leaned the gun against the wall and pulled her 9mm pistol from the holster.

There was a thud to Tammy's right and the muffled curse of a man. Someone had bumped into something or fallen. "Samuel?"

"See him, shoot him," he answered, his voice low and calm.

One of the shadows to Tammy's left suddenly moved and became a figure rushing at her with a raised knife. Reflexes kicked in and she aimed the pistol and fired, the bullet catching the man in the throat. He fell at her feet and clutched at her leg. She put a second slug into his back and looked up to see another shadow moving toward her. She loosed a shot in his direction without knowing if she hit the target.

Samuel suddenly lunged forward and slashed at a dark spot in the fog, his blade catching a man in the shoulder.

"Ambush!" A shot rang out. "Get low!" There were sounds of bodies hitting the ground.

Tammy reached behind her, touching Samuel's back for a feeling of security. The man at her feet was making gurgling sounds, bleeding to death from the wound in his throat.

"Spread out!" The voice came from behind the tower. "Sam Donachee, are you there? Dexter sent us to keep you company. He said you might be waiting for his return and he was afraid you might get lonely. But don't worry, we're not here to do you harm. Dexter wants us to being you back to SkyeEden with us. You do want to see him again, do you not?"

"Shut up!" Tammy screamed into the dark. "Shut up!

Samuel placed hand on her shoulder. "Shhhh. It's a trick. They want us to talk so they can locate us."

There was another loud gurgle from the man she had shot. *My God,* she thought. *I've just killed a man!* Her mind raced. Her eyes flicked from side to side. She was almost gasping for breath. Another gurgle. Please … just die!

"Samuel Donachee, why do you fight us? We mean you no harm."

314

A man on his hands and knees suddenly came out of the shadows toward Tammy. She couldn't get the pistol aimed at him quickly enough and the bullet whizzed off harmlessly into the darkness. She tried to move back but a hand grabbed her foot and she tripped, falling backwards and landing on a rock.

Samuel whirled, made a slashing movement with his sword and the man's hand holding a short knife was suddenly gone. The man looked up at his attacker, the stump of an arm spurting blood. A second later and the sword had slashed again, putting him out of his pain.

Samuel turned to help Tammy, but before he could reach her two men came out of the shadows and attacked him at once. He stumbled over the woman and crashed to the ground. Tammy, still stretched out on her back where she had fallen, got off two shots at one of the men. The other made a slashing movement with his knife that Samuel blocked with his arm. Before the attacker could recover, Tammy had pumped a bullet into him. The man's body jerked and an arch of blood sprayed across Samuel's chest.

Three more of the men charged and Tammy used only three bullets to take them down.

Samuel pulled Tammy to her feet and whispered, "Let's move to the steps." They couched low to the ground and moved to the new location. When they paused, they could hear the wounded men groaning and cursing.

"Where are ye?" one man shouted. "Come out and fight us, you coward!"

They had barely reached the steps when Draconis began to glow. The sword grew brighter and Samuel could feel it trying to rise on its own. He released it and they watched as the sword moved across the lot, pausing, and then moving again.

"It's taking stones from the dead men," Samuel whispered.

Almost before the words were out of his mouth, one of the men slammed into Samuel from behind, knocking him to the ground. Tammy grabbed at them and was pulled down also. The attacker rose to his knees and died in midair as Tammy shot him in the face, the wound making his face bloom like a morning glory.

Samuel was stunned from the fall and having trouble breathing. Two more men suddenly came out of the fog and Tammy didn't even think. She just pumped four bullets into them and they crumpled to the ground.

Samuel pulled himself up, shaking his head to clear it, and Tammy grabbed his hand and helped him rise. They watched as Draconis continued to collect stones from the dead men, and then rose high in the air, moving in a strange ritual of celebration. Samuel was hoping the sword would return to him as he knew there were still more of the assailants in the area.

"Run, Donachee!" and man shouted. "We'll find you. You are a dead man!"

They reached the pickup and Tammy got under the wheel. Samuel turned and shouted, "Draconis, come!" He silently urged the sword to hurry and held his hand out to accept it. "Take your time," he said sarcastically. "No hurry." He climbed into the truck, but left the door open. "Wait," he said to Tammy, who was trying to insert the key into the ignition with a shaking hand. "I'm going to get out, and when I do, turn your head lights on bright."

"What?"

"Just do it."

"Okay."

Samuel got out of the truck and knelt by the door. "Now! Turn the lights on."

The headlights lit up the area in front of the truck and a man a few yards away from it tried to shield his eyes from the blinding glare. He was holding a knife in one hand.

Samuel came in low and with an upward slash sent the blade of the sword into the man's armpit. He withdrew the sword and drove it into the stomach. He yanked the blade free and the man crumpled to the ground on his face.

"Get in and let's get out of here!" Tammy shouted. But Samuel wasn't ready.

"Not yet," he said. "We have to get the stone." He released his grip on Draconis and the sword rose in the air above the dying attacker. The knife the man had held began glowing and seemed to rise to meet the sword. A bright crimson stone began emerging from the center of the blade. Draconis was glowing fiercely blue, yellow, red and purple and the colors spewed forth and swirled. An arm of light moved downward to the knife and engulfed the freed stone, pulling it toward the sword.

"Jesus, Samuel, we can't wait much longer!"

The stone melded into Draconis and Samuel reached out and grabbed the hilt of the sword. "Okay," he said, sliding into the passenger seat and slamming the door, "let's go!"

Tammy made a tight turn with the pickup, its wheels spewing dirt and gravel as she gunned the engine. The truck reached the paved road and Tammy breathed a huge sigh of relief as she leveled the speed off to a safe pace.

"Are you okay?" she asked, and Samuel grunted a reply. She began assessing her own injuries, finding aches and pains she hadn't realized existed. "Jeez," she complained, "I'm hurting everywhere. My knee, my head, my leg. She reached down to feel her left ankle and brought back her hand smeared with blood. "Oh, God, I've been cut!"

"As soon as you find a place where you can pull over, stop and we'll take a look," Samuel said. He wasn't feeling too well himself. His left shoulder felt as though a boulder had slammed into it and he could feel warm blood running down his back. His shirt was blood-soaked and his hands were red with it.

"I'm not stopping!" Tammy half screamed. "Some of those crazy bastards are still out there!"

"I know," Samuel said, keeping his voice calm, "but we're a couple of miles away from them and they don't have transportation. Okay, go a little farther, and then stop."

Tammy was nearing hysteria. Her shoulders shook with uncontrollable sobs and she was gasping for breath. "I killed some of them," she said, her voice trembling with emotion. I killed people, Sam!" I had never even fired my weapon anywhere other than on a range before tonight. I KILLED people!"

317

Samuel placed a hand on her shoulder and gripped it firmly. "Stop the truck, he said, pointing to a widened shoulder area ahead. "Right there. Pull over."

Tammy pulled off the road and braked to a halt. "Okay, just take few deep breaths," Samuel said. "Do you have a flashlight?"

Without speaking, Tammy reached over and opened the glove compartment. He reached in and pulled out a long, black flashlight. He opened the door and got out, then went to the driver's side and opened the door. "Let me see your leg," he said.

The beam from the flashlight revealed a long gash between the knee and ankle on Tammy's left leg. It was bleeding freely, but not with the rush that comes from a severed artery.

Samuel examined the cut and said a silent prayer of thanks. The wound was a superficial one, ugly and painful but not crippling. "You're going to be okay," he said. "We just need to get this cleaned up. I want you to move over and let me drive. Okay?"

Tammy was still hyperventilating. "God! All those men I killed! I'm going to be sick!"

Samuel put an arm around her and pulled her to him. "You didn't have a choice," he consoled. "They were going to kill you."

"But there are bodies everywhere back there, Samuel; bodies all over the place. God! Did you hear that one making that gurgling noise? I'll have nightmares of that!"

"Come on, Tammy!" Samuel's voice was harsh. "Get it together, Ranger! You're going to have to guide me out of here. I'm lost."

"Okay. Just get me home so I can wash all this blood off me."

"I will, but stay alert. I don't know the turns."

They had traveled in silence for a couple of minutes when Tammy sat upright. "Damn it! I left the shotgun!"

Samuel chuckled. "Don't worry about it. We'll get it in the morning."

"No way!" Tammy said. "I'm never going back to that place. Can you imagine what it looks like with bodies everywhere?"

"There won't be any bodies there, Tammy."

"What do you mean?"

"Trust me. Dust to dust and ashes to ashes."

"What?"

"Never mind. Just take it easy for a while. You're almost in shock."

"You really think they'll be gone?"

"Yeah. I think the ones who are still alive have gone home crying to Dexter."

"Oh great! Then one of them will probably take the shotgun back to the 14th century. Can they do that?"

"I guess they can."

They reached Tammy's home and Samuel lifted her in his arms and took her to the door. She gave him the key and he carried her inside. "Take me to the bathroom," she said, looking up at him with eyes that appeared haunted. "There's a first-aid kit there."

"I'm going to run some water and get in the bathtub," she said. "I have to get this blood off me. I don't even know how much of it is mine. Would you please bring me a bottle of rum? Screw the mix; I'm taking it straight."

When Samuel returned with the rum, Tammy was naked in the tub. The running water was turning red with blood. She reached for the rum and drank from the bottle. She leaned back in the tub and closed her eyes. Samuel was embarrassed by her nudity but tried not to let it show. The martial arts training must have worked wonders with her body. The breasts were firm and jutting, even without a bra, and the muscles in her stomach were defined. He closed his eyes and tried to quiet his racing pulse.

"Is it bad?" Tammy asked.

"You'll probably need some stitches and you'll have a scar, but on you it will look good."

For the first time in hours, she smiled. "Pour me a glass of the rum," she said. "I'll try to drink it like a lady this time."

Samuel poured and handed the glass to her. She turned it up and emptied it in one gulp. She grimaced, smiled again, and said, "Would you please get my cell phone? I'm going to make another call to the vet. Crissie is going to love this."

Samuel gave her the phone and she looked up at him as she was pressing the keypad digits. "Are they going to come after you again, Samuel? Will you ever be safe?"

Samuel pondered the questions for a moment, then shrugged his shoulders. "I really don't know," he said. "But it would probably be better if I leave you here. You've already been caught in a bloodbath and I don't want you getting hurt again. I think it's better that I be alone."

Tammy held up a finger to silence him and spoke into the phone. "Hi, Crissie. Yeah, it's me again. Look, I'm sorry but I need your help again." Her voice broke as she spoke to her friend. "No … everything's okay now. It's just, well, I have this cut on my leg and it needs stitches. No … I can't. Not right now. Please don't ask … I'll fill you in later. But right now I need you, Crissie. Thanks."

Tammy dropped the phone on the rug by the bathtub and leaned her head back, closing her eyes. Samuel used a towel to press against the cut on her leg and slow the bleeding. It had almost stopped, so nothing vital had been damaged.

"When your friend gets here, I'm out of your life," he said in a soft voice. He closed his eyes, fighting back tears. "I can't keep on losing the people I care for. Do you understand?"

"I understand, but I don't agree. You need help and I'm the only one you can trust right now. No one else is going to believe you. This is bigger than you, Samuel or me. There's too much at stake. If we don't stop this Dexter jerk, God knows what the long-term effects will be. Yeah, I'm scared and I'm hurt, but I'm in this now and I can't walk away."

"But look what I've already done to your life. You were at peace and enjoying your work until I came along."

"That doesn't matter. None of that matters, Samuel. This is fate and we can't fight it. It's obvious that you and I have been brought together for a reason."

"You are a special person, Tammy lass. I've never known a woman with your bravery."

"I'm not brave! I react out of fear and self-preservation. I killed people tonight, Samuel, and in my heart, I have no regret. They were going to kill us."

"Yes, that's true. However, it will never end until I can kill Dexter. That's why I had to have you wait while Draconis collected the stones from the men that we killed. I am going to need more power to match his strength."

Tammy raised her head and opened her eyes, still seeming oblivious to her nakedness. The running warm water was soothing and was no longer turning red from her blood.

"We're partners now, Samuel, whether you like it or not. I'm just a park ranger and I was content with just watching the squirrels play, but this is important. This is something that can change the course of history. And most of all, this Dexter character is one wicked devil. I'm convinced he has to die before our lives can return to normal. Whether you kill him with your sword or I pump a couple of nine-millimeter slugs into him, he has to go.

"Here" she said, offering her empty glass, "pour me rum, please. I want to be numb when Crissie gets here with her sewing kit. One more ought to do it."

Samuel shook his head, smiled and leaned over to kiss her forehead and then left to get the drink.

It was almost half an hour later when Cristine arrived, wearing a pair of faded blue jeans, a long-sleeved flannel shirt and a perplexed look on her pretty face. "What is with you guys?" she asked. Tammy was wearing a robe, relaxing in the recliner. Samuel was perched on a barstool. Both held glasses partially filled with rum. "Are we having a party here, or what?"

"More like a wake," Tammy said, showing a weak smile. "Sorry to interrupt your beauty sleep, Crissie, but it seems it's my turn to bleed." She pulled the robe aside and removed the towel from her leg.

"Wha…?"

"Don't ask," Tammy broke in. "I had an accident."

321

"No shit!"

"Hey, it's complicated, Crissie. Much too long a story for me to tell right now. In fact, one more glass of rum and I won't even remember it."

"Okay, be that way, girl. But believe this; I'm getting tired of sewing you people up. Obviously, you've got some stuff going on here that needs taking care of, so why don't you call the sheriff? You're a deputy, for Christ's sake, Tammy."

"It's not that easy, Crissie. It's complicated."

"Yeah, I'll bet it is." The lady vet sent a mock-angry glance Samuel's way and he smiled. But it was ghastly smile that did nothing to ease her concern.

"I'm going to step outside," he said, and left the room. Outside, he lit up a tobacco stick and added smoke to the enclosing fog. It was uncanny how Dexter seemed to know every move he made. Still, if the bastard was going to come back through the portal, he would have to do it at the tower. There was no doubt that he would return, knowing that Samuel was wounded and not at full strength. He wouldn't miss an opportunity like that.

"You coming back tomorrow, Dexter? I hope so. This time you're gonna get stoned!"

CHAPTER 37

HOUSE CALL

Samuel was playing with the controls on the microwave oven when Cristine came out of the bedroom carrying her medical bag. "She'll be okay, I think. Whatever happened, though, she's pretty traumatized over it. I gave her a sedative and when she wakes, make sure she takes it easy on that leg. I had to use 11 stitches." She gave Samuel an inquiring look. "How about you? I'd better take another look at that back."

Samuel grimaced as he unbuttoned the shirt and let it fall to his waist. It was Cristine's turn to grimace. "Damn!" she muttered. "I haven't seen this much sliced meat since the last time I was at the deli. You guys have got to quit going to the wrong places. Jesus! Look at this bruise! It looks like a mule kicked you right on that cut. Your shoulder looks like a purple birthmark! Sit down, man, and let me take a look underneath the dressing. You've been bleeding again."

"How long have … Ouch!"

"Oops! Sorry about that," Cristine said.

"How long have you and Tammy known each other?" Samuel asked through clenched teeth as she removed the bloody bandage.

"We were friends in high school. We met as freshmen and then we were roommates at Appalachian State. She left before I did because I stayed a couple of years to get my vet degree."

"The lady is something special."

"You bet she is. She's my best friend and we've held each other's hands through a lot of stuff. Tammy never really dated anyone until college. Then she met this guy, fell hard for him and when he graduated two years before her, he said goodbye. Broke her heart. She's been a little disgruntled ever since. Hasn't really had a serious relationship. She's an independent little shit and says what she thinks. I think most guys are afraid of her. You know, the big, bad ranger with a mad on. She doesn't even associate too much with the other rangers, either. Doesn't let them anywhere near her personal life. Drives them a little buggy, I think. Here's this cute little trick that they'd love to be hitting on and she just shuts them down. She loves her job, but there's something missing. She's like a rebel without a cause. She's afraid of commitment, doesn't seem to want to let anything exciting into her life."

"Oh yeah? You should have seen her last night."

"I'm sorry. Didn't mean to get carried away. It's just that I care very much for her. I don't know what you've brought into her life, but you have to end it. It's obviously dangerous and I don't want her going through this kind of stuff."

"You're right," Samuel said. "It won't happen again."

"I hope not. One more time and I'm calling the sheriff myself. There, I've done all I can do for you." Cristine placed the tape and leftover bandages, needles and anesthetics back into her black bag.

"She's lucky to have a friend like you," Samuel said. "One more thing before you leave; could you show me how to operate the washer. I really need to wash my clothes."

Cristine rolled her eyes. "Men!" She went to the washer and pointed out the controls. She found a box of detergent and poured some into a cup. "Put the clothes in here, and then put the detergent here," she said. "When the cycle is finished, take the clothes out and put them into the dryer. Here." Again she showed him the controls. "Where do you wash your clothes? A creek?"

"How did you know?"

Cristine threw him an amused smile and headed for the door. "Gotta go. Tell Tammy to give me a call when she wakes up. And no more middle of the night sewing classes, okay?"

"I promise," he said, adding an aside to himself, *If I can keep her from going with me.*

Samuel took off his soiled clothing and placed it in the washer, pushed the right controls and walked naked to the bathroom. He ran the tub full of hot water and eased his aching body into it. A half hour later, he got out of the tub, toweled himself off and padded back to the washer. He moved the clothes to the dryer, punched the buttons again and went to Tammy's room. She was still asleep and he moved quietly, not wanting to disturb her. He opened the closet door and removed a robe. It was too small, but he could squeeze into it.

"Sam?" Tammy was awake and staring at him in the dim light of the table lamp. Her voice was small, almost childlike, and blurry from the sedative. "Sam, would you hold me? I'm shaking."

Samuel hesitated, and then moved to the bed. He clutched the robe around his body and lay down beside her. She turned, rested her head on his chest and was asleep within moments, snuggling close to him for warmth.

Samuel struggled with his emotions. It had been almost two years since he had held a woman. He lay with his eyes open, staring at the ceiling. He and Heather had never had the opportunity to sleep together as man and wife. He smiled as he remembered the touch of her auburn hair caressing his face like feathers. He closed his eyes and indulged himself in the memories. In his mind, the woman beside him became Heather. He stroked her hair and drifted into a state of ecstasy.

Samuel dozed off and it was daylight when he awakened. He gently removed Tammy's arm from his chest and got up, padding to the washroom and removing his clothes from the dryer.

Tammy's arms were around his before he knew she had followed him. "Thank you," she said, leaning her head against his back. Samuel turned and pulled her against him.

"Are you feeling better?"

"Oh yes, but we need to get dressed and get back to the park. I have to find the shotgun."

"Maybe I should go alone."

"No way! The way I live the rest of my life depends on what's out there. I have to go there as soon as possible. Get dressed and I'll go change."

She turned to leave, then said, "Thanks again for holding me. I needed that."

Samuel smiled and thought, *Me, too.*

CHAPTER 38

SCENE OF THE CRIME

I t felt good to be back in his clothes. He had thrown the soiled black coat into the washer. Now back in his clothing, he felt as though a part of his soul had been restored. The clothes were warm and smelled clean and fresh.

"We need these machines back in SkyeEden," he said, smiling at the thought. "Maybe not, though. The women would have too much free time and would have to find some way to entertain themselves."

Tammy threw him a dirty look. "Chauvinist pig."

The drive back to Mount Mitchell was uneventful. Tammy had made the drive so often that it was automatic. She sat behind the wheel of the Chevy pickup and mused over the happenings of the past 24 hours. Was it real? Was it a dream? Was she insane?

It must be real, she thought. *I've got a 9mm in my hostler* and *a .45 on the seat beside me* . She gave Samuel a glance from the me corner of her eye. *And a hunk in the passenger seat that I don't know whether to hug or shoot.* She chuckled at the thought and decided to concentrate on her driving.

The early morning fog had lifted; and, the sky as clear enough for the three-quarter moon to be seen, still hanging low the sky. As they drove along the Blue Ridge Parkway, Samuel could see houses perched on the hillsides and down in the valleys. They reminded him of the stone home Nathan had planned on building on the mountain overlooking the village. Instead, his home had become a stony grave.

Tammy slapped a hand against the steering wheel. "Oh, great. We left the gate open last night," she fussed. The parking lot was empty, however, and she breathed a sigh of relief. She didn't need any more demerits on her record. She cut the engine of the Silverado and coasted into a parking place. "Maybe we can sneak up on them," she said, grinning at Samuel.

They left the truck, leaving the doors open to avoid noise, and separated as they neared the tower. Tammy held the .45 at ready, while Samuel had drawn his sword, brandishing it in front of him as they walked. The sight of the huge sword brought strange thoughts to Tammy's mind. It made her feel uneasy, much more than a gun would have. She was familiar with guns. *But this blade ...*

It had a presence about it. She knew that it could reside in Samuel's body, but how? It seemed that the man and the sword co-existed as host and parasite. But who was living off whom? The blade seemed to have a life of its own and Samuel gave it commands as though it was a dog fresh out of obedience school. She wondered if a woman could ever come between the two. *Would Draconis allow it?* Could the sword sense the affection its master might feel for a woman? Cause of death? It was heat of passion, sir. Jealous sword. Poor girl never saw it coming.

The ranger shook her head, trying to clear it. The sword had been forged in the Highlands of the 1300s and yet it looked new. And if the stone had invaded the sword as Samuel said, what history did the stone possess? It had fallen from the sky as a huge boulder and then broken into thousands of pieces in search of hosts. So what animated the stone? Why did it merge with another sword as well as its host? Had some higher intelligence sent these stones to Earth for entertainment? What the heck am I thinking about? I've returned to the scene of the crime to see if I can find the men I killed last night. *Am I crazy?*

The fog of last night was now dew on the damp ground. The rocks in the ascending steps toward the tower appeared glass-coated. A feeling of dread and disbelief flooded through the ranger as she reached the spot where she had fired point-blank into the man's face. There was no body, just a smudge of soot on the rocks. Yeah, blood that burned away. Blood from a man's body that she had taken the life from with two squeezes of the trigger. She felt nausea rising and paused to take a deep breath. She reached out a hand and steadied herself on the railing.

Samuel was ahead of her. He reached the top of the steps, paused and studied the surroundings. Seeing nothing suspicious, he began a slow approach to the tower. It appeared deserted.

"Have you seen the shotgun?" Tammy asked.

"Not yet."

"Do you think they could have taken it back with them?"

"They must have. I just hope that the first time they fire it, they have both barrels pointed at Dexter."

"Oh, God, you've got to get it back," Tammy said. "I don't want to be responsible for what they might do with it. You have to get it back."

Tammy stood in the spot where she had fired at the attackers and shuddered at the memory of the gurgling sounds the dying man had made. *But where were the bodies?* Actually, she was relieved that the area wasn't scattered with dead men. How many? She had no idea. She shuddered again.

Samuel saw the expression of horror on her face and said, "Don't be too hard on yourself. What you did was self-defense. They were coming for us on orders from Dexter. They would have taken us to him and we would have been executed in cold blood. He is a man with no compassion driven by a passion to dominate and kill."

Tammy nodded, not trusting herself to speak, and joined Samuel in policing the area for shell casings. The casings were cool from the night air and smelled of gunpowder. They had all come from Tammy's gun. She was still trying to rid herself of the feeling of dread. This was one of her favorite places in the world and now it had been tainted by death. *Death that she had caused.* She felt that her soul had been tainted. Maybe Sam was right, and she had really not done wrong. What could she have done differently? Officers of the law were sworn to protect, and she had certainly been protecting Samuel and herself. She carried a firearm for the use of deadly force when it was deemed necessary. Anyone would have deemed her actions last night as necessary for survival. At least she didn't have to stare at the bodies. What had happened seemed like some kind of foggy dream.

"You need to leave," Samuel said, breaking into her reverie. "It would be better if I'm here alone when they come back."

"Just walk away and leave you, huh? You know I cannot do that. I'm too involved now."

"It's okay," Samuel said. "They won't try anything during daylight in a public place like this."

"Yeah? So why are you going to hang around?"

Samuel threw her an amused look. This was one spunky lass. With an attitude like that, she might have been labeled as a witch in the 14th Century. "Just in case," he said. "Come on; let's go back to your truck. I want you to drop me off just outside the gate."

"What are you planning, Sam? You're not going to do something really stupid, are you?" A sudden thought flashed through her mind. "I am going to see you again?"

"Of course you will. In fact, I'd like for you to pick me up a little after six tonight."

Samuel watched until the truck disappeared around a curve and then left the road and followed the path that led to the nearby campground. He veered off the path into the woods until he spotted a boulder near a spruce tree. He sat on the boulder and leaned against the trunk of the tree. Patience. It was a virtue.

A few minutes later, the bored Samuel decided to kill time by doing some whittling. He summoned Draconis with the intention of doing some whittling with the knife he had attached to the sword. He had made the sien du and another like it for his brother Robert in his father's ironworking shop.

However, when Draconis had solidified, the sien du was missing. There was a nick in the area of the sword's hilt where he had attached the knife with the leather thong. One of the blows from the assailants had apparently severed the leather and the small knife had been lost.

Great. One of Dexter's men must have picked it up. The carved buckhorn hilt would have made it an attractive prize.

It was few minutes after 8 a.m. when the park ranger replacing the suspended Tammy arrived. Several tourists had already gathered and were waiting outside the gate. Samuel decided to go on a scouting expedition and began a circular walk around the exterior of the park. He would be close enough to sustain a vigil but wouldn't be obvious to the park visitors. The last thing he wanted was to attract attention to himself.

He pulled the pouch of tobacco from his pocket and rolled a smoke. The morning air was brisk and invigorating and the overcast was beginning to burn away in the morning sun. It was going to be beautiful day. The trees were a black-green on the horizon and the scents of spruce and damp earth were heavy in the air. Purple thistles amid groups of white and yellow heather lined the path he was walking.

He reached an area that provided an open overview of the surroundings and the striking resemblance to his beloved Highlands made him long for SkyeEden. No wonder so many of his people had taken refuge along the Black Mountains. A pang of sadness settled in his heart as he thought of his dead brother. Young Robert had never had a chance to pursue his dreams. He had been a big brother and a father to Robert, but he hadn't been able to save him from the bloodthirsty Dexter. He remembered how the two of them had made funny shapes from their shadows as they walked among the sun-drenched hills. Now there was only one shadow and there was nothing funny about it. "I walk alone," Samuel said to himself.

When he had regained a view of the parking area, a strange sight greeted him. Some tents had been erected at one end of the lot and women in long brown dresses and white aprons with white bonnets were stirring the contents of a couple of cauldrons that were simmering over the barbecue pits. Several men dressed in jeans, plaid flannel shirts and suspenders were playing dulcimers. The men had heavy beards and wore their hair in ponytails.

The other tourists were dressed in an array of outfits. Some wore winter clothing with jackets and coats while others were wearing shorts and T-shirts. Samuel smiled. At least no one would pay much attention a stranger in a long black coat and wide-brimmed hat. Just another weird native.

Samuel mingled with the crowd, taking out the compass Tammy had given him to check for uninvited guests. The needle held steady on North. Good, there had been no Rippling yet. He had left the Lightning ball plugged into the lighter outlet in Tammy's truck. The ball had shown nothing either, except for a lone stone carrier that had appeared to be miles away. When one of Dexter's men or anyone else who was carrying stones came within range, the ball would begin emitting tiny blue-white lines that merged. When Dexter himself was in range, the lightning lines grew in intensity and formed a single blue-white light that pointed straight up. The single beam was brighter and thicker than it would be for ten of Dexter's henchmen. The murderer's collection of stones must number in the hundreds. In addition, with each stone, he gained power, both physically and mentally.

Samuel's presence also caused the ball to glow, but the beam identifying him was much weaker than Dexter's. Still, Draconis had made several stone collections over the past few days and Samuel felt his own strength should be growing. He knew he was still overmatched by the villain, but he had faith in his skills and in the magic that his sword held. Dexter had been the victor in each of their four previous encounters and each time had leered over him. "I let you live to grieve. I let you live to hate me and to remember the loved ones that I have taken from you. I want you to relive the day I killed my father before your eyes."

It made no difference how many years the Ripplings put between the time he had witnessed the butchering and where he emerged from the portal, the memory was as vivid as the day it had happened. He could still see the Swordslinger collapsing on the platform as his entrails spewed from the cuts to his abdomen. The look on Nathan's face had been one of love and serenity, but the horror and evil of the moment remained fresh in Samuel's mind.

Nathan still lived in Samuel's inner-world. He often consulted with the Swordslinger when troubled by a difficult decision in life. Nathan was always there, and the advice he offered was always sound. Samuel hated Dexter with every fiber of his being. The thought of his archenemy changed his vision to multiple hues of blood red.

The music by the dulcimer players broke through Samuel's murderous thoughts. The song was Amazing Grace. What a wonderful melody. Samuel found an empty chair and sat down to listen, watching the musician's fingers perform along the strings and wood.

The song ended and the musicians took a break. One of the men pushed a button on a small box and the sound of wailing bagpipes filled the air. Samuel's heart quickened. This was uncanny. He smiled as the notes flowed and weaved into sweet melodies. He smiled at the memory of Robert's pitiful efforts with the bagpipes. He could see his little brother's cheeks rising and falling, elbows moving in and out, his foot tapping to the rhythm.

He recalled the night Robert had convinced the Vikings and the Manteo Brothers that they were surrounded and how he had ridden nude on the big horse garbed in weeds and thistles. Boy, that must have been a frightening sight!

He recalled how Nathan had laughed after their seeming impossible survival, the exhilarating feeling of pure joy and exaltation. And he remembered how the arrow from the hidden archer would have taken Nathan's life had it not been for the wooden slat across the back of the chair.

The ringing of the cell phone in his pocket startled Samuel. He pulled it out and pressed the button Tammy had pointed out. "Yes."

"Are you okay?" Tammy asked.

"Aye, doing great. Just listening to the band. No Dexter."

"Good. I'm going to meet my boss at the park. I'll bring you some lunch."

"My stomach says thanks already."

They said their goodbyes and Samuel put the phone back in his pocket. If only they had something like this back in the Highlands. What a tactical advantage this device would offer. Charges and attacks could be timed perfectly and catching Dexter's men off guard might be possible.

With time to kill, Samuel decided to search for his sien du again. He trudged back up the steps to the tower, taking his time. He wasn't sure he had yet identified all the aches and pains in his body.

The only traces remaining from the previous night's conflict were the dark smudges on the ground. Samuel climbed the cast-iron stairs of the tower and stood on the balcony. It was here that he had been saved from an almost sure death from Dexter's sword by the arrival of Ranger Tammy Swain. Aye, he owed that lass. He clenched his jaw in anger and frustration as a he recalled how he had failed once again to rid the world of a great evil. If only he could once get the advantage on Dexter, he could end his life and free himself from the dread that followed him around like a huge black cloud.

Come on, Dexter, show up again and give me one more shot. I'm waiting. He was eager to test himself against the devil now that Draconis had merged with several new stones. Maybe their powers would be more equal.

There were a few tourists on the observation deck, checking maps and trying to locate points of interest listed. The sky was almost clear, just a few puffy white clouds over the mountain peaks and the wind had died down to a gentle warm breeze.

The view from the tower again reminded Samuel of his homeland. He had climbed up to Nathan's burial place many times and sat and talked to his old friend. What a beautiful spot the Swordslinger had chosen for his home site. He was sure that Nathan could hear him and would spiritually direct him to make the proper decisions. It was a comfort.

It had been six years since the murder of the Swordslinger when the 20-year-old Samuel had decided to build his own house on the property. It was a rugged trip down the mountainside to the village, but the solitude and serenity were worth the effort. The place was just too beautiful not to take advantage of it, and he made his own hours in the ironsmith shop, where he had nurtured a flourishing business.

As he stared out from the tower across the peaceful landscape, he wondered if he would ever be able to know that tranquil feeling in his homeland, where every waking moment was tinged with fear of an attack from Dexter's violent men. It was a gift of nature that the land's grass was able to remain green instead of being stained red by the bloodshed. He longed for his homeland, being able to sit by an open fire, cooking venison and watching the smoke unfurl and rise from the chimneys in the village below.

Most of all, he missed his love, Heather. As much as he had loved his brother, his father and the Swordslinger, it was Heather that he longed for most. Damn Dexter! That piece of donkey dung had taken everyone he loved away from this earth. *Dexter, my enemy, my nemesis, my blackness, my hatred!* The acid of hatred seared his soul, burning away the compassion and the ability to experience the emotion of love.

He thought of Ranger Swain and how special she was. Under different circumstances, he would have been attracted to her. However, he was too jaded for romance. No. There could be no one after Heather. He gripped the rails of the tower until his knuckles whitened. If only he could squeeze the pain from his heart. Oh God … Heather. Tears ran down his cheeks and he closed his eyes only to see the blue-green eyes. The gentle wind caressing his cheeks could have been the touch of Heather's hair on his face. He touched his lips with his fingertips and remembered the softness of her lips. He could feel her body pressing against his, her heart beating against his chest. All that gone forever, thanks to Dexter. *Oh, God, give me one more chance to send this bastard to hell.*

Samuel opened his eyes and returned to the present. All around him people were talking, laughing, and making plans. A small smile curled Samuel's lips as he recalled the building of their home. They had used stone and he had placed a large window for Heather to look from as she worked in the kitchen. The window overlooked the garden he had planted. The garden thrived with vegetables and the bees from nearby hives spent their days pollinating the plants. He roamed the nearby countryside searching for wild flowers with the brilliance to match the woman he loved and would be taking for his wife.

Samuel proved to be an even better ironsmith than his father was, and the business thrived. Men from surrounding clans traveled many miles to have him forge swords. He took great pride in his handiwork, saved his money and invested in more land and livestock. He dreamed of having children with Heather; maybe even starting his own clan.

Now he was standing on tower in a faraway land hundreds of years in the future, feeling alone and bloodied. Dexter. Always Dexter. He was like a deep pain that you lived with, slept and ate and breathed with. Sometimes you could ignore him but he was always just under the surface, ready to strike and kill again. Dexter, a man so vile that he had butchered his own father. How many of his own clan had he been forced to hear uttering their death cries as they were being struck down by Dexter? Samuel knew that he had reached the point of no return. He must either kill Dexter or die from Dexter's hand. Nothing else mattered to him. Life was nothing more than hauntings and an unreleased rage that made him gnaw at himself like a hyena chewing its leg to free itself from a trap.

So come on, Dexter. Let's finish this now. Where was he? He had leapt from the tower at almost this exact spot and disappeared into the portal. Where was he now? Who was he killing now?

The laughter of a child broke Samuel's chain of thought. A father lifted his son to his shoulders and the lad was awestruck by the dizzying height. "I can touch the sky, Daddy. I can touch the sky!"

Heather and I should have had sons by now. Samuel tried to recall their last moments together and the pain was so acute, so sharply etched in his heart that he slammed the door on that memory. He reached into his coat pocket and brought a tobacco stick to his lips. The trembling of his hand made it difficult to light the smoke.

"Can I look through the telescope, Daddy?"

"Sure, kiddo, let me put you down."

Samuel had to turn away from the father-son scene. He returned to the stairs and retraced his steps to the bottom. He left the stairs and again began scanning the ground for the sien du. Someone had made off with the knife and shotgun. He gave up and returned to the parking lot, where some 50 people were milling around in various stages of arriving and leaving. The strangely dressed group was still there and a young man was playing the dulcimer. Women stirred the apple butter in the cauldrons. The aroma made Samuel's mouth water. He sighed and checked the compass again. The needle was still pointing north. It was going to be a long day.

Samuel was going over the grounds once again in his fruitless search for the knife and shotgun when he heard his name being called. It was Tammy, standing near one side of the parking area and motioning for him to come to her. She was wearing a backpack and was slightly limping as she approached.

"Beautiful day," she said, mouthing a shy smile. "Seems we've stirred up things around here. I talked to the chief; and, he says he received a call from a man who claimed he was involved with the tower incident. Told the chief it was just an elaborate prank and he and his partner were having fun at the expense of the dumbass woman ranger."

"What does your chief think?"

"He's wondering where the hell my head was to let all this stuff go on around me. And he wants to know if I've been smoking something funny. But he is worried because Manny seems to have completely disappeared. Can't pick up a line on him and his truck is still in the parking lot. The chief is pissed that the suspect I had handcuffed was able to escape." She wrinkled her nose and gave him a mock glare. He's doubly pissed that this guy had the nerve to leave the message on his answering machine about this all being a prank. And, he wants to know, if this is a prank, then where the hell is Manny?"

"Sounds like the chief is not a happy man."

"Oh, he's more than unhappy. He says he doesn't want to see my face for the next three days. Told me to take three days of my vacation and let my leg heal up. Oh, yes, I have been written up for all this. It's now a part of my official record."

"Sorry," he said, grinning, "I thought the call might help you."

Tammy threw him a dirty look and led him to one of the wooden picnic tables. She removed the backpack and took out a box of fried chicken, some roasted corn and a couple of homemade biscuits.

"You can cook, too?"

"Shut up and eat. This is straight from KFC. Enjoy."

Samuel had never eaten fried chicken before and he found the crunchy texture delicious. He bit into a drumstick and smiled. "This is great," he said.

"What, they don't have KFC in the 14th Century?"

Tammy watched him polish off the chicken leg, and then turned serious.

"Any signs of your friend Dexter?"

The smile faded from Samuel's face. "No, and I also discovered that I've lost my knife. Your shotgun isn't the only thing missing."

"Yeah, I'm going to have to report that missing. The chief is really going to take a bite out of me when I tell him it was stolen by our mystery guests."

"Don't report it missing just yet," Samuel said. "I'm going to be returning to my homeland soon and maybe I can find it. I'm sure those guys will be waiting for my visit. They may be hanging onto the gun."

Tammy's face clouded. "You're leaving?"

"Aye. If Dexter hasn't shown up by tomorrow night, I'm going hunting for him. I don't like not knowing what he's up to and I just may have a little surprise for him."

"I wish you could just let him go. How long have you been chasing him now?

"Forever, it seems. But especially for the past two years."

"He could kill you, you know."

"Aye, that he could. However, I'm not going to let that happen. Thanks to Dexter's clumsy men and your marksmanship, Draconis has been feasting on stones recently. I'm looking forward to our next encounter."

Tammy sighed. "The last time I saw him he was about to run you through with a sword."

"Oh, he enjoys his advantage and he seems to take great pleasure with taunting me. Nothing seems to be as good for him if I'm not around to suffer from the act. But I'm thinking the next time may be different."

Samuel finished the last piece of chicken and licked his fingers. "This was good," he said. "Who's the fat man on the box?"

"Oh, that's Colonel Sanders. He started this business. Don't know what kind of colonel he was, though."

"Doesn't matter, he must have earned a medal for this recipe."

Tammy laughed and shoved the empty box toward him. "Look, I'm going to have to get out of here and get off this leg for a while. I'll be back after the park closes and we'll check things out again."

Samuel watched her leave, favoring the injured leg as she descended the steps. Had there been room in his shattered heart, he would have found a place for her. She was a feisty woman. Spirited. Honest. Determined. All the things he admired in a person. He thought of what Cristine the vet had said about Tammy carrying a grudge against all men because one had broken her heart. Too bad. She was obviously a woman capable of giving and receiving love. And the body isn't bad, either, he found himself thinking. He felt a stirring in his chest. *Emotion? For another woman?* He shook his head as if to clear it.

Tammy reached the bottom of the stairs and turned to give him a farewell wave. He returned the wave and then averted his eyes, staring off across the mountains. In his peripheral vision, he saw her pause and look at him for a few seconds. He could feel her presence and he was tempted to leave the tower and join her. However, he couldn't. There was no room for feelings for another person in his heart. He couldn't play games with another person, no matter how much he might like to taste the forbidden fruits. He didn't

338

want to give Tammy hopes for a future with him. He steeled his emotions, drawing on the inner strength and focusing on his single-minded ambition. He spoke only truths, and when he committed, whether to love a woman or to slay an enemy, that commitment was total.

Tammy finally turned and walked to her truck, her eyes cast downward. Emptiness settled in Samuel's chest. He sighed and pulled the compass from his pocket once again. Back to business. The needle pointed unwaveringly to the north. He studied the visitors below; they came in all shapes, sizes and colors. The license plates on the vehicles were just as diverse. Canada, New York, Georgia and Florida. They came from all parts of this great nation and moved about unthreatened. In his homeland, they would be carrying arms as they traveled, wary of bandits and ambushes.

A young couple approached and complimented him on his long coat. European cut, they wondered? Had he been to the Renaissance Fair? Another man asked about the black hat. Would he like to sell it? Samuel politely responded to the inquiries but encouraged no further conversation.

He listened to the folk songs and mountain tunes, the music lightening his spirit. He had discovered earlier that he liked the taste of Pepsi, and ventured to a refreshment stand to purchase one. The burning sensation of the soda was pleasant and the caffeine lifted his sense of awareness. *"I need to take this formula back with me."*

The day passed slowly and he tired of standing. He found a seat on a bench and rested, the compass placed on his lap, the needle still pointing north. It had been a boring, wasted day.

As the sun slowly sank into the western horizon, Samuel rose and began walking toward the entrance gate. He had just reached it when the cell phone rang again. Tammy was calling to tell him that she was almost back at the park to pick him up. Seconds later, he saw her truck approaching.

"Get in," she said, and handed him a thermos of coffee. "Try this; it'll singe the hair off your tongue."

Samuel poured some of the black liquid into the plastic cup and sipped it. He marveled at how hot it was. Tammy noticed the expression and said, "Yeah, this new world is just full of surprises, isn't it? Guess you don't have thermos bottles where you come from, huh?"

"I have no idea what you're speaking of," he said, smiling and taking another sip of the smoking brew. "But tell me, do you have any camping gear?"

"Of course," she said. "Little ol' Tammy is a wannabe Boy Scout; prepared for everything. Whatta ya need?"

"Well, it's obvious that Dexter isn't going to risk a Rippling during the day when so many people are about. My thinking is that he'll try it tonight. I want to be here when it happens."

"Oh." There was disappointment in her voice. "I thought you'd be starving, so I've got homemade spaghetti and a bottle of wine waiting."

"Spaghetti?"

Yeah, you know, strings covered in sauce with hamburger balls in it."

Samuel made a face. "Hamburger balls?" Doesn't sound too appetizing to me."

"Oh, stop it! And you need a break. We're going back to my place and eat and then you can come back and hold your vigil. Nothing's going to happen for a while."

Ranger Swain didn't look too official now, Samuel thought. She had washed her tawny hair and it was buoyant. He could smell her perfume and a little of his resolve melted away. He felt his pulse quicken and he tried to fill his mind with other thoughts. The women in this country were bold. They wore tight jeans that hung on their hips, revealing Celtic knot tattoos on their lower backs and pierced belly buttons. Some even had those horrid things piercing their noses and lips and eyebrows. What a strange culture!

But Tammy was none of that. She sat behind the wheel of the Silverado, looking and smelling great, alluring and intoxicating without even trying. He breathed in the scent of her and sighed. She was wearing a low-cut blouse that revealed the beginning slopes of her breasts and tiny stones hung from her ear lobes, glinting in the fading light. He

340

couldn't admit it and he certainly couldn't acknowledge it, but Samuel was stricken by this young woman.

When they reached Tammy's home, she said, "Go take a shower. You'll find some clothes in the bathroom. I guessed at your size but I think they'll fit. When you finish, dinner will be ready."

The hot shower was heavenly, and Samuel was once again wondering how he could take this knowledge back to SkyeEden. The hot water washed away the soreness and tightness of his muscles and he lathered himself in the cleansing soap. He relaxed, exulting in the luxury.

Wonder what Dexter is doing now?"

The thought hit him like someone pouring cold water over the top of the shower curtain. It was as if a snake had slithered from beneath the bed. Guilt engulfed him as he thought of the man he hated. Was he killing someone even as Samuel was pleasuring himself? He had no right to pleasure as long as Dexter was still breathing.

The mood shattered, Samuel turned the water off and stood dripping as he pondered the situation. Finally, he reached for a towel, dried himself and began putting on the new clothes. Tammy had bought a pair of Wrangler jeans and a light blue sweatshirt and both fit perfectly. The woman's talents were unending.

Damn Dexter. How could he be wasting time here? Dexter may already be back at the park. There was no time to be dawdling here at this woman's house. Damn Dexter!

Samuel entered the dining room and found it candlelit. The room glowed from half a dozen red and blue candles and there was rich incense of jasmine in the air. Tammy made a gesture towards a chair and he sat down at the table. She filled his glass with a red wine and then appraised his new look. "You look great in jeans and a sweat," she said, grinning impishly, "and they even fit. Try the wine on for size."

Samuel lifted the glass, and then paused before it reached his lips. A bitter anger surged within him. *What am I doing? I should be on the hunt, not here in this woman's home preparing for a feast.* He understood that Tammy was trying to

341

help him, but she didn't understand that she was interfering in his single-minded quest to rid the world of Dexter. Yes, he needed her help. Without her, he would probably be dead already. Nevertheless, he would not allow himself to become indebted. He would have done as much for her had the tables been turned. His mind raced. The ranger was a wonderful woman, a lovely woman. In addition, he had made her look like a fool in the eyes of her superiors. Because of him, her job was in jeopardy. He thought of Manny, Heather's father, now nothing but another smudge in the mountain cabin, and bitterness welled in his chest.

Enough of this! Gain control. This is a good woman. Honor her.

Samuel brought the glass of wine to his lips and sipped. Instead of the bitterness, he had expected because of his mood, the wine was sweet and smooth, a stark contrast to his inner feelings. He smiled in Tammy's direction and took another sip. The liquid soothed him and he became aware of how taut he had been. He was a burning fuse of vengeance. The thought reminded him of the nude boy on horseback with the lighted firecrackers and he couldn't smother a bemused chuckle.

"What's so funny?"

Samuel sighed. "Just an old memory," he said.

"Want to share it?"

Samuel smiled. "Oh, it's nothing; just me naked on a horse."

It was Tammy's turn to smile. "That sounds interesting. Tell me more."

Samuel drank from the wine glass and lowered his inhibitions. Why not? Who was she going to tell that would make a difference to him? Tammy refilled his glass with wine and he began relating the adventure with Nathan and the Manteo Brothers.

He was on his third glass of wine and the candles had melted half an inch by the time he finished the tale. Tammy's eyes had grown large as she listened to the story and found herself spellbound. *Amazing.* His words floated in the air like dust from a century-old chest that had just been flung open. The wonder of the transcending worlds was magical but almost incomprehensible. Yet, she knew it was the truth. She listened in wonder as he told of his love for the strange man called the Swordslinger and how he had been turned on by the villagers and then slain by his own son.

The wine bottle was empty when Samuel paused and Tammy rose from the table. "Fascinating," she half-whispered. "I think I need more wine. Want some?"

"Why not?" He was beginning to feel mellow and the tension and hatred seemed to have drained from his body and soul.

She used the corkscrew and poured their glasses full. "Now, tell me more about the Highlands."

"You would love them. Green meadows, purple mountains, clear sparkling streams, thistles, rolling terrain, gentle breezes. My home is on the side of a mountain overlooking the valley of the clan's village."

"It sounds wonderful."

"When I was on the tower today, I was reminded of it. It's only been days since I was last there, but I do miss it. All of these gadgets — your TV's, your radios, your cars and planes, all of these are nice — but I prefer the old way of life. You are closer to the land and nature there. Here, you are indoors or in your cars and you rarely even feel the breeze. In addition, when you do, it smells dirty. Even from the tower today I saw brown, dirty smog hanging over the terrain. We do not have that in SkyeEden. The air there is clean and fresh. You have spruces dying on your mountaintops here from bad air and tainted rain. We do not have that. Your trees are stripped from the earth. Your roads are littered with trash and unsightly billboards."

"Oh, come on. We're not that bad."

"It's just that I am disappointed. I travel hundreds years into the future and I'm not sure it's a future I would like for my descendants. True, your technological advances are incredible, and there is a freedom in your country that I envy, but your television news is filled with violence and life seems to be so cheap in places such as the one called Middle

East. I have seen pictures of dead and wounded and there seems to be carnage everywhere."

"It can be scary," Tammy said. "I find it ironic that those who claim to be the most religious are among the most violent people on earth. Man can be a beast. That's why I enjoy working up here in the mountains, trying to protect our greatest heritage from destruction by mankind."

"You are well-suited for the profession," Samuel said, taking a rolled cigarette from his pocket and preparing to rise and go outside.

"It's okay," Tammy said, "go ahead and smoke. I'm little nicer after a few glasses of wine. Do your people know about cancer yet? Probably not."

She paused and watched him inhale the smoke. "Do you have a wife waiting for you?"

The question startled Samuel. He stopped the wine glass halfway to his lips, set it on the table and pondered what she had said. The drinking of the wine was pleasurable and he could allow himself no pleasure as this sacred but horrifying memory was dredged up. He would not allow himself to feel any pleasure, any desire, anything but hatred until he had found vengeance. He raised his eyes to meet Tammy's and saw the reflection of the candle flames in her yellow-brown orbs. The fuzzy warmth that he had been feeling was drowned in an icy chill.

"Yes. Her name was Heather," he said in a low, distant voice.

"Was? What does that mean?" Tammy pushed her glass aside and reached out a hand to touch his fingers that held the wedged cigarette, the curls of smoke forgotten in the moment. He pulled his hand away and took a draw from the cigarette, holding the smoke for a long moment before exhaling.

"She was murdered."

"Oh, Sam." Tammy was crestfallen. She realized she had just opened another old wound in this man that she was begging to feel close to. I'm so sorry. It was stupid of me to ask you that."

"No," he replied, his voice muted. "It's only natural to inquire. I just keep the memory buried inside. I have forbidden myself from thinking of it."

"Then don't. You don't have to tell me anything."

"I feel that I should, though. Perhaps it will help you to understand some of my actions."

"Leave it to me to waste a bottle of wine and spoil a mood." Tammy raised her glass and drained the last of the wine.

Samuel drew a deep breath and leaned back in the chair. He stared at the blue flame of the candle, into its scorching heart, and began to speak in words and sentences as fragile as the spun filament of a spider.

"It happened long after the falling of the huge meteor and rumors of Dexter's dastardly deeds began reaching our village," he began. As he spoke, the candle flame began to blur before his eyes and spread until it had consumed him. He pictured himself back in SkyeEden and he vividly relived the moments, the emotions, and the horror.

CHAPTER 39

THE WEDDING

Robert laughed and slapped his brother on the back so hard that Samuel spilled his cup of mead on the table. "How are you enjoying your final day of freedom, brother?" he chortled. "I suppose I will be an uncle soon, huh? I can see it now; wee ones crying and crawling after you with their mouths gawking like hungry baby birds. Are ye sure ye are ready for this?"

The brothers were in the dining area of the recently completed house Samuel had built on Nathan's dream site. Samuel and Heather were to be wed in the evening and this would be their home.

"Stop your teasing, Robert. I'm too nervous for joking around. The evening is going to be here before we know it."

"Aye, that it will. Why don't you get dressed and I'll check you out to make sure you're presentable to the bride."

"Go ahead, have your sport, brother. Your day will come soon. I've seen you and that young maiden exchanging glances. Have you set a date, yet?"

"No way!" Robert exclaimed. "I'm going to be a swordslinger. You'll be an old married ironsmith and I'll be roaming the countryside protecting villages from bandits."

"Right. I can see that happening. The only thing you can do is blow your pipes, baby brother. You'd have a better chance chasing bandits away with your bad notes than with your sword."

"Oh, really? Would you like to go spar a little before your wedding? No, better not. Heather would slay me for sending you to your wedding night with your body bruised and your energy spent."

Robert grew serious. "I'm going to miss you, Samuel. The old house is going to be lonely without you. Don't know if I'll be able to sleep without your snoring. Tonight will be like the first night without father."

Samuel went to his brother and embraced him. "I'm proud of you, Robert," he said. "Despite me, you've grown into a fine young man. The girl you choose for your bride will be a lucky lass."

"I won't be getting married," Robert said, glancing at his brother to see how he would greet this news. "I've been talking to Father McFarley a lot recently and I'm thinking my future is with the church."

Samuel was taken aback. He knew Robert enjoyed singing the hymnals and seldom missed a church service. However, nothing his brother had ever said had made him think he was considering a life in the church. That would mean no marriage and no children. His heart and soul would belong to the church. "Really? And when did you make this decision?"

"About the time you and Heather announced you were going to be married," Robert replied. "I figured it was time I began thinking about what I was going to do with my life. I'm okay with the ironsmith work, but it is not enough to support two families. And, besides, it has never been the joy for me that it is for you. It just isn't in my heart to create weapons to be used to kill.

"At our last village meeting you said that we must continue our lives despite the raids from the bandits. You said if we don't find happiness, our lives are meaningless. Then you backed up your words by proposing to Heather in front of all the villagers. I was proud of you for that. I'll never forget the look on her face."

Samuel smiled at the memory. "Aye, I surprised her that time."

"Yes, but you also set an example for the rest of us to go on with our lives. We cannot exist if we're afraid to make a commitment because we're afraid that Dexter Frasier will show up. Your determination to become a husband and a father is a model for how we should live. But I'm convinced my way is the path of God. I can share His word, instill hope, and love in the hearts of our people. When danger comes, you assume the role of protector, but I am not a man of the sword. I've always been a man of music whose desire is to bring happiness to the heart and soul. Are you okay with this? Do I have your blessing?"

Samuel made no effort to hide the smile on his face. He had never been so proud of anyone. It wasn't just that Robert had chosen the priesthood as a profession, but he had made a decision on the role he would fulfill. It was a sign that his little brother had truly become a man.

"You have my blessing, brother. I think God will be delighted to have such a pure-hearted man as you to help lead his flock."

"Thank you, Samuel. Today you commit to Heather and I commit to God."

Samuel looked closely at his brother. He almost failed to realize that Robert was indeed a young man, not a boy. He was a handsome man, with clear blue eyes and slim build, only an inch shorter than Samuel was.

"You're going to break that young lass's heart," Samuel joked. "I'm sure that she'll be so crestfallen that she will never marry and will only want to serve you in whatever capacity you will allow."

"Yeah, sure," Robert said, his eyes gleaming. "Truthfully, had I not chosen the church, I probably would have married her. She's a fine young girl and I only hope she understands my decision. I have no doubt that seeing her with another will cause me discomfort, but I must follow my destiny."

"I guess I'll just have to accept that you're no longer my little brother," Samuel laughed. "Actually, you were like my son. In a way, I feel you are as much as my son as my brother."

"I wouldn't let the local gentry hear me talking like that. They may think strange thoughts about ye and mother."

"Robert! Remember, you're going to be a priest."

They laughed then gradually sobered. "When we walk out this door, we will go our separate ways," Robert said. "I…" his voice began to crack. "I guess I never really thanked you for taking care of me when I was younger. Somehow, you got us through. I've always admired what you did that night with Nathan and the Manteo brothers. You stood alone for what you thought was right and ye went in the face of danger. I think that day you made your own path away from father."

The sun had set by the time the brothers reached the village center. Heather was already there, a vision of loveliness standing near the well in a long beige linen dress. The dress had long sleeves and was delicately embroidered. A garland of blue heather had been braided into her auburn hair. She stood with her mother, holding hands, and watched the brothers approach. Her father came from the pub bearing three mugs of mead.

"We men have to make a toast," Manny said. Samuel thought he had never seen the man so clean and well groomed. His skin glowed like a full-moon reflection off still water. He offered two of the mugs to Samuel and Robert. "Here," he said, "think ye lads can handle this?"

Robert faked offense. "Have ye forgotten, sir, that I was reared by my father, who suckled me on mead?"

Heather laughed at the remark and Samuel thought he had never seen her appear so glorious. His heart was pounding with joy, love, and excitement. This would be his wife tonight and they would consummate their love. The act would bring her into womanhood and him into manhood. He felt himself stirring from anticipation and his face reddened with embarrassment. He hoped Heather and her parents didn't notice his discomfort.

Even as he drank, Samuel could not keep his eyes off his soon to be wife. Her beautiful eyes, those moist, red, pouting lips that he could taste. He felt like a leaf floating on a pond of water. His yearnings for her were emotionally deep and physically obvious. He had dreamed of her thousands of nights; and, now she was, at last, going to be his. His heart raced with excitement.

"Och! We must make a toast to this union," Manny said, his face glowing with pleasure and happiness. You never had a chance, me lad. This woman wooed you from the first time you met as babes." Manny lifted his mug high and began speaking:

"Tonight my own flesh and blood, me daughter

349

Fine a woman as her mother
Whose heart is true will never falter
Ne'er will she love another
Only to her one true love Samuel Donachee
To whom I give me daughter free
May ye live long and prosper
And list many a son on the rosters
Tonight ye are husband and wife
Bound together till the end of your lives."

Manny clinked his mug against those of Samuel and Robert and they drank. Their eyes met over the rim of the mugs and it became a contest as to who could finish quicker.

They finished in unison, all gasping.

The women laughed. "Don't make him sick, father. He's got a long night ahead of him," Heather said, smiling coquettishly.

Samuel blushed, wiped the foam from his lips and said, "I guess we should see Father McFarley now."

Manny reached out and embraced his new son-in-law. "Ye were always like a son to me," he said, tears moistening his eyes. "Now I can officially welcome you to our family."

"It is an honorable family that any man would be proud to become a member of," Samuel said, and turned to his betrothed. Heather beamed a smile and lifted her arms toward him, opening and closing her hands in a gesture that she had made to him even as a toddler.

Samuel felt his cheeks burning again and the scene took on a surreal appearance for him. He felt as if he and Heather were bodies moving in a dream. He took her hands in his and said, "Shall we, Mrs. Almost Donachee?"

"Aye, we shall, me darling Samuel."

The couple entered the church, knelt at the altar and made crosses to the statute of Mother Mary. Father McFarley stepped from a cubicle and stood between the couple, placing his hands on their shoulders.

"Father God, Mother Mary, Sweet Jesus, this couple comes before ye, seeking thy blessing before they become man and wife. If ever there were two that truly loved, it is these two. We thank you, Lord, for your consent and for the bestowed blessings to come. In Jesus' name, we pray, amen."

Samuel and Heather rose and Father McFarley embraced them. "I knew this day was coming many years ago," he said. "I've known both of ye as wee babies and I've watched ye grow from seeds to trees. And tonight, ye have honored me and God by coming here. Ye have all my blessings. Your bonding gives us hope amidst the murders and darkness that seem to have fallen upon the Highlands. Ye shine so brightly with love that the shadows of evil will flee. I am very proud of the both of ye. Now go, as man and wife."

Heather lifted Father McFarland's hand and kissed his palm, then leaned forward and kissed his cheek. "Thank ye, Father."

Samuel felt as though his chest had expanded double its normal size. He held out his hand, but Father McFarley embraced him instead. "Good luck to ye, Samuel. Now, go and live ye life."

"Aye, I will, Father. Thank you."

As the newlyweds left the church, Robert began ringing the church bell. Heather's parents embraced them one last time.

Without speaking, Samuel and Heather followed the westward path almost a quarter of a mile to their special place, a stream by Loch Myst. Heather held the hem of her dress up to keep it from getting wet and they waded out to the boulder where they had been lying the night they saw the stone fall from the sky.

The enthusiastic Robert was still tolling the church bell and they could hear it clearly even from this distance. "I hope the villagers won't think we're under attack," Samuel said, as the ringing echoed around them."

"Are we really man and wife, Samuel?"

"Well, not quite yet," Samuel quipped, "but that will soon be rectified."

"Oh yeah? And just how is that going to happen, me darling husband?"

They had reached the boulder and Heather climbed up with Samuel following. She grasped his hands and began dancing around him, pulling him along. "I'm so happy!"

"Me too, my love, me too." He pulled her to him and the furious beating of their hearts became one. She raised her face, the full lips parting slightly, and they kissed deeply.

Moments later, their lips separated and Samuel held her face between his hands. He loved staring into the blue-green eyes and he could feel her pulsing blood through his fingertips on her cheeks. Her eyes were bands of green with irises of sea blue and they stared back at him with an intensity of love and trust and a purity of soul. There had never been another for either of them since Heather's mother had brought her to visit Samuel's mother. Heather was lying in a basket and she had reached out a hand and wrapped her fingers around his thumb. That had been their bonding and it had never been questioned.

The mothers had been best friends and they spent many of their days together, sharing chores and laughs. Heather and Samuel played together and babbled as their mothers worked or gossiped. When they grew older, they played games as husband and wife. Samuel would pretend to hunt wild animals or fight battles against intruders and Heather would feign excitement over his conquests. She would prepare mud pies for their enjoyment when he returned from his trips. *The innocence of childhood.*

Now they stood in their special place, brought here by destiny and knowing that this time they weren't play-acting. Tonight was for real and they were beginning the next stage of their lives as husband and wife.

"This is the happiest day of my life, Samuel."

Samuel's nerves were jumping. His heart pounded like that of a cornered rabbit. The moment was at hand and the new husband had no idea how to proceed. He had never been given the benefit of a father-son talk. He had witnessed the mating of sheep and dogs, but he couldn't compare that to making love to the love of his life. He was a virgin, and a very frightened one. He had vague memories of lying awake and listening to gasping and groaning from his parents'

352

bedroom. However, he was at a loss as to what consummation of marriage meant. He and Heather had spent many hours holding each other and kissing, but they were truly a pair of innocents.

"I love you, Heather," he mumbled, his voice barely audible.

"Yes, I know, and I love you, my husband. I will be a good and faithful wife." She put her arms around him and rose up on her toes to give him a kiss on the lips.

"I … I'm not sure how … you know … I don't know how …" His face was as red as summer apples.

Heather laughed and kissed him again. "Don't worry my love. It is as simple as breathing. My mother has explained everything to me. Don't worry. It will just happen."

"I love you, Heather."

She quieted him with anther kiss, this one deeper and making his breath a harsh rasping in his throat.

Heather broke the kiss and turned away from him, returning a moment later with a blanket. "I was here this afternoon," she explained, giggling. She spread the blanket on the ground and made a swirling movement that had her dress billowing. The movement sent scores of fireflies into flight and a fluorescent light rose above the boulder island.

She danced among the fireflies, which seemed to serve as stage lights for her performance. She moved toward the entranced Samuel, slowing her movements and undulating her hips. Some of the fireflies perched in her long hair and she seemed to be wearing a sparkling tiara. Laughing, she took a graceful stride that brought her back to Samuel, her hair brushing against his face. As she turned, he grabbed her from behind and pulled her to him, kissing the back of her neck.

"Make a wife of me," she said, her voice soft and tantalizing. She turned to face him and he pulled her close in an embrace. Her hands were suddenly under his kilt, gripping his buttocks and pulling him tight against her. He felt her proud, firm breasts against his chest and he moved his hands to her buttocks. The sheer dress seemed only to be an extra skin. They kissed deeply, a lasting kiss, unlike anything they had done before. Time stood still. The warmth of her mouth consumed him. He ran a hand through her long hair and they both moaned.

"It's time, Samuel," she whispered, and pulled him down to the spread blanket.

"I've waited for this moment all my life," Samuel said.

They reached for each other and their flesh was hot. Samuel couldn't separate the sensations surging through him. His body tingled, tightened, bulged, and he shivered in anticipation.

Heather freed herself from his embrace, rose and began to loosen the shoulder straps of her gown. The rest of the world ceased to exist for Samuel. He watched the gown fall away from the beautiful woman that was his wife and thought only of how much he loved her. He felt himself stirring and the rush of blood made him dizzy. He helped her remove the gown and was stunned by the feeling that swept through his as he saw her in the delicate wedding undergarments. He was going to faint.

Heather brought him to his senses, asking, "Are you not going to get undressed, my husband?"

Samuel mumbled something incoherent, stood up and began loosening his shirt. He pulled it over his head and when his eyes were uncovered, he saw that she had removed the rest of her clothing. He knew he was going to faint. Her breasts swelled with each breath, and then she made the gesture again, reaching toward him, opening and closing her hands in that familiar gesture.

They stood facing each other on the blanket and Samuel knew he was going to faint when she moved close enough for her nipples to graze his chest. He pulled her to him and the touch of their bodies was electrifying. His hands moved slowly down her back and her hands traced that movement on his own back. Again, their mouths met in a long kiss. Samuel moved his lips to her throat and felt the pulsing of her blood. He kissed her earlobes and then moved to the back of her neck and down to her shoulders. His hands were on her breasts and she was moaning again.

They lowered themselves to the blanket and continued the embracing, the kissing, the moaning. "Make me your wife, Samuel."

There was nothing else. There was just the two lovers, exploring, enjoying, and experiencing delectable true love. Time passed. It could have been a minute. It could have been an hour. It was a lifetime. Neither knew and neither cared. Ecstasy was not measured in time. They found new ways to reveal their love for each other and finally they were drained, satisfied. Swept away into a world neither had even known existed.

"Oh, Samuel, my mother never told me it would be like this!"

Samuel held her body tight to his, not wanting the moment to end. He felt her warm breath on his naked chest. "We are one now, my wife," he said gently. "We will never part."

The clapping of hands sounded like thunder to the young lovers. Samuel leapt to his feet, staring into the darkness. "What …!"

"Bravo, Mr. and Mrs. Donachee. That was a grand show you gave us!"

The voice sent cold shivers down Samuel's spine. He could make out the figures of several men in the dark, standing almost knee deep in the water surrounding the boulder island. Heather scrambled to pull the blanket around her.

"Dexter Frasier?"

"Aye, ye remember. How touching."

"What in the name of Satan are you doing here?" Samuel asked, trying to keep his voice from quavering. "This is our wedding night! Have you no decency?"

"Decency? And what might that be? Nae, Samuel, I have come a long way for you. I've had a craving for your stones for a long while now. I think that your stones will be delightfully tasty since you were so close to my dear departed father."

Heather rose, clutching the blanket around her. "Please, we are no threat to you and we have nothing here with us that you might want. Please let us go."

"Och, Samuel, have you no pride? You allow your woman to plead for your life?"

Samuel picked up his kilt and pulled it on, covering his nakedness. The hatred for Dexter surged through as strongly as the desire of a few minutes ago. "Is this a challenge?" he asked. "If so, I accept."

"Samuel!" Heather screamed her protest and reached out to clasp his arms.

"It's okay, my love," he said. "This man has to be stopped and now is as good a time as any."

"Ah, Heather, don't you see? I have to be stopped." Dexter's tone was mocking. "Don't worry. When I have killed him, I will take his stones and then I will take you. I did admire your enthusiasm before we so rudely interrupted."

"Go to hell, Dexter!" Samuel shouted. "Don't sully my wife with your foul mouth. This is between us. Let's do it!"

"Ah, Samuel, ye of such naïve bravery. You know, I know, Heather knows, and these dozen men with me know that I will kill you. You would have a better chance going against all my men at once than with me."

"That's a coward's speech," Samuel said. "Come on! Me and you!"

"Please, Samuel," Heather was almost hysterical. "Leave us, Dexter," she screamed. "My father will hunt you down and kill you like the dog you are if you continue with this."

Dexter laughed, and his men joined in. Their laughs echoed along the pond and wove through the trees like a hundred insane ghosts. When the laughter subsided, Dexter drew his sword and the moonlight glinted on the steel blade.

Samuel placed a hand on Heather. "Stay back," he warned, and took a step toward the men.

"Ye don't have a weapon," Heather whispered.

Samuel paused, staring down at Dexter still standing in the shallow water. The man appeared evil and menacing in the half-light. Was this really happening? Maybe this was a dream. If not, where had the man come from and how had he found them.

Heather was terrified and moved alongside Samuel. "He has no weapon!" she screamed. "Leave us!" We can't harm you!"

Dexter laughed. "Now your woman is going to defend you?" he taunted. The men laughed.

"Damn you, Dexter. I'll fight you without a weapon." Samuel moved closer to the edge of the water. Maybe he could catch the bastard by surprise and plant a fist in his evil face.

Dexter raised a hand in a halting gesture. "Hold it," he said. "I am a fair man." He glared at the men, who had begun to laugh again. He motioned to the man nearest him. "Give me your weapon." The man handed him his sword. "You know why I am here, Samuel Donachee?"

Samuel no longer cared why. He was ready to break Dexter's back with his bare hands. The bastard was here, spoiling the happiest night of his life and terrifying his new wife.

But Dexter was not to be denied. "I have such a hatred for my father that it will not die, even after he has died. He died too quickly for me to obtain the satisfaction I needed. He didn't suffer enough pain. But you had become like a son to him in only a few days and you will serve to satisfy my vengeance. When I heard you were wedding tonight, I thought the timing couldn't be more perfect. So here I am … the best man!"

"Okay, you're here. Let's finish this."

"Aye," Dexter said, cocking his head to one side. "Ye are right. We are wasting time. He brandished the sword his henchman had given him. He held it by the tip of the blade, the hilt toward Samuel. "Take this weapon. I don't want to take advantage of an unarmed man."

Samuel reached for the sword, fighting the impulse to grab it and slash his enemy at the same time. However, that would not be honorable. There must be honor even among deadly enemies.

Dexter suddenly drew the sword back and tossed it. Before Samuel could react, the sword was upon him, barely missing his left arm.

Heather's cry curdled Samuel's blood. He turned to his wife and she had already fallen to her knees. She clutched the blade with both hands where it entered her body. Her face was pale in the moonlight and her eyes expressed shock. This was her wedding night and she was impaled on an intruder's sword.

"Ohh, Samuel, look what you have done," Dexter wailed mockingly. "Look what you have done!"

The terror of the moment entered Samuel into a state of paralysis. In what felt like slow motion, he dropped to his knees beside Heather and clutched the hilt of the protruding sword.

"Heather!" Samuel's hands were clenched on the sword, but he was afraid to pull it free. The blade had pierced the blanket and pinned it against her body. She was quivering and her eyes were blank.

"Samuel?" The voice was weak, barely more than hoarse whisper. She tried to raise her arms toward him and her hands clenched and unclenched in the gesture he loved so much.

"Oh, Heather!" Samuel leaned forward and grasped her hands. She moaned, closed her eyes and seemed to relax.

"Ah, Samuel," Dexter needled, "ye are such a coward. Ye let your wife catch the blade. No wonder my father loved ye so. Ye are his spitting image."

"Shut up, you bastard," Samuel cried, remaining kneeling by Heather. He released Heather's hands and gripped the sword again, this time pulling it from her body. A gush of blood followed the blade. Heather gasped and her eyes opened, expressing the fear of the unknown. Samuel pressed the blanket against the wound in her stomach to stem the bleeding and felt her rapid but shallow breathing. "Hold on, my love," he whispered. "Please hold on."

Heather's hands found Samuel's arms and gripped them with surprising strength. "Kill him," she wheezed, the words ending in a gurgle. "Kill him now. Go. I will be fine." A trickle of blood ran from the corner of her mouth.

The rage that consumed Samuel turned everything into a red haze. He rose to his feet, holding the sword that he had removed from Heather's body, and turned to face his tormentor.

Dexter was smiling. He lifted his arms and arched his eyebrows in an expression that said, "Well?"

In his mind, Samuel saw himself take a mighty swing with the sword, saw a headless Dexter still standing, his grinning head catapulting across the water and bouncing, then sinking.

Dexter's shout brought Samuel back to the present. "Get him!" the madman shouted to his men.

Samuel moved first, leaping into the shallow water and swinging the sword at the nearest foe. Issuing a guttural scream, Samuel swung the blade and made a 360-degree spin, feeling the resistance as the sword cut into first one man, then another. Both went down, their blood turning the water red.

Two more of the intruders came at him and Samuel feinted, slashed the blade across the abdomen of the first, and deftly blocked the sword of the other. He stepped backward and as the man's sword lost contact with his, made a lightning thrust that sent his own blade into the man's heart.

Samuel felt, rather than saw the next two opponents. He ducked and a sword swished just above his head. The momentum of the swing cost the man his balance and before he could regain it, his head was almost severed by Samuel's sword. The other man never had chance. He froze for just an instant as he watched his friend's head fall from the body and died a second later as Samuel's sword slashed his midsection.

There were only eight of the men still mobile and they were huddling around Dexter, who was watching the fray with an amused smile on his sinister face. No one seemed eager to challenge the crazed young man who fought with the skill of a swordslinger.

Samuel weighed the odds and decided he might be better off on land if they all decided to charge him. He began backing toward the bank of the stream, keeping his sword raised toward the men. "Don't let him get out," Dexter commanded, and two of the men started forward. Still backing up, Samuel let them get within a couple of yards before making a move. He feinted left, moved right and swung his sword with a mighty swoosh that sliced one man's chest and caught the other in the upper arm. The first man dropped to his knees, a glazed look appearing in his eyes. The other man bellowed in rage and made a fatal mistake, lurching toward his antagonist. Samuel took an evasive step to his left and brought his own sword smashing into the man's face. The dying dropped and began thrashing in the water.

Six to go.

Samuel made it to the bank and stood glaring at the enemy.

Four of the men broke from the group and began sloshing toward him. They didn't seem quite so eager to attack now, however, and Samuel could see the doubt and fear in their dull eyes.

The four men had almost reached the bank when Samuel attacked. The knee-high water slowed their movements and Samuel moved into their midst, slashing, thrusting, parrying and screaming. He was a blur among the slower assailants his sword slashed with an unleashed fury. Flesh severed. An arm flew into the air. A head fell from a body, leaving it standing momentarily in the stream. Samuel was mindless. He acted as man who is already dead and has nothing to fear. He swung the sword with a strength he had never before possessed. Instincts honed by hate and emotion kept him free from the frantic slashing of his attackers. It was over in a less than a minute and four more of Dexter's men lay dead, emptying their veins into the stream.

Two to go.

But where …?

Dexter and his remaining henchman had disappeared. A wary Samuel scanned the area but could see nothing in the dim light. Where had they gone? Surely, the boastful Dexter would not have skulked away into the night, leaving his loyal men to die.

Nothing.

The adrenalin began to subside and Samuel allowed himself to relax. He reentered the water, returning to the boulder island and Heather's side. But a sudden glow emerging from the water startled him. A stone from one of the dead men rose above the surface, paused, and then quickly approached him. Even as this stone came toward him, Samuel saw the other stones from the dead men coming. They didn't enter the borrowed sword he held, but instead went straight for his body. They peppered his chest like ice pellets in a hailstorm. He dropped his sword and his body was hot. He could feel the stones like hot coals inside his flesh. He screamed from the pain searing his chest and frantically tore at his flesh in an effort to remove the stones.

Just as suddenly as it began, the pain was gone. Breathless, the strands of his wet hair streaming across his face, he made his way across the water, stepping carefully around the partially submerged bodies. *Heather.* Was she still alive? His heart raced and his soul filled with dread at what he feared he would find. He moved through the water like a zombie, growing weaker by the moment as the adrenalin oozed from his aching body.

He collapsed just before reaching the boulder and pulled himself onto it. Heather was lying as he had left her. "Heather," he moaned, and saw her eyes flicker open. "Heather!"

She was lying on her back, her head turned toward him. He crawled to her, leaving a trail of his own blood on the rock, and took her face in his hands. Their eyes met.

"I'm so sorry, Heather ..."

Tears ran down her cheeks but she smiled. She tried to lift a hand but it fell back to the blood-soaked blanket covering her stomach. "Sam ... was I a good wife?" Bloody bubbles formed on her lips.

"No, no. Not was. You are a good wife, Heather." The pain in his heart was almost unbearable. He caressed her lovely cheek.

"I'm dying, Samuel."

"No ... don't say that. I'll carry you back to the village and we'll get help. You'll be all right."

"No, it's too bad, my husband. I'm so sorry."

"Oh, Heather, it's my fault. I should have caught that sword before it hit you."

"No, it wasn't meant for you. His aim was true, Samuel. I ... I wanted to have your children. I wanted us to make our home at Nathan's place. I ... wanted ...""

"We will, Heather! You are not going to die!"

"Samuel ..." Heather shifted her head and the trickle of blood from her mouth became larger. Her flesh was ghostly pale in the moonlight and the blood on her chin and her lips were in vivid contrast. "Will you ... keep my garden, Sam? Plant a purple thistle ... for me?"

Samuel couldn't speak; he could only gaze upon the face of his one true love.

"Remember me when ... you see the fireflies. Dance with them for me."

"I will," he murmured, tears streaming down his face. He caressed her cheek with the back of his hand.

"Samuel ..."

"Yes."

"If there is a Heaven, I will wait for you there."

"I know you will." His voice was quavering.

"Don't forget the fireflies." Her voice was just above a whisper now.

"Heather." His voice failed and his body was wracked with deep sobs.

She lifted her gaze to his eyes one last time and he had to strain to hear her last words. "I love you, husband."

It was dawn when Samuel walked into the village with Heather in his arms. A crowd began to gather. Women wailed and wrung their hands in anguish. Robert came running and met Samuel at the well. A minute later, Manny and his wife Martha arrived. Heather's mother collapsed to her knees and took her daughter in her arms.

Manny was stunned, standing like a frozen statue as he unashamedly cried. Slowly, his eyes rose to meet Samuel's.

The sadness in the man's eyes was more than Samuel could bear and he fell to his knees. Robert put his arms around his brother and tried to console him. Manny sat on the ground by his wife and helped her hold their dead daughter.

CHAPTER 40

THE FUNERAL

The notes from the dirge Robert played on the bagpipes hung in the air. The sky was overcast, adding to the funeral atmosphere. The entire clan gathered around the village well to say goodbye to one of its favorite daughters. Heather's body lay on a table, dressed in her favorite blue dress. She was wrapped in white gauze.

Martha stood beside her daughter, holding one of her hands that were folded on her midriff. She patted the hand, then wiped at the steady stream of tears flooding from her eyes. Manny placed a hand on his wife's elbow and led her away from the body. He returned to the funeral table and placed a hand on Heather's forehead. He raised his face heavenward and said a silent prayer, then leaned forward and pressed his face against that of his daughter. He straightened and moved to Samuel, embracing his son-in-law before joining Martha.

Samuel moved to the table and stared down at his beloved Heather. She appeared to be sleeping and there was a sweet smile on her face. Leaning forward, Samuel kissed her lightly on the lips. He straightened and sprinkled a handful of tiny heather flowers over the body. He had gathered the flowers from the spot where she had danced the night before.

As tears rolled down his cheeks, he moved back to join the grieving parents. Robert had finished his mournful tune and placed an arm around his brother. Samuel lifted his eyes to the profile of the purple mountains and then upward to the cumulus clouds. He felt he could see Heather's spirit ascending into the heavens.

The family led the procession following the funeral wagon along the road to the site of the boulder island. The men of the village had removed the bodies of the 12 slain attackers and the scene was peaceful in the subdued afternoon light. Samuel relived the bliss of his brief honeymoon.

The wagon pulled to a stop at the edge of the stream, the horses panting after the exertion of pulling the body and the load of stones that had been placed on the wagon. Samuel, Robert and Manny unloaded the burial stones, carrying them to the boulder island as the onlookers watched in reverent silence. When they had completed the task, Robert climbed onto the wagon and lifted Heather's body, handing it over the side to Samuel. The grieving husband took her in his arms and waded into the water. He held her in his right arm and with his left hand beneath her head walked slowly toward the boulder. When he was halfway across, he paused, looked into the beautiful face and whispered, "One last dance, my love." He began turning, moving her body gently above the water, swaying to an unheard tune.

As he danced with the lifeless body, he remembered how he had looked into her blue-green eyes the night before and how she had bestowed the most precious gift of his life upon him — that sweet smile. Now they were having the last dance, a rite of passage, and her soul was drifting to the hereafter.

Her body was so light. So lifeless. His wife. She would never bear his children. He issued a low mournful wail and pulled her to him, placing his warm cheek against her cold one. Hot tears poured over their faces and he fell to his knees in the shallow water. He cradled her in his arms and cried.

Finally, he rose and carried Heather to the boulder. He placed her on the spot where they had made love the night before — an eternity ago. He folded her arms across her chest and straightened the funeral clothes. He replaced a stray strand of the auburn hair.

Samuel and Robert had prepared the grave earlier that morning and now Robert brought two shovels from the wagon. The brothers lifted Heather's body and gently placed it in the wooden coffin beside the grave, then gently lowered it. They stood, one at each end of the grave, and bowed their heads in prayer. Moments later, they began filling the grave. They used the shovels to smooth the mound of dirt and then began placing the stones on it. The sun was setting when they placed the last stone and the mourners began filing back to the village. Robert took the shovels back to the wagon and looked back at his brother. Samuel knelt by the gravesite and bowed his head. Robert motioned for the wagon driver to leave and waded back across the stream. He watched in silence as Samuel grieved.

It was dark finally and still Samuel knelt by the grave. At last, he raised his eyes and saw a group of fireflies hovering above Heather's resting place. "Come to say farewell, too, eh?" He held out a hand and one of the fireflies settled on his palm. As he watched, the firefly blinked several times, then flew away to join the others, they moved out over the stream and appeared to be performing a water dance.

Robert moved to his brother's side and gently placed a hand on his shoulder. He gripped his arm and helped him to his feet. They embraced, then waded out into the stream and began the long walk home.

CHAPTER 41

THE FORGING OF DRACONIS

There was no sleep for Samuel that night and he rose early the next morning. Robert was still sleeping and Samuel quietly dressed and left the house. He saddled his horse and began the long ride to Loch Myst Mountain and Nathan's home site; the house that would never be a home for him and Heather.

He tethered the horse to the headstone he had placed at Nathan's grave and began removing the stones. Once he had done that, he took the shovel he had attached to the saddle and began digging. Within minutes, he had reached the wooden coffin and cleaned the dirt from the top. He removed the lid and reached inside for the cloth-covered bundle on the dead man's chest.

He removed the wrapping and placed the broken pieces of the sword outside the grave, then carefully replaced the dirt and the stones. He picked up the broken pieces of steel and weighed them in his hand, willing the emotion of his suffering into a vengeance that he hoped would transfer to the metal. He relived Nathan's telling of his wife's rape and slaughter and his own hatred for the murdering Dexter. He held the broken steel above his head and vowed vengeance. His hands shook with frustrated rage and he vowed to obtain justice for Nathan and Heather. He would search out the evil and extinguish it. For Nathan. For Heather. For all the innocent people who had died at Dexter's hand. And yes, by the gods, for himself.

When he returned to the village, it was past noon and Samuel went directly to the ironsmith and closed and locked the door behind him. A short time later, Robert came to the shop and tried the door. He pounded on it and shouted, "Samuel, you okay?"

"Aye, I'm working on something."

"Are you hungry?"

"I'll eat after I finish."

The fire in the kiln was blazing and Samuel began melting the pieces of white-hot steel. Drop by drop the blade formed in the mold and two hours later, he was cooling it with air from the bellows. He shaped and honed the blade for hours; and, when he was satisfied that it was perfect, he had been in the shop for almost two days. Now that it was finished, he was exhausted but exhilarated. He held the gleaming sword above his head with both hands and felt the weight and balance.

"I christen ye Draconis," he said. "Let your fire be my rage. And from this moment onward, my mission is to rid this world of the evil that is Dexter Frasier.

"Prepare yourself, Dexter, for the Swordslinger cometh!"

CHAPTER 42

EMPATHY

"Oh Sam," Tammy sobbed, "I am so sorry; how horrible to have to go through that." Her face glistened with tears in the candlelight. No wonder you want to kill that crazy bastard!"

"Now you understand."

"I understand, but I feel helpless. I don't know what to say or do."

"You've listened," Samuel said, "and you've heard things no one else ever has. I have not talked of this since the night of Heather's murder. Even now, I can see her — that sweet smile — like the sweetest wine. I miss her and will never get over losing her." He lowered his head.

"If you don't kill that lunatic, I will." Tammy's voice was brittle. "I'll never forget what he looks like, and if I see him, I'm going to just walk up and shoot him. No warning. Just shoot."

"My chance will come," Samuel said, his voice quiet.

"And then, after you kill him, then what?"

"I will live the rest of my life in serenity. And I will be able to think of Heather without the hatred for him ruining the memory."

"I've never known anyone to carry such a love," Tammy said. She sighed. She had finally met a man she could love and he was forever bound to another. "I would think there are many others who would like to kill this animal."

"Aye, of that I am sure. He has destroyed many families and ruined the lives of wives and children throughout our land. But I know that I can stop him now. My strength is the greatest it has ever been. The stones Draconis has collected over the past few days are a powerful force."

Tammy reached for the wine glass and drained it. She sat it down and asked, "Mind if I have one of your smokes?"

Surprised, Samuel asked, "Are ye sure?"

"Aye," Tammy said, smiling as she mimicked his dialect. He gave her a tobacco stick and lit it. She inhaled deeply and allowed the smoke to curl from her mouth. "You know what? I'm going to help you hunt this guy down."

"Nae, lass. That cannot be."

"Why not?"

"You have your own life here. You are young and you are not tainted by the violence and vengeance that is my world."

"Sam, I was at the tower, remember? I fought there. I killed men."

"Yes, but …"

"But nothing. You have become a part of my life and I care for you. Anyway, I'm kind of like a swordslinger myself. I am a protector. And don't say no because I'm a woman. I'll bash your face in. I got involved in this as part of my job and it still is. I'm here until it's finished."

"I can't …" the words were strained, deliberate. "I can't have another person I care for die. If you're with me, I'll be distracted. I'll be better off alone."

"Damn you!" Tammy rose to her feet. "Don't you worry about me! I could tell from your talk that Heather had a little spirit in her, too. I think she would be going with you. So don't you dare say no to me!"

"Tammy, you are a good person with a good heart. But you don't need this in your life. Your veterinarian friend is getting tired of making house calls."

"Look, this is no time for making jokes. I'm not going to just sit around and watch men being gutted for their stones. Yes, I'm a woman, but I can still kick ass. I'm trained in martial arts and weaponry. You may have noticed that I can shoot straight. And, just for your information, I can use a sword and throw knives. Frankly, I think I could have done a better job against Dexter than you did."

Samuel smiled. "Aye, you are lovely when you're angry, lass."

"Grrrrr! You ain't seen nothin' yet, me fine lad. Tell me, what if Dexter doesn't show tomorrow? What then?"

"I don't know."

"Oh yes you do! You're planning on going back to wherever it is you came from, aren't you?"

Samuel stood and put his arms around the woman. "I really don't know," he said. "I guess I will return. I can't leave him over there to continue killing my people."

"Well, tell me this; why, after all he has done, are you the only one trying to stop him? Why don't you guys form a posse and hunt him down? He couldn't be too hard to find, unless he's another Bin Laden."

"The people are afraid, lass. For the most part, they are just villagers who don't even carry weapons. They work, mind their own business and raise their families. They don't know how to fight against someone like Dexter. And he has grown so powerful now from all the stones he's collected that they feel he can perform magic."

"Magic?"

"Yes, he …" the image of Robert's face tense with death throes as his chest had been pierced by the stony spikes made him shiver. He turned from Tammy, shielding the emotion on his face. "He can send his stones to kill for him, send them to spy for him, and God knows what else. He killed my brother Robert only days ago as we were preparing a Rippling. The portal had already opened, but he unleashed stones from his sword and they formed themselves into spikes and drove into Robert's back. I was looking into his face when he died.

"This monster has taken everyone I ever loved, Tammy. Nathan, Heather … Robert. My hate for him consumes me. It tears me apart inside. I can't think rationally. My every moment is spent being haunted by my loved ones crying out for vengeance."

"Samuel, we'll get him. You aren't alone anymore. We'll hunt him down and we'll kill him."

"I can't involve you, Tammy. "I can't."

"You can and you will. I'm not giving you a choice. Don't you understand? If Dexter lives, he can change the course of history. All that is now may never come into existence. If he gathers all the stones, there will be nothing on earth that can stop him. Right? He'll be like a god."

"Not a god; a devil."

371

"Okay, well you can just face this, Samuel Donachee. From now on, I am your shadow. I am not leaving your side or taking my eyes off you. If you do a Rippling, I'm Rippling right along with you."

"No!"

"Shut up, Samuel. Don't you understand? I love you. When you hurt, I hurt! When you bleed, I bleed! I know that your heart belongs to Heather and that's okay. I can love you as a friend. You can't do this alone, dammit! And I can't, for the sake of my world, allow you to fail."

"But, Tammy …"

"But nothing." She placed a finger on his lips.

"Nae, listen. I have to get back to the campground because I'm sure Dexter or his men will show tonight."

"Okay, we'll be there waiting for them."

"This could be dangerous."

"No shit?"

"I can't talk you out of it?"

"No way."

"Okay, we'll do it your way. But you're going to have to let me call the action. I am not going to have your blood on my hands, too."

"Don't worry about me. You may have noticed that I can handle myself. But you have to promise me one thing."

"Yes?"

"You aren't going to do this Rippling thing and try to leave me." Her voice and the look on her face were defiant."

Samuel was silent.

"Promise me! Either you promise me or I'm making a call to headquarters and have every law enforcement agent in the county on Mount Mitchell!"

"Very well." He smiled. "I promise not to leave without ye, lass."

"Well, me lord, I shall cease bugging ye, then," she mocked, her face brightening. She went into the dining room and blew out the candles. The television was still playing in the den and she went to turn it off. The evening news was on and the local broadcast was a live scene from Gene's Gun and Pawn Shop in Charlotte. The façade of the

372

building was lit up by blinking blue lights from the police cars. Policemen were swarming in the parking lot. She thought of what Samuel had said about how disappointed he had been to learn that time had not eliminated the violent nature of mankind. *We're no better than they were in the thirteen hundreds,"* she mused. *"Probably worse.*

Samuel retrieved his long black coat and the wide-brimmed hat. He felt bad about lying to her and hoped the brim of the hat could hide his intentions from her. There was no way he was going to take her on the Rippling. Had Dexter known of their relationship, she would already have been killed. The thought made him feel ill. No, he would not take her. He couldn't afford the distraction of having to be concerned for her safety. Well, he would deal with it when the moment came.

"I'm ready," he said, entering the den. She shushed him, holding up a finger for quiet, and motioned toward the television.

"Members of the special operations team fired flash-bangs and entered the pawn shop building," the news reporter said in an excited voice, "but they found no suspects. Authorities are issuing a statewide bulletin asking law enforcement personnel and citizens to be on the alert for a group of men, possibly as many as eight, who are transporting stolen weapons and ammunition. Here with me now is Captain Edward Farrow of the Charlotte Metro Police Department.

"We're trying to piece everything together," the captain said. "A squad car answered an alarm at the pawn shop and when he got here observed a group of suspects inside the building. Because of the number involved, he called for backup, and while he was waiting, he noticed several bright flashes of light from the building, but heard no explosions. Moments later, we had several police officers on the scene and they entered the building from both the front and the back. Unfortunately, the suspects had already fled, although we aren't sure how they managed that. The only entrances are front and rear and we had both of those covered. Somehow, they eluded us and escaped with the firearms."

"Could these men have been terrorists attempting to build an arsenal?" The reporter's voice sounded almost hopeful.

"Until we have more information, I can't tell you what their motives were," the captain said, obviously annoyed. "If you'll pardon me, I need to get back and help coordinate the search."

"Do you have a description of the men or their vehicles?"

Captain Farrow turned back to the reporter, facing the camera. "We have nothing other than what I told you. They pulled a disappearing act and we're doing everything possible to apprehend them as quickly as possible. Thank you."

The camera focused on the smiling face of the reporter. "So, police have no descriptions of the suspects," he said. "They seem to have simply vanished into thin air. Once again, our police officials seem to be chasing ghosts, something that has become all too common in our city in recent days. That's it for now; I'm Jim Hanadoff speaking to you live from ..."

Tammy pushed the off button and the screen went black.

"What do you think about that," she said, looking at Samuel. "Sudden flashes of light. Men disappearing into thin air. Sound familiar?"

Samuel didn't answer. His mind was racing. The strange visitors had stolen guns and ammunition and then just disappeared. His blood ran cold as he pictured Dexter and his band of outlaws with those weapons.

"Let's go," he said calmly. Inside, his nerves were playing leapfrog.

Their ride to the park was a silent one. Tammy drove up to the gate and stopped the truck. "What now?"

"I don't know. We just wait and watch."

Tammy retrieved the lightning ball from behind the seat and plugged it into the cigarette lighter outlet. The beams were scattered and wriggly. Nothing unordinary was disturbing them. She placed a hand on Samuel's shoulder. "If Dexter comes ...?"

374

"We'll know."

"And if he doesn't come?"

"Then I will go to him."

"Okay, but don't try to go without me."

"Of course not," he lied.

They sat in the truck for long minutes, listening to the chirp of invisible insects. Samuel stirred and looked at the woman.

"I've promised you that I won't leave you here," he said. "And if Dexter's men do come back, I'm certainly going to want you by my side. But I think it would be better if I scouted the area."

"OK, I'm going to trust you against my better judgment. However, be careful. If you see anything or need me, just whistle and I'll bring the cavalry." She put an arm around him and pulled him to her. "Good luck, Highlander."

Samuel opened the truck door and stepped out. He paused to get his bearings and began walking along the path to the campground. "Draconis." He spoke the sword's name softly and it immediately began forming in his right hand. He gripped the hilt firmly and, reassured by the weapon's heft, walked briskly along the trail.

Within minutes, he was nearing the late Manny's cabin. He entered the building and waited for his eyes to adjust to the deeper darkness. He drew a deep breath and said, "I sense your presence, Manny. I can smell ye. I'm sorry I wasn't here to protect you."

A kerosene lamp sat on the wooden table and Samuel took out a match and lit the wick. The flickering flame put out a yellow-white light; and, as it brightened, Samuel noticed the drawing hanging on the wall. It was a crude sketch of him and Heather sitting on the boulder in the stream that Robert had done what now seemed like an eternity ago. Robert's signature was in the bottom right corner.

Samuel reached out and ran his fingers over the signature. Then he moved them to Heather's face, wishing that somehow he could feel her warm flesh.

"I miss you, Heather. All of you ... Nathan, Manny, Martha ... and dear Robert. He pulled a chair back from the table and sat down. Moments later, he pulled the brim of the black hat down over his brow and closed his eyes. The images of Heather and Loch Myst began forming.

CHAPTER 43

LOCH MYST

"Wake up, husband!"

The sound of the familiar voice drew Samuel from the depths of sleep.

"Samuel, open your eyes!"

He sat up, wide awake, his eyes wide in disbelief. He was lying on the sandy, damp ground and it was dark. The mist was hugging the ground, creating eerie images from the bushes and boulders. The sound of water lapping on the bank told him he was near the loch. He rose, a little unsteady on his feet, and tried to locate the voice.

"Heather, is that you?" He moved toward the loch, waving a hand in front of him in a futile effort to clear the mist. "Heather?"

"Aye, husband. I am here."

Samuel moved toward the water, eyes straining to see through the mist. At last he saw her, standing almost waist deep in the water, dressed in her wedding gown and wearing a crown of heather, hundreds of fireflies blinking around her. Her lovely auburn hair curled over her shoulders and she lifted her arms toward him.

Samuel was stunned. This couldn't be! But there she was, alive, vivid as a hand before his face. As real as he. As real as the trees, the mist, the boulders, the water. "It is you!" he said, his voice rasping. "My God! It is really you!" He ran toward her, not allowing the water to slow him as he splashed through it. The water sprayed against his chest and his face. His boots were filling. But it didn't matter. Heather was here! Alive!

He fell to his knees in the water and reached up for her, but she was just out of his grasp. "Ssshh! Stay my love," she cautioned, placing a finger to her lips.

"What do you mean? I don't understand. God, I've missed you so. I'm so sorry! It was my fault that you died."

"No my love, don't blame yourself. Listen," she paused and glanced nervously over her shoulder. "The wheel is turning back. What has past is here again. Prepare your heart and steel your courage. Then blade will meet blade. I love you," Samuel."

He bowed his head. "I love you, too, my wife. I will ..." He lifted his head and she was gone.

Samuel woke and shook his head to clear it. He went outside and reached for a tobacco stick. A cloud had descended on Mount Mitchell and it was misty here, too. His heart was racing. Heather had been so real, so alive, in the dream. He could still see her and it was both a blessing and a haunting. Yes, to see her once again, look into her blue-green eyes and see the way she had lifted her arms to him. Yes, it had been her. So real. He took a deep breath, hoping to discover a lingering aroma from her presence. So real. The hair, with the heather still there from their wedding day. So real. But it wasn't real and the opening of the lid to the container of his emptiness was killing him. Seeing her again only intensified the love he felt for her.

The wheel is turning back. What has passed is here again. Prepare your heart and steel your courage, then blade will meet blade.

What had she meant by that? *I love you, Samuel.* He could still hear her voice.

"I love you, too, my wife."

He walked back into the empty cabin that Heather's father had built and sat back down. He closed his eyes and tried to go back to sleep. He was hoping to find Heather again. However, this was a dreamless sleep.

CHAPTER 44

THE INVITATION

Almost two hours had passed when Samuel woke again. He checked the compass and it was pointing true north. He went to the wall and removed the drawing. It had been sketched on linen and he folded it and placed it in his coat pocket. He stretched and received a reminder from the bruised shoulder blade and the still sore cut on his back. He yawned.

Tammy! He had not thought of the ranger since his dream of Heather. She must be worried about him; it had been hours. He had separated from her in hopes that if he found Dexter or some of his men, Tammy would not be involved. He had already visited too many of his problems on the woman. He sighed. He was better as a loner, but he had to admit that she had certainly carried her own weight in the battle in the park. In fact, she had probably saved his life and been injured in the process. He owed her, but how could he repay her? By allowing her to get even further involved?

Well, she was one feisty woman. He smiled at the memory of her fighting spirit. That had been her first contact with war and she was aghast at the carnage, the killing of human beings, and knowledge that they were living targets for an enemy she didn't even know. She had been terrified, of course, but she had handled herself well. Her training and her instinct for survival had reaped a huge benefit. Their lives.

It was still not morning, but there was purple hue spread across the eastern horizon that promised a dawning. This was to be his last day here. Either Dexter was coming to him or he was going to Dexter. And, promises to the contrary, the lady ranger was not going with him. He felt a momentary pang of remorse. *"I'm going to miss her."*

He made his way back down the trail and soon spotted the truck still sitting near the gate. He approached and

379

tapped on the window. Tammy unlocked the door and he got in, entering a vacuum of silence.

"I'm back," he said, trying to break the ice.

"No shit, Sherlock."

"I'm sorry. I know I shouldn't have been gone so long, but I had to do some thinking."

"Oh yeah? Well, I've done a little thinking too. You know what? You suck!"

Samuel knew he should try to explain, but he wasn't sure how. "Look," he said, "let's move the truck out of sight and when the ranger gets here and opens up the park, we'll go in with some of the tourists. I don't want to attract attention."

Tammy glared at him. "Yes, Massa, whatever you say, Massa." She started the pickup and drove it a few yards down the trail. "Is this okay, Massa."

"I'm sorry …" Samuel began, then decided he'd be better off keeping quiet until Tammy had gotten over her anger.

The sun made its glorious appearance over the top of the mountains and a few minutes later the first of the tourists arrived, stopping at the gate to await the park ranger. Within 15 minutes, four vehicles were in the line, their occupants chatting impatiently. They wanted to view the arrival of morning from the tower.

Samuel was trying to gather himself. He had to be alert and ready for action. But he couldn't neglect the woman beside him. She had done so much for him, had saved his life, kept him company, bathed his wounds and given him sanctuary. The knowledge that he was about to betray her was not a comforting thought. "Stop this!" he scolded himself. Sentiment makes one soft. He was involved in a war and there was no time for sentiment. He could not even allow himself to enjoy the beauty of the morning while there was still vengeance to be gained for the deaths of the people he had loved.

Samuel lowered his head, the hat brim covering half his face, and pondered what lay ahead. *My life is cursed*, he thought, and gave himself a mental kick in the pants for the negative mindset.

The park ranger arrived, opened the gate and drove inside, followed by the impatient tourists. Tammy started the truck and pulled into the traffic. She parked the truck between two SUVs, trying to hide the park ranger emblem on the side. "Now what?"

At least she had dropped the "Massa" bit. Maybe she was relenting.

"I know you're not going to like this, Tammy, but we need to separate again." She threw him a killer glance. "You stay with the truck and keep your weapon ready. I'm going to walk around the perimeter of the park and see if I can spot anything strange."

"Do whatever you like," she said, her voice cold. "But be careful, please."

"I will, and I won't be gone so long this time. I promise."

He left the truck and walked to the outer edge of the park. It took him almost 45 minutes to reconnoiter the area, stopping several times to make a compass check. Afterwards he hurried back to the truck. Tammy saw him coming and opened the door.

"See anything?"

"Not a thing. But I worked up an appetite and the restaurant is open now. How about some breakfast while we wait?"

"Good idea for a change."

Smoke snaked from the roof vents of the restaurant as they approached. The aroma of bacon permeated the morning air, making them ravenous. "At least if there is to be a fight today, we will go into battle with our bellies full," Samuel said.

Tammy didn't smile.

They went into the restaurant and found a table with a view through the large window overlooking the Mount Mitchell peak and the Black Mountains across the valley. They could see for miles with their vision hampered only by the puffy wisps of clouds. A gray hawk soared over the peak, rising and falling with wind currents.

They both ordered eggs over-medium and bacon with grits and toast and as they ate, Samuel studied the other diners. There were several couples in the room, two with children. The kids were playful and impatient to get out in the park on the tower. The mother's ssshhh'd them and the men read the sports pages in the local paper and "USA Today". Life was good in 2005. Samuel noted the array of different hairstyles on both the men and women and smiled. Everyone in SkyeEden wore their hair long, men and women. The clothing amused him, too. Both the men and women were dressed much alike, blue jeans and sweat shirts, or for the braver ones, tee shirts.

Samuel was adding jelly to the final piece of toast when he saw it. A flash of light from the mountainside, almost invisible in the glare of the morning sun. It came from a wooded area a few hundred yards outside the park.

"They're here," he said to Tammy, who responded with a jerk that sloshed coffee from her upraised cup. Samuel rose from the table and went to the door, leaving a frantic Tammy pawing through her purse to find money for the breakfasts.

Samuel's heart was pounding. Dexter was here! He walked as quickly as he dared to avoid attracting attention and headed in the direction of the flash. Behind him, Tammy paid the breakfast tab and hurried outside.

I'm going to finish this once and for all, Samuel thought, digging the compass from his coat pocket. He held it face up and watched the needle spin crazily around the dial. Hatred and adrenaline surged through his system He fought the urge to summon Draconis. He couldn't have one of the tourists witnessing that. He would wait until he was in the wooded area. How much farther? Maybe a quarter mile? Was the enemy moving toward him?

"Samuel!" It was Tammy, trotting toward him, motioning for him to wait. He couldn't allow her to be involved this time. There was going to be a killing and he didn't want it to be the young ranger. He paused, waited for her to catch up.

"Tammy, I can't let you go any farther."

"You listen to me, Sam!" her eyes were flashing anger. "I'm in this! Now you can bust my chops and leave me lying here in the parking lot or you can let me go with you. I am not going to watch you go into this alone."

Samuel's mind whirled. He didn't have time to argue with the woman. And maybe she could be of use. Anyway, she knew what the dangers were. If she insisted on going, he couldn't very well stop her without creating a scene and probably drawing the on-duty park ranger to the scene.

"Okay, I obviously don't have a choice. But be careful, please? I don't want any more of our blood being shed."

"Gotcha, pal." The smile was back. Tammy the Ranger was back in form.

Samuel turned and led the way, half-trotting. He couldn't get there quickly enough. Dexter! *Oh, it is going to be different this time, you bastard!* Dexter had always managed to come out on top in their previous confrontations, but this time was going to be different. Draconis had collected many stones since the last encounter and his powers would be greatly enhanced. If Dexter makes one mistake or underestimates his foe, he will be a dead man. Samuel's spirits soared at the thought and he quickened his pace, forcing Tammy to run to keep pace. *"Going to get you this time, Dexter!"*

Another few yards and they were out of the parking lot. They had passed the ranger's office and a food stand set up for the tourists. A vendor had set up a booth and was selling mountain music CDs. Some of the tourists were cooking their bacon over open fires and the aroma filled the air. But the only thing Samuel smelled was blood. A reel of memories played through his mind and he saw Dexter slashing with his swords, heard the screaming of the dying and the mourning of the survivors. He saw Nathan's face — the shock and amazement as his son ran the sword across his belly, spewing his guts onto the gallows floor. And drowning out everything else was the expression in Heather's eyes as she ...

"Ahhhhhhhh!"

Samuel's scream startled the straggling tourists and destroyed the movie playing in his mind. Tammy reached for his hand and people stopped what they were doing and stared at him. *Oh great!"* he thought. *"Let's make sure Dexter knows we're here.* He fought to regain control over his runaway emotions. He checked the compass again and the needle continued to spin. Still here.

"He's in the wooded area just outside the fence," Samuel said, keeping his voice quiet. He continued moving; only a few hundred more yards. They entered the wood line and he summoned Draconis. The sword came quickly, seeming as impatient as its master, the mercury-tinted liquid flowing from his right hand.

They were close now. Samuel could feel the hair on the back of his neck standing. Nothing. Everything was quiet and undisturbed. Had he been wrong? Could the flash have been from a car? No! He knew a Rippling flash when he saw one. In addition, the compass had verified it.

They entered an opening in the foliage surrounded by spruce trees. Samuel paused, sniffed the air. It was hardly noticeable, but it was there. The smell of steel and flesh. Just a hint, but enough, if you knew what you were looking for.

Samuel reached a hand back to Tammy, who was almost against him. "Be ready," he cautioned.

He turned his attention back to the clearing. "Where are you, Dexter," he said, his voice low and deadly. Are ye hiding from me now? What are you afraid of?"

"Careful, man. I've not come here to kill you, just to deliver a message."

Samuel and Tammy whirled to see who was speaking from behind them.

The man was a head shorter than Samuel, but well put together and muscular. He was wearing leather-stitched pants and a linen shirt stained yellow under the armpits.

"Don't know how I missed smelling you," Samuel said, wrinkling his nose. "Who are you?"

"Dexter sent me."

"Who else? Samuel asked with sarcasm.

"Guess I'm the reason for all of this stuff that's happening," the man said, his voice almost apologetic.

"I recognize his voice," Tammy broke in. "He's one of the guys who attacked us at the tower!"

"Aye, you're right, lassie. I was there. My name is Mickey." He grinned, showing a gap where at least one tooth was missing. "I made a big discovery that night, thanks to you, me lad."

"Oh," Samuel said, his lips curling in a cold smile. "And what was that, scumbag?"

"Well, ye might listen to this. I think you'll have some interest. With all the fighting and the noise banging this lass was making, I stayed out of the fray. When it was over, and you had left, I found the bang-stick and a dirk. You had left, so I figured, what the shit, I'll take it. So I grabbed them up and the knife had a leather thong attached, so I tied it to my sword. Then after checking the bodies and finding everyone else dead, I figured it was time to get my arse back to the Highlands. I made a Rippling and everything went as usual, except that I came out in an ironsmith shop. And damned if you weren't there, pounding on a piece of hot steel. I popped up right behind you, my sword and the dirk were on the floor, and I was still holding the bang-stick.

"I don't know who was shocked worse, you or me. I said something like, 'What the fuck?' and you almost jumped over the anvil." Mickey's laugh sounded like something that might come from a weasel. "You and me just stared at each other. My first thought was to run you through with the sword, but then I thought that wouldn't be right. This wasn't the tower and Dexter hadn't given me an order for this. Hell, I wasn't even sure what was happening. The timing was all wrong and I knew what I was living was something from the past. So, I just said 'Excuse me,' and ran out of there. I must have run dang near a mile before I stopped. I couldn't figure how I had done a Rippling that took me back too far. I must've scratched my balls for an hour trying to figure out what to do."

Samuel seemed in shock, staring slack-jawed at the man. Tammy recovered first and asked, "What did you do?"

"Well, the only thing I could think of doing was to create another portal, so I threw my sword and whoop-de-doo, there I was, right back home with Dexter and my friends."

Samuel's mind was racing. Could this be for real? Could you really go back to a previous time in your life? Was that any more improbable than going from 1305 to 2005?

The ruffian was still talking, seemingly intent on blabbing everything he knew. Good. Let him rant.

"Dexter is brilliant, you know. I had no idea what had happened to me, but Dexter, he figured it out right away. You get it?"

"No, I'm confused, man." Samuel wanted to hear the rest of the tale. He tried to hide the exhilaration building inside him. "How did it happen?"

"Well, listen up, you dumb ox. This is important. I gave the bang-stick to Dexter and told him how I had been in your ironsmith shop. You should've seen his eyes light up, laddie. I'll swear his eyes glowed like the stones just before they merge. He wanted me to tell him everything I did before I made the Rippling from the tower." Mickey paused, checking Samuel for a reaction.

"I'm listening." Samuel tried to appear nonchalant, but his insides were quivering with excitement.

"Well, let's see if you're as brainy as ol' Dexter, me lad. As hard as it is for you to pay attention, I doubt you're going to figure it out."

"Just go ahead with your tale, please. You're beginning to bore me."

"Well, I told Dexter about tying the dirk to my sword before using it to make the portal. That's when he told me to hold on. Just like that, he says 'Hold on.' Then he asked me for the knife and he just sat there, looking at it, turning over in his hands and thinking. 'You sure this is the knife,' he asked, and I said, Well, it sure ain't my bagpipes. Thought that was funny, but ol' Dexter doesn't laugh. He's still staring at the dirk, as if it was something about to take a life of its own, you know?

"Suddenly, Dexter just jumps up and summons his sword and ties the dirk to it. Then he throws them to make a Rippling and jumps through the portal."

Mickey paused, studying Samuel's face. He couldn't believe his story wasn't getting more of a reaction.

"You want to hear the rest, laddie, or would you rather I left you sleeping?"

"Oh, I'm sorry," Samuel said. "My mind just drifted for a moment, Go on with the story." Samuel struggled with his emotions, but didn't want this man to think he really cared about what had happened. Just keep him talking. Could this story be true? Had the dirk taken the man back to the time of its conception? Did that mean he could return to a time when Heather and Robert and Manny were still living? This couldn't be possible! This Mickey had to be raving, foaming at the mouth, howling at the moon crazy!

"Anyways, we're all still standing there, wondering where he's gone, when a few minutes later, here comes Dexter back through another portal. He runs up to me and kisses me right on the lips!" Mickey wiped his lips with a sleeve. "I ain't the boy-buggering type, mind you, but ol' Dexter was just excited. He said he had been in your ironsmith shop and that you were standing outside, talking to a red-haired lass."

Samuel felt his heart skip a beat. Heather was alive!

"I've never seen ol' Dex so lathered up unless he was getting ready to gut somebody. He was pacing up and down until he wore the grass right off the ground. Then he comes up to me and grabs me by the shoulders. 'You're a genius!' he says, and then he goes on to say how smart it was of me to bring back the bang-stick. Said he had seen one of those things work and that if we had a few more of them, we could really get some things done. Said the bang-stick was more powerful than his sword. Then he said he wanted some of us to make a Rippling back to that city with him. So we did and found this store with hundreds of bang-sticks. Dexter went inside and had the dealer show him how to use them, and explain which ammunition to use. When the man had finished, Dexter says, 'Thank you, I'm going to try it out now.' Then he shoots the dumbass right between the fucking eyes. Yuck! You ever seen a sheep's intestines after it's been torn open by a wolf? This was worse.

"Anyways, we took all the bang-sticks — the man called them guns — and ammunition we could carry and were leaving when the police came flying up with their cars wailing and blue lights flashing. Dexter just laughed and said let them figure this out, and he made a Rippling and we all went through."

"Interesting," Samuel said, pretending to stifle a yawn.

"Yeah? Well get this. We've got an arsenal now like nothing the Highlands have ever seen. We are kings. Nobody can touch us. But you want to hear the crowning piece?"

"Pray tell, what could that be?"

"Okay, Dexter says now that we know how to travel back in our own time, we're going to use the knife to take us back to before the stone fell from the sky." The man was gloating. "We're just going to wait until it falls and everyone has gathered around it and the stones have entered them and then we're going to show up and gun them all down with the bang-sticks. Once they're dead and we've gathered their stones, our power will be so great that nothing can harm us and we'll live forever."

Tammy, who had been so quiet Samuel had forgotten she was there, gasped. Samuel gave up the pretext of being disinterested.

"Is it only my sien du that takes you back farther in time?"

"Oh hell no," the man said, flouting his superior knowledge. "Where's your brain, man. Any knife or sword that you throw with your own will take you back to the time and place where it was created. I was with Dexter and the others at your village before coming here."

Samuel's blood turned to ice. What would Dexter and his men be doing right now? "Why would Dexter want to do that?" he asked, but answered his own question. By going back in his own time, Dexter could get the thrill of killing everyone all over again. *He wants me to know that he's killing my loved ones again.*

Mickey snickered. "Dexter sent me to tell you that he wants you to come to the place where the stone is going to land. He wants you see what is going to happen. Get it?"

Samuel's face was pale from dread and hatred. "Yeah, I got it. So how do I get back there?"

"Ahhh, more good news for you. Dexter went to the house you built on the mountainside. You should've seen him, he was spectacular. He opened up the grave there and pissed on the bones. Then he went into the house and found your wedding sword. Nice job, by the way. Really admired your work. Anyhow, Dexter tells me to find you and instruct you on how to join him. He says if you want to talk to him, you can find him where the great stone will land again." Mickey smiled, showing the gap where the missing teeth had been.

"So what does my wedding sword have to do with anything?"

"Ohhh, you are dumber than dirt, Samuel Donachee. You made that sword before the falling of the stone. Remember, you engraved the date on it."

Samuel's mind was overloading. If Dexter was able to slay all the men who came to view the fallen asteroid and gained all their stones, he would be unstoppable. He would be a superman. However, maybe there was hope. If he could go back to the right time period, maybe he could give Dexter a stone where he wasn't expecting. Like in the heart. His heart swelled at the thought of seeing Heather and Robert again.

"He has to be stopped," Samuel said, reaching out and pulling Tammy to his side. "All of you bastards have to be stopped."

Mickey laughed. "Dexter wants you to try," he said. "One of the things he enjoys most is kicking your arse, lad."

Samuel grabbed Mickey by the front of his shirt and threw him against the trunk of a tree. "I can even the odds a little by getting rid of you right here, you toothless bag of wind!"

Tammy placed a hand on Samuel's arm, trying to calm him. Samuel shoved Mickey hard against the tree and turned to her. "I have to get back to my village," he said. "I have to get my wedding sword."

"Okay, let's do it."

"No, I don't need you for this." His voice was cold and distant.

"You're going back now?" Samuel lowered his eyes in response to her question.

"Then I'm going with you."

"That's not possible. It's too dangerous."

Tammy saw red. "What can I do to convince you that I can take care of myself, you big dummy? If you go, I go! End of story!"

Mickey watched the two and decided to take advantage of their ignoring him. He slid his right hand into the right side of his pants and pulled out a large knife. Samuel saw the movement and turned to him, holding Draconis at the ready. He waved Tammy out of the way. "I don't need you, Mickey," he said, "but I can't just let you walk away. I'm giving you a choice: break with Dexter right now or die."

"Yeah, right! And how long do you think I would live if I defy Dexter? You've seen what he does to the unfaithful."

"Then die now." Samuel raised Draconis above his head. Mickey panicked and lunged toward Samuel. The foot came out of nowhere and slammed into his face, crushing his nose. He sat down hard on the ground, dropping the knife and putting both hands to his ruined face. Tammy regained her balance and turned to the startled Samuel.

"You can't just kill him," she said.

"I gave him his chance."

Mickey was frozen with fear. His broken nose was bleeding profusely and he was having trouble breathing. His breath whistled through the gap where the teeth had been.

"Samuel," Tammy said in an even voice. "Let it go. You don't need to kill him. You're not like Dexter."

Samuel relaxed and lowered his sword. Mickey breathed a little easier. Two children, a brother and sister, suddenly appeared several yards away, stopped when they saw the three people in the clearing and stood there, staring.

"People, people everywhere," Samuel muttered. He kicked the knife Mickey had dropped farther away and commanded Draconis to merge, turning his back to the gaping children.

"If I were you, Mickey lad, I would spend a little time here. Because if I see you again in the presence of Dexter, you will be the first I kill. You are a dead man, understand?"

The dazed Mickey shook his head. He put a hand to his face to feel the damage to his nose and counted his blessings.

Samuel gave the man a look of disgust and faked a kick at him. "Get out of here," he said, his voice low and dangerous. Mickey scrambled to his feet and scrambled away into the trees.

Samuel turned to Tammy. "I'm going now. Thank you for everything, but I don't think I will be returning."

Tammy placed hand on his arm. "You have to do this?"

"I have to. It's my only chance to stop Dexter."

"Then I'm going with you."

"No. I can't risk losing another person I care for."

"You know what! You're a self-centered son of a bitch! All you think about is yourself and how you feel. Well, I have news for you, Samuel. This isn't all about you anymore. The entire course of history can be changed. I'm not going to just stand here like some meek little woman and let you screw up the only chance we have of stopping it!"

Her words stung Samuel like bees. He knew there was truth in them. He took a deep breath, exhaled and looked her in the eyes. "All right. You win. Let's move deeper into the woods so people won't see us."

"Okay." She smiled. "I'm going."

"Aye, but hurry."

"All right!"

"Okay, stay here and watch those kids. Make sure they don't come down this way and I'll find a spot for the Rippling."

"You're going to leave me here?"

"Just until I find a spot."

"I don't trust you."

"Trust me. I'll call you."

"Okay, one last time."

Samuel turned and walked into the trees until he was out of sight. He summoned Draconis again and checked to make sure that Tammy wasn't coming. The sword formed in his hands and he said, "Take me home," and flung the sword end over end. The fabric of time burst into a bright white light and the portal opened. With no second thoughts, no remorse, no silent farewell, he stepped through the portal alone.

Tammy came upon the scene just as the portal opened. She screamed, "NOOO!" and ran toward it as Samuel disappeared. "Damn you!" Running full tilt she reached the portal just as it was closing and hurtled herself through it.

CHAPTER 45

BONES TO WEEP ON

The sword came through portal opening first, then the man in black. Samuel staggered as his feet hit the earth, but regained his balance in time for the horrible scene to make him scream. His sudden appearance startled a flock of blackbirds that rose like a veil being lifted by a magician to reveal a wonderful surprise.

However, the surprise wasn't wonderful; it was the horrible sight of Robert's corpse tied to a post. The orbits of his eyes were picked clean. Shreds of flesh hung from the wounds where the stones from Dexter's sword had ripped through his body. His clothes lay at his feet, revealing a sunken, decaying body that crawled with flies and maggots. His arms hung away from the body, almost seeming to reach out for Samuel. The fetid smell was overwhelming. A sign hung around his neck and on it were the words scrawled in blood, "Embrace me, brother."

Samuel fell to his knees, eyes riveted on the hanging corpse, so distraught that he didn't even notice the park ranger when she tumbled through the portal seconds after him. He raised his eyes heavenward and wept. He had known that his brother had been killed, but he was not prepared for anything as horrible as this. The blackbirds "cawed" overhead and to him the sound was that of Dexter cackling. The world spun, went black for a few seconds and Samuel grasped at the grass to keep from keeling over. He glanced at the blackened body again, wanting to believe that it had just been some dreadful nightmare, but it still hung there, the open mouth emitting a silent scream. The hovering blackbirds continued to express their outrage at being interrupted from their feeding, swirling in a frantic dance macabre.

Samuel suddenly sprang to his feet, grabbed his sword and began swinging wildly at the birds. They scattered, retreating to nearby treetops where they perched, waiting ...

Tammy Swain stood silently, unnoticed, and watched with anguish the ritual being played out before her.

Samuel tried to gather his wits. Obviously, the devious Dexter had planned this scene as a "welcome home" party for him. But why? Just to torment him further? Had God forsaken him? He lowered his head and wept again.

It was time to stop grieving and take some action. *But what?* He had to face it; Dexter had won. The only reason he had allowed Samuel to live was to see him mourn his loved ones and suffer in the aftermath. It was just part of the evil one's master plan.

Steeling his emotions, Samuel used Draconis to sever the ropes holding Robert's mangled body to the post. The stench of the rotting flesh made him ill, but he doggedly kept at the task. He used Robert's discarded clothing to wrap the stiff body as he removed it and placed it on the ground.

The Murry River that ran nearby brought cold water from the mountains and carried it to the sea. Now he wanted to use its waters to clean his body of his dead brother's stench and the humiliation forced on him by his archenemy. He went to the bank, peeled off the jeans and sweatshirt, and stepped into the fresh mountain water. He splashed the water in his face, then dry-heaved. The stench was still with him. He dove into the water, and came up gasping for breath, splashing himself and trying to wipe the smell and the memory from his body and mind.

"Samuel."

What? Had someone called his name? Was it Heather?

"Samuel."

Tammy! He was astounded to hear the ranger's voice. How? God, she must have followed him through the portal. He wanted to scream at her for such a foolish act. However as he looked at her, he saw the empathy on her beautiful face, and felt a need deep inside that cried out for help. He was falling into an abyss of self-pity and loathing and her voice was a rope to cling to, a final straw of hope before being engulfed by the jaws of eternal hopelessness.

"Tammy," he said in a voice that cracked with emotion. "Oh, Tammy …"

The ranger came to meet him at the river's edge. She was clenching the 9mm pistol in her right hand. "Who was that, Samuel?"

He looked at her, his eyes once so bright and alive now appearing almost dead. "It's Robert." He buried his head in his hands again.

"Dexter did this?" She stuck the pistol in the waistband of her cargo pants and stood with fists clenched. She appeared ready to attack, something ... somebody ... anything.

"Who else?"

"Oh God, Samuel. I'm so sorry. What are you going to do?"

"First I have to bury my brother. I'll dig a grave by Nathan's side and bury him there."

"Are we near your village?"

"Aye."

"Well, why don't we go there and get a wagon or a horse so we can carry the body. Maybe get something to cover him."

"Aye."

"Oh, Samuel. I'll stay with Robert until you get back."

Samuel suddenly turned to her, his face black with rage and hurt. "Never call me that again! Samuel is dead." He turned to walk past her and Tammy reached out to touch his arm, her fingers grazing him as he passed. "I'll be back," he said, and walked away, disappearing into a wooded area.

Tammy knelt on the riverbank and splashed water on her face. She rose and glanced around nervously, her mind racing. This was a foreign land ... this new world. The temperature was cooler than her native North Carolina and there was a constant breeze. She watched the hungry ravens circle overhead and grimaced. What if Samuel doesn't come back? Suppose someone kills him in the village? How would she get back to her own world? What would she do if she was attacked? Suppose Dexter and his men should suddenly appear? She patted the butt of the 9mm pistol for assurance and gave herself a mental pat on the back for thinking to stuff the three extra clips in her pocket. The pistol should protect her from anyone armed with a sword. If the men were the ones who had robbed the gun store in Charlotte and had her out-gunned, well, shit happens.

She grimaced, trying to ignore the odor emanating from poor Robert's corpse. It was a sickening smell. Leaving the body lying there with only the bloodied clothes partially covering it, seemed indecent. She went to the nearby wood line and found a broken branch, dragged it back to the body and covered it. She tried not to look at the ravaged remains, but was unable to keep her eyes averted. The image burned a new file into her memory bank. She was holding her breath to avoid the odor, but the smell seemed permeate everything near it and she knew it would cling to her body. She backed away, and then hurried back to the banks of the Murry. She stood there, shaken, tears streaming down her face, occasionally glancing back at the body beneath the tree branch. She shuddered.

Tammy was not an overly religious person. But she did believe in God and now seemed like the perfect time to ask for his intervention. "Oh, God," she prayed silently, "please help us to get out of this. I promise to be a better person if you do." She opened her eyes and looked at the body again. Another world. A dead body. All alone. She shook her head in revulsion, hoping to clear it of the muddled thoughts. What of Samuel? He didn't even want her using his name again. What was that all about? Didn't the dummy know she was in love with him? Hadn't she followed him to the ends of the earth? And beyond? God, how could she be so stupid? Even if everything else wasn't so screwed up, he was a married man. It wasn't fair! She had been so careful, kept her emotions bottled up, refusing to be hurt by another man. Now this? Jesus, even when she was with him, she felt as though Heather was watching them. She imagined how it must be for Heather, if she could somehow see another woman trying to woo her husband away.

But it wasn't all about her love for Samuel, either, was it? There was the small matter of trying to save the world from history being rewritten by a mad man, an evil man, the worst kind of tyrant that one could imagine. *A killer with no conscience.* Oh yes, the grandiose idea of falling love with a man from a different time and saving the world from the terrible Dexter had been exhilarating back at Mount Mitchell. *Hey, Mom, look at me! I'm here to save the world!* The futility of her position and the helplessness that she felt was overwhelming. She was in a foreign land, alone except for one man who didn't even want her to use his name. And her life depended on him making the right decisions. Jesus!

Time crept by and her mind began playing dirty tricks. What if Samuel never came back? She shrugged and let her mind drift, back to her college days and Bobby Brown. Bobby Brown, the first guy she had loved and the first to break her heart. *Oh, great memory. Comforting.* But that had just resulted in a broken heart. This time there was lot more at stake than an achy-breaky heart. Her whole world could be lost this time; not just a love that never had a chance anyway. The last thing Bobby Brown had said to her had been "I love ya, Babe." And those words had haunted her for years, as rancid as the smell of Robert's corpse.

Samuel had tried his best to keep her from this. He thought he had left her behind at Mount Mitchell. She cursed her decision to follow him in the Rippling. *Stupid!* And he was so distraught now that she wasn't even sure he was in his right mind. Suppose he decided to go in search of Dexter or Rippled himself into another time period. What could she do? Nothing. The thought left her confused, grasping, and anxious. She began pacing, aggravating her wounded leg. She glanced back toward the body and it was shrouded in black. The damn birds had returned! She ran towards them, screaming and waving her arms. They didn't seem to be bothered by her presence, ignoring her. She stopped a few yards away, drew her pistol and fired into the swarm of birds. Feathers flew and one of the ravens fell to the ground, thrashing its wings in death. The other birds took flight and returned to the nearby trees.

The echo from the shot rang through the trees. "Have I just fired the first shot in this world?" she wondered. "Samuel, please come back. Don't leave me here alone. I can't handle this." She went to one of the spreading oaks near the riverbank and leaned against it. The last time she had felt so desolate and helpless was when she learned that Bobby Brown had left town immediately following the graduation ceremony without even saying goodbye.

They had hugged when he left the stage and he had smiled that great smile and said, "I'll meet you at the dorm, Sug. We'll do something special this evening and then we'll make some plans. Okay."

Okay? God, anything he did was okay with Tammy. She loved him more than life.

"I love ya, Babe," he had said and left with his parents, leaving his sophomore sweetheart standing alone in the crowd, wondering why she wasn't being invited to go with the family. But it was okay. The family wanted to spend some private time together. She could understand that. She walked back to her dorm, hands stuffed in the pockets of her jeans. It was okay. She would have Bobby to herself later and their time would be sweet. They were in love and that was all that mattered. She had given her virginity to him because he had promised they would be together forever. The plan was for him to get a job near the university and wait until she graduated in two years. Then they would marry and pursue their careers. Two making one.

"I love ya, Babe."

Those were his final words and they haunted her for years. Still did at times when she lowered her guard. She had waited in her dorm room all night. Sleepless. Wondering. Heart aching.

The next morning, while it was still gray outside, Tammy put on her jacket and placed the small ring box in the pocket. Bobby had lost his Appalachian State class ring while they were playing tennis one day and despite searching for hours, they couldn't find it. Tammy had secretly begun saving money from her salary at the university bookstore and when she had enough, ordered a new ring. Her plan was to give it to him for a graduation gift. It had diamonds implanted around the ASU and had his initials engraved on it. It was stunning, and so was the price of $800, a fortune to a struggling student.

When she arrived at his apartment, she found it vacant. The curtains were even gone from the windows. No lights. No cars outside. She peered through the window and the inside looked like a mausoleum after a group of goblins had celebrated New Year's Eve. Papers littered the floor around a broken recliner. An over-turned trashcan, its contents spewed about. Bobby Brown was out of town.

It took a while before Tammy could accept the fact that he was no longer part of her life. She wrote a dozen letters, left tearful messages on the answering machine and finally, heartbroken, gave it up as a lost cause. She wanted to die. If a broken heart could kill, she was a dead woman.

Her roommate and best friend Crissie saved her life. Crissie came back after a visit with her parents and found Tammy looking like a ghost of herself; long hair hanging in her face, old eyeliner streaking her cheeks. She hadn't eaten in days. Crissie the vet to be shaped her up, cheered her up and propped her up until she had recovered enough to face the world.

Tammy leaned her head against the trunk of the oak and tried to refocus on what had happened to her. She was a survivor. Somehow, she would survive this. But there would be no Crissie to the rescue this time. This time she was on her own. She would find a way. She would survive! If Samuel didn't return, she wasn't going to just sit here and shrivel up beneath the oak. *Hell, no.* She had been left alone before. And she was a lot tougher now than she had been then. So okay, there was no more Samuel. Fair enough. The guy was really a stranger anyway. Right? Moreover, he certainly wasn't going to be thinking about poor little Tammy when he was on a quest to find the man he hated more than anything on earth. *Face it, Babe, you're all alone.*

She folded her arms across her chest and stared blankly ahead. She had to think, had to gather herself for what lay ahead. She would find some way to make a rippling and return to her world. All she had to do was find one of Dexter's men, kill him and take his sword. Screw you, Mr. Don't Call Me Samuel! Who needs you?"

She tried to relax, hoping the calmness would help her to be rational. Instead, a new sense of dread began forming inside her. Something was wrong! Samuel was in trouble! Something horrible was about to happen!

"Oh dammit!" Tammy rose to her feet and began running in the direction Samuel had gone.

CHAPTER 46

FROM HOPE TO ASH

The horror of Robert's corpse had only been a prelude to what awaited Samuel. He came into the village like a dead man walking and nothing short of a bolt of lightning could have penetrated the anesthesia of shock that ensconced him.

He moved along the graveled road that led to the village with his head down. Nothing was real for him anymore; not for a dead man, not for a man who had lost his family, his wife and his mentor. He was a ghost ship, empty, haunted and drifting along on the currents of the River Dexter.

He crested the knoll in the road where it seemed a century ago the Manteo Brothers and the Viking outlaws had planned their assault on the village and their tormentor, the Swordslinger Nathan. He raised his eyes and noticed the poles alongside the street. The poles appeared to have bundles attached.

The bolt of lightning struck him the instant he saw the street of the village. The poles held only a small part of the carnage. Bodies were strewn everywhere as the villagers had fallen where they died. These were people Samuel had known all his life; people he had cared for and who had cared for him and shared their homes and food during his troubled youth. As he moved among the bodies, another horrible fact emerged. All of the victims were women! Mothers, grandmothers, daughters, wives. The bundles were women who had been impaled through their chests and hung from the poles. Dried blood pooled beneath them.

Samuel knew that it was no coincidence that the body on the first pole was that of Martha, Heather's mother. A fist-sized stone that Manny had carved had been stuffed into her mouth, breaking the teeth as it was forced in. The shock, piled upon the earlier ordeal of finding Robert, left Samuel numb.

Young girls, some just babies, were impaled, looking like water bugs pinned with their little arms dangling, poised for

401

a science class dissection. Samuel walked on, passing at least thirty corpses lying in the street. His brain was numb. The scene had taken on a surreal quality. Nothing existed other than this nightmare. He no longer even felt the road beneath his feet. Was he breathing? Was his heart beating? If so, it was only reflex. He had no sense of himself or anything else existing. He walked along, searching the dead faces, looking for Heather.

Had a sword been run through Samuel, he would not have felt it. All the misery, the tragedy, the heartaches and sadness prior to this had been nothing more than foreplay. This was madness, even for a mad man like Dexter. These helpless women had been no threat. They didn't even possess stones to be taken. They were killed for no reason other than to torment Samuel. And from appearances, they had been alive when they were impaled on the poles. Their bodies were twisted in knots of pain and agony. Dexter had crossed the line. This was pure evil. What had been bad was worse. The knowledge that all these people had been slain by Dexter just added to Samuel's pain and grief that was almost unbearable.

There would be no turning back now. It was better that he died in an effort to kill Dexter than to have this go on. If every time he escaped the madman's clutches, he was going to respond with an atrocity such as this, it was better that he was dead. Maybe if Samuel died, Dexter's rage against his people would subside.

"I'm coming, Dexter," Samuel said in a hoarse whisper. "I'm coming, you bastard." He walked past the bakery and went to his ironsmith shop. The door had been broken from its hinges and the tools were strewn across the dirt floor. None of the swords that had hung on the wall remained. The shop had been vandalized and stripped.

Samuel went back outside and turned his gaze toward his home on the mountainside. He began walking in that direction, flowing along the Dexter Stream. He passed his father's home and heard the ghostly laughter of Robert. He thought he even heard his father calling his name. But he didn't pause. He picked up his pace, walking purposefully, and summoned Draconis. The sword appeared and he gripped the hilt tightly. Dust rose when his boots struck the path. His coat flapped in the breeze. Draconis glistened in the afternoon sun.

He left the village and its death scene behind. The road climbed gently into the foothills that he had once thought of as God's steps going up the face of the mountain and into the Heaven beyond. *One more Rippling to go.* A portal that would open before the night of the great stone falling from the sky. He would use his wedding sword to gain entry and nothing else mattered. The possible horrors that might await were of no concern. Nothing could be worse than what he had already experienced. Until now, he had been a mere walking windstorm. Now he was the eye of a hurricane. The winds no longer blew. Instead, there was a deadly calm in a place that Samuel had never walked before. His mind functioned like that of a shark, moving with a calm instinctual black, haunted-eyed directive. *Kill Dexter!*

"Samuel!"

The voice stopped him in his tracks. The woman had followed him. She must have run all the way to catch up. He turned and saw that she was breathless, her face flushed. "Wait for me," she pleaded. "Don't leave me again, Samuel."

She reached him and collapsed against him, clutching her arms around him. "Oh, Samuel. Those poor people! What can we do, Samuel?"

"We have to face him."

"Face him? He's too powerful, Samuel. What can we do?"

"It's better that we die trying to rid the world of him than to allow him to continue this murdering. He's doing it to torment me."

"But, Samuel, he isn't going to fight you fairly. He'll have some ambush, some trick. I've never known anyone as evil and treacherous as he."

"Neither have I. But it has to end. Now."

"Samuel? Was one of those women your Heather?"

"No. Only her mother."

Tammy was silent and Samuel resumed walking up the mountain trail, quickening his pace.

"Where are we going?" she asked.

"Home," he answered.

A while later, Tammy said, "I don't think God has brought us through all this hell for nothing, Samuel. Fate brought us together and between the two of us, we make a whole. Together, we can defeat this madman."

"You're too much of a romantic."

Samuel quickened his stride again and Tammy had to trot to keep pace with him. Finally, she spoke again. "How are we going to find Dexter?"

"You heard what that scoundrel Mickey said. "I can make a portal with my wedding sword and go back to a time where we change all this."

"Oh, my God, is this for real? If you do this, Dexter will be there?"

"Aye."

"His men will be there, too? With the guns they stole?"

"Aye."

"You're going anyway?"

"Aye."

"Oh Samuel, don't you know that he has done all this to provoke you into such a state of mind that you'll just come to him without regard for your own life?"

Samuel stopped and whirled to face her. "Stop it!" he said pointing a finger in her startled face. "You have no idea of the hatred within me. I'm aware that this is a trap, and you know what? I don't give a damn! This has to stop now and if it's God's will for me to prevail, I will. If not, at least I will no longer be alive to grieve and feed Dexter's perverse desires."

"Okay! Okay. You're right. But you can't just go barging right into them. That would be crazy. Not to even mention suicide."

Samuel made a snarling sound like a cornered animal, and Tammy was afraid he was going to strike her. What she saw in his eyes frightened her. He glared at her with the glazed eyes of a beast about to make a killing strike. She shrank back, but refused to back away. Instead, she raised her right hand and slapped him across the face. Hard. The sound was like that of a leather strap hitting a concrete block.

The blow stunned Samuel. It knocked the glaze from his eyes and made him blink. He reached for the trembling Tammy and pulled her to him. "You have to understand," he said. "I am a warrior and I will fight as Nathan taught me. He stood before twenty barbarians and won the battle. I will do what I have to do."

"I have faith in you, Samuel, "but I don't want you going off half-cocked." He raised his eyebrows at the strange expression. "You know; he just wants you to come at him crazed and not thinking."

"I know his intentions. But it is time for the confrontation."

"Okay. But let's do it right, Samuel. Let's plan. Let's do some scheming of our own. Let's act instead of reacting."

Samuel smiled, took her hand and began walking up the mountainside again.

An hour later, they were approaching the house. The sun had just passed midday and there was a dark, brooding storm front moving in from the west. The storm would be upon them in a few hours and its darkening clouds cast a shadow that steadily advanced across the land.

The two weary, emotionally drained travelers reached the homestead, the muscles in their legs aching from the steady climb. The view was breathtaking and Tammy knew instantly why first Nathan and then Samuel had chosen the spot for a home.

In one direction lay the village, its horrors hidden by the distance. In the other direction lay the ocean, its color reflecting the darkness of the stormy sky, its waters a seething black. Samuel paused when he saw the open grave with Nathan's bones scattered beside it. Tammy reached out a hand to his arm and he stopped, his chest rising and falling as he breathed deeply.

"Is that Nathan?"

Samuel didn't answer immediately, but dropped his head. Then he raised it and looked heavenward. He removed his hat and wiped a hand across his forehead. "When we return, we'll give him a proper burial. Come with me." He walked purposefully toward the house, opened the door and they went inside.

Dexter's friends had done their job well. The wooden table and the chairs had been smashed as well as the bed frame. Pieces were thrown across the floor. Pottery had been shattered, clothes scattered and urinated on. Samuel moved quickly to the fireplace where the wedding sword still hung over the mantle.

Without speaking, he stepped over the ruined pieces of his home and took the sword down. He held it, staring at it, feeling its weight and reading the date inscribed on the hilt — August 24, 1302. This sword had been created on the day the asteroid had crashed into the mountain and now it was going to serve as a weapon to defeat Dexter. He ran a finger along the honed blade and smiled. It was the first time Tammy had seen him smile in an eternity. And she wished she hadn't seen it. It was ghastly.

Samuel walked outside, still saying nothing. He held his wedding sword alongside Draconis and hurled them simultaneously. They tore the fabric of time and a searing white light spilled from the wavering portal. "Let's go," he said, speaking at last, and stepped into the light. Tammy went through with him.

CHAPTER 47

HOMETOWN BURNING

The troubled young Scotsman and the angry young American park ranger entered the portal expecting the worst. They came out of the Rippling with weapons drawn, ready to do battle if necessary. Hearts pounding, they tumbled into the brave old world of August 24, 1302.

Samuel stumbled, gained his balance and went into a defensive pose. He blinked his eyes to clear them, peered through the rising heat waves and found that the village had been decimated. What? There was the carcass of a cow lying near the well. Chickens were scattered everywhere, their bloodstained feathers moving in the summer breeze. The remains of a dog lay in the street.

Tammy was still trying to catch her breath. She had grown used to the urban rapid transit, but this was a totally different kind of travel. She spun around. "This is your village? The same one we just saw earlier?"

"Was."

"Ah… he's already been here?"

"Aye."

Tammy stared at the glowing embers and back husks of buildings. The stone facades that remained were covered with black soot. "Where is everybody?"

"I don't know. It doesn't make sense." He studied the remains of the building that had been his ironsmith shop.

"So, where's Dexter," Tammy asked.

"I know where he is," Samuel said, sighing. "He's waiting where the stone will come tonight."

"Are we are going there?"

"Aye."

"Good, I want to kick some ass."

Samuel looked at the ranger and smiled, "Then let's do it."

They followed the street through the center of the village to the north. Ahead, the graveled road disappeared into the forest.

"Hey, there's your home up on the mountain! But … I can't see the roof."

"It hasn't been completed yet," Samuel said.

"Oh, God, Sam, all of this is some creepy stuff."

"Aye, it is," his voice broke. "You know, I thought, if I could come back to this day I would find Heather, my brother, and the others alive. Dexter has massacred that hope. He seems to always be a step ahead of me. But I will find him today and one of us will die."

"Maybe two of us," Tammy said to herself.

Samuel picked up the pace to a semi-trot. Tammy, thankful for her exercise routine, managed to keep pace. Both of them kept a wary eye on the roadside, half-expecting Dexter's men to open fire on them with their "bang-sticks" or attack them with drawn swords. *I'm going to die today*, Tammy thought, and she felt surprisingly calm. *If I do, it will be for the right reasons. And I won't go alone.* She shook her head as she mused over the change in her life in the past couple of days. No boring eight-hour shifts here.

A dark cloud suddenly obscured the sun and Tammy marveled. This couldn't be the storm cloud that had been threatening before they had made the Rippling. Or could it? Hell, what did she know? This was some confusing shit. Lightning flickered in the western sky and the smell of rain was heavy.

"Sam, if we're in the past, won't your other body be here?"

"Christ, woman, I don't know. I've never traveled backwards before."

"Oh, my God, you don't think we're going to round a curve and find Dexter holding a young Samuel with a sword to your throat, do you?" Her mind boggled. What would happen if Dexter was able to kill the young Samuel? Would this Samuel just vanish? God! This is crazy! Okay, settle down. Whatever happens will happen. Destiny. Even a lopsided crazy as hell destiny. *Jesus! If I go, I'm fighting and*

408

screaming, she thought. *That damn Dexter is going to know he's tangled with a wildcat.*

After another few minutes of walking, Samuel stopped and pointed to the left where a small trail led toward the side of the mountain. In the distance, Tammy could see what looked like a body of water with a boulder in the middle of it. "Down there is where Heather lies," Samuel said, his voice sad and strained. Tammy nodded, but said nothing. *She isn't there now,* she thought. *Unless ...*

They continued on their journey and the clouds became more threatening. It was going to rain. The wind whipped and swirled the purple and white wisps and a bolt of lightning split the sky. The winds gusted through the oaks, creating a mourning tune.

"It rained the day of the stone," Samuel said, "but for only a short time. It will clear soon." The first of the raindrops fell upon the brim of his hat. Tammy tucked the pistol back in the waist of her cargo pants. The crowns of the oak trees began whipping wildly in the wind. Birds dropped like stones from the black sky to seek refuge in the trees.

The heavy raindrops seemed to come straight down despite the gusting of the wind. The water was cold as it ran down the neck of Tammy's shirt, but it was a pleasant relief from the August heat. The raindrops trickled down her back. She shivered, but not entirely from the cold droplets.

Lightning flashed so nearby that they both jumped, and a branch from one of the huge oaks splintered. The thunder roared a second later. The lightning continued, sending sheets of light through the branches dancing in the wind and shadows skittering and retracting. The world moved and shifted in a staccato dance.

The heavens opened and the rain soaked them immediately. The water ran from the brim of Samuel's hat like a fountain. Tammy wanted to laugh, but this wasn't really a laughing time. Another lightning bolt struck nearby and she grabbed Samuel's arm, squeezing it hard. They kept moving, the raindrops pelting their faces.

The surroundings had become surreal, a menagerie of bone-like tree branches lit up by the lightning. Even the stones on the ground seemed to move and shift in the eerie light from the raging storm.

Samuel suddenly took her arm and said, "We cut through here. Be careful, we've got about two miles of rough terrain."

"No shit," Tammy muttered. *What had it been so far, a picnic?* She could feel the rough texture of her socks pressing into the soles of her feet and against her water-wrinkled toes. Her black tee shirt wrapped around her like a second skin, and the cold water made her nipples stand out against the restraints of the bra. *God, I must be a beautiful sight*, she thought, pushing her drenched hair back out of her face.

Samuel was right. The terrain was rougher. Rocks rose to her knees and they had to be careful not to trip over them. The landscape was so scattered with the rocks and small boulders that Tammy wondered if a mountain standing here at one time had exploded and scattered over the area. The few trees that rose from the garden of stone were so gnarled and twisted that they gave the appearance of being in agony. At least the rain was letting up.

The boulders were getting bigger, and in trying to get around one, Tammy slipped and struck her chin on the top of the rock. "Damn!"

"What!" Samuel's voice was anxious.

"Nothing. I'm okay. Bit my tongue and cut my lip, but at least I'm still able to feel it."

"Let me see. Aye, you lost a little skin there, lass."

Tammy spat to get rid of the coppery taste of blood and stared him down. "Don't worry about me. I've had a busted lip before. I'll be fine."

"Okay, good. The storm is almost finished and we have only about another mile to go. The stone came from over there and went in that direction," he said, pointing.

Making sure Samuel wasn't looking; Tammy ran her fingers over the nick on her chin. Probably have a scar, but what difference did it make? Dexter wouldn't care. She stifled a sarcastic giggle. Yeah, must look like a real warrior now. Maybe the scar would show at her wake. Or would she be left for the ravens, like Robert? She shivered.

Their progress was slowed by the steeper terrain and they were able to enjoy the brilliant sunset. The sun seemed to be making a statement, as if to tell the retreating storm that it was still the master of the elements.

"It's beautiful," Tammy said. "I always was a sucker for a great sunset. That's one reason I chose the mountains for my home. I've seen some in better circumstances, though."

Samuel laughed. "Complain, complain. That's all you do, lass." He offered her a hand and helped her over another large rock.

"I'm worn out," she said, thankful to have him talking again. "When we get wherever it is we're going, I'm just going to collapse."

Samuel chuckled. "Ah, you're a regular mountain goat, girl. Don't use up all your energy; chances are we're going to have some real excitement very soon."

"Oh, God, I was trying to forget that. I hope they don't hear us squeaking in these wet clothes."

A few more hundred yards and Samuel whispered, "Shh. Keep low and follow me."

They worked their way single file around a huge boulder and a clearing appeared some fifty yards ahead. "We make it through that clearing and the next small stand of trees and we'll be there," Samuel whispered. "Be careful. Don't make any noise. They may have people out scouting for us."

"I can feel him," Tammy said. "It makes my skin crawl."

Samuel chuckled. "Dexter does have that effect on people." He held his hand out and summoned Draconis. The sword flowed from his hand and formed before them. "Hello, old friend. I hope to feed you well this evening."

Tammy drew her 9mm pistol from her waistband. "I've brought a friend, too," she said, and they both smiled.

"Whatever happens here is going to end this once and for all," Samuel said. "We need to rest before we go any farther. And if you have any sins, you'd like to confess, this is your chance. I can't promise you that either of us will live through this."

"Well, thanks for the positive thoughts. Mind if I quiver a while? Look, Samuel, I'm at peace with this. We don't have a choice. If we die, at least we die trying to do what we both know is right. If we live, well, the next round is on you."

They sat and rested. Tammy closed her eyes, bowed her head following Samuel's suggestion. She prayed. She asked God to give them the strength and wisdom to defeat the Devil that awaited. She asked him to watch over her parents and Crissie. She even told God that she was forgiving Bobby Brown for breaking her heart. Then she asked for forgiveness of her sins. *I am your warrior,* she prayed. *I fight for all that is good and the defeat of evil. This man is a Satan on Earth and if he goes unheeded, I grieve for the world to come. Amen.*

She raised her head and Samuel put a reassuring hand on her knee. "We may have one advantage," he whispered. "I don't think they know you exist and they'll only be expecting me. You stay behind me and watch what happens. Don't make your presence known until you have to. Maybe we can do some real damage before they are ready for us."

"I want to go in by your side. I've been left behind too often recently."

"Look, I know I have been unfair to you, but I thought it was for your good. I'm sorry. But for us to succeed, I really need you to follow my instructions now. Okay?"

"Well, I don't like it, but you've got a point. I'll do what you say and I'll keep your back covered."

"Thank you. It's time." He smiled slightly and took her hand. "Thank you for your aid and comfort and your trust."

"Thank you for giving me purpose in my life again. Bobby Brown is a history note."

"What?"

"Never mind."

"If things go right, you can be back in your world by morning."

"That's good. It would be nice to see another sunrise at Mount Mitchell."

Samuel squeezed her hand and rose to his feet. "See you," he whispered. "When I get to the trees, you start across. And be careful."

He moved away crouching to remain as much a part of the rugged terrain as possible. He came to a boulder and knelt behind it. He lifted his head to peer over it and suddenly jerked it back down. He held his sword at ready by his side. He turned his back to the boulder, holding Draconis in front of him. He waited. A minute passed. Another.

Tammy was becoming impatient. She wanted to be moving. The sun had fully set and it was almost dark. A flock of ravens suddenly took flight to her left. Pistol in hand, she released the safety. There was no further sound and she had seen nothing. She glanced back to Samuel. He was tensed, head bobbing slightly as though he was counting.

Suddenly, he whirled, catapulted himself over the boulder and brought his upraised sword down. There was a muffled cry from the other side of the boulder and a flurry of movement. Tammy was going insane, unable to see what was happening. She broke from her position and made a crouching run toward the boulder. She heard another noise to her left and glanced that way. There was something or someone over there, but she had committed now. She had to find Samuel. Quickly! She reached the boulder, paused, drew a deep breath and darted around it.

Samuel was kneeling over a man who was gasping for his final breaths. He looked up at Tammy and motioned for her to join him. Together they moved the dead man behind the boulder.

"There's someone up ahead, to the left," Tammy whispered."

"Yeah, I saw the birds."

Samuel scanned the wood line, but could see no evidence of anyone. He held a finger over his lips to caution Tammy, then crouching, ran toward where the birds had taken flight. He slowed to a creep, holding Draconis ready for a strike.

A huge man in a kilt suddenly stepped from behind a rock. He saw Samuel and made a move for the rifle strapped to his back. Samuel made a move toward the big man, but

Draconis was not cooperating. The sword pulled itself from his hand and began moving toward the man that Samuel had slain moments earlier. The dead man's sword had emitted its stone and Draconis was going to take it.

The other man had the rifle now and was taking aim with it. He was obviously still not familiar with the weapon and his fumbling saved Samuel's life. Just as the man was taking aim and preparing to squeeze the trigger, a shot rang out and he grew a third eye. The man's mouth fell open in a surprised look. Then he dropped to his knees and toppled over.

Tammy gave Samuel a thumbs-up sign as the shot from her pistol echoed through the trees and rocks. He eyed the ranger, shook his head, and held out a hand to welcome Draconis back. He looked at the still glowing sword, and said, "Don't ever do that again, Draconis, you're going to get me killed!" He turned to Tammy, who had joined him. "Thanks," he said, "but we'd better get moving. That shot will attract a lot of attention."

Sound wasn't the only thing traveling. The flutter of wings sounded as flocks of birds took wing. Men were shouting to each other.

Tammy picked up the dead man's rifle and held it out to Samuel. "You should take this," she said.

But Samuel had never fired a weapon and wasn't ready for a crash course. He preferred the familiar sword, if he could keep it from leaving him at the wrong time.

They could hear the men thrashing their way through bushes and the snapping of branches as they approached. "Find a place to hide," Samuel whispered to Tammy. "They still don't know you're with me. The surprise can work to our advantage again."

Tammy moved to a nearby boulder and crouched behind it, holding the newly acquired rifle to her shoulder, ready to take aim and fire.

Samuel suddenly rose and charged toward the wood line, screaming like a madman and twirling his sword before him. A bullet whizzed past, ricocheting off one of the boulders and whining away. Two men came from the trees,

414

both armed with swords and pistols. Samuel was within ten yards of them when he dove to the ground. They fired the pistols but their aim was poor and they missed. Dirt kicked up inches from Samuel and he rolled toward the men swinging his blade and clipping them across the legs. Draconis ripped into both legs of the man on the right and slashed the calf of the other man's left leg. The men screamed in pain and toppled to the ground.

Samuel jumped to his feet and ran into the trees, ducking behind a huge oak. Seconds later, five men came out of the woods and entered the clearing between the hiding Samuel and Tammy. "He's out here somewhere," one of the men shouted, and another five men left the trees and joined them. Tammy peered from behind the boulder and watched as several more men left the woods and joined the group in the clearing. They were facing in the direction of the oak that Samuel was hiding behind.

The men talked among themselves for a few seconds, and then fanned out to form a line. They held their rifles and pistols at ready and began moving in Samuel's direction.

Tammy was close to panicking. What could she do? There was no way Samuel could fight off that many men with a sword against rifles and pistols. She breathed a silent prayer, gripped the rifle firmly and prepared to step from her hiding place.

"Hold it!" The man's voice rang out with authority. He stepped from the shadows of the trees and Tammy immediately recognized him as the man who had been dueling with Samuel at the tower. Dexter! He was wearing a kilt with breast armor and wristbands adorned with metal spikes. The men stopped and looked at their leader.

"Samuel Donachee! Is that ye?" Dexter had moved ahead of the line of men and was facing the big oak. "I ask ye, Samuel, is this the gratitude, the thanks I get for all the effort I have made to give ye such a fitting homecoming?" He laughed with the sound echoing among the trees.

Tammy rose from behind the boulder and rested the rifle on it, drawing aim on the center of the big man's back. *If I shoot him, his men will probably scatter and disband,* she

415

thought. Good. This could truly be the shot heard around the world. Her finger tightened on the trigger.

Samuel stepped from behind the oak, standing straight, the brim of his hat pulled low, the long black coat rustling in the breeze. He held his sword at his side, pointed downward. Tammy eased the pressure on the trigger and held her breath.

Dexter was speaking. "Ah, there ye are. We meet again, mine enemy." Dexter clapped his hands. "Hope ye enjoyed the warm welcome I prepared for ye at the village. Wasn't that a beautiful sight? One I will always remember. Hope you do, at least for the rest of your life." He laughed again. "Tonight is the night, you know. The night the big stone falls. Do ye remember what ye were doing when the stone fell from the sky?"

"Cut the crap and let's get on with it," Samuel said, raising his sword.

"Well," Dexter said, laughing. He was obviously enjoying his moment of triumph. He reached up, loosed his flowing hair from the ponytail he had been wearing it in, and shook it free. "Ye are the stubborn one, Samuel," he said, moving his head slowly back and forth in wonderment. "How many times have we met now when I have defeated you?"

"Too many," Samuel said. "But not this time."

"Oh, relax, Samuel, I am not yet ready for you to die. There is so much more I want you to see. I want you to witness the landing of the stone again. And then I want you to witness the birth of a god. Me. Once we have killed all the men who gather here and gain their stones, I will be a god with an invincible army. But then, you must think I am already that, eh?"

The men roared with laughter and shouted out a chorus of "Aye!"

"Tell you what, Samuel. Once the stone gathering is over, if ye still want me, ye can have me. I will await you and grant your desire."

"I want you now, you murdering bastard!" Samuel took a step forward and the line of men raised their weapons.

416

"Ye must be patient," Dexter said in a condescending voice. "I will not deny ye the opportunity to see a man become a god."

"I only wish to see you become a damned dead man!" Samuel lunged toward his tormentor, sword raised.

Dexter quickly stepped behind his line of men. "Stop him, but don't kill him," he ordered.

Tammy again drew an aim on Dexter. Now! "Die you, son of a bitch," she screamed and squeezed the trigger. The rifle recoiled and blazed in the twilight.

Dexter was a dead man. He heard the woman shout and spun around, but there was no time to evade the bullet. The aim was true and the projectile sped toward its target. However, Dexter's sword of many stones was loyal to its master, and it rose of its own accord to block the speeding bullet. The metal-against-metal clang rang through the woods. The bullet ricocheted into the woods, cutting through leaves and finally burying itself in the trunk of a tree.

Dexter had lost his balance and fallen to his knees. He looked at his sword, and then slowly raised his eyes to the woman who had tried to kill him. His smile was blood curdling.

The ranger wasn't through, though. She squeezed off another shot. Another. And another. Each time Dexter's faithful sword sent the bullet caroming off into the woods. Dexter, still on his knees, howled in laughter. Behind him, the men were converging in a circle around Samuel. Tammy kept firing, getting only the frustrating clangs as a response, until the hammer clicked on an empty chamber.

Dexter cried out victoriously and rose to his feet, holding his sword with both hands high above his head. His eyes blazed with insanity. He began walking toward the woman, who remained partially hidden behind the boulder.

"Who are you?" he shouted. "Another woman for the brave Samuel to hide behind? How many women must I slay to get to him?"

Tammy weighed her options. Both of them. Stand and die or run and hope to fight another day. She chose to run.

But where? Her best chance was to try to make it to the trees on her left. Decision made, she dropped the empty rifle and sprinted toward the trees with Dexter in pursuit.

Meanwhile, things were looking desperate for Samuel. The ring of some thirty men was closing in with swords drawn. They obviously preferred their trusty blades instead of the new "bang-sticks" for close-up work. They were being cautious, though. Dexter's order not to kill the man made their work dangerous. No one had ordered him not to kill.

They stared at their quarry for a moment, then a man with wild red hair suddenly yelled and they all converged on Samuel.

Samuel swung Draconis in a huge arc, feeling the blade cut into three men. Then he was engulfed in a mass of humanity. They swarmed over him, pinning him to the ground. Someone's knees pinned his sword arm and he felt Draconis being torn from his hand. "Merge," he screamed above the melee, and the sword began to liquefy and flow through the fingertips of his right hand.

Fists pummeled his face. Dexter had not said "Don't bruise." A boot landed against the side of his head and everything went momentarily black. A deep black with stars in the background. Then hands were pulling him upright, and continuing to lift him until he was held above their heads, arms and legs stretched out. Helpless prey.

Tammy was running for her life. The ache in her cut leg was forgotten. She surged through the bushes and undergrowth, using her left arm to push the branches out of her way. She was fast and her ranger training had given her durability. Maybe she could outrun Dexter. She never had the chance. Dexter didn't believe in chasing. He liked to send for people. So, he raised his sword in her direction and commanded, "Fetch!

The sword left his hands in a blur, flying hilt first toward the fleeing girl, easily evading the clutching branches. Within seconds, it reached her, the hilt banging against the back of her head. Tammy was one step from reaching the next clearing when her head exploded and she was knocked unconscious.

CHAPTER 48

THE FINAL CONFRONTATION

Four of the men carried Samuel through the finger of forest to the clearing where Dexter was standing over the unconscious woman.

"Ah, Samuel, we are together again. Such sweet pleasure. And look, my men hold ye in such high esteem that they do not allow your feet to touch the ground. We welcome you to our little festival, my dear friend, and I would like to thank ye for this little gift." He reached down took a handful of Tammy's short hair, pulling her face up for Samuel to see. A trickle of blood ran from the wound in her head and across her face. Laughing, he pulled the 9mm pistol from her waistband and tossed it to one of his cronies.

"Ah, Samuel, you know that my father and I loved the same woman. My mother; his wife." Dexter cocked his head to one side so that his eyes would be on same angle as Samuel's, who was still being held aloft by the four men. "My father was a coward, you know. Ran away and left his wife — my mother — to be raped and slaughtered. I vowed that I would someday rape a woman before him in his name, but unfortunately the circumstances of his death would not allow me that pleasure. But now, methinks, the opportunity to reap my vengeance has been presented. Such is the pleasure of a god. Given that ye held my father in such high esteem, I grant ye the honor of watching me avenge his cowardice as I rape your woman."

Samuel spat in the madman's direction. "Do what you like, you insane bastard. This woman means nothing to me. I tried to leave her in the other world, but she followed me of her own stupidity. Rape her! Kill her! I don't give a damn. Free me and I will kill her myself. She has been nothing but an albatross for me."

Dexter roared with laughter, pressing a hand against his side. "Oh, Samuel, the games you would play!" He addressed the men holding Samuel. "Place him down, but hold him. I want him to watch." The men dropped Samuel roughly to the ground and he rose shakily to his feet.

Dexter prepared to remove the armor from his upper body, then paused. "Why bother," he said laughing. "All I need do is pull up me kilt." He grinned evilly at Samuel. Okay, some of you men hold this bitch down just in case she regains her senses. Get those clothes off her and ready her for me."

Samuel stood, a brute on each side holding his arms, and moaned quietly. He was helpless. "Why don't you fight me first," he rasped. "Then you can enjoy her without my distraction."

"Oh, you're not a distraction, Samuel. No. You are the main attraction. All of this is for the benefit of my father's adopted son. I will pleasure you with a bout later, my friend. But first I must pleasure your whore." He used his boot to nudge one of the men attempting to undress Tammy. "Come on! Don't take all day. I am beginning to get impatient. Rip the clothing from the bitch and don't be too gentle. Because that's the way I'm going to take her!"

The men began ripping at Tammy's shirt and the movement brought her awake. She screamed and kicked one of the men in the ribs before they pinned her to the ground. One of them yanked at her bra and her breasts sprang free. Dexter chortled. Another man used his knife to cut the cargo pants off her. Another stripped her panties off, leaving her nude and helpless on the ground.

"Stop!" Samuel tried to scream the word, but it came out as a hoarse rasp. Dexter uttered another demonic laugh.

"Ah is life not so sweet!" he said. He stood over Tammy, now being held spread-eagle on the grass, and raised his kilt. He turned his face to Samuel and winked. "Hold her men, but bring the whore to her knees."

Samuel struggled against the men holding him and shouted one last insult. "A coward such as you will never be a god, Dexter! Some king you are, hiding behind your men at every encounter. You are nothing more than a pathetic weakling who has to have others hold a woman because you aren't man enough to take her on your own! Have you ever even made love to a woman? Or are you capable of nothing more than rape with a bunch of animals looking on?"

The insult struck a nerve. Dexter whirled and glared at Samuel, who pressed his advantage. "With all your stones, you are still too much of a coward to make love to a woman or to fight a man that you have already bested four times. I wonder what your faithful men really think of you."

"Shut up!" Dexter shouted, dropping his kilt and moving a step toward Samuel.

"You're pitiful, Dexter," Samuel continued. "She's just a helpless girl, lying naked at your feet, and you can't even take her without the help of thirty men. Some god you will be!"

"Enough!" Dexter was rattled, his face red with anger. "I planned to save you for dessert, fool. But if you don't be quiet, you're going to be the main course!" He turned to the men holding Tammy. "Release the whore! Step away from her! She will submit to me of her own free will!"

"Fat chance, Dexter," Samuel continued taunting. "You're too afraid of her to do anything. She's naked and unarmed and you're still a coward!"

Tammy had risen to her feet and was standing nude before them. She stood straight, proud, arms crossed over her breasts.

"Come to me, whore," Dexter snarled at her. "Submit to your master. I will be your king; your god. And if you don't do as I say, I will certainly be your death!"

Tammy stood, defiant and unblinking. "You want me, come and get me," she said in a flat, quavering voice.

Dexter's men snickered and some of them oohed and aahed. Dexter face turned a deeper shade of red in the half-dark. "Oh, I will come and get you, bitch. And I will give you a night to remember for the rest of your short life." He handed his sword to one of the men and started toward her.

Tammy turned her back to him. The move stunned the men because they all knew that turning ones back on the feared Dexter was to make a death wish.

Dexter lost the remainder of his composure; his face went from red to black with rage. "You dare turn your back on Dexter?" He stepped up behind her and seized her throat with both hands. Some of the men felt their muscles spasm in response. Tammy made no move to evade him, hands hanging limply by her sides.

Dexter yanked her hard against his chest armor. One of the spikes on his wristband made a slight cut in her neck. "What are your thoughts now, whore?" he raged. "You are mine and I will …"

He didn't complete the threat. Tammy drove her right fist with a backward uppercut into his groin, whirled, and as he dropped his hands from her throat, placed her right foot behind his left leg and shoved with all her strength. "No, you're mine," she shouted, as Dexter slammed to the ground so hard that his breath left him in a loud "whoosh!" Tammy grabbed his right hand, raised it, twisted it, and drove a foot to his armpit.

Dexter cried out in pain. His men stood, as they had been, some with their mouths open. Dexter was their leader and he had not ordered them to interfere. So they watched, some gleefully.

Dexter, still on his back and agonizing from the pain in his crotch and beneath his arm, screamed at the idle men. "Get her!" he bellowed. Three of the men grabbed the woman and restrained her. Dexter rose slowly to his feet and brushed the dirt and twigs from his clothes. His eyes were bulging and the whites were red with anger.

Samuel laughed, drawing the madman's attention. "My king," he mocked. "Have I just seen you defeated by a mere lass? Indeed, I think I would like to test your battle skills myself."

Dexter paused. He glared at Tammy, and then turned his gaze to Samuel. "I think I have finally had enough of you, Samuel Donachee. You have humiliated me before my men and I will not abide with that. It was my pleasure to toy with you like a cat with mouse and to keep you around for my enjoyment after I had collected all the stones. But I've change my mind. You are going to die now and I will save the woman for my dessert. You want the fight? I will give you the fight. Sword to sword. Our paths will not cross after this day. It ends now. There will be no more play!"

Samuel felt the adrenaline rush through his body. "Bring it on, butcher!" he said between clenched teeth. "Bring it on!"

Dexter motioned to the man holding his sword. "I am ready," he said. "Free him."

The men released Samuel's arms and he flexed his hands. He raised his right arm and said, "Draconis! The liquid metal spewed from his hand and the blade formed. His arm ached where the men had driven their knees into it during his capture, but this was no time to admit pain. This was the moment he had lived for. The arrogant Dexter had played right into his hands without realizing it. "This is my last chance," he said to himself, and assumed a fighting pose. This would be his last sword fight.

The two antagonists walked toward each other, crouched, ready, each eyeing the other warily. The men closed around them in a tight circle. Tammy had found her ripped shirt and pulled it on trying to cover her nakedness.

All of the men carried swords and knives and many of them had firearms from the raided gun shop. However, they were not interfering in this duel to the death. Dexter was their leader, but he had earned that status by killing anyone who got in his way. This was another such test. They were loyal men, but only to the winner.

The fighters moved in a circle, each waiting for the other to make a move. Instead of moving closer, Dexter was backing away, increasing the distance between the two.

Samuel decided to wait no longer. The adrenaline rush was in full force. Every instinct was functioning. He could feel the power emanating from Draconis. The hours he had spent practicing the swordslinger moves Nathan had taught him were being called on. He suddenly lunged toward Dexter and their weapons clanged together, the sound ringing through the night. They whirled, metal rasping against metal, turned and moved together. Samuel went into a move that Nathan had called the "undefeated", faking a right over-shoulder strike, bringing Draconis down between him and Dexter, then bringing the sword up, leveling it off in a motion meant to decapitate the foe.

Dexter blocked the blow, stunning Samuel. No one could block that move! Nathan said it had never been done. Yet Dexter had fallen for the fake and committed himself to the feint, yet recovered in time to make the block coming from the opposite direction. Samuel's confidence wavered. It had to be the sword. The same sword that had blocked the bullet's from Tammy's gun. The sword that had chased the fleeing Tammy and knocked her unconscious. The sword that had swallowed so many stones. The knowledge left Samuel with a nauseous feeling. The strength of those stones had given the sword a life of its own.

Dexter pressed his advantage, circling to his right. Samuel followed. Dexter thrust his blade to Samuel's left, forcing him to parry off balance in an effort to block. Dexter leapt to Samuel's right, and without turning, drove the sword from behind him. The blade cut into Samuel's side. It wasn't a deep wound, but it was painful. Samuel moved away, and regained his balance, trying not to grimace from the pain. He could feel the blood running down his side and it felt as though someone was holding a flame to his flesh.

He forced a smile and said, "Come on, Dexter. You can do better than that."

"The fifth and final time," Dexter said, the evil grin returning to his face. "Prepare to say your farewells to the world."

Samuel lunged forward, coming over the top with a blow meant to split Dexter's skull. However, Dexter again blocked it and their eyes locked. Samuel eased the pressure, allowing his blade to slip from the other and the downward strike sliced into Dexter's upper arm. He uttered a curse and stepped back. The wound was deep and bleeding profusely. For the first time, Samuel saw doubt in the man's face.

"Now, Sam!" an excited Tammy yelled, and a pair of grimy hands seized her arms.

"How dare you strike me," Dexter yelled as they exchanged parries. "I have spared you four times and you do this to me with an imbecilic strike. You are a dead man for sure now!" He paused, looked at his sword and commanded, "Blind him!" The obedient blade began glowing, the light growing in intensity until Samuel could only see a white glare. He swung blindly and Dexter easily blocked the move. He backpedaled, hoping to get far enough away from the blinding light to regain his sight.

"You can run, but you cannot escape," Dexter gloated. "Prepare to die!"

Tammy was screaming from the side. "You cheating bastard!"

Samuel retreated until he had backed into the wall of men surrounding the fighters. Someone shoved him in the back and he stumbled forward, falling to his knees and into Dexter's sword. The blade entered the stomach area, but wasn't deep enough to prove fatal. Dexter stopped the thrust, leaving the blade in Samuel's flesh. Samuel tried to bring his sword up for a counter blow, but Dexter laughed and kicked at the blade. He pressed it to the ground and placed a foot on it.

"Samuel!" Tammy cried out in terror. She wrestled to free herself to no avail and cringed as she waited for Dexter to strike the killing blow.

But Dexter wanted to gloat one last time. "You and your stones are mine now, Samuel. And the girl will soon be mine. Too bad you won't be around to see that."

Draconis, still pinned beneath Dexter's boot, suddenly began to glow and liquefy. The blade merged into its master's hand and disappeared.

Dexter chortled, the laugh of a madman who thinks he has conquered the world. "See, Samuel," he said, "even your sword knows when it is over." He leaned forward and placed both hands on the hilt of his sword, the tip still buried in Samuel's midsection.

"Game over!" he shouted. "You die!" He put all his weight into the move and shoved the hilt of the sword toward the kneeling Samuel. However, the sword didn't penetrate further. A surprised look appeared on Dexter's face, and he pushed at the blade once again. Tammy screamed and fell to her knees.

Again, Dexter thrust the sword forward, but it would not move. Samuel remained on his knees, staring at the man trying to kill him. What was happening? The area around the sword's entry into Samuel's abdomen suddenly began to glow and a silvery liquid oozed from the wound where Dexter's blade was. Dexter, reacted by jerking at his sword to free it. The sword came free, bringing with it Draconis, which had attached itself to the Dexter's blade.

The startled Dexter froze, staring at the two swords that had seemingly mated. Samuel reacted by seizing Draconis by the hilt and rising to his feet. The swords parted, and Samuel lunged and swung the sword high, changing the arc in mid swing and going low. The blade bit into Dexter's lower leg and the big man fell to his knees, his eyes registering shock at the turn of events.

Dexter raised his sword and made a powerful swing at Samuel, who ducked back, dropped to one knee and felt the wind of the blade as it almost skimmed the top of his head. Off balance from the power of his swing, Dexter left himself unguarded and Samuel made the most of the opportunity. He drove Draconis forward and upward, catching Dexter in the midsection. Dexter grunted, and his sword dropped from hands.

Samuel placed both hands on his sword's hilt and rose to his feet as he thrust the blade through Dexter's body. The tip ripped through the intestines, the liver and exited through a kidney. Dexter was impaled on the blade, his eyes blaring, the ruddy face draining white.

Samuel gave the sword another thrust and said, "This is for Heather, for Robert, Manny and all the others you've murdered. And especially for Nathan, your father who taught me how to kill you!"

"He's got a knife!" Tammy shouted, and Samuel saw the dying Dexter reaching for a dirk. Before he could use it, however, Samuel thrust Draconis once again, and Dexter's hand fell to his side, the dirk falling to the ground.

Dexter slumped forward until his head was only inches from Samuel. "You have not won, Samuel Donachee," he whispered through a bloody froth. "I live in other times and you will see me again." His eyes closed and he collapsed as Samuel withdrew Draconis from his body. The sword that

427

had served Dexter so valiantly burst into a brilliant, blinding light and rose from the ground, then exploded into what seemed to be hundreds of stones. The stones took on lives of their own, screeching and squealing as they swarmed above the lifeless body.

Samuel loosened his grip on Draconis and the sword drifted skyward, the stones following like the tail on a comet. The sky was now cloudless, but lightning bolts suddenly flashed and thunder roared so loud that Dexter's men screamed and cowered on the ground.

Tammy ran to Samuel and put her arms around him. They watched the spectacle playing out in the night sky as the stones formed into what looked like a glowing lightning bolt and struck Draconis. The sword blazed blue-white as the stones embedded themselves in the blade. Then it grew still, hovered for a moment and gracefully returned to Samuel.

Dexter's men had disappeared into the night while Samuel and Tammy had watched the stones-sword merger, and the two were alone in the clearing. Tammy was in his arms, sobbing quietly.

As soon as Samuel could quiet his nerves and Tammy's tears, he began trying to assess their situation. There was no longer any danger of Dexter slaughtering the men who would come to look at the big stone. All that remained was finding a way to return to his own time.

Tammy was searching the ground, hoping to find a piece of clothing to help cover herself, when she saw the dirk Dexter had dropped during the final stages of the battle.

She held the knife out to Samuel and he took it with shaking hands. It was his sien du, the one he had lost in the battle at the park and the one that had opened the portals to the past.

"Thank you!" he said to Tammy, and pulled her to him, kissing her squarely on the lips. "Are you ready for another trip?"

Samuel gripped Draconis with the dirk and threw them into the darkness. He grabbed the dead Dexter under the arms and stepped through the portal of light. Tammy went with him.

CHAPTER 49

A SECOND CHANCE

They exited from the portal into Samuel's ironsmith shop. Samuel stumbled and dropped Dexter's body. Tammy crashed into him and he grabbed her to keep her from falling.

Samuel took the girl's hand and led her away from the spot where Dexter lay. "Be careful," he said. "When one of us dies in a time other than our present, the body incinerates."

As the last words were uttered, Dexter's body burst into flames and was immediately reduced to a mall heap of ashes.

"Oh, my god!" Tammy murmured. "I thought nothing else could shock me."

There was noise at the door and Robert ran into the shop, followed closely by Heather. They stopped when they saw Samuel and the semi-nude woman.

"What's going on here?" Heather demanded with a frightened look on her face. She stared at Samuel, then at the strange woman. Tammy pulled the shirt together as best she could and crossed her arms to hide her breasts.

Samuel and Tammy stared at each other.

Heather's face was beginning to redden. "Methinks you have some explaining to do, Samuel Donachee," she said. She was in such a state that she didn't notice that Samuel's clothes were blood-soaked.

"Ah … she just came by to look at some knives," Samuel offered lamely. She got too close to the flame and her clothing caught on fire. I had to roll her on the ground to put it out."

"Amazing. Seems she escaped any burns, though."

Samuel pointed to the ashes from Dexter's body. "See, that's where her clothes burned." He could contain himself no longer. "Oh, my God, Heather!" He ran to his love and took her in his arms. He reached out a hand to Robert and pulled his brother into the embrace. "Robert! Oh, it's so good to see both of you alive!"

430

Robert pulled free, staring at his lunatic brother with wide-eyed wonder. "Fire must have scared you pretty badly, brother. And what is wrong with you? You're covered in blood."

"Just a scratch from the blade I was working on when the accident happened," Samuel said, smiling sheepishly. "I'm fine. It looks worse than it is."

"Heather, I think your would-be husband has gone off his rocker," Robert said. "You sure you want to marry him when you could wait for me?"

Heather nestled in Samuel's arms and smiled. "That depends on whether I find him with another nude woman."

Tammy was mollified. The scene she had just witnessed coming on the heels of the horrific episode she had just escaped from was more than she could handle. "I'm sorry," she muttered. "I don't belong here."

"It's okay," Heather said, still secure in Samuel's embrace. "Robert, give the woman an apron or something to cover herself with."

Robert quickly grabbed an apron from a hook on the wall and handed it to Tammy, who mouthed a "Thanks." She pulled the apron over her head, wrapped it around her body and flashed an embarrassed smile. "I hope what they say about first impressions isn't true."

Robert and Heather exchanged looks and shrugs. This strange lass also had a strange speech. Robert was having trouble keeping his eyes off the woman.

"Oh," Samuel said, breaking the awkward silence, "by the way, Tammy — that's the lady's name — comes from a far distance. She is from a village on the coast that is ruled by the English. She didn't like the English and left to find another home. I think she's considering settling in our village."

Tammy raised her eyebrows. Had Samuel read her mind? She glanced at the younger brother. Samuel hadn't bothered to tell her handsome he was.

Heather broke the embrace with Samuel and turned to Tammy. "Where are you staying," she asked.

431

Tammy shrugged. "Well, I haven't exactly found a place yet."

"Do you have some more clothes?"

"Not here," Tammy said, feeling her face redden.

"Well, I can remedy that," Heather said, eyeing the scared girl. "We seem to be about the same size. Come to my home and I'll find you a dress. Besides, if we stay here any longer, Robert is going to stare holes in you."

It was Robert's turn to be embarrassed. "Come on, Heather," he said.

Heather moved to give Samuel a goodbye hug and he embraced her again. "Don't be long," he said in a voice filled with emotion."

"Why, Samuel, you act as if you hadn't seen me in a century."

"You could almost say that," he said, smiling.

Heather led Tammy out of the shop and toward her home.

With the women gone, Samuel turned to his brother and unashamedly began crying. Through the tears, he said, "Oh, Robert, I thought I would never see you again."

"Did the fire scare you that badly?"

"Aye, I guess it did." He reached out and embraced Robert, who stood with arms by his side, wondering what was going on with his older brother.

"Why all the sentiment?" he asked.

"Listen, little brother," Samuel said. "You have to trust me with this. I need your complete support and understanding. No questions asked. Can you promise me that?"

"But I don't understand. What is going on? What has happened to you?"

"I can't tell you that right now. You just have to believe that everything is all right and accept the way things are for now. Someday, perhaps when we are old men and are taking care of our grandchildren, I will tell you a tale."

"Jesus! You have gone nutty, Samuel."

"No, listen. I had a vision that I know is going to come true. Not long from now, a gigantic stone will fall from the sky and bring with it evil and death for people. Through this vision, I know where this stone is going to hit, and we must convince Chieftain Bruce of the danger. When this stone hits, it will dig a deep hole in the ground, and we must cover it with dirt before it begins to spread its evil."

Robert had a glazed look in his eyes. "Okay … I think."

"Please. I have never been more serious in my life. This is something we must do if we are to survive."

"Brother …" There was pleading look in Robert's eyes. "When did you become a prophet?"

"Robert, have I ever lied to you? Have I ever acted insane?"

"Well, not before today."

"Then you will help me. You're my brother. You have to trust me."

"Okay, Samuel. I believe you, and I also believe that omens are not to be taken lightly. I will do whatever you ask."

"Thank you, Robert. God, I missed you, brother."

"Yeah," Robert said, laughing. "You hadn't seen me since you left the house this morning. That fire must have really scared you."

"It did."

"Oh, Samuel … that girl … Tammy. She's a lovely lass. Do you think maybe …?"

Samuel laughed. "Go for it, brother, but methinks you will have your hands full with that one."

"Ah, nice to have your blessing. Tell you what, big brother. While you're cleaning up your mess here, I'm going to check on the girls. Maybe I can talk them into fixing us some supper."

Robert left, hurrying in the direction of Manny's home where the girls had gone. He had to force himself not to break into a run.

Samuel gathered himself for a moment. There were still decisions to be made. Chieftain Bruce had to be convinced of the danger that lay ahead. And Tammy was going to have to make her own decision. Could she remain here and make a happy life with Robert, or would she be too homesick for the 21st century? She really wasn't going to have a choice, was she? If he was successful in his arguments with the chieftain, the stones would never exist. And without the invasion of the stones, there would be no Rippling. No time travel.

Decisions.

Samuel eyed the debris on the floor and the small pile of ashes and closed his eyes. Nothing that couldn't wait until tomorrow. He wanted to be with his loved ones. He was reaching for the peg where he usually hung his wide-brimmed hat and long coat, when he realized he had left them in another time period. He laughed. He wouldn't be wearing black anymore, anyway.

He went to the door and paused. He thought of the death and destruction that had filled the street the last two times he had been on it. He shook his heads as if to clear it, patted the wooden building lovingly, and stepped outside. He brushed the dust from his clothes and felt the dried blood from his wounds.

He began walking along the graveled street, hearing the comforting crunch made by his footsteps, and suddenly remembered the night the nude boy had ridden the swordslinger's horse.

He smiled as he saw the scene in the street. A group of men was gathered outside the bakery, laughing at some story or joke. Children were playing in the street, two of them chasing a cackling chicken. Their laughter rang among the buildings. A woman was gathering clothes from the backyard where she had hung them to dry that morning. Six centuries later, the scene would be a Norman Rockwell painting.

Samuel smiled and picked up his pace. Life was too short to spend time alone in the street. He was eager to get to the McGuire house and see Manny and Martha. They had to make plans for a wedding — or two.

With his first step outdoors, he realized something was amiss. Tensing, he glanced around for any signs of immediate danger. His joy a moment before was replaced by something close to panic. To the left two children ran through a group of chickens, behind him was the empty shop. A flock of ravens rose in a chorus of haunting caws. What was it? His clenched fists opened, willing Draconis to come. Draconis. That was it. He flexed his hands as a man would when trying to wake tingly fingers of sleep.

Samuel sighed. He drew in a deep breath, a highland cool breath. "Dragonis, my old friend. You are back in the arms of your master," he said to himself. 'Though ye drove me crazy at times, you were once a part of me." A smile crossed his face, the merging, the sky stone, all the deaths, they haven't happened yet. "And not going to on my watch. It's a beautiful day and I feel wonderful." In the future times he realized there were no flock of birds in the sky. Here, there were annoying chickens and quail for weekly meals and rabbits and deer. Here, there be ravens circling above. That was odd. Ravens usually flew short distances from tree to tree. These were fifty, sixty of them flying above in a circle. *You don't see that in Charlotte, North Carolina*, he thought.

He passed Heather's home and could hear Heather and Tammy laughing. Poor Tammy without a cell phone or computer or Facebook and QVC, this was going to get interesting. His heart raced when he saw his old place intact. It would be too much to endure reliving the times ahead. It seemed like moments ago he was staring into Robert's raven pecked eyes. The stone had made a ten-foot hole into the earth. They would have to dig a twenty-foot hole. Men came from all around that night. Samuel remembered standing for hours mesmerized by the stone. If the curious men were held back, would they fight? Would there be enough time to cover the stone completely? What if the stone lulls the men through the dirt to dig for it?

What if the stone breaks apart on its own, pushes through the earth, then slides, and rolls over the terrain until it finds a man to merge with? All of it would start over again. These thoughts dampened his happy homecoming mood. *I'll have nightmares for the rest of my life*, he thought.

One more time….this second chance to have his life, this good life before the sky stone fell. Who knew what was going to happen. All he knew was at this moment in time; he had Heather, Robert, his village back. What had happened can never happen again. Tomorrow, he would begin taking every action possible to prevent the killings.

All was at peace now. Everything was normal. In fifty yards he will be opening the door to his old home, have supper with his brother, then spend time with Heather. After losing so much, it could not happen again. It was like waking from a dream that all you loved was lost. He loved Heather, his brother, the people of the village a hundred times more. Never would he take one moment for granted. Each moment alive was precious. He could not and would not let it happen. Heather was going to be his wife. They will have children. His brother and Tammy could possibly work. It was wonderful just thinking of possibilities. His eyes grew wet with all the emotions he was feeling.

Wiping his eyes with the sleeve of his shirt, he saw the rise of mountain and the cliff with Nathan's grave. "I'll come visit you soon," he said, then froze. There was someone by Nathan's Standing Stone.

Samuel's hands instinctively opened.

NEWS RELEASE

Feb. 15, 2013. Chelyabinsk, Russia. A meteor the size of a bus exploded in the atmosphere over the Russian Urals city of Chelyabinsk Friday, terrifying thousands with blinding light flashes and powerful sonic booms that shattered windows, damaged buildings. Injuries may be heading toward 1,000, mainly due to flying glass and debris.

Thanks to the proliferation of new technologies like CCTV and dashboard cameras in cars, the dazzling meteor shower that hit the far-western Siberian region may be the first event of its kind in history to be filmed from almost every angle.

Dozens of videos have cropped up on YouTube and other social media, and they offer an astounding glimpse of what happens when a huge hunk of rock, estimated at about 10 tons, plows into the atmosphere at a speed of 30,000 miles per hour. It disintegrated in a series of bright flashes while still several miles above the Earth's surface.

According to eyewitnesses quoted by the Ekho Moskvi radio station, the event began around 9 a.m. local time, when it was not yet full daylight. The station said that thousands of people rushed into the frigid streets, looking up at the fiery contrails in the sky, with many wondering if it was an air disaster, a missile attack, or the end of the world. - Christian Science Monitor

Feb. 15, 2013. Chelyabink, Russia. The area where a meteor struck outside of the Russian Ural city Chelyabinsk was blocked from public access around 10 a.m. Military and local law enforcement officers assisted the area populace with a mandatory evacuation. According to eyewitnesses by the Ekho Moskvi radio station, dozens of officials at the zone of impact were fleeing the scene shouting at others to escape. One soldier was recorded on a video that has gone viral on YouTube that the meteor began to vibrate and crumble. In letterbox translation from Russian to English on the video, the soldier said, "It began to crack and break into pieces like the size of your hand. They started moving over

437

the rim of the crater and...(unable to translate....) going inside the men. Run. Go now!"

That has been the last video and radio report from the city of Chelyabinsk. The Russian government announced a media blackout of the city has been given until the situation has been investigated and controlled.

News media across the world were replaying the videos with commentary from newscasters, doomsayers, scientists and laymen. Fox News began playing video clips from the movie War of the Worlds with the movie's soundtrack as bumper music.

This was the first time in recorded history video recordings have captured actual impact of a meteor of this magnitude. There are craters around the world from large meteors striking before recorded history such as in Ural, Russia, America, and the Highlands in Scotland around 1300 where several villagers wrote their eyewitness accounts of a ball of fire coming from the sky. Archeologists noted the populace of the village had vanished soon after leaving a great mystery for the inhabitants.

(This news release will be continuously updated.)

AFTERTHOUGHT

Way back to 1989, the Light to write novels was extinguished. My dream of becoming a successful novelist was shelved. Until about three years ago, I was riding back from a Plein Air art event in Florida listening to Celtic music and whoosh, while driving up I-95 I see a man with a fedora and long black coat with his back against the wall, sword drawn and waiting for his enemy to emerge out of the darkness. Drums are beating; the singer is doing a kind of strange mid-eastern chant to the pipes. That's how it started.

I am a huge fan of the Highlander Series and Movies. I did an art show in L.A. at the Highlander Convention and had a photo with Adrian Paul to donate a painting I did so we could raise money for the Haiti people after their big storm. I loved the first Highlander movie and TV series. The other movies never captured the magic as the first…well that might be said about a lot of other series movies and other things. All I know was that I had a story to tell that was banging in my head to get out. I wanted to start writing again. I was terrified I would lose the feeling so I launched right into it.

I didn't want to write another Highlander. I wanted to start a new story. When you go into the romance sections, you see a man in kilts time traveling. I didn't want Samuel to be immortal. I didn't want quickenings that give the winner the lower's soul and power. So, out of the sky falls this huge rock. It has a spirit within. It breaks into pieces, melds into highlander's weapons, and forges this kind of spiritual/material blending into the two. And as the swordsman discovers, the more kills the more magical qualities the sword possesses…..but so does the spirit of the sword, having a mind of its own that can sometimes come in conflict with the owner's will. Being mortal rather adds to tension of your fighting. Time travel is a wicked thing to write about. You can talk for hours on hypotheticals about as wearisome as a religious debate. I did the best I could. Swordslinger is just your everyday mortal for the 1300's Scotland. When you first meet him, he's been to Charlotte several times already and has learned enough about banks and getting transportation. He is somewhat busy being chased as he hunts.

Night and day, I worked on this story....then Samuel goes to the highlands in memories when he was a boy and met the first Swordslinger. It was about then the story walked on its own. I was no longer the writer but the reporter. Suddenly, the book was finished, leaving me like a winded marathon runner. It had been over 20 years since I wrote a book. 20 years??? Since my accident, I've had trouble reading over a couple of pages at a time. I listened to every audio book I could to keep up with the fantasy/horror genre.

Five months ago, I was hit with another flash to right, "The Raven's Light." Several days later, I met a director who happened to walk into my studio and told him of my idea. He said he loved it and sounded like it should be a series. This story centers in a mountain town in North Carolina and suddenly turns into this massive Lord of the Rings/Game of Thrones fantasy tale with a kind of portal between Earth and another world I call Skyeden. As a character in Stephen King's Gunslinger says, "There are more worlds than these," which is the case for Raven's Light. I'm working on Raven's Light now. I did a screenplay first, but now putting it into book form. The book form grows and starts its own walk and about finished with the first book as I write this. Karen is in the living room putting Swordslinger together in proper format before we send it to the publishers.

A doctor told me that sometimes an injured brain could sometimes heal a year, ten years, 20 years later. I don't know what happened, but I am writing feverously night and day. My father, an editor for a newspaper, used to edit my earlier novels as we prepared to send them out to the world. Well, I got Dad working for me again.....It's like the old days. We've gathered up 10 whole and parts of unpublished novels that we will be updating and adding on. Not including Swordslinger, The Raven's Light, I Saw The Light (movie script); we have 10 novels scheduled for publishing within the next four years.

This is over a 20-year dream. I made my living as an artist the last 15 years and hope I can do the same through my stories. Swordslinger is the book that makes my lifelong dream come true. I have the storyline for two more Swordslingers and imagine ideas for another two will come.

In Book Two: a big surprise is waiting for Samuel. While he is dealing with this surprise, the motive and plot of his enemy if carried through will change the course of history for mankind. It begins with the clashing of swords like a "Go!" pistol shot for the 50 yard dash. It's an emotional, very thought provoking, action packed tale – and that's just the beginning.

Better, get back to work. I need to do about 15 illustrations for some Swordslinger promos. I am working daily on the Raven's Light. After The Raven's Light, I will be working on a novel called "Crematory," then back to book 2's of Swordslinger and Raven's Light. I lost 20 years and I want to get my stories out at last. My Grandfather Roy Duncan was a man I worshiped as a child. He died when he was 56. I was born in 1956. I always thought that when I turned 56 that something was going to happen and I guess it has. The dream to publish has come true. Special thanks to all art collectors and friends that have hung on through the ups and downs.

The morning of February 15, 2013 "Swordslinger" was to be published; we saw the reports of a meteorite crashing in Ural, Russia. Since there is a similar scene in the book and future similar events in the epic, we decided to use some of the press releases. We changed the names of the writers and added a few lines here and there into the reports to fit our story.

In addition, the other day, the Pope announced that he was going to retire. A little later lightning struck the Vatican. Many felt this was a sign from God. Well, with a little imagination we thought the meteor was one of our very own Swordslinger sky-stones.

Stefan Duncan
February 15, 2013

Stefan Duncan and Adrian Paul of the Highlander series

Stefan donated this original Highlander themed painting entitled "Bonnie Portmore" to The Peace Fund, Adrian's charity. The painting was the showcase of the Fund's auction and raised over $1500. Stefan is dubbed "The American Van Gogh."

ACKNOWLEDGEMENTS

The Swordslinger is my first official published book of a dozen sitting in my stack that represents a lifelong dream for me. Though the last 15 years I have made my living as an artist, writing novels has always been in my heart. I'm elated that I'm riding this horse again and so thankful that at last I am writing again and publishing books. At last my time has come. I plan to ride this horse full gallop until the end. That is my promise to you.

I want to thank my Father, Howard Ward, retired Sports Editor of the Fayetteville Observer and Golfer Hall of Fame Sports Writer for always having the faith in my storytelling and countless hours of editing my stories through the years. As I had told him, it was as if I made the stew but he added the seasoning or say "sprinklings" of spice. It also has always been the link that kept us together and has brought pure joy to me to share with him.

My Mother, Betty Ward is a retired teacher at Fayetteville Technical Community College. She has always been my safety net. And to whom I attribute my waking from my coma by the will of her prayers. She has always been the one in the bleachers cheering me on and the first to wade through my battlegrounds to patch up me if I fall. Thank you for everything. Love ya, Mom.

I want to thank my high school sweetheart, Karen Troutman, an OR Nurse, whose support and love has helped me secure a steadfast launching pad to send my novels out into the world.

The people of the Highlander series are also on my list for thank yous. When I was learning to walk again, the Highlander series TV and Movies were a great inspiration with their wonderful stories and hero that always sought to be on the side of right. I had the chance to meet Adrian Paul and writers of the TV series.

I want to thank all my friends who have stood by me throughout the years and been supportive my dreams. In addition, to you my readers- Thank you for allowing me to entertain you with my story and those yet to come. Each of you is contributive to my dream coming true.

Stefan Duncan

Stefan Duncan
Author and Artist

ABOUT THE AUTHOR

Stefan Duncan lives in Charlotte, NC. He has an English and Art Degree. He was dubbed the American Van Gogh by http://www.vangoghgallery.com He created the impressionistic styles of 'Squiggleism' and 'Illuminism'. He is an internationally known artist who has sold around 1000 original paintings. His mission is to give the world more Light through his paintings. With Light brings hope for the human condition. Stefan is in galleries and establishments around North Carolina and the nation. He works out of his studio at the Charlotte Art League in Charlotte, N.C. and his home. Stefan was featured as one of America's rising artists in Art Business News Magazine. He has appeared on Fox News and Papers, Crafts, Paints TV show on PBC. Mr. Duncan supports various charitable organizations by donating original paintings to their fund raising efforts. Local listings and events are on his website at. http://www.stefanduncangallery.com

As the recipient of an Associate Press Award, Stefan's dream has always been to become a successful published author. He had signed the rights to hold six of his book of unpublished books for movie projects prior to being involved in a car accident that placed him in a coma. With many broken bones and head injury, Stefan's dream was side tracked. He discovered (from a talking goose – that's another story one day) to become an artist as a means of expression. What concentration was lost with writing had moved to the art side. After many years of being unable to express his creativity through his keyboard, Stefan recently rediscovered his ability to paint a picture with words once again. Overall, he calls his work a 'Living Spirit Art.' Stefan is currently writing an epic fantasy screenplay/novel that will include his paintings. The writing has just begun. There is much more to come

Karen Troutman, Editor

READER'S REVIEWS

Emotionally charged and riveting, this spellbinding tale is about the son of a blacksmith who faces the ultimate question, "How far would you go for the one chance to return all that was loved then lost.

Time travel, romance, sword fighting - the Swordslinger series belongs on the shelf between the Stephen King's Dark Tower series and the Highlander movies

True love will always draw one back home to family regardless the cost of what one may endure to get there.

I thought this was going to be one of those action stories. Then, a character mentions something and you're left with your mouth open with this big massive shocker that lets the reader figure it out before the Swordslinger does. It's one of those Oh, My, God! moments. Love the book. It's Samuel, the Swordslinger, and his ravenous sword against the world. This book sits among my favorite fantasy books.

This book has excitement and romance. I didn't want to stop reading after I started it. Days after finishing the book, I was still thinking about the characters. I hope that there is a sequel

Stefan Duncan is expanding his artistic repertoire. Known as America's Van Gogh, this painter has tried his hand at the sword and sorcery genre, and has proved himself a talent to watch. This certainly is not the tired old quest that has been redone many times, but is a chilling and attention grabbing thriller that will keep you up all night. I was unable to put this book down, and am anxiously awaiting more works by Stefan. Long a fan of his painting, he has now proven his genius in painting a tapestry with words. Thank you Stefan for one of the best reads I have had in a long time.

Once the book is opened, one can't put it down until reaching the last page. The "Swordslinger" will take you on his journey as if you were there with him. At times you will catch yourself holding your breath not believing what is happening. It is worth the read, because you will breathe a sigh of relief and feel that you have just found the secret of what it is to be loved by someone who will go to the ends of the earth for you. With a very surprising ending, you will see that love is magical and eternal.

Riveting. Spellbinding. Master storytelling. 10 Stars .My favorite living artist has just become my favorite fantasy writer. It's really a wonderful story. I can't wait till Book 2.

This book is hot! I love it. Get it now cause it is on its way to be a big hit.

http://www.swordslinger.net/

PREVIEW

The next book in the series
SWORDSLINGER

SWORDSLINGER

BOOK TWO

FOR THE GLORY
OF LOVE IS DEATH

Stefan Duncan

SWORDSLINGER

Book Two: FOR THE GLORY OF LOVE IS DEATH
Stefan Duncan
Copyright © 2013 Stefan Duncan
All Rights Reserved

Publisher: Raven's Light Publishing
Charlotte, NC
Published February 2013
Cover illustration:
Editing: Howard Ward
Final editing and digital formatting: Karen Troutman
Available as digital e-book

Find out more about the author and upcoming books online
http://www.swordslinger.net/
http://www.stefanduncan.com

CHAPTER ONE

How many times will you die in my arms as I watch
the light fade from your eyes, and feel your last
breath lay to rest upon your lips?
How many times must I feel your face grow cool
beneath the warmth of my tears?
And how many times must my heart die within as
you die again?
Is there no Light that shines forever
No time just to hold you for an hour or two
Before winter settles into you
And the spring slips away?
Is there no sorrow for love so pure and lost
To hold back the hands of time
Where for a moment you can be mine?

Feb 1st, 2014. Charlotte, N.C. Charlotte Motor Inn,
N. Tryon St.

    It seemed that a moment to rest was as distant
a dream as the memories of the highlands. Samuel
removed his hat, ran his fingers through his long
black hair, and leaned his head against the bathroom

wall of the hotel room. The sounds of Charlotte traffic on North Tryon Street could be heard. Tires dividing pools of rain on the road continuously splashed water. He was so weary and exhausted that his blue eyes were dark and sullen. Where he sought within himself a source of energy and life, he found only a reservoir of heartbreak.

Of all the happiness and moments of elation, cradling Heather's face in his hands and gazing into her eyes as their climatic wave rolled and spread from them to the universe...all of it... only reminded him of his sense of loneliness and the bitter vile tasting venom of unsatisfied vengeance. Vengeance was just a name for hollow victory and a treasure for fools. It never gives back what he has lost. The feel of her lips against his. Hearing the sound of her laughter. The spark of life in her eyes that always showed adoration and devoted love. He pressed the side of his face against the cool gritty concrete wall and gently reached up with his blood stained hand then lightly ran his fingertips across the surface of the wall as if it was her face. He had to acknowledge a newly discovered truth that some events were rooted and anchored down in the flowing stream of time thus leaving a wake. And if one removed an event from the stream, the water filled into the wake to create a kind of chaos that ends up pretty much as the original event. Or, that changing a major event to save a wife could bring a ripple of refilling that would lead to horrific events.

Once, a long, long time ago, in the land of Skyeden, there stood a man on the mountain side amid a field of purple thistles, He knelt before the standing stone and ran his fingers across the encryption, "Heather Donachee, beloved wife of Samuel." He raised his gaze overlooking the mist that hung low in the valley concealing the loch beneath. The only hint of water there was the lapping of waves upon the gray pebbles on the beach. Though the new village was in the same place as the old, its sense of home no longer remained.

Only the loch now gave him that sense and the small jutting ledge that over looked the village where the grave of his old friend laid buried. The village below was asleep, with wisps of black smoke rising from a night low of burning embers from the hearths of the stone and mud homes. The first crowing of the roosters sounded as the first hint of daybreak yellowed the horizon of purple skies.

A hundred yards away, a man named Amos climbed on top of the "wailing stone", a protruding boulder that looked like an old man's last gray tooth.

"I saw you come into the village last night. I figured you come to visit her this morning. I'll play a lament for you. Peace be with you, Swordslinger. Sorry for your loss." He raised the pipe to his lips then said, "Sometimes I think I see her standing there. She waits for you, you know."

As the first wailing notes haunted the valley, Samuel looked over his shoulder of the hundred plus standing stones. He leaned toward the standing stone and kissed her name HEATHER. "Soon, my love. There is one last thing I must do."

Thunder rattled the stainless steel frame of the bathroom mirror startling a roach from its hiding place. Swordslinger opened his eyes and wiped away his tears. The cool water from the faucet revived him a little. He watched the last of the blood on his hands grow thinner in the descending swirl of water of the drain. He toweled dried his hands and walked to the end of the bed and looked at the items laid out before him. His sword, Draconis yearned for him to touch it, pulling at him like an undying nicotine habit. *No. Stop it.* Instead of taking the oxen horned handle, he pulled his hand back and looked at the lance.

The television played in the background. The mumble became words as Swordslinger began to focus on what the newscaster was saying.

"Authorities will not comment any further except to say they would be reviewing the recorded video footage of the Discovery Place security cameras. All we know at this time is that the Holy Lance alleged to wound Jesus is missing. This has left many of the Christian faith in a state of shock wondering who in the world would have the audacity to steal such a holy relic."

"Dear God, forgive me for what I am about to do," Swordslinger said.

Made in the USA
Charleston, SC
05 April 2013